Returned to Devil's Island

Returned to Devil's Island

Chris Nand

COPYRIGHT © 2011 BY CHRIS NAND.

LIBRARY OF CONGRESS CONTROL NUMBER: 2011915996
ISBN: HARDCOVER 978-1-4653-6226-1
SOFTCOVER 978-1-4653-6225-4
EBOOK 978-1-4653-6227-8

All rights reserved. No part of this book may be reproduced or transmitted in any form or by any means, electronic or mechanical, including photocopying, recording, or by any information storage and retrieval system, without permission in writing from the copyright owner.

This novel is a biographical fiction. The names of some places, characters and incidents portrayed in it are the work of the author's imagination. Some resemblance to actual persons, living or dead, events or localities is entirely coincidental.

This book was printed in the United States of America.

To order additional copies of this book, contact:
Xlibris Corporation
1-888-795-4274
www.Xlibris.com
Orders@Xlibris.com

I dedicate this book to my late aunt Ram Kali and the brave Catholic missionaries who had dedicated their lives to save lives of others on the island of Mokagai once known as the Devil's Island.

CHAPTER 1

One of my earliest childhood memories is of playing on boulders large enough for me to hide behind. These were great rounded stones scattered close to our village situated on the far side of the dirt track we knew as The Kings Road.

It was here where local children congregated and became the preferred place for acting out childhood fantasies. Here was the ideal place to climb, practice our jumping skills; to be pulled up amidst shrieks. We would then slide to the ground with a bump whereupon the tears would flow but mostly with joy and laughter. It was a perfect place for childhood play; an activity that would keep us occupied for hours on end.

It was also a place of wonderment where on those warm tropical nights before nightfall settled in we would sit atop as tigers might. From those lofty heights we had the advantage of height and could marvel at the panoramic view of the world as seen from a village. Ours was a magical world the adults had left far behind them. They gave our fantasy kingdom scant recognition when threatening to punish us should we fail to return immediately to our homes and beds for the night.

To the north of our village there was a backdrop of mountains with their rain forests cloaks and often shrouded in clouds. To the south of our village the track wound its way back down the hill away from the village before disappearing into the forest. To the east the vastness of the deep blue Pacific with its far distant horizon that whetted our imagination with dreams about what might lie beyond.

With the passing of time we were face to face with a shocking revelation about that place we had come to consider our own small children's kingdom. It started with the arrival of the U.S. military.

I will never forget the arrival of the convoy of armoured trucks and varied vehicles, each painted in jungle green and which covered in flumes of dust jerked to a halt outside our homes. As they did so, men with white faces and others that were much darker than our own, poured from their trucks before enthusiastically shaking our hands. There were many friendly gestures and passing the candy around. One huge black man picked me up as though I was feather light and sitting me first on his shoulders he then placed me on his back whilst pretending to be a horse. Some of them took photographs of the boulders and urged others to pose on them to give a better idea of perspective.

CHRIS NAND

The unaccustomed noise brought parents rushing from the village huts; concern was written on their faces as they wondered what the commotion was all about. It was then we were told that the war that we had heard about had now entered the Pacific following the Japanese bombing of Pearl Harbour. By this time Singapore and Java had already surrendered to the Japanese invaders and Fiji could be next. The Americans were there to protect the islands from any invasion force.

To our delight they set up camp in the nearby fields. From this point on a steady supply of chocolate for the kids and cigarettes for grown-ups could be relied upon. Rides on open-top jeeps became a normal part of village life and the sound of English songs sung by Americans replaced the Hindu prayer songs we used to sing. English wasn't spoken in our village so communication with the soldiers was limited to smiles, gestures and the exchange of foods. They were as fascinated by our way of life as we were of theirs.

They gave us home baked bread, butter, jams and biscuits in return for chickens, goats and pigs given to them by villagers. They were not given cattle. Our grandfather, a staunch Hindu, would not allow the infantrymen to slaughter cows but as fish were plentiful the Americans showed little interest in the cattle.

They played in the lagoons; we improved our swimming skills and learned how to better dive for oysters and gather the large black crabs from the mangrove bushes nearby. In the evenings we would watch attentively as the Americans cooked their food on open fires and drank beer following which there was much singing and dancing.

We children were not allowed to join the servicemen after darkness had fallen but we soon learned to peep from behind the coconut grove and we laughed at their capers. Sometimes we saw them dance whilst holding bamboo canes close to them as they might a partner; how strange we thought. Others among them sang and strummed guitars.

My favourite activity was watching them exercise in the mornings. Some jogged along the beaches, others boxed or played football. Afternoons were spent swimming with them at the river's estuary; a place where there was fresh clear water from the nearby Queen Victoria Mountain.

I vividly recall one afternoon in particular. We children were splashing around in the river beneath the waterfalls. Leaping from high rocks we clasped our knees to our chests as we plunged into its current. We would then be swept down river until we were able to scramble back to the rocks and repeat the process. Further downstream some GI Joes were swimming and paddling or scouting along the riverbank looking out for fish worth trapping.

There was the day when from out of nowhere the heavens opened in the hills following which the river began to quickly swell. Terrified by the unexpected surge of waters the children began to scream. The GIs dived into the water and plucking the children from the river threw them onto the river—bank. "Run fast, get out of here," they screamed with an urgency no one dared to question.

We set off running across the valley towards our homes with the GIs right behind us, some of them were carrying children under both arms. We had run a good way up the hillside and well away from the river before we stopped. We still had little idea why we had been urged to leave in such haste but we will never forget the sight that met us when we looked back down the hill. By then the river had violently overflowed its banks to the tops of the rocks from where we had been jumping; the torrent was now flowing over the pathways we used.

Heavy rainfall in the mountains had caused the deluge a GI told us. "Let's get the hell out of here before it is too bloody late to do so."

Urging the older children to run as fast as they could we scurried across the valley. We were now aware of the ominous ridge of dark clouds working its way towards us from the mountain tops. As they moved towards the village they cast great sweeps of shadow over the landscape. By this time the sun was completely blotted out; the heat of the day was replaced by a damp chill wind followed in seconds by torrential falls of rain accompanied by thunder and lighting.

Making our way through the valley with the help of strong American arms we followed a path that was often submerged in great pools of water. By the time we reached the plateau at the top of the hill we were exhausted. Stopping briefly we turned round to gaze back on the scene of devastation below. The river we had been playing in was now a raging violent flow of white water rapids. The waterfall, which once fed the river from a sheer vertical drop was now gushing in an outward arc like some gigantic breached damn.

We were stunned and watched whilst clinging to out GI saviours. All we could hear was the deafening relentless sound of a billion raindrops as we realised our lives had just been saved.

As we followed the escarpment to our homes the weather deteriorated further. It gave the impression that we were running into rather than away from the storm. The rain was coming down heavier and instead of dripping from tree branches was flowing in thousands of small streamlets. The wind was howling and it was now near impossible to walk without leaning into its pressure. The path we were following was now strewn with the debris of forest saplings; palm and banana leaves ripped from their trunks by the fury of the storm.

Occasionally we had to wade through rising waters or negotiate fallen trees blocking the path. For me the most frightening aspect of the perilous journey was the relentless noise of the storm's fury and the expectation that it could only end in one catastrophic explosion.

On drawing close to the village we were met by several fathers who were understandably anxious. There were no formalities exchanged as both groups met; but there was much hugging and an overwhelming feeling of relief washed over us all.

The Americans apologised to parents and made their way as best they could to their canvas camps. There they were needed to help secure their own tents which were now likely to be torn from their anchor points by the storm. Had they lost them there would be little chance of recovery from the sea.

CHRIS NAND

Once safely home we huddled together as a family, with mother and father comforting my four-year old sister Sabita and Malti aged two. As we cowered we listened expectantly to our battery-operated radio. Fiji Broadcasting Commission was repeating the storm warning in three different languages. First in English; this was followed by native Fijian and finally in Hindi. The announcer told listeners that the storm could develop into hurricane conditions with the possibility of a tidal wave striking lower ground. It was their recommendation that those living in coastal areas should move to higher ground and as far away as possible from the raging Pacific surf. The storm's fury continued and we screamed as our grass roof was torn away and seemingly vacuumed up into the night sky. This was followed by the copper aerial strung between palms crashing down to the ground; the radio went dead. My father was extremely apprehensive for our safety but the sound of the American voices reassured us that help was never far away.

Finding us in distress and taking our hands the soldiers led us towards their huge army trucks. By this time the entire village was a scene of devastation; villagers including our grandparents, uncles and aunts and the rest of our extended family were crammed into huge army trucks which then set off for the Catholic Mission Church of St Nicolas nearby.

The drive to the church was a difficult one as debris from fallen trees was blocking the dirt track leading to the top of the hill where the black concrete place of worship was perched. Hundreds of GIs dressed in waterproof rubbers and Wellington boots helped clear the road for our small convoy as we drove through.

On our arrival at the church we could hear its bells tolling. This was caused by the hurricane force winds swinging the tower bells from one side to the other; ding-dong, ding-dong as though a bell ringer was hard at work calling the faithful to prayer.

Pausing in a darkness so profound we could hardly make anything out we heard voices nearby and in the truck's headlights the strange pallid faces of men dressed in dark clothes were now rushing towards us. One took me in his arms and rushed with me into the dimly lit building. Soon we were all grouped together in the corner of this odd but protective building. Within minutes we were greeted by two men dressed in black and a woman covered from head to toe in dark blue clothes.

"Hello everyone: I am Father O'Donnell," said the rotund and cheerful looking priest. These are my companions, Father Marcel and Sister Henrietta. You are all welcome to stay here in the church until the hurricane clears. You are safe now."

Father stepped forward and shook their hands as he thanked them for their kindness. Hot chocolate and bread was then served up and warm blankets passed around. Only after having assured themselves that we were safe and had eaten did the GIs hurry back to their camp. There was a necessity to collect their comrades and bring them to the sanctuary of the strongest building too.

Now out of harms way we huddled together on the coconut matting covering the church floor. As I cuddled into my father's embrace and tried to sleep I was aware of extraordinary figures and faces looming high above us from where they sat on cement tables; they were staring right straight at me. I was disturbed at the sight and melting further into my father's chest closed my eyes and finally fell into a deep sleep.

It was dawn when I finally awoke and got a clearer view of the strange figures on the tables. I screamed with alarm. At that moment Sister Henrietta entered the church door. Many more children were now beginning to cry and to hide away from the strange dead figures perched along the inner walls of the church.

"My dear children," chuckled the sister: "Don't be frightened. They cannot hurt you; they are statues, images made from plaster and cement. We put them up there to remind us of our Lord God and the saints."

Not surprisingly this information was welcomed by us; we all had vivid imaginations but we were still too panicked to get close and have a proper look.

After a breakfast of bread, jam and hot lemon tea, we ventured outside in search of the toilets and bathrooms. Sadly the bamboo walls and grass roof that once covered the toilet was no more; it had blown away leaving the loos exposed. We gazed in disbelief as father urged us to use it before the tempest returned. As to set an example the men made use of the facility first. Then the women began to giggle nervously between themselves before surrounding the cement seat with their saris and making use of it.

The weather remained peaceful for awhile and we were allowed to play on the grass lawns outside. Then, as quickly as developed the first storm a second appeared but this time with even greater force. It seemed disaster was turning into catastrophe. Running inside the church we peered through the gaps in the church's doors. From our sanctuary we saw grass structures and the corrugated metal roofs of surrounding buildings flying through the air. Huge tropical fruits from laden trees began to bounce off the church walls like footballs before joining other debris and then the radio in the vestry went dead. The copper aerial strung from a crucifix high above the church roof crashed earthwards and now only whistling and crackling sounds came out from the device.

As the afternoon progressed the winds abated and father timidly ventured out to set up the aerial. We sat huddled around the Bush apparatus listening to the news and weather reports. We then learned that the hurricane and tidal waves that followed in its path had overwhelmed parts of Fiji. The warnings came loud and clear for everyone to stay in safe places as hurricane conditions were predicted to last for several days.

Seeing carpets in hallways, cutlery and china plates; paintings on walls not to mention doors with locks and handles there was great excitement. We had never before set foot in the church.

The nuns who tended us were friendly and taught us nursery rhymes, prayers, hymns and how to make the sign of the cross. They also showed us posters of King George VI and Queen Elisabeth that were fixed to the inner walls of their school. "This is our royal family; the king and queen and the two teenage princesses are Elizabeth and Margaret." Sister Henrietta proudly explained. We were then shown the Union flag and taught to sing the national anthem; God save our Gracious King.

CHRIS NAND

The hurricane returned again and again for the next fortnight after which time it was at last safe to return to our homes. Thanking the missionaries for their kindness and hospitality we said our goodbyes and left. The American troops drove us back to our shattered village and it came as no great shock to see the extent of the damage. We had expected it. We immediately set to work searching for any remnants that may have been trapped in the surrounding palm groves.

With help from the infantrymen our village was rebuilt in no time. The bamboo walls were woven, roofs re-thatched and our homes miraculously made ready for habitation soon afterwards. The renovation had taken us just two days and this included the village building known as the Big House.

Fortunately, the pots and pans along with the kerosene stoves and fuel had been saved. The men had had the foresight to bury the basic essentials before we had left for the Mission Church.

Each village has a Big House built in the centre; it will typically be surrounded by many smaller huts in the same manner as Fijians traditionally built their villages. There were no tables or chairs in this house and its floor was covered with coconut matting. Inside the men would sit crossed-legged on the mats. These houses were used for meetings, weddings, funerals and the settling of fights and feuds. Only male members of the village gathered here each evening; there they would chant the sacred versus of the Ramayana, the Hindu mythological epic. In the past similar houses were used by the indigenous Fijians as temples; places for sacrifice, sexual orgies and cannibalism.

In appreciation for their help father invited the Americans for a drink of kava and a feast on the beach. While the drinks were being prepared our visitors sat crossed legged on the powdery white sand and from there watched curiously. "I believe kava comes from the root of the yanggona plant. Is that true?" asked one soldier named Brad.

"That is true," replied father. "It's a native plant, only found in the South Sea Islands."

"Do you have any growing on your farms? Can we see it?"

"Yes, sure but first you must try some."

Father mixed the crushed roots of kava in a huge turtle shell filled with fresh water as one of the Americans remarked that it looked like muddy water.

"It sure does but wait till you try it; it is very potent," father grinned: "In the old days fresh branches of the yanggona were taken from the plant then chewed by young women and spat it into a large turtle shell. It was then mixed with water and drunk by the men of the village in cups made from coconut shells."

"It sounds disgusting,"

"Perhaps it is but we love it," father smiled. He then explained the native custom of drinking kava to our visitors.

"The first bowl of kava must be poured into the sea or on to plants in the garden as an offering to our gods and ancestors. Now, everyone must clap three times before receiving the shell full of kava and again after drinking it."

He then scooped the full bowl and with a grin presented it to the young soldier. Brad dutifully clapped three times, bravely took the bowl and drank from it. He then passed the empty bowl back to father and again clapped three times. The GIs joined in the clapping and soon everyone was served with bowls full of kava. Before long there were over one hundred all singing and dancing Americans who were relishing their kava. Photographs were taken of men wrestling on the sand and playing with the children.

The noise attracted the attention of the residents of nearby villages. Ukuleles appeared out of nowhere and more kava was served whilst young women began to dance and ululate. Their grass skirts shimmied perfectly as they sang along to the thrust and wiggle of their hips. The beads covering their tops that swayed in all directions according to the dancers' mood; their bare breasts could clearly be seen as they flicked their beads upwards or tossed them sideways.

As darkness fell several campfires were lit and more kava was served. The light from the campfires attracted crabs, prawns and fish which the Americans quickly scooped up. Father meanwhile slaughtered a goat and placed it on the campfire to roast along with yams, tapioca, taro and sweet potato.

Soon we relaxed on the beach and ate food placed on banana leaves that served as plates. Everyone was quietly enjoying their supper when we heard soft voices in the distance and raising our heads our party could see four canoes heading towards us. We stood up to take a closer look.

"Who are they?" asked Brad.

His question was met with silence. We watched as the men from the canoes hauled their boats onto the beach before walking casually towards our gathering. When we saw the enormous figure of the man leading them we hid behind the grown-ups and peeked out from between their legs.

"My name is Riaci. Riaci Udre Udre and these are my friends from the mountain village up there." As he spoke he indicated towards a distant village in the mountain. "We saw the campfire, heard the singing and dancing and we have come down river to join you in celebration. Our village was also devastated by the hurricane but we sought sanctuary in the mountain caves. After the storm had run its course we rebuilt our village."

The village elders stepped forward to welcome Riaci. "Please be our guests and join us in our feast," father smiled.

"Thank you! We have brought canoes full of food." Riaci grinned as he pointed towards the four canoes, some of which were filled to the gunwales with an array of fish. Others were weighed down with bags filled with live wriggling crustaceans and chunks of freshly cut meat. It all cooked well on the campfire. Again grandfather advised us not to eat the meat as he smiled politely towards the visitors making sure not to offend them.

The visitors were welcomed and more kava was served to the sound of clapping, singing and music on the ukulele. Riaci was the tallest man I had ever seen. He had broad shoulders, curly crinkled hair and was wearing a leather covered machete that dangled from his waist. Wearing just a loincloth there were beads around his neck. Towering over everyone he grinned happily; chewed tobacco and every so often spat noisily on the sand. I was enthralled and couldn't keep my eyes of him.

Our conversation took place in three different languages: Fijian from the natives, English from the Americans and Hindustani from our village elders. Somehow everyone understood each other amidst much gesticulating and laughter.

After the feast and to a backdrop of deafening chirruping from a million crickets and lit by fireflies that illuminated the night sky, everyone formed a circle around Riaci and listened intently as he spoke.

"I am the supreme chief of all this land," he told us. The Colonial Sugar Refining Company took our land away from us and leased it to you Indians. Some day we will reclaim our land. It belonged to our forefathers and now it belongs to us and our children and our children's children. My great grandfather Ratu Udre Udre is buried over there."

"He was the supreme king and he lived here on this very spot where you Indians now live." As he spoke he pointed towards the boulders where we so often played. He glared at us children as he spoke. "That tomb is a sacred place. No children must ever play there again." he growled.

We listened in silence while a few of the village elders coughed nervously. They were clearly concerned about what they had heard and were terrified of losing their land, which was their livelihood.

"Our parents have leased this land from the Colonial Sugar Refining Company (CSR). We were born here, our children were born here: This is our home and the only home we know," replied father with a firm and challenging voice.

"Yes, yes, I know that." said Riaci. "Please don't worry about losing this land right away. We will re-claim it back after your lease has been terminated. That is written in the contract."

There was a near audible sigh of relief from the audience. "Where is the contract?" father asked.

"The contract is with the Colonial Sugar Refinery Company and kept at their head office in Suva the capital."

Brad butted in and the subject abruptly changed tack: "Is it true that your grandfather, Ratu Udre Udre was responsible for three hundred and fifty human sacrifices on this land, sacrificed on those boulders over there?"

Riaci glanced at his three companions and smiled before looking at Brad's curious face and laughing nervously. "Yes, that's true but bloodshed was the custom of the land then. Father killed son and brother killed brother to compete with each other and to become supreme king of the land. My grandfather was only doing what he felt he had to do."

"How about the women and children who were raped and the blood sucked from their battered limbs, their tongues sliced out for your grandfather to eat?" said Brad coldly.

Riaci chuckled: "You know these stories?"

"We read your country's history before coming here but we weren't expecting to meet descendants of Ratu Udre Udre. This is a real surprise to us all and very exciting I must say."

Riaci grinned. "Look here, my friend. We are not to blame! We weren't even born when that happened. It's all history to us. Now we are Christians and God fearing people belonging to the Wesleyan Church. You must come to our village and meet our pastor. He speaks fluent English and will explain everything."

Hearing the eye-opener about what happened where we now lived we children clung to our fathers and were too frightened to even look towards the old tomb again. Even the grown-ups were nervous. In the past they had heard rumours about our little village and the land upon which we lived but my family had stopped believing what was said to have happened here. It was now late when we finally shook hands with some of the crowd and left for the comfort of our beds. Before we left, we heard Riaci invite the Americans to the mountain village for a native style feast.

"Come on Sunday, join us in prayer before the feast and bring your Indian friends, if they want to come along?"

"Thank you, sir, we shall be there," the soldier replied courteously.

Back in our grass home my parents were quiet as we prepared for bed. Obviously, they were concerned about the revelations from our newly discovered landlord who had turned up on our beach that day. I was petrified and snuggled up to my dad before falling fast asleep. The following morning, after breakfast of freshly made chapattis and vegetable curry, we went back to the old tomb; this time not to play on it but look at it in awe and with apprehension. No one dared to set foot on that tomb ever again.

The next few days were spent watching the adults as they went around whispering to each other, discretely trying to protect the children from the horrors of what had occurred. Father assured us that the natives have been down to see him before and we have a long lease on the land and mustn't worry.

Sunday came and grandfather tried to exert his influence. "No one must go up there to that Fijian native village," he growled. "Cows will be slaughtered and cooked and who knows they could be still bloody cannibals."

"No" said father. "We must go. They extended their hand in friendship and it's an opportunity to get to know them better; especially when we have been living here on their land for so long. We must learn about their customs and how those hundreds of human sacrifices were made on this land."

Grandfather was outraged and protesting as we made our way to the mountain village. Some jeered at us for visiting those cow eating natives. On our way we called in at the canvas village the American servicemen had set up and then together our party headed for the riverbank and then followed the cinder path up to the native village.

As we arrived there Riaci and some men, each carrying bibles, came to greet us. All were dressed in white sulus; a wrap around waist garment; white shirts and ties but no shoes. Before long we were gathered together in the communal house similar to the one we ourselves had but several times bigger. The villagers were friendly towards us and came out in droves to meet us. Many were curious about the Americans as this was the first time they had seen European faces. Brad introduced his own pastor to Riaci; an older man known as Padre Victor.

He joined the village pastor in prayer at which women cried out loudly as prayers were said and hymns were sung. Standing barefoot next to my dad I was fascinated by the spectacle and wondered why there was so much grief during this strange ceremony.

As prayers ended we were greeted by deafening sounds of drumbeats booming from the village centre. Inquisitive I ran outside to investigate where the throbbing monotonous sound was coming from. I was astonished to see two men beating a massive canoe shaped tree trunk. They were using solid chunks of wood shaped like Indian clubs. Soon I was joined by the Americans who were also curious.

"These drums are called lali drums," remarked one of them. "It's a hollowed tree trunk tuned like steel drums to create different sounds. Certain sounds are created for births, deaths, and marriages. Someone listening far away can tell the difference between one occasion and another. In the past these drums were used in ceremonial human sacrifices."

"I bet this drum can tell a story or two if it could talk," smiled another of the infantrymen.

Cameras could be heard clicking as the group of servicemen posed with Riaci and his family as they were all gathered around the drums. I was fascinated by the sound as I had listened to this distant sound of drums since I was born but never knew until now how the noise was created. When the clamorous sound of the drums died down we were led to a clearing where I noticed smoke seeping upwards from mounds of freshly dug earth.

Riaci pointing towards some coconut matting laid flat on the ground and invited us to sit. We did so as young women showed up and served us with bowls full of kava whilst the men folk clapped noisily. After a few bowls of kava everyone was at ease and father allowed me a full bowl. It tasted awful but determined to be a man I screwed my eyes up and gulped it down; I then clapped the required three times just as the adults did.

After the ceremonial kava drinking session the men removed the mounds of soil from where the smoke was seeping. To my amazement I saw bundles of green banana leaves taken out of this primitive oven and placed nearby. One of the men then came forward and opened the bundles with his sharp machete and as he did so he smiled broadly at us. "Help yourselves." He shouted. "Eat whatever you can. There's plenty more where it came from."

The GIs moved towards the oven as father and I took one step backward, hesitating. "What is it . . . is it cow?" I asked.

"Wait here let me have a look. There might be some fish in there," father said as I waited as he identified some lobsters and fish for us to eat. Sitting cross-legged on the mat we ate straight off the banana leaves, using them as plates but with our bare hands for utensils.

The GIs ate whatever came out of the earthen oven and devoured every morsel of food, joking and laughing as they ate. When dinner was finished Brad curiously looked at the earthen oven and addressing Riaci asked how the system worked.

"Yes sure! The oven is called a lovo. First a large deep hole is made and lined with medium-sized boulders. Then wood is placed on top of the stones and set ablaze. Once the wood is completely burned and the stones heated, the food wrapped in green banana leaves will be placed on the hot stones. It is then covered with more leaves and then buried with earth for several hours until the food is steamed well enough and ready to eat."

Brad, fiddling with his beard and looking nervous, had another good look at the oven, and asked cheekily. "Sir . . . were people cooked this way?"

Riaci roared out laughing. "You are still curious. You don't give up, man, do you?"

"I don't mean to offend you, sir. We are all interested in the history of these islands."

"Are you writing a book about us?

"Well there is so much history here in your village," the soldier replied thoughtfully without answering the question directly.

"Yes, Brad. To satisfy your curiosity this method of cooking was and still is used throughout the islands. It's the only way to cook meat around here. We don't have the privilege of your fancy cooking methods do we?"

"And was the Wesleyan missionary Rev Thomas Baker cooked in this way?" Riaci began to chuckle and his shoulders heaved with humour. I didn't think it was so funny but I smiled politely.

"Yes, just for the record, the reverend was killed and baked in this manner but not by our tribe. He met his fate in the high mountain village of Navosa."

"I read somewhere that he came to this village before he took the coastal road to Navosa."

"I don't know anything about him to be honest. He came to this village and converted our people to Christianity. It was well before I was born."

"Do any of the villagers remember him?"

The village spokesman smiled and told him there were two elderly ladies who remembered him to which Brad asked if he could chat with them. "Yes you can but not now as I have to see them first to arrange a meeting."

As other preparations were now under way we took a stroll around the village and from the edge of the forest could see our village in the distance lower down the coast. The white sandy beach and the mouth of the river where we swam looked like an oil painting. It was a perfect day, the sun shone brightly and the deep blue sky above us was magnificent. The GIs worked their dinner off by playing rugby followed by more kava drinks.

CHRIS NAND

Before darkness fell we were ushered into the big house again. Some of our elders said their goodbyes and left but eager to listen to the rest of the story I stayed behind with father. Kerosene lamps were lit and two very old women were introduced to us; sitting cross-legged on the mat we listened. This time it was Padre Victor who spoke and did so speaking fluently in the native language with the old ladies.

"Please can you tell us about Rev Thomas Baker? Did you meet him?"

"Yes, we met him. He was a tall, strong and a very good-looking man who spoke to us gently in our own native tongue and taught our young men to play rugby. Because of his beautiful white complexion we thought he was god. After teaching us the Christian way of life he helped to build a small church here on this very spot before rowing the mission boat up river. He had told us he was going to visit the high mountain village of Navosa. We waved him goodbye and that was the last time we saw him. When we heard the news that he was killed we wept."

The Padre thanked the two ladies after which we said our goodbyes and left their village. As we did so Riaci lit kerosene lamps and escorted us all the way to our own village. On the way back Padre Victor asked him why the women were so emotional during prayers that morning."

"They were distressed because seven of our village sons are in Bougainville in the Solomon Islands including my two sons. They are fighting the Japanese. They joined the Fijian military three years ago; they were hoping to travel and see the world. Now the fighting has intensified and we are worried for their safety."

"Have faith in God, my friend. He will protect them from evil and bring them back home. Look at us: We are here and away from our homes and families. We Americans will fight the Japanese and defeat them if they ever dare to invade these islands. We are much more powerful then the bloody Japanese. The Lord will protect us."

Riaci stayed morose and walked along with us till we arrived closer to home. There we parted company with a thoughtful goodnight and watched as the big man disappeared behind the tall palm groves. He was swaying from side to side as a consequence of perhaps a little too much kava.

As the days passed more revelations began to unfold about our little village and its former inhabitants. Brad had acquired much information and came daily to the beach to tell us the horrifying history of the land. Much of it he had picked up in the vast library situated at his army training camp, which he told us was called West Point.

He explained: "Ratu Udre Udre used to send his men to the nearby villages and select children and young women for his own entertainment. No one refused to give up their children to be used in ceremonial sacrifices. Parents felt proud that the king had selected their offspring for the ovens. This way they believed that the souls of the sacrificed would join their gods to protect them from evil spirits, hurricanes and tidal waves."

As he talked I was speechless and horrified at the thought of the final moments of those poor children.

RETURNED TO DEVIL'S ISLAND

"If a king's home was built then four young and strong men of the village were selected and buried alive under the corner posts of the home to protect the residents. If some men of high rank died virgins were buried alive to accompany him to the spirit world. All marriages and birth celebrations were celebrated with cannibalistic feasts." He paused for a moment before continuing: Do you know that Ratu Udre Udre had over a thousand wives? Thousands of people in these islands are related to him."

Father told him he knew nothing of the history of the islands. "We were told stories about cannibalism on these islands but didn't begin to suspect it happened here where we live. I am not sure we wish to live here anymore. The women want us to move away as they think the souls of the dead may still be here."

"Where will you move to?"

"As far away as possible"

In the short time since the Americans had arrived our lives had been turned upside down. Now no one dared to venture out in the dark knowing too well that hundreds of innocents had been cruelly slain here. Children had been grabbed by their legs and smashed to death on the very same boulders that we had so often played on. How could we live here knowing the truth about the land we cultivated and the grass we played upon; the brilliant white sand where we sunned ourselves?

Streams of blood from so many victims must have flowed like rivers where we were now standing. Whether it was history or not we felt we had to get away from there and find new places to live. Everyone thought the same; all wanted to get away but it wasn't that easy to leave. Days turned into weeks and weeks into months. There were more meetings with Riaci and his village community and as our friendship grew we learned to live with the island's past.

One afternoon in July 1944 as we played on the beach with the GIs Padre Victor came running to tell us that several Fijian soldiers had been killed in the Solomon Islands. Shocked and horrified we ran back to our huts and listened to the news on the radio. The programme in Hindustani reported that sixteen men had been killed in a frightful battle with the Japanese. Names of the dead had not yet been released as their families had to be notified first. We sat terrified in a huddle around the radio and prayers in Hindi were said for the safety of the brave men fighting the Japanese in the Solomon Islands.

We waited patiently until we heard the sound of lali drums from Riaci's village. From the tone of the drums' beat father knew that someone had died. Then the names of Riaci's sons were announced on the radio. It was Revuka the eldest boy and then Revula the youngest. There were four dead from Riaci's village; all were descendants of Ratu Udre Udre. Revuka was only 26 years old when he died and destined to succeed his father as High Chief. He had left a young wife and four small daughters behind, all of them under the age of twelve. Revula wasn't married but had fathered many children in and around neighbouring villages. He was known as the wild one.

Although we didn't know them personally others who did described both brothers as gentle giants; tall and strong like their father and just as handsome.

CHRIS NAND

A few days later we gathered at the old tomb and saw the dark wooden coffins of the four servicemen being lifted from the back of an army truck and placed around the tomb of their great grandfather. Then, one by one they were carried through our village to the beach and after being placed in war canoes were gently rowed up the river to their village. There, the coffins were wrapped in homemade coconut matting and left in the communal house for a week before burial. We went up to the mountain village to share the sadness and pay our last respects to the dead.

Shortly afterwards the Solomon Islands campaign came to an end after many brave allied and Fijians soldiers had lost their lives. We mourned the dead with our native friends. Instead of spending time playing together the kindly Americans set up a school in their tent and taught us English. Each morning we made our way to one of the army tents. There, a blackboard was fixed and lessons began. We sat on the floor cross-legged and listened to the GIs before imitating whatever they said. It wasn't long before we were singing Yankee Doodle Dandy; Old McDonald had a farm and the American National Anthem. We sang at the top of our voices, mimicking every word and strutted proudly whilst singing the songs we had learned.

One morning as we were singing Ring around the Roses the Catholic missionaries arrived from the church that had provided us with sanctuary during the hurricane. We recognised the missionaries and running to their jeep shook hands and shyly said a few words in English.

"Well done," said Sister Henrietta as she clapped and smiled. "And where have you learned how to speak English may I ask?"

"From the Americans," we chorused.

"Ah, I see: How very smart of you. Would you like to learn more? How to read and write in English?" asked Father O' Donald.

"Yes, Father, we would."

"Then you shall, my son. You shall." he laughed. When father saw the missionaries he invited them to sit in the shade of the mango tree outside our front door before offering them refreshments. We had no chairs or tables so wooden soapboxes were provided for them. Excited at the unexpected arrival of the missionaries we sat on the surrounding grass. I was wondering if they had come to take us to their school adjacent to the church.

Father Marcel was the first to speak. He told us he was French and had come to Fiji many years previous to educate the native people. He chuckled nervously as he explained. Father O' Donald's story; he had spent much time in India and because he spoke Hindustani fluently was sent to educate the local Indian population and spread the word of Jesus Christ.

"I am from Ireland and speak only English," Sister Henrietta told us before adding: "But I am learning the native and the Hindustani languages." She then blurted out a few words in broken Hindi in parrot fashion which made us laugh.

"The Bishop of Fiji, Rev Foley has sent us here," we were told: We are to talk to your village elders so we can take the children to our boarding school and give them a sound education."

Father agreed that it was an excellent idea but grandfather grumbled that it would be only over his dead body: "We Hindus will never let our children become Christians and eat our sacred animals. Please leave us alone and go away," he said as he turned towards the missionaries. I frowned and looked down at my feet. I wanted to go to school and hoped grandfather wouldn't have his way.

It wasn't long before a row broke out. "For the good of my children, I am sending them to the Christian school. I don't care if they have to eat elephants to survive," my father yelled. My maternal grandparents Chand and Gulbi angrily stormed out of the meeting but my paternal grandparents, Lal and Rani stayed and gave their support to father.

Soon a prized goat was slaughtered, portioned and cooked into a curry dish. Rice and chapattis were then made and served followed by Indian sweets. Having no utensils for the missionaries they devoured the goat curry using their bare hands as sweat poured in rivulets down their bright red faces. The missionaries then drank much water to wash the food down whilst theatrically pretending they were enjoying every bit of it. I wasn't so sure.

As soon as dinner was over we helped them wash their hands in buckets full of water and then talk of our education began. "Do you have a birth certificate, young man?"

"Yes, Sister, said father."

"May I see it, please?"

Mother rushed into the house and brought the postcard size paper and gave it to her. "So you are named Krishna?"

"Yes, he is, said mother. "He is named after Lord Krishna." Father added that the name was given by a Hindu holy man when he was born. The man had predicted that he would travel the world in search of fortune and fame."

Father O'Donnell began to laugh. "Yes, I know the history of Lord Krishna. According to your holy scriptures, the Ramayana, he spent much of his time with the young ladies of the village playing a flute to entertain them all."

The missionaries burst out into laughter. "Sounds like he was a bit of a Casanova" said Father Marcel. Again they laughed. We had no idea who Casanova was but we laughed all the same.

Raising his eyes from the document the father said softly: "According to your date of birth I see you have just had your fifth birthday. Is that correct?"

Father agreed and then before I had time to realise what was happening I was given a battered old leather bag and lifted into the mission jeep with Sister Henrietta holding me tightly to her as we drove off. As I looked back over the sister's shoulder I could see my mother and my two sisters running behind the jeep. They were wailing as they waved and called my name. Before long the military-style vehicle was back on the dirt track throwing up clouds of dust as we headed towards the mission school.

On arriving at the mission church Father Marcel and Sister Henrietta smiled goodbye and stepped from the jeep. I realised then that the school I was being taken to was not here but somewhere else and began to sob. Half of me wanted to return home as the other half wished for me to go into the unknown in search of excitement or whatever promise may be out there. After all, Brad and his fellow Americans had left their homes which were thousands of miles away. I must do the same and be grown-up like they are? If I didn't like it there I could always come back.

As we drove off Father O'Donnell smiled and passed me sweets. I took them half-heartedly but was bewildered and wondered where he was taking me. The friendly priest smiled and kept on gathering speed on the long and dusty road into the unknown. He tried to jolly up the journey by singing to me. We drove for several hours and just after nightfall arrived at a cluster of buildings constructed of timber but with corrugated tin roofs.

"This school is called St Mary's Primary School and it is run by Marist missionaries. You will be taught in English by European nuns and from time to time by me."

As he spoke two friendly looking European nuns emerged from the dark and smiled a greeting at us; they were both dressed in white. I was then led into a long wooden building that had rows and rows of metal beds that resembled a colonial hospital. By this time I was nervous, homesick and hungry. Tucking me up under an old blanket spread on a metal spring bed they both left me to my thoughts and the long night ahead.

As soon as they had gone other kids who had been pretending to be asleep jumped out of their beds and surrounded me. I was horrified at their appearance for they all had bald heads: I began to shiver and cry. To me they looked like little monsters from the children's stories my grandmother used to tell me. Some shook my hand while others opened my bag and searched through my belongings. "Don't be frightened," said an older boy. "The nuns shave everyone's heads to keep it clean and free from lice."

I kept quiet and tried to hide beneath the bed sheets.

"What's your name?"

"Krishna,"

Everyone laughed. "Krishna what?"

"Krishna, that's all I know."

They giggled as they repeated my name. The journey had made me tired and I lay there quietly with my own thoughts. I was missing my family and friends; I was miserable that I didn't have time to say goodbye to my American friends. I had no idea that this was to be my home for the next ten years and that I wouldn't see my family for at least two years. Nor was I to know that I would be on the receiving end of excessive violence at the hands of some of the nuns teaching at the school. My detention there, for that was what it was, would set a pattern for the rest of my life in one way or another. Sleep comforted me after a little sobbing.

As dawn broke early next morning I was awakened by the sound of bells. There was pandemonium all around me as children jumped from their beds before rushing to the bathroom and toilets to wash and dress. "It's six o'clock," I heard a boy shouting.

RETURNED TO DEVIL'S ISLAND

"Come on, Krishna, get ready. We have to go to mass. The nuns will be here soon to take us there." I didn't understand what he was on about but quickly dressed myself.

Soon afterwards two nuns entered the dormitory ringing small hand-held bells and praying as they did so. We formed a long line before they marched us to the church. This took about ten minutes as the church was at the far end of the school compound. First we passed the large low building that was the school itself and then we passed the canteen, kitchens and the convent where the nuns slept before finally reaching the church.

Inside we were surrounded by statues, candles, flowers and wooden pews for us to sit and kneel on. Father O'Donnell conducted mass. Afterwards we were taken to the canteen to receive two slices of bread and butter each with a large mug full of tea. Immediately afterwards we were taken to the gardens. These surrounded the school and the church and there we were set to work.

The older children mowed the lawn with a hand-held lawnmower. Others picked fresh flowers for the church. I was taught to weed and brush the cement paths around the long stretch of garden. After that a gentle and kind nun by the name of Sister Mary took me by the hand and sitting me on the school veranda shaved my head clean whilst I protested and cried. "Don't cry, little boy we won't hurt you. We're just trying to keep everyone clean and healthy; that's all."

Showers followed the gardening tasks. As I took my shirt off Sister Chang noticed I was wearing a Hindu medallion around my neck. Rushing over to me she snatched the pendant from my neck and threw it in the overgrowth close to the shower cubicles.

"What is this?" she screamed. "Some sort of idol worship? You come here and want to be fed and educated. How dare you bring this pagan filth with you?" I was then handed a new toothbrush and some toothpaste. Then rage over, patting me benignly on my head, she handed me a blue shirt and a pair of khaki shorts. "Wear these, young man, and then get into line for school."

Outside the school there were more prayers chanted. Hymns were chorused and there was the honouring of the British union flag under which we sang the national anthem, God Save our Gracious King. We were then marched off in our bare feet to our classrooms: 'left, right, left, right'. Once at our desks more prayers were said before we settled down and lessons were begun.

My first few days were spent learning the prayers, hymns and catechism. Then taken to mass on my first Sunday morning I was baptised. My name was changed to James and the head nun required that I renounce the name of Krishna.

"You must only answer to the name of James. No one must ever call you by that pagan name again. Do you understand, young man?" said Sister Magdalene the headmistress. I assured her I did understand.

"What's your name, young man?"

"My name is James, sister"

"And don't you ever forget that. Do you understand?"

After the baptism I was treated to a feast of chocolate cakes, ice-cream and jelly before being told to rest awhile in the school's library with the other children. Sunday was to be our only day of rest as no one was allowed to work on the Sabbath. We read books and prayed most of the time.

At twelve noon the bell rang and the children then rushed to the canteen for lunch. I followed and took my seat at a long wooden table. The girls were sitting at similar tables behind us. It was when we were settled and quieted that two young lady cooks began to serve curry and rice on our dinner plates. These were already laid on the tables in front of us. One of the ladies served some rice and curry on my plate and seeing the meat I remembered what my grandfather had once said about eating the sacred animal.

I was still staring stubbornly at the meat when a boy named Francis advised me: "You better eat the meat before Sister Chang comes. She will ram it down your throat. They give beef to all the newly converted Hindus to be sure you're not a Hindu any more. It's no big deal. We all had to do it. You will get used to it."

I hesitated and began to eat only the rice and leave the meat on the side of the plate but true enough Sister Chang did arrive on the scene of the crime. Seeing what I had done she was beside herself and screamed: "James don't you want to eat? You can stay hungry if you want, I don't mind."

I looked up at her florid face but mulishly refused to eat the meat. Contemptuously she grabbed my knife and fork and deliberately cut the meat into smaller bits. Then with one hand she grabbed my cheeks and with the other force-fed me whilst yelling repeatedly; "chew, chew, chew. Come on swallow. We don't have all day. Hurry up, little boy."

Swallowing the meat I rushed out as soon as lunch was over and was sick in the flower bed. Soon I was surrounded by other children who included a small European child who appeared from nowhere and popped a sweet in my mouth. "This will make you feel better," she said and then ran away. I chased after her but she disappeared into her classroom.

There were over two hundred boys sharing one dormitory and seventy four girls of all ages sharing another. Every morning beds were inspected and those who had wet their beds were lined up and beaten. The hard wooden floorboards and the corrugated tin roof of the building created a terrifying echo from the screams of children receiving a good hiding. Unfortunately, most of the children were either orphans or were unwanted by their parents; some were very poor and had nowhere to run away to. I wasn't unwanted or an orphan but I was of a near destitute family.

It was some days later that I learned that the little European girl who had given me the sweet was named Susan. Her Australian mum and dad had been through an acrimonious divorce and left their daughter with the nuns until they were in a position to have her re-join them in Australia.

Even though friendship between the boys and girls was discouraged Susan and I became the best of friends and stayed close to each other whenever possible. The education was free and I had little choice but to remain there for my own good. All that was required of us was that we learn, pray morning noon and night, and work hard in the school's plantations in our spare time.

As I settled in I got used to the frequent beatings but watching some toddlers suffer was more difficult for me to understand. Everyone had to obey the nuns' commands; especially those of Sister Magdalene the head nun. She could quickly get into a sadistic mood and beat the children with sticks, leather belts and even fists for the smallest misdemeanour.

In the school's plantation we grew everything we needed for our food supplies except meat. Meat was bought from the local butcher and I was now used to eating the dreaded beef. We were fed on oxtail soup, beef stew, beef curry and rice. After the hard work in the plantations at such an early age we were constantly famished and had no choice but to eat whatever there was on our plates. Beggars are never choosers.

We were not allowed to speak in either Hindi or Fijian; here only English was spoken. Anyone overheard speaking in another language was severely punished by Sister Magdalene. She would make us bend over and touch our toes following which she would beat us with a broomstick on the seat of our pants. Once I was beaten so hard that the welts on my buttocks took months to heal throughout which I was in a great deal of pain. At times like these I felt frightened, sad and missing my family and often cried myself to sleep at night.

There was no home contact as there were no telephones. We weren't allowed to listen to the radio or read newspapers. Indian songs were banned and replaced by Latin hymns and prayers. Our only contact with the outside world was the regular visit by the red bus known as the Royal Mail. This was the same bus that pulled up outside our old bamboo village next to the old tomb. I remembered the very fat middle-aged Indian bus driver we called Ram. But no one called him by his name; he was affectionately known as "Fatty". Ram was not only fat but was a jolly man too who always had time for us children. He taught us to read the words painted on the side of the Royal Mail bus. He told us the G.R. painted on the two front doors of the bus stood for George Rex, our king.

Occasionally he brought me a food parcel sent by my parents; sometimes a few shillings that mother had sent but there was never a letter inside. I later discovered the reason for this was their being illiterate; neither of my parents could either read or write. In their childhood days there were no schools nearby. When in their early teens they were forced by the Indian elders of the village into an arranged marriage even though they were strangers to each other.

Following my first year I made my Holy Communion and was confirmed. I was given yet another name so I was now James John. I was also a little taller, stronger and a little wiser; at least I thought so. Father O'Donnell taught me to serve mass and soon I was a regular altar boy.

One day after serving mass I was left alone in the church vestry to clean and tidy the place up. Suddenly I began to tremble with hunger pangs and my knees felt weak

CHRIS NAND

I had to eat something fast to recover or faint. I hurriedly opened the cupboards and took a hand full of Communion wafers and wolfed them down and gulp a little red wine that was used to signify the blood of Jesus during mass. As I recovered I saw the collection plate full of coins and with trembling hands I stole a few coins and put them in my pocket. I knew it was wrong of me to do so but I was overcome by hunger and temptation.

During the 1947 Christmas holidays I was finally allowed a home visit. It was my first break after two years of hard work, constant punishments and unremitting discipline. It was sad to be separated from Susan but I had little choice in the matter but to visit my family. Before I boarded the Royal Mail bus the nuns handed me a bible and a rosary along with several medals of Jesus, Mother Mary and the saints; this so I could pray daily and not revert back to my Hindu beliefs again.

As I clung on the old bus chugged along belching out diesel smoke. The smell of dust and dead frogs littering the dirt track made me feel drowsy. We passed through rolling hills, acres of sugar cane plantations and coconut groves. There were people selling home-grown products by the roadside and smiling women carrying babies on their backs while tending to cattle. They would wave cheerfully as we passed them by. Across the landscape of farms the herds of goats crossed the dirt track as bare footed men and boys dressed in loincloths smiled and waved to Fatty. The bus spluttered and heaved along its dusty meandering country lanes until eventually I spotted the familiar old tomb and home. As the bus pulled up alongside the boulders I stepped out and knocked on the wooden door on my bamboo home.

On the door opening my sisters looked startled as they saw my bald head but then there was immediate recognition and we hugged and kissed and a few tears were shed between us. When my mother set eyes on me she broke down and wept too. Her hands were stroking my bare scalp over and over again as she kissed and hugged me to her bosom: "Krishna, Krishna my son, what have they done to you?"

"My name is James John," I told them speaking like some sort of a robot with a programmed voice box.

Soon other members of the family on hearing the commotion emerged from their homes to greet me. Grandparents Lal, Rani and Gulbi, each hugged me and kissed me but my grandfather Chand, refused to touch or even look at me. In his eyes I was now a Christian. I had eaten the sacred animal and I was now recognised as an untouchable by Hindu standards.

When father arrived home he embraced me. My education being uppermost in his mind he instructed me to take up the Fiji Times and to read it so everyone could see the progress I had made As I did so he sat proudly on a soapbox listening to me read and there were tears in his eyes as he did so.

"Well done my son. We didn't have the chance to be educated but you have and when you return please learn as much as you can; it is for your own good."

"I will father. I like learning," I told him. The effect of my reading to him struck a chord in me too. It seemed to make all my troubles worthwhile.

RETURNED TO DEVIL'S ISLAND

On that Christmas Eve I walked to the hilltop to attend midnight mass at our local church of St Nicolas. Sister Henrietta and Father Marcel were both delighted to see me and I was asked to visit the confessional box, serve mass and to take Holy Communion. I did so but stopped short of confessing mortal sins already committed, especially stealing the wine and communion wafers from the church. Had I done so I would have been severely punished by Sister Magdalene and expelled from school.

Christmas Day we had a traditional dinner of goat curry and rice set out on the beach. It was then I asked about the American servicemen. Father told me the war in Europe was over; hostilities had ceased not long after I left for boarding school and most of the Americans had returned to the U.S. Only a few remained and were employed at the sugar mills and gold mines of Vatukola nearby.

I was sad to hear this news and strolled to where they used to camp. The tents had by now disappeared and the land was overgrown. All that remained where the ghosts and the memories of the fun we had together. I felt a sadness creep over me. Perhaps I had changed too.

In January 1948 I returned to St Mary's and realised that being close to Susan brought me an experience of exhilaration. It wasn't just her natural prettiness for this could be said of any youngster; there was an unfathomable appeal about her. Blonde, despite the relentless sunshine there was fairness to her skin that would never betray her lineage.

It was her eyes that truly set her apart for although I had seen many Europeans I had never before seen eyes like Susan's. Her eyes were brown but a light brown; a little like the colour of a lion's hide. Most intriguingly of all her right eye showed a delightful dark freckle or speckle. My eyes were constantly drawn to hers and my fascination never wavered.

Even though we weren't able to be alone together, just being aware of each other's presence and exchanging scribbled notes gave us a wonderful feeling of mutual affection. We had our secret places to hide notes and often she would leave a sweet or two she had received from the nuns.

Our backbreaking work in the plantations didn't bother us as it gave us a few extra minutes to be close together. We were both studious and ambitious and I think our closeness helped us to become achievers. Sister Mary had by then introduced us both to children's story books. Susan and I avidly read novels about Robin Hood, Sir Lancelot, Rebecca, King Henry V111, The Knights of the Round Table and Dick Whittington.

We both had an appetite for Australia where we hoped to find Susan's parents and with our yearning we shared a dream to travel to London. Sister Mary was born in Australia but had spent her childhood living with her grandparents in Dublin where she was ordained as a nun before she was transferred to Liverpool and finally to St Mary's. She was the one who had brought Susan up since she was abandoned at St. Mary's as a baby. She had also fired our imaginations and wanderlust with stories of her visits to Liverpool and London. In London she had actually seen Buckingham

CHRIS NAND

Palace and Tower Bridge. She had also seen King George, Queen Elizabeth and both the young princesses, Elizabeth and Margaret from a distance at least for they had waved from the balcony of the palace.

"You also have a good chance to travel and see such places when you become a priest," she told me.

That was news to me. I was unaware that I was being prepared for becoming a priest. However, the thought of travel did appeal and I decided to go with the flow as it where. From that day onwards I constantly dreamed about seeing places I had so far only read about.

On religious holidays and each Sunday we were allowed to use the school library. I never missed an opportunity to take advantage and read as many children's books as I could lay my hands on. I was fascinated by the adventures and explorations of Captain James Cook RN; the English adventurer, and to learn of Captain Bligh's visit to the South Seas.

On the morning of the of January 31, 1948, when working in the school gardens the solitude and silence was shattered by loud cries from Indian shopkeepers' who worked in the nearby town of Valabala. They had heard the news that Mahatma Gandhi had been assassinated and Hindus throughout the world were mourning his death. Thousands of people came out in the streets and it seemed each was wailing and obviously distressed at hearing the grim news. Many were beating their chests and calling out the Mahatma's name.

At the beginning of 1949 Father O'Donnell took retirement and was replaced by several young Irish fathers from an order called the Colombian Fathers. I never did find out why they were called Colombian and the fact that they came from Ireland only served to confuse me further.

They were fit young men and their purpose was to build a college nearby which was to be called St Joseph's College. Now confirmed Catholics we were not allowed to attend Hindu colleges to further our education. We had to be taught by Catholic missionaries only.

Attending our school was a good mix of ethnicities and nationalities. Some were indigenous Fijians whilst others hailed from China. There were Rotumans and Tongans, Samoans but most were Fiji born Indians. Susan was the only European and there were two small boys of mixed race. Their father was an Indian and their mother English. Apparently they were abandoned by their parents.

As we grew older we boys took boxing lessons from a new priest who had recently arrived from Ireland. Father John had been an amateur boxing champion before he became a priest. He also took us jogging and sparring with him; our thinking was that it was important to keep our bodies as healthy as our minds. On days on which it rained we either read books or had discussions and debates about race, language, culture and the less pleasing aspects of Fiji's gruesome history.

A young boy named Tomaci, whose family lived on the tiny island of Bau, had the most blood-curdling yarns to tell us. "My ancestors," he told us, "were cannibals. They were the finest of warriors and likely the best spear throwers in the region. Whenever they conquered a neighbouring village they would routinely kill the men and children. The young women were saved to be used in sex orgies before being sacrificed to the gods. After this ghastly end their cadavers were chopped up, cooked in ovens and then eaten."

"How do you know these stories?" we asked horrified.

"Our villagers always talk about the past. There is nothing to be ashamed about. Remember they were possessed by witchcraft and superstition. Such thoughts flooded their kava crazed minds and it is said that under the drink's influence they heard voices in their heads which ordered them to kill each other. They really believed that was the only way to survive in those days."

I found this a little unconvincing and echoed the others in asking what happened at the orgies.

"After the young women had been repeatedly raped the men sucked their broken limbs for raw blood before they were cooked and devoured by the villagers."

We youngsters sat there listening to these accounts with our faces screwed up in disgust and our eyes wide open, aghast as we listened to Tomaci's stories.

"Our predecessors believed that by sucking the blood from virgin limbs they would be granted eternal youth. As children were produced by them life itself came out of them," he explained quietly.

"And the corpses of the men and boys?" we asked.

"They were dragged back to the village by hand if the dead were on land. But when they raided islands they brought the dead back by canoe. Back at the village their bodies were placed in sitting positions and displayed. This was done by thrusting spears through their bodies to keep them upright. The bodies of children were hung upside down in the war canoes much like a display of fish caught from the ocean."

"That's nothing," called out a student we knew as Rambuka. "Wait until we start on you bloody Indians. We will skin you alive, fuck your curry-filled arses, chop your balls off and roast you like pigs."

We chuckled nervously as the natives roared with laughter at the unwanted interruption and threat. "We are Fijians too," I pointed out hesitatingly. "We were born here and our parents were born here."

"No bloody way! You are Indians and always will be but please don't concern yourselves; I was only joking."

Bunisa was the next to offer his version of local history. "They all had different traditions. In my village our ancestors after capturing the enemy trussed them before torturing them by chopping their limbs off while their victims were still alive and even cooking the severed limbs as their agonised victims looked on. Many of them, again whilst still alive, were wrapped in dry coconut leaves and cooked over open fires until well cooked and ready to be eaten."

"But the murdered were your own people; they were your own flesh and blood?" I remarked.

"Yes, I know that now but everyone had to kill. It was a kill or be killed culture and only time was going to change that. It had been the way of doing things for maybe thousands of years.

"How dreadful!"

"Wait until you hear what happened to Reverend Thomas Baker."

"I know: Reverend Baker was the first visiting missionary to be killed and eaten but I don't know exactly how it happened," I told him as other young children gathered around us to listen.

"Well, I'll tell you," interrupted Tomasi. "The Reverend Thomas Baker arrived in Fiji in July 1859 and began converting the natives by the thousands. One day he made his way up to the mountain village of Navosa.

"People had warned him not to venture there as the villagers were notoriously ferocious and they were known cannibals too. But filled with self-confidence the reverend wouldn't take advice. He got together seven young volunteers and off they went.

"As they arrived a ceremonial sacrifice was taking place. He just pushed his way into the crowd of onlookers. He was carrying a huge wooden cross and as soon as he saw what was taking place he tried to stop the human sacrifice. The natives didn't like being told what to do by a strange looking white skinned man. One of them approached from behind and struck him down with a battle axe and he was then mutilated on the spot. His face, genitals and stomach were cooked and eaten by the cannibals.

"What bastards! How could they do such awful things?"

"It is absolutely true! If you are ever in the capital city of Suva then you should visit the museum. His Holy Bible and battle axe used to fell him are there as tourists attractions."

"I will go there and see for myself. Do you know of other missionaries who were killed?"

Tomaci turned to answer my question: "No. Baker was the only one killed and eaten. There were two missionaries who trail blazed their way here before him. One was David Cargill and the other William Cross."

"What happened to them?"

"They were partly successful in stopping sex orgies and cannibalism but the natives became increasingly threatening and so they departed which was probably a wise decision. The Reverend Cargill went on to the Tongan Islands and Cross returned to England."

"This happened way before Fiji became a British Crown Colony. By that time cannibalism was already history," said Rambuka. "Our people are now church going and God fearing."

"Thank goodness for that," I muttered fervently beneath my breath.

* * *

It wasn't until 1950 that I next returned to our village for Christmas holidays. Susan was still at St. Mary's. Unfortunately five years had passed and there was still

RETURNED TO DEVIL'S ISLAND

no sign of her parents ever returning for her. Susan had written to them regularly but her letters were always returned. That Christmas I was heartbroken to leave her behind but there was nothing I could do but pine for her.

On this occasion when I arrived home I was amazed to see the changes that had taken place during my time away. Father had bought a small Austin van; an old battered vehicle but it was at least running. He had also bought an old fashioned gramophone of the type seen in His Master's Voice advertisements. Also a household iron fuelled by benzene.

The sound of Bing Crosby's Dreaming of a White Christmas made us look at the old Christmas cards the nuns had given us and wondered what it must be like to experience snow. Village people sang or whistled the English and American ballads without any real understanding of what it was all about.

Other changes had taken place but on a far grander scale. A timber and corrugated roofed town had sprung up in the valley. It included a small post office, police station, a dispensary and a wooden hut called The Theatre.

It was there I was to see my first movie; a film called Cobra Woman. The main characters were John Hall, Maria Montez and the little Indian elephant boy, Sabu. Before the film started we saw Bud Abbott, Lou Costello and the Pathe News from London. We also watched a film of the marriage of Her Majesty the Queen Elizabeth to Prince Phillip. This had taken place on November 20, 1947.

On returning St Mary's I penned an essay about the film but this didn't go down at all well with the sisters. "No young child should ever be allowed to see those filthy films," screamed Sister Magdalene. "All that hugging and kissing will corrupt your young little minds and lead you into temptation. James: Look at me, promise me that you'll never go to watch a filthy movie again?"

"I promise, sister. I promise," I spluttered as I wondered what on earth I had done wrong.

"Now off you go and pray in the church. You must ask Almighty God to forgive you for yet another sin committed."

A few days later we were allowed to visit the theatre, not to see 'filth' as the sister described it but to watch the movie Our Lady of Lourdes. To reach the theatre the nuns marched us through the dusty streets in our brand new multicoloured flip-flop sandals and arranged for us to sit tidily in front of the big screen. Two hundred scruffy head-shaven small boys and seventy two girls of similar age, we were surrounded by a group of nuns dressed immaculately in white. It must have been quite a sight.

* * *

December 1953 I was again given approval for a home visit; by then my father's enterprising little venture was beginning to prosper. He was not only selling clothes but Eno's Fruit Salts, Epsom Salts, Ovaltine, Rickets Blue and Berwick's Baking Powder. The latter used by Indian housewives to make chapattis and gull-gulla, which is a doughnut like cake.

When I arrived he had not long returned from a trip through remote mountain villages and had sold a van load of his goods. He couldn't stop smiling at his enterprise and its success. "They would have bought the shirt of my back if I had let them, Krishna."

"My name is James now, father."

"You'll always be Krishna to us. According to Father O'Donnell James is the name of one of the Saints form the bible."

"How do you know that, father?" I asked.

"Father O'Donnell came to see us one day and he told us they had changed your name to James. He said that you were named after a very special Saint so that he can guide you throughout your life from evil spirits and bring you back to us if you ever decide to leave us and travel abroad."

"Yes, I am named after Saint James and no one must call me Krishna again," I said determinably.

"Whatever, you'll always be Krishna our son and that is all that matters to us: Do you understand?"

I didn't reply but instead quietly helped father to unload the van. He had bartered goods in return for homemade mats, woodcarvings, baskets and other artefacts. The indigenous people in remote villages didn't have money so father part exchanged goods with them knowing he had a ready market for goods bartered.

"We'll go to Suva at the start of the royal visit; there we will sell these things to the tourists. They will purchase anything Fijian," he told me. Laughing at his high spirits I went inside the house as hot bowls of tea and bread was being served.

The six o'clock news on the radio reported that manganese has been discovered on the nearby hills of Nadi. This was land that belonged to Mr Hari Charan, an Indian street vendor. I was pleased for him as I had met him once outside our school. His sons' Biren and Akhil were at boarding school with me. Theirs was a real rags to riches story for they had become millionaires overnight.

The Fijian government had loaned them the necessary cash to build a small mine to extract the manganese for export. Machinery was supplied, jobs created and the small town of Nadi prospered as a result of the discovery. Good fortune had certainly bestowed its favours on the community; it was at this location that Fiji's first international airport was built.

The main news that evening was that Her Majesty Queen Elizabeth and Prince Phillip were on their way to Fiji. After visiting Australia and New Zealand they were due to arrive in Suva the capitol on December 17. The news reader spoke of the excitement in the streets of Suva. He also described the main street linking the wharf to the government buildings. Everywhere in Suva was decorated with thousands of fluttering union flags. Some of these were strung from lamppost to lamppost and others from palm trees.

Just a few days before the visit father and I drove to Suva in our rickety old van and parked close to the market, where we sold everything to the visiting tourists as father had once predicted. With his pockets full of ready cash father and I sneaked through the crowd and waited close to the main wharf. There, thousands of people from the surrounding islands had lined the main street leading from the quay to the Grand Pacific Hotel; they were there to give Her Majesty the Queen the best of South Sea Island welcomes.

Father hurriedly picked up two Union Jacks from a nearby stand and soon we too were waving flags and cheering. Fiji's military band dressed finely in red tunics and white frilly sulus began to play the national anthem. The Royal yacht Britannia gently tied up against the huge rubber fenders dangling from the wooden wharf.

Greeted by a twenty-one gun salute from the Fijian military Her Majesty Queen Elizabeth stepped ashore and immediately onto the red carpet lay before her. There she was welcomed by a small girl who placed a garland of flowers over her head. A few steps behind followed the queen's husband Prince Philip. The crowd were cheering at the tops of their voices as the royal couple were greeted by the governor of Fiji, Sir Roland Garvey.

We watched in awe as the famous pair stooped and stepped into the royal car and driven slowly towards the Grand Pacific Hotel. Leaving father by his van I followed the crowd now running behind the car to the hotel. On arrival the Queen and Prince Philip were met by masi-clad Fijian High Chiefs. They were carrying spears, battle axes and dancing in jubilation as a kava drinking ceremony was begun.

As deafening clapping began I squeezed through the crowd for a better look at unfolding events. From where I was peering I could see a High Chief kneel in front of Her Majesty and present her with a coconut bowl full of kava. She dutifully clapped three times, cupped the bowl with both hands and drank it before handing the empty bowl back and clapping three times again. The din of applause was quite thunderous.

One by one the Fijian royalty; high chiefs and dignitaries took their turn in the kava drinking ceremony. After the ceremony the elite royal guards took up positions to escort Her Majesty to the Governor's Residence.

That evening father and I joined the thousands of people assembled at Albert Park overlooked by the Grand Pacific Hotel; we were there to listen to the queen's speech. Later, father and I had dinner in an Indian restaurant and drove home. A few days later I was back on the bus to boarding school.

On arriving back at St. Mary's I was punished for being two days late. Led into the yard by Sister Chang I was ordered to chop firewood for an hour before being allowed to have a shower and have dinner.

It was by then dusk and the evening sun was setting behind the tall crucifix situated in the school's playground. I was alone so I stripped off and wrapping a towel around my waist I slipped into the shower cubical. Turning on the cold water I thrilled to the cascade of spray. As I showered my mind drifted to Susan and I wondered what it must be like to tenderly kiss and make love to her.

The thoughts of doing so aroused me and in a trance-like state I closed my eyes and began to gently masturbate. Only when I had reached orgasm did I open my eyes to see a face peeping at me from over the roofless shower. I am not sure which of us was the most aghast; me or Sister Chang. Her eyes were bulging and she was clearly horrified. She must have crept in and was standing either on a chair or a box and watching me over the shower cubical. I hadn't heard her arrive due to the noise made by the shower.

At that point she began to scream. Hurriedly wrapping my towel around my waist I wished for the ground to open and swallow me. I instinctively new I would get severely punished for committing the 'sin of the flesh' the most dreaded sin the nuns frequently worn us about.

"James, you filthy little pagan: How dare you abuse yourself when we are trying our best to bring you up as a good Catholic?"

Sister Chang then began to scream hysterically for Sister Magdalene to come and punish me. "Sister Magdalene, Sister Magdalene, please hurry. I have seen him committing the sin of the flesh? Please Sister Magdalene. Come quick and see for yourself."

The Head Sister, sensing an outrage against decency arrived on the scene carrying with her a baton. Both nuns arm-locked me and dragged me out from cubicle. Manhandled I was forced to bend forward and touch my toes before taking the full force of the first hit on my buttocks. Involuntarily jumping as a consequence of the excruciating pain the towel fell to the floor but she didn't stop flailing until my tortured flesh was red raw.

My screams of agony brought other boys running to the scene but they couldn't interfere as they had all been victim to the head nun's outbursts and beatings. When she finally calmed down she was breathing heavily from her exertions. Taking a contemptuous look at me she then casually walked away with a sort of silly grin on her face. As soon as the nuns left some older boys helped me to dress and guided me back to my bed in the dormitory.

*   *   *

Next morning I could hardly walk due to the pain and stiffness felt from my waist down: somehow I managed to falteringly walk to the church. There I was ordered to confession by the nun before being allowed to serve mass.

In class that morning it was Sister Chang's turn to teach us. On arriving in the classroom she stood at the room's head as usual and greeted us.

"Good morning sister," we chorused.

The sister was breathing fire and walked straight to my desk and ordered me to stand atop it, calling me a 'filthy child' as she watched me climb up on to the desk lid.

The desk was uneven and wobbly and my knees buckled with fear from my uncertain perch. It was then that she started to prod my groin with a ruler and scream: "This boy here is the reincarnation of the devil. I have seen him with my own eyes, committing the sin of the flesh."

RETURNED TO DEVIL'S ISLAND

Some of the boys and girls in the class began to giggle at her words whilst others, their eyes filled with curiosity, balefully stared at me. Naturally I was embarrassed and felt like leaping from the desk and making for the door but thankfully the arrival of a new nun changed Sister Chang's mood. Gesticulating she ordered me to step down and resume my seat. I was still in pain from the previous evening's beating and struggled to take my place on the desk's seat. The new nun curiously watched me as Sister Chang introduced us to her.

"This is Sister Angela," she informed us: "She has come here from Australia to be in charge of the medical department of our school. She is a doctor."

Despite my discomfit I was quite taken by the new sister's charm and prettiness. Tall and slim she was dressed in a brilliant white habit. Only the crucifix around her neck and the shoes she was wearing contrasted for they were black. Her sapphire blue eyes twinkled as she smiled and I think we were all taken aback by the whiteness of her teeth and the warmth of her smile. She was to us like a vision. We looked at her almost disbelieving of our own eyes; it was as if an angel had suddenly descended upon us.

"I am pleased to meet you all," she said demurely.

"Pleased to meet you Sister," we called back. Not only was she very beautiful, she had also arrived in time to stop my very public humiliation. After a brief chat with Sister Chang she smiled at the class and disappeared from view. Just than the bell rang for morning prayers and I was so thankful for my lucky stars to be saved by the bell.

During the next few days we were inspected for lice and our beds checked for bedbugs by Sister Angela. She had chosen Susan to be her assistant as a trainee nurse. Not surprisingly the school surgery suddenly became very busy as more and more teenage boys arrived with every kind of undiagnosed malady imaginable; and I too made the pilgrimage to see our two angels of mercy.

Susan always met everyone with the same charming smile; a twinkle in her eyes and a gentle kindness in her voice; my knees wobbled each time our eyes met. I often wondered if everyone found the fleck in her eye as appealing as did I. It was then that I knew I was in love with her. At this stage I was thinking of her day and night and fantasised about her constantly. I was truly obsessed with her charm, personality and serene beauty.

In January 1954 I was beaten again by the head nun. She had caught me perusing an exercise book full of Indian love songs and was summoned to her study. That day there were three of us outside her study, each waiting for punishment. All three of us were wearing double pairs of shorts each; this was to cushion the blows to our buttocks when the full force of her baton landed. An older boy named Francis was to be the first to be called. Then it was the turn of a boy named Thomas: I would be following him.

On entering the study I was again ordered to touch my toes. As I did so the nun barked out that I was nothing less than a little monster. "Go on! Touch your toes," she screamed.

I had little choice but to obey and trembling like a leaf did so remembering the earlier beating I had received. Holding aloft the wooden baton with both hands she brought it savagely down and hit me so hard I fell to the ground. I tried to crawl away from her but she kept on hitting me.

"Stand up, stand up, you filthy little boy. What did I tell you about filthy pagan songs?"

As I staggered to my feet she frenziedly struck me again and again. The more I screamed the harder she hit me. It seemed to satisfy her that she was administering the punishment as she thought she should. By this time she was out of her mind and in a sadistic frenzy.

After ten strikes on my backside I again fell to the floor and this time I couldn't rise to me feet. Hauling me to my feet by the collar of my shirt she violently shoved me out of the study. I stumbled several times and tried to walk but couldn't. Some kind soul took pity on me and helped me back to the dormitory, there to leave me lying face down on the top of my bed. I was still sobbing and whimpering when I heard the rear door of the dormitory creak open and glancing sideways saw Susan approaching my bed.

This increased my fear for what if the nuns caught her visiting me? I could see the fear in her ashen face too as she drew closer. She must have been thinking the same fears. Her beautiful white face was now turning crimson. I tried to get up, to take hold of her but I couldn't. Placing her finger to her lips she handed me a small jar of ointment.

"Here rub this on the welts. It will ease the soreness," she said.

Impulsively I grabbed her hand and kissed it before she vanished as silently and as quickly as she had arrived. As she rushed away from my bed she left an aroma of fresh talcum powder. I watched her silently as she disappeared through the back door. Being beaten by the head nun might be a blessing in disguise. It had certainly brought Susan and me closer.

During the Easter holidays that year I was selected to carry a heavy brass crucifix heading the Easter procession through the Hindu town of Valabala. From there we would make our way to the hill top. Leading the procession I was followed by the boys and then the girls and taking up the rear the nuns. Behind these were about three hundred local men, women and their children. At the tail end of the procession there were two prayer chanting priests sprinkling holy water on the Hindu onlookers from the neighbourhood.

After ten minutes we crossed the railway crossing separating our school from the shanty town. It was then that I began to feel very hungry and weak; my baggy red robe became entangled with my flip-flop sandals and stumbling I fell to my knees across the metal tracks of the railway.

Fortunately the shiny heavy crucifix missed my head by inches as it fell to my side. Susan rushed to my aid and tried to help me to my feet but Sister Magdalene gesticulated fiercely for her to get back into line and rejoin the procession. Susan bravely defied Sister Magdalene and helped me to the school dormitory to recover.

Once inside the deserted dormitory Susan noticed I was no longer limping. This seemed to make her angry and yelling at me she called me a fake and added that it was no wonder I was always getting into some sort of trouble.

I pleaded with her: "I needed to be alone with you Susan. I can't think of anything but you. I love you Susan and you know that don't you?"

"Jamie, I love you too but we'll be both severely punished when Sister Magdalene returns. I can't stand it when you get beaten; sometimes I cry myself to sleep thinking about you."

Unable to control an impulse I reached forward and grabbed her tightly and kissed her: it was the first time we had ever done so. She held me as tightly to herself and returned my kisses before grabbing at my hand.

"Let's go," she urged me before leading me towards the door.

"Where too?"

"To my dormitory. It's safer there," she whispered defiantly: "There's no way I can catch up with the procession and to hell with Sister Magdalene. She can punish me as much as she likes."

As soon as we entered the girl's dormitory we rushed to Susan's bed and kissed a marathon of kisses before we were consumed with passion and made love. It was the first time for both of us and it was so scary especially when the nuns used to preach daily about committing the sins of the flesh and burning in the everlasting fires of hell. Afterwards we were both shivering with fear as we held each other for comfort. In a state of panic I tried to persuade her to run away with me but it was futile: Susan says she has to stay with the nuns until she finds out the truth about her parents. She confessed to me that she constantly worries that the nuns were hiding something from her; about her parents abandoning her and their returning back to Australia. She had a theory that she could be an illegitimate daughter of one of the nuns. Now I was even more scared of the consequence if Susan became pregnant? History could be repeating itself if what she had told me about her mother being a nun was true. Suddenly Susan felt her groin and saw blood on her fingers and began to sob. I held her tightly and nearly jumped out of my skin when the church bells began to toll, an indication that the mass on the top of the hill has finished and the procession would be returning back to the church. Susan ran in the bathroom to clean and tidy herself fast. I hurriedly grabbed a black and white picture of her that was standing on a small table at her bedside and ran back to my dormitory and dived into my bed.

The procession passed the dormitories and made its way slowly towards the church. It was then that the bells began to chime for the second time, which was indication that the procession was over. Soon everyone would congregate in the school canteen for a late lunch.

Afterwards Sister Angela came to inspect my ankle and told me that it was a minor strain and assured me that no bones were broken. She also told me that Susan was in Sister Magdalene's study and being punished for defying her and helping me to the dormitory.

CHRIS NAND

I lay in bed shivering with fear, absolutely terrified what might happen to Susan and me if blood was found in her underwear or her dress. My fears worsened when I heard footsteps of someone running towards the dormitory door. Suddenly the door was flung open and David my class mate arrived screaming to my bedside.

"Sister Magdalene has chopped off Susan's hair and is slapping her hard on her face. Please Jamie, do something. She's insanely angry and will be coming to punish you soon."

Not long afterwards I heard approaching footsteps. The door slammed open and Sister Magdalene stormed in followed by a hundred or so shaven headed boys like a people train. I took off at a run and hid in the boys' toilet. In she came after me and viciously kicked the toilet door open as would a man. Her eyes were bulging with irrational rage as I held the drainpipe tightly to prevent her from pulling me away from the toilet.

After struggling for awhile but failing to dislodge my grip she unfastened her shoe and began beating me with it whilst yelling: "I want you to report for confessions first thing in the morning, before serving mass again. Do you understand?"

After she had stormed out I staggered out of the toilet and slipped beneath the blanket on my bed. Life had now become unbearable. All I could think of was absconding but the thought of leaving Susan prevented me from doing so. It seemed I had to endure whatever came my way just to be close to Susan.

I was now deeply in love with her and felt deeply that I had to stay and help her find the truth about her mother and father. It was degrading for a Hindu to be beaten by a woman, especially with her shoes but I was now a Catholic and for Susan's sake I had little choice but to bite my bottom lip and stay.

I was still deep in thought of what had really happened between Susan and me in her own bed. We were both trembling with fear when making love and talking excitedly. Yes, I had felt penetration when Susan had gasped and held me tightly. I felt her fingernails dig into my shoulders but it was all over in a few minutes. There was blood on her fingers so we really must have made love? All kinds of questions were coming thick and fast when suddenly a group of boys stormed the dormitory and surrounded my bed but before they had time to speak to me Sister Chang and Sister Mary appeared. "I have brought you some lunch." Sister Mary placed a dish of beef curry and rice on the bedside table.

"Thank you, Sister but I am not hungry."

"You haven't eaten since breakfast."

"I just don't feel like eating anything."

"Please, James, eat up. We have some very important visitors coming to visit our school next week and all the older boys including you will have to serve mass and assist them throughout their stay here at St. Mary's, you understand?"

"Yes, Sister, I do but my ankle hurts when I walk."

"You'll be fine by next week, I am sure of that," she smiled pleasantly and patted my head.

As soon as the Sisters realised everyone had gone down to the shower rooms they headed towards the shower cubicles. I watched them till they disappeared through the dormitory door.

That night when the children were asleep I rose from my bed and gathered up my spare school uniform. Then, making my way for the door I stopped before opening it. I just couldn't bring myself to leave. I did venture outside and silently sat beneath the mango tree for a while before returning to my bed.

The following morning my whole body ached from the beating I had received from Sister Magdalene's shoes. The children by then had left for mass but I stayed in bed. Thursday arrived and was of course the fourth day after Easter Sunday. Throughout the day I lay in my bed; I was sorely missing Susan and impatiently I waited for her but there was no sign of her.

David brought my lunch and told me Susan was being punished on a daily basis by doing the nun's laundry and ironing their habits. At other times she had been spotted cleaning the convent and serving at the nun's dinner tables. On hearing this news I felt utterly dejected. I even thought of forcing my way into her dormitory where I might grab her hand and go on the run with her, maybe to some remote island. I was absolutely besotted by Susan and never went to sleep without thinking of her. The next morning, I woke up to the sound of bells and Sister Chang's voice. "Come on, hurry up and get in line for church."

As she came past my bed she stopped and came closer to the bed. "James, get up?"

I turned around whilst grimacing and pretending to be in great pain. "I can't Sister, my ankle hurts."

"Let me look?"

I took my foot from beneath the bedclothes and showed my lower leg to her and as I did so she prodded it with her fingers. "It looks fine to me. Please stand up and let me see if you can walk?"

Standing unsteadily on one foot I hopped around the bed. I wasn't doing it very realistically. She looked at me with contempt and told me about the visiting VIP guests who were due.

"James, Sister Magdalene would like to see you at mass on Sunday: Not only you but Francis, Charles and David too. She wants all the experienced boys to be there because Cardinal Heenan from England, and our own Bishop Foley, are visiting our parish. You four have been chosen to serve mass. Do you understand me?"

"Yes Sister, I do?

I was about to doze off again when the deafening sound of children approaching woke me from my reveries. I pretended to be asleep but within minutes there was pandemonium and excited children surrounded my bed. "Jamie, Jamie, guess who is coming to visit our school on Sunday?"

I pretended I didn't know. "Please tell me who is coming to visit us on Sunday?"

"Cardinal Heenan from London and our Bishop from Suva, they are both coming to visit our school."

Feigning surprise I didn't let on that Sister Chang had told me about the impending visit. Soon the children had brushed their teeth and were tucked up in their beds.

That Friday morning I went to confession but there was no way I was going to confess that Susan I had actually committed the sin of the flesh. Afterwards I entered the church and saw Susan for the first time since we had consummated our love for each other in her dormitory. I could see her kneeling with the other girls and earnestly praying. Her pony tail had gone but even with cropped hair she looked as beautiful as ever. When she looked up our eyes met and I felt very miserable for not being able to take her in my arms and comfort her.

During prayers and hymns we managed to catch each other's eye but the look on Sister Magdalene's face put the fear of God into both of us. Susan looked so beautiful and serene as she stood there singing hymns and praying. After mass we had to work in the gardens outside before breakfast. Later, having finished eating the bread and cup of tea given to us Sister Chang announced that the sisters were taking us to the beach to trap fish and black crabs in the mangroves. What was planned was a seafood banquet for the cardinal, the bishop and their entourage.

Hurriedly we changed into bathing shorts, formed a line and marched off towards the beach. There we spent the entire morning trapping fish, crabs and various crustaceans before bringing our haul back to the kitchen.

On the Saturday morning as soon as mass was over we had breakfast in the school canteen before being marched back to the church again. Not to pray this time but to clean every surface before the proposed visit took place. Some children were delegated to brush the wooden floor and dust the pews. Others decorated the altar with red and pink roses and white water lilies. I worked in the vestry with the nuns.

Once all the preparations were completed we returned to our dormitories to shower, change our clothes and return to the church for a rehearsal, which went on until lunch. Afterwards we were taken to the school's plantation where we were to dig up fresh sweet potatoes, yams, tapioca, fruit, green beans; to then carry it back to the school's kitchen before helping Maria the cook to prepare Sunday's banquet.

We older boys washed the yams, sweet potatoes; cutting them up and placing them in large metal pots ready to be boiled. Meantime Sisters Chang and Mary took the younger children to be showered and readied for Evening Benediction before a late meal.

Once we had finished helping Maria in the kitchen we too went to the showers and were made ready for events that were to take place that evening and especially the following day. Father John conducted the Benediction prayers and spoke about the important visit that was to take place the next morning. By the time we took our seats in the canteen for our late dinner some young children were crying or whining whilst those really exhausted fell asleep with their heads in the dinner plates. After such a long day we were all glad to be finally in the dormitory and in our beds.

Sunday morning the chimes of the church bells woke me suddenly from a coma-like sleep. We were so pleased to see Sister Roselyn and Sister Agnes, regarded for their sweet dispositions, on morning duty instead of the old dragon Sister Chang.

RETURNED TO DEVIL'S ISLAND

Both sisters were broadly smiling as they hurried us along to wash and ready ourselves for mass. Stepping out of dormitory we saw in the distance Sister Chang and the girls marching towards the church. We soon caught up with them and in high spirits entered through the two side doors of the church.

The church was almost filled with local parishioners and many more were still standing in line trying to get in from the main entrance of the church. As soon as everyone was seated the prayers were said and hymns were sung before us altar boys and the priests, assembled outside the main entrance of the church. Moments later Bishop Foley and Cardinal Heenan with our parish priests arrived and a signal was given for us to enter the church.

We were followed by the Bishop finely and impressively dressed in church purple. He sprinkled holy water on the parishioners as he passed down the aisles. Immediately behind him was the cardinal dressed in a black robe and with a black mitre perched on his head. This senior figure carried a large brass cross in one hand and blessed the worshipers with the other. Following immediately behind us, walked the priests and carefully selected members of the parish.

As soon the cardinal arrived at the over resplendent altar we joined him to serve mass before he made his way up to the pulpit for a sermon that put the fear of God in me. The effect on the parishioners was likely the same.

He spoke and emphasised the importance of the Ten Commandments and told the assembled congregation how the heathens and sinners would certainly burn in the deepest fires of hell. Listening to his every word I discreetly managed to glance at Susan standing a few steps away. She was looking very edgy, occasionally biting her bottom lip and with her hands clasped tightly around a small hymn book. The puckered brow and her deathly white knuckles suggested that she believed every word the Cardinal was saying.

I thought I could see sorrow if not pain in her eyes and my heart went out to her. I was passionately in love with Susan, which was fuelled in some part by my sorrowful empathy for whatever fears she was holding inside her. I longed to take her in my arms, to kiss and comfort her but that was not to be. Deep down in my heart I knew that it would be difficult for us to ever meet in private or even enjoy the briefest of chats ever again.

I was relieved when the sermon was finally over and with lifting spirits we formed a line before being marched into the canteen for breakfast after which we retraced our steps to the church. There was a big clean up and we were to be the cleaning squad.

I was in the church vestry when I came face to face with Susan. There was intense emotion between us as our eyes met but it was impossible for us to say even a few words. Keeping a little apart as we worked our furtive glances and expressions do our talking. Our clandestine attempts at telepathy didn't go unobserved as whilst gazing longingly at Susan I was grasped by Sister Magdalene and taken outside the church and severely spoken too. "Why are you always looking at Susan?"

I was non committal to the point of near denying it but the sister was well aware of the mutual attraction. She told me in no uncertain terms that I had better keep my eyes off her otherwise I would be severely punished.

The next few days were spent avoiding each other, not by choice but by circumstance for we were being buffeted by fate. We did infrequently meet in the classrooms where we might nod and smile at each other but there was no physical contact. The raw emotion was becoming unbearable and in a vain effort to take my mind off her I studied, read extensively in the school library and fortunately passed the entrance exam to St Joseph's College with flying colours.

Once the exams were behind us the nuns gave each of us a treat and took us to the theatre to see the movie St Bernadette. The boys sat in the front close to the large white screen; the girls sat directly behind us but still there was no contact between Susan and myself. I didn't want to make it too obvious so I avoided the temptation to turn around and look at her. In some way knowing she was there and close to me was in itself comforting. The nuns watched us like hawks.

After the afternoon film we walked slowly back towards the school. I walked as close to Susan as I could without touching her physically and wretchedly not close enough for me to express my feelings. I am sure she knew it anyway but it would have been nice to express the depth of my love for her.

Days passed and I made a few visits to the small dispensary where she helped heal the sick and the ailing but it seemed we were destined never to be on our own. By the time Christmas was upon us I had made a firm decision to leave the boarding school. I entertained the thought that if I got work and was able to support myself I could return and take Susan with me. I was a good sportsman and boxer: I could even get work as a pugilist and earn good money. I had once heard Father John telling Sister Magdalene what good boxers David and I were. I felt that I was not cut out for the priesthood and determined to put as much distance between me and all things ecclesiastical as I could.

Packing my belongings and placing them carefully into my old bag I said my farewells to children who had been such good friends during the time I had spent there. There was nothing but poignancy felt for my orphan friends as the school, whatever their feelings were to be their home until they reached maturity.

After the leave-taking rituals I took a stroll past the girls dormitory hoping that I would be able to get a last glimpse of Susan; I desperately needed a last image of her that I could carry with me. Sadly there was not a sign of her and no telling where she might be. Turning my step towards the convent door there was just one more thing to do; that was to say farewell to the sisters.

Knocking on the wooden door I could soon hear footsteps approaching. When it swung open I found I was face to face with Sister Chang. Her face clouded over as soon as her eyes went from me and then to the battered old leather bag I was clutching: It was the very same bag as I had arrived with so long ago. You don't forget such things and I suppose it spoke more eloquently than I myself could. "Are you going on holiday, James; somewhere nice I expect?" There was no sincerity in her voice and if anything she was a little sarcastic.

"Yes, I have decided to return to my home village, sister. The school has nothing more to offer me. I intend to find work and to eventually travel to England. I am not cut out to be a priest."

"But, James," she said meaningfully: "Have you forgotten? We have spent many years of our valuable time instructing you in the ways of the church and the priesthood. There is only one way you can show how grateful you are and that is to remain here. What is the point of your going back to the primitive life of a mud village from which we rescued you? Here you have been given food, shelter and care not to mention an excellent education to which you haven't contributed any payment at all. Have you thought this through? You cannot be serious about giving up all this to return to what . . .". The sister left the term primitive hanging in the air.

"Please don't get me wrong, Sister Chang. Of course I'm grateful but I have made up my mind and I must go. David has already gone and I am catching the Royal Mail bus as soon as it arrives."

"But, James; you do realise that Father John will never allow you to leave St Mary's. There has been too much invested in you. He will come and find you and he will bring you back. This is your home and we have good plans for you."

I looked at her steadily: "It is my life, sister; not Father John's or yours. I am not a slave; I am not something that you own and can use as you see fit. The bus will be here very soon and no one can stop me going."

Children aware that something unusual was taking place were now gathering and whispering at the spectacle of the sister and me debating my future on the convent steps. It was then that Sister Magdalene arrived on the scene. Seeing my bag on the floor at my feet she kicked it aside causing it to fly open. She looked scornfully at the few items that fell from it she turned her face to mine. Her eyes were filled with contempt as though I were a naughty dog. I am sure she regarded me as being little more than a possession. Grabbing me by my collar she was clearly intending to forcefully drag me back to our dormitory.

"You, James, have been nothing but trouble since the first day I set my eyes upon you. I should have sent you packing then."

"Then you will be happy to see me go." I exclaimed as I struggled to free myself from her grip.

It was then that Susan arrived on the scene and burst into tears as she realised what was happening; clearly in view my clothes were now scattered across the ground and clear evidence of my intentions. Weeping, the young girl began to collect the spilled clothing and to stuff them back into the bag. At seeing her do so Sister Magdalene became incandescent with rage; she hated seeing her authority questioned.

"Susan! Get away from that pagan monster and get back to the washhouse right now. I want all the laundry washed and ironed by this afternoon."

Turning her attention to the gathering children she snarled that they too must get back to their work. For once unfolding events were more compelling than were her threats. The children refused to move although they shuffled and increased their distance from her to avoid being singled out. There were few of them who hadn't suffered at the sister's hands. Such open rebelliousness encouraged Susan for she too defied the sister and she carried on placing my stuff back in the bag.

It seemed that the sister was losing it as again and again she ordered Susan back to the washhouse or else suffer the consequences. I had to do something to break the impasse and grabbing the bag I turned to make off. Susan was now very much distressed and crying pitifully as she begged me not to leave her and the school. She was going to be abandoned the second time which was unbearable for the both of us.

"Jamie. Please don't go. I love you, Jamie, I really do. You can't leave me here: You are the only one I have."

"Susan, I can't stay here with these crazy people ramming their stupid religion down my throat."

Enraged at hearing my contempt for her religion the sister's arm swung like a battleaxe and I felt the stinging slap across my face. "How dare you talk to me like that? I am going to telephone Father John to come here and knock some sense into your thick scull."

The words were hardly out of her mouth when she disappeared into the convent, presumably to telephone the priest. I was furious and shouted after her that she should go to hell where she would be very welcome. Rising to the occasion I bellowed inside the still open door: "I've had enough of your constant beatings and the praying, morning, noon and night."

Just then the Royal Mail bus lurched to a stop a few feet away. Susan reached out to grasp my arm but Sister Angela was quicker. The nun had appeared from nowhere and had taken one of Susan's arms. Ram, the bus driver had some mail to deliver to the convent. I begged him to wait just for a minute or two. He just smiled and maybe not wanting to be involved dropped the mail off and climbed back into the driver's seat and released the handbrake.

The upset had certainly caught the attention of the passengers on the bus who were now gawping through the windows and peering at the spectacle occurring at the convent gates. This was destined to be the talk of the town.

Overwhelmed by my love for Susan I grabbed hold of her and held her tightly to me; longing to board the bus with her and leave that God forsaken mess behind us. Tenderly I kissed her on her lips. At the sight of such 'blasphemy' the three nuns unsuccessfully tried to separate us by force.

"Jaldi . . . Jaldi." I could hear the bus driver calling: "Hurry, hurry!" Breaking free of Susan I shouted to her: "I love you more than anything in the world; you alone. I will be back for you; I promise.

Running towards the bus, which by then was revving up and beginning to move I scrambled up its steps and ran to the back of the bus and in distress watched the poignant scene through dust and smoke I was leaving behind. As the bus pulled away the sight of the three nuns dragging poor Susan back to the workhouse filled me with horror and the scene was to never stop haunting me.

CHAPTER 2

The bus took me up and along the narrow overgrown and dusty route whilst I was wracked by guilt mixed with a sense of liberation. I sat with jaw set and my own thoughts at the fickleness of fate. Such was my mood still when we finally reached my old village, steeped in tranquillity, near to the lapping waves of the Pacific Ocean. Could there possibly be any place on earth more idyllic or welcoming?

Being home again was a relief in many ways. It was of course wonderful to be back with my parents and my small sisters, Sabita and Malti. There was sadly much pain and heartache in so many other ways. Did freedom have to carry such a high emotional price tag I thought as I emptied my bag of garments Susan had placed in there? The pain of missing her was unimaginable; it was heartache of a depth I had never before experienced. I knew that the love and the regret; the betrayal and the images of what she must be going through would haunt me for the rest of my life. I decided that for all the education I had received I wished I had remained in our village.

The days went by during which I again took up fishing and diving for oysters. I would swim in the mouth of the river where the Americans once had taught me how to master the sea waters. Many of my uncles and aunts, along with their children, had now moved to a town nearby called Vaileka. They were now living in safer homes with timber walls and corrugated metal roofs. Father too was in search of somewhere different to live. He too yearned to move on and distance himself from the past.

In our hut there was still no running water nor was there an electricity supply; the radio was still battery dependent. The clumsy telegraph poles the P.W.D. had erected were strewn hideously along the King's Road and were there primarily for the commercial units along the length of the highway. Only the sugar refinery and the Emperor Gold Mines of Vatukola had running water and electricity.

Well no one in their right mind was going to supply grass huts with electricity would they? I found it difficult settling back into traditional village life after being at boarding school. There I had taken for granted running water on tap and electricity. My dreams of leaving home and crossing the seas became more compelling. The years spent at the boarding school had changed me and whetted my appetite for more worldly experiences than those of a peasant villager. The happy-go-lucky little boy had become educated but sullen, or so the villagers told me. I smiled and told them it was just wanderlust.

That I should find paying work and save money; enough to enable me to travel was their advice. I had considered furthering my education at St. Joseph's College but decided against it: Besides, my parents couldn't afford the college fees. St Mary's had been free but the college was not. I had little choice but to get a job.

That evening before going to bed I listened to the news on the radio. As it came to an end my parents and sisters said good night and went to their beds. I twiddled the station finder and opted for the BBC World Service before finally getting into bed.

As dawn broke to the din of tropical birds making their presence known I took a peep through the window. From there I could see the mynah birds, black crows and the large black pigeons common to that part of the world.

I was still taking in the view when I heard someone turn on a radio. The sound of Hindu prayers could be heard. This was followed by the news and then the congratulations for the newly born and finally commiserations for those who had become bereaved.

It must have been eight o'clock when I heard mother's voice calling that breakfast was ready. Hastily cleaning my teeth I stepped through into our small kitchen. There we would sit crossed legged on the coconut matting and enjoy breakfast together as a family. Between mouthfuls of chapatti and vegetable curry we talked between ourselves. I couldn't keep up with the flow as my thoughts were totally focused on Susan.

Late that afternoon I received a letter from St. Joseph's College. It was congratulating me on passing the entrance examinations and the signatory looked forward to seeing me at the start of term. Father was adamant that he could not afford the fees; that I would have to remain at home and find paying work.

On the following Saturday evening the family as usual listened to Hindi programmes on the radio. It must have been a charming sight to see us as a family sitting on the matting quite enchanted by the sounds of tabla drums, sitar and violin accompanied by love songs.

Most of the Indian songs are about love but conversely young females were never allowed to meet boys of their own age. All Hindu marriages were arranged. In the unlikely event a young Indian girl was to fool around and become pregnant then their chances of marriage would be remote. Some committed suicide whilst others were passed on to older men who hadn't yet married; such unfortunate girls were cast out of their parent's home as untouchables.

The freedom of courtship was the sole preserve of males. There was no bar on my sleeping with any consenting female as long as they were from another race of people and not Indian. So for the teenage Indian girls life could be a period spent in self denial. The only enjoyment in their restricted lifestyle was to watch Indian films and listen to Indian music. That was until they were old enough to be required to take part in a marriage that had been arranged for them; often to a total stranger. I didn't like the idea but could not argue with the village elders.

On first travelling to the Fijian islands from India my grandparents had brought with them their own strict Hindu customs and made it clear that we all respect them. In India my maternal grandfather's father had died at the age of forty-six. Then the uneducated Hindu conformists had gathered around his home and demanded that his surviving wife should share the funeral pyre and burn on it with the body of her husband. They had caught her and drugged her before tying her to her husband's dead body. Then they had piled wood over them both and dousing them with paraffin cremated both my great-grandfather's corpse and his suffering wife. This barbaric custom was called becoming a sati. As widows were classed as untouchables they had to be disposed of in this manner. No Hindu man would ever have married such a woman.

My now orphaned grandfather, Chand, went off to live with his two elder brothers and their wives. There he was mentally and physically abused by his sister-in laws who used him as they might a slave until he was fourteen years of age. The drudgery didn't stop there. He was then used as an indentured slave delivering letters for the village Post Office.

On one of his deliveries he had met Gulbi who was to become my grandmother. The pair had fallen in love and eloped. Later they discovered the recruiting office in Calcutta where they were to sign up to a new life in Fiji. It was an escape but only of sorts for they boarded a rat infested ship called the Leonidas that chugged across the Pacific carrying labourers to wherever the British Empire needed them.

Grandfather was then just fourteen-years of age; Gulbi was thirteen. Had they not eloped both would have been forced into marriage to someone they neither knew nor necessarily liked.

The wooden vessel, overloaded with its 495 passengers, slipped its Calcutta moorings in February 1879. After ninety days in what can only be described as the voyage from hell the slave ship, for it could hardly be described otherwise, eventually moored in Fiji. The two had little idea of the world's geography; the distances involved or the different cultures. They had been tricked by a fast talking recruiting officer who was likely on a commission. This clerk had given no indication of the long arduous trip or the appalling conditions they would endure during the long voyage lest he lose his commission. On the way some passengers had succumbed to cholera or dysentery; others had jumped ship on arrival at ports the ship called in at; several had taken their own lives. Bodies were routinely tossed overboard. Four hundred and sixty-three souls did make it, which was a good survival rate for the times.

When those who had made it arrived in Fiji they were taken to a sugar cane plantation in the district of Navua. There they were set to work for the Colonial Sugar Refinery Company; they were to be contracted labourers for five years.

My paternal grandparents Lal and Rani had made a similar journey on a ship called the Syria. It had made most of the way to Fiji but had capsized and foundered a mile offshore on reaching the island.

CHRIS NAND

They were both fortunate to be plucked out of the raging surf by natives in canoes from which point they were taken to Navua where they were to meet Chand and Gulbi, my maternal grandparents.

The five years they spent working together can only be described as a living hell. Once their contracts had expired they were brought to Raki Raki to work the land under a lease arranged by the Colonial Sugar Refinery Company. The rain forest was to be cleared and replaced by sugar cane plantations. A refining mill was built nearby and sugar was to be exported across the world. Most of my relatives were then employed at the mill including my father. He was a steam locomotive driver who delivered freshly harvested sugarcane to the mill. Once he had used his savings to buy the old van he left the mill to become a mobile shopkeeper.

Having the first and only mobile shop in the village was fun. It gave me a chance to travel around the islands and visit remote villages, calling in at street markets to buy and sell whatever was in demand. Our own Saturday morning street market was my favourite as I would receive a shilling pocket money to spend. Six pence would go on a matinee and the remaining six pence on ice cream and jelly from the Chinese shop.

One day after seeing the Hindi film named Aawara I came home to find father counting his pounds, shillings and pence. Everything he had taken to the market had been sold and not surprisingly he was beaming ear to ear. We celebrated with some bottles of Fiji beer he had purchased at the Chinese store.

Back then it was illegal to sell and buy beer. Consumers of alcohol had to have an alcohol drinker's permit issued by the Fijian government. This permit looked like a small passport and bore the permit holders photograph. Only the Europeans and Chinese people were allowed to drink freely in the one and only bar attached to the Raki Raki Hotel. But bootleggers were rampant and alcohol and home grown marijuana was plentiful.

Necking a bottle of the beer father poured a tumbler full and passed it to me; the rest he drank straight from the bottle. We sat around listening to the Hindu programme on the radio until the sound faded without warning; the battery was flat and so replaced. When the programme finished I listened to the World Service on the BBC. Father explained that in England a radio had been invented that showed moving pictures. We laughed: Mother thought the beer had gone to his head. She ridiculed him: "Moving pictures on the radio may I ask?"

When I eventually crept into bed my thoughts again were to dwell on Susan. I had no regrets about leaving St Mary's but she would be confined to a bare dormitory with no radio, newspapers and no loved ones to spend time with; just a regimented life of prayers, prayers and more prayers in between beatings and cruel hardships.

Morning came and strong winds turned to tropical rain and rather than go to the markets we remained inside listening to the radio. Apart from the big house every village had their 'little houses', a euphemism for the lavatories. Basically it was a pit; a long drop with thatched roof over it, seats made from shaped boulders or cement and a bamboo wall built around it for privacy.

There was no running water or electricity. Hindus carry water in large fish cans to wash their backsides with after which they wiped themselves dry with newspaper or masi. This was done using the left hand only; afterwards washing the hand thoroughly with carbolic soap. The right hand was to eat with, touch food and of course to shake hands with.

Even though we were poor and benefiting from limited facilities hygiene was of the uttermost importance. We washed and bathed in the river. Household utensils were scrubbed with coconut husks using ashes until they gleamed. Before we had toothbrushes and toothpaste we cleaned our teeth with a twig that had been chewed into a shape of a small paintbrush. This was combined with charcoal dust from the wood we had earlier used for cooking. After cleaning our teeth the twig was split in half and used to scrape our tongues clean. It's a Hindu custom where people who scrape their tongue create a lot of unnecessary heaving and coughing noises, which I find disgusting. Indians still do it in Fiji and indeed all over the world. Many people around the world still complain about having Indians neighbours who make such a disgusting noise while cleaning their teeth and scraping their tongues every morning.

Some coastal villages had little huts built on trees leaning over the sea. Those who lived in them would climb up into them and sitting on specially shaped branches relieve themselves much to the delight of the fish shoals in the waters beneath.

When the tourist boom first began postcards were made of the tree toilets. The visiting Europeans would flock to the villages just to photograph and laugh and to tell their children about the village toilets in Fiji.

On Sunday evening everyone gathered in the village big house. Prayers were said and kava was drunk. Some of the elders lit a chillum (earthen pipe) and marijuana would be smoked. I had known about the marijuana smoking but didn't take any notice of father and some of my uncles who walked around with permanent grins on their faces. According to the Hindus this was the food of the gods. It is believed to be sacred like kava is to the indigenous Fijians and only to be used in prayer or ceremonial sacrifices.

The men smoked and talked about our Hindu gods but father was always questioning the Hindu faith. He told us the Hindu scriptures are very well written and as a matter of fact are beautifully written. No normal person can write such incredible stories unless they were under the influence of marijuana. He at least thought they were hallucinatory.

In those days I remember Hindu families praying to the sun god and offering a brass tumbler full of water to it every day. Dad advised them not to do but they still did.

"That's no sun or moon god out there. It is just another planet, a lump of rock." He told them. Years later he was to have the last laugh when men were to land on the moon. There were lots of heated arguments between the grownups, mostly based on religion. But after a few cups of potent kava and marijuana they used to giggle like children and tell silly jokes. When that happened, it was time for us the children to head for our beds.

CHRIS NAND

*   *   *

Next morning I gathered firewood from the forest as it was the major source of fuel for daily cooking. I then cut open dry coconuts and scraping the white meat from the shells readied the milk that is used in cooking fish and other curries. Later I went to the river mouth and dived for oysters and crayfish which we were to have that day for lunch. As I was about to dine with mother and two sisters father arrived from one of his sales trips.

Looking at me sternly he said: "Krishna, have you been out looking for jobs yet?"

"I am going to the sugar mills this afternoon to see if they are hiring. If not I will go to Suva and find employment in the city, I promise."

It was enough to keep him off my back for awhile. What I really wanted to do was travel to Suva the capital of Fiji. There I might find myself some work and earn some cash to help the family. As an older brother I was expected to put something towards my sisters' marriage dowries. This was yet another ridiculous Hindu custom brought from India. Even though we were third generation Fiji born Indians we had little choice but to follow the customs of our forefathers.

Men should pay dowries to women before marriage and not the other way around. Many poor families couldn't afford a dowry and some unfortunate young girls were just given away to older men and got rid off that way.

That evening father was still going on about my finding a job. "Krishna, you know very well that we need more money than I am earning, just to get by and to get your sisters married."

"But father, Sabita and Malti are too young to marry and as I told you before I am planning to go to Suva to find a job soon."

"How soon is soon?"

"I will be sixteen in a few days time and will leave just after my birthday, I promise."

"Stop dreaming about going to Suva. It is far too expensive to live there and where will you live? Do you know anyone there?"

"Yes, father I do. Some boys from my school live there."

I was thinking of David, my best friend from school. He looked at me as he really didn't believe a word I was saying and then turning on his heel he disappeared into the house. I followed him in and sat on a mat next to my mother.

"Krishna," she asked: "Do you really know someone in Suva. We will be worried about you when you go and us not knowing where you will work and sleep."

"Yes, a friend from school, David lives there. I can stay with him until I find a place to board. I'll be alright ma, please don't worry about me."

After dinner of prawns curry, chapattis and rice I lay on the bed listening to the radio and began to plan my trip to Suva. I was serious and on the day following my sixteenth birthday I said goodbye to my parents and two sisters before making for the bus stop.

RETURNED TO DEVIL'S ISLAND

Clutching my small suitcase in one hand I climbed board and waving happily to family and friends I felt that adventure beckoned. As I looked out through the rear windows I could see the billowing dust cloud kicked up by the vehicle's wheels now obscured the view. Who could know when I might see them again?

The two hundred miles journey took me along an inland route and meandered through rough country terrain. Eventually we reached the banks of the Wainibuka River. This mighty river snakes in and out of the steep mountains passes and rolling hills. Scattered along our way and in between stops there were grass and bamboo huts similar to our own village life. There were no bus stops as such; the driver stopped wherever someone put their hands out. Sometimes when he pulled in the villagers would come out to greet us as if we were long lost members of their family. Given a short break we walked around their village and bought bananas, oranges and pawpaw. We also used the facilities of their small houses. These were similar to our own toilets.

Within two hours we had reached the small town of Korovou and after the briefest of stops took the road to Suva. Crossing the bridge that spanned the Rewa River we finally came to a narrow tarmac road. This was pockmarked with flattened frogs and occasional dead mongoose. Indians street vendors were sitting at the roadside selling freshly cooked curries and chapattis. Some were calling out to attract us to their stalls whilst others just seemed to daydream or were clearing their throats and spitting on the tarmac.

An hour later I arrived at the long wooden building with its rusty tin roof which according to signage was Suva Bus Station. I was pleased the four hours journey was over and I was finally getting away from the Indian man who had sat next to me. My fellow passenger had chewed tobacco all through the journey and spat out of the large open windows of the bus. Many sitting at the back of the bus complained as they had to duck and dodge the dark brown spit splatter that came their way as a result of his repeated spitting. Alighting from the bus I was immediately surrounded by Indian street vendors. Some with strings of live crabs, fish, roasted peanuts and spiced peas. Many were shouting at the top of their voices; they were desperate to make a sale.

Clutching a small portion of roasted peanuts in one hand and my overnight sized suitcase in the other I made my way into town. As I did so I passed the Suva city market avoiding the vendors' protestations that they really were the cheapest and it was their best price. 'Lying bastards,' I thought to myself as I strolled on my way.

Everywhere there were goats and chickens; live turtles turned on to their backs. There were lobsters, shark fins and tropical fruit. The livestock in their cramped and dry enclosures made me want a beer. I did go up to the bar at the Metropolis Hotel but they wouldn't serve me as I was under age and anyway I didn't have a drinkers permit.

It was then that I saw the clock tower of the department store called Burns Philips. It was the tallest building I had ever seen; all three stories of it. I glanced through the store's windows and could see pretty Indian and native girls busily serving customers.

Several smartly dressed policemen strolled past. I noticed they were dressed in white ankle length sulus, black tunics with silver buttons and open toed sandals. To me they looked magnificent.

Soon I was in Cumming's Street and was taken aback by the sheer number of people thronging the top of the road. Curious, I forced myself through until I reached the front and saw the no entry sign and stopped. "What's going on?" I asked an Indian man.

"All Hollywood is here. They are shooting a movie called His Majesty O" Keefe.

"But they are all Chinese."

"Yes; they are Chinese extras needed for the film."

Peering over shoulders I could see at least one familiar face: "Look there's Burt Lancaster." I said. "I saw him in the movie "From Here to Eternity"

"Yes I see him too, and the actress Joan Rice they are seen around the pubs most evenings. They are staying at the Grand Pacific Hotel next to the Albert Park."

It was explained to me that the entire street had been designed to resemble a street in Hong Kong. Apparently Burt Lancaster deals with Chinese businessmen in Hong Kong.

I managed to make my way a little further forward where I witnessed a filmed fight scene. Lancaster was beating the crap out of a group of Chinese shopkeepers and was surrounded by a group of cameramen. Feeling sad and admittedly a little alienated I wandered through the streets of Suva and entered Suva Lodge, the Indian restaurant. After enjoying something to eat I was shown to a dark and dingy room at the rear of the building where beer was served illegally. I spoke to the manager about employment prospects.

"It is your lucky day, son" he told me. "I need a waiter right away. You will be paid one pound per week and all found."

"All found?"

"You can eat as much as you can and sleep upstairs in the corridor."

Smiling at my good fortune I thanked him and depositing my suitcase upstairs made an immediate start. This will do for a while I thought, until I find something better.

During my employment at the Suva Lodge I worked as general dogsbody. Each day I washed hundreds of dishes, huge metal pots and pans and then cleaned the restaurant from top to bottom. Work started at six in the morning. The first hour was spent helping in the kitchen, mixing and kneading flour for chapattis then serving the tables from seven until ten in the evening. For two hours after that I was set to work cleaning pots and pans again.

Eventually I was to meet up with David, my old friend from St Mary's. He helped me to find employment at Bish Limited. He worked there as a welder. David had already made his debut as a professional boxer and won his first four fights by knock outs. The boxing lessons from Father Kelly had served him well and I started to turn up at his boxing club and to train several times a week. My evenings and weekends were now free.

I wrote several letters back home to my family and also to Susan. I did so knowing that Sister Magdalene would read and destroy my letters unless Susan got to the mail bus first. It was a chance worth taking.

Whilst working at Bish Limited I met several Australians who were on secondment from the company's head office in Australia. They had been sent to Fiji to train the locals. There was an age gap between us for I was just sixteen while they were in their early twenties but my familiarity with the Australian way of life and language had begun.

"Fuck this, fuck that, mother fucker and wanker were commonplace expression and whatever I heard I imitated. They took David and me to dance halls, parties and sly grogs. These are seedy back street unlicensed bars where one could drink freely without a permit.

Even during work the Aussies were good humoured and took very little seriously. They taught us our jobs well but always found time to tell us jokes and make us laugh. One particular day we were all laughing when suddenly we felt the earth moving beneath as though we were on a dysfunctional elevator. The workshop lights began to swing and flicker.

"Earthquake!"

Running for our lives to reach comparative safety outside we saw the water from the river that ran parallel to our workshop being sucked towards a huge whirlpool that had suddenly appeared in the sea. Scrambling to shelter on higher grounds nearby we reckoned we were out of immediate harm's way. Fortunately, the earthquake stopped within minutes but as we gazed back towards the ocean we could see a huge tidal wave of black water lift up out of the Pacific and start to advance towards us: the force that lay in it was incomprehensible; it was truly an awe-inspiring phenomenon.

Within seconds the river swelled its banks and small anchored fishing boats were sent crashing against the cliffs just below where we were standing. Holding on to each other we watched in horror as the debris created by the tidal waves brief invasion of the coast began to return back to the ocean: Within minutes the sea was back to normal again. The police arrived on higher terrain directly behind us and indicated that all was clear. "Please go back to your homes and do not return to work until further notice."

David and I rushed to the seaside bedsitter where we lived and saw what little we owned had been vacuumed up by the Pacific Ocean. Happily for us we soon met a young Tongan boxer by the name of Tom Hini. A smiling and friendly chap he accompanied us both to the Tongan part of town where he provided us with food and shelter. The three of us shared a small room and were grateful for his generosity of spirit.

The next day the Fiji Times reported that there were no fatalities. One old lady had been washed away but found safe and well clinging to an over turned boat. The city of Suva was fortunate: It is built on high ground and the residential areas were safe. The earthquake had registered 3.4 on the Richter scale and the tidal wave was the result of a large coral reef that had disintegrated during the quake. It was my first experience of an earthquake and tidal wave; it was not something I ever wished to experience again.

When I returned to the welding shop at Bish Limited I was surprised to see the old building still standing. This in itself was worthy of celebration. The river had absorbed most of the tidal waves impact and damage to the concrete walls was minimal.

Moving to the Tongan part of the town we had found our lucky break. Tom Hini introduced us to the heavyweight boxing champion of Tonga, a fighter by the name of Kitone Lave. I had by this time seen his picture in the Fiji Times and had followed his boxing career so it was a privilege to meet him as a person. On his last visit to Fiji he had beaten several Fijian heavyweights by knockouts including the champion named Miliano. He had just returned from London where he had knocked out the British and commonwealth champion by the name of Don Cockell in just two rounds and was now prepared to fight any heavyweight in the world, including the world heavyweight champion Rocky Marciano.

Travelling with Lave was another renowned Tongan named Johnny Halafifi; the light heavy weight champion of Tonga. Following a brief stopover in Fiji they were both due to fly to New Zealand and return to London where they both lived.

We became good friends and it wasn't long before David and I joined their boxing gym and spent most evenings training with them. It was far healthier and more fun than painting the town red with our Aussie friends and my boxing career was back on track. We were now sparing with Tongan champions and working out at the gym. We were also feasting Tongan style; mostly on a diet of suckling pig, fish and oysters. Within weeks I put on muscle and grew far stronger than I had ever been.

It was in August that my grandmother Gulbi fell ill. This obliged me to return to the home village to be with my family. It was nice travelling and on this occasion the trip was taken on a brand new bus called the Sunbeam. It was a big improvement on the old Royal Mail boneshaker.

This bus had sliding glass windows and rubber mats on the floor. Better still it had reduced the travel time to my village by an hour because there were no mail deliveries to slow the journey up.

After a ten day visit I was about to return to Suva when my grandmother passed on. We kept her body overnight in the big house and then carried her on a stretcher made of bamboo canes to the shores of the Pacific where she was cremated. As night fell that evening our family stood outside our homes and watched the fire's glow until the early hours of the morning. The next morning we gathered her ashes and according to Hindu faith scattered them into the last resting place in the blue lagoon that had been so much a part of her life and ours.

Within days I was back in Suva to see my Tongan boxer friends leave for New Zealand and England. Together with David, Tom Hini and other Tongans we waved as the cruise liner Oransay sailed off to take them to whatever fortunes awaited them. I vowed to follow them one day.

Tom Hini won the Fijian Heavyweight title and David was matched against Josepo Sitiveni for the middleweight championship of the South Sea Islands. It was during this time I made my debut as a professional boxer. I was billed to fight an up and coming middleweight named Leweni Waga. So far he had fought and won four fights and I was understandably nervous; I had no desire to become his fifth slaying but was determined to fight him as I needed to earn some extra cash towards my travels that I had planned.

On fight night I apprehensively stepped on the scales at the Lilac Theatre and at last came face to face with Waga. He glowered, tried to stare me down; intimidate me but I avoided eye contact with him and looked over his shoulders. The doctor examined us both and deemed us both fit to box.

I was pleased that Waga was seven pounds heavier than me as it meant our fight was cancelled. It was a blessing in disguise for I knew in my heart he would have demolished me and possibly have put an end to my dream to leave Fiji. My fight was rearranged with a substitute opponent named Sireli Bau.

When my turn came to climb into the ring I was accompanied by my new Tongan trainer known as Big T. Bowing to the crowd of several hundred I took my place in the blue corner. Wearing black boxing shorts with white stripes on each side I had a borrowed red dressing gown that hung freely over my shoulders.

Standing in a small box full of grit I was rubbing the soles of my boxing boots when Bau entered the ring, smiled across at me and stood in the red corner. Immediately after the ringmaster's introduction the referee checked our gloves and waited in the middle of the ring for the bell to ring. When it did so I felt nervous but flew out of my corner and started throwing fast left jabs to Bau's face. I could hear my workmates and Australian friends too cheering and calling out my name.

Moving around the ring I hit him with fast left jabs and counter punches, ducking, dodging and evasively letting his punches fly into thin air. He did catch me a few times but nothing too hurtful. I was becoming more confident by the time the bell signalled the end of round one. Big T took control from there.

"You have a heavy punch, Jamie. Go out there and hit him with heavy combinations of punches and knock him down. What the fuck are you waiting for, man?"

As I sprang from my corner my uneasiness evaporated and I felt stronger and more confident. I did exactly what Big T had asked me to do. For the next two rounds I bombarded my opponent with heavy combination punches. Then, admittedly to my amazement Bau went down in the third round after I had caught him with a heavy right cross to his jaw. He staggered as I heard voices from my Australian friends. "Hit him Jamie and don't let him off the hook."

As soon as he staggered to his feet I let fly with a few left jabs and hit him again with a right cross that dropped him to the canvas. That was it: The referee counted to ten and lifted my hand in victory. Hurriedly dressing I slipped unnoticed back to the ringside to watch Leweni Waga beat the shit out of a guy named Joe Momosewa.

CHRIS NAND

After that bout I rushed back to be with David in his corner with Big T and Tom Hini; his was the main event of that evening. As the challenger, David had to enter the ring first and wait for the champion to make a grand entrance. We waited in the blue corner before Sitiveni arrived and began to shadow box in his corner. At the ringmaster's announcement we stepped out of the ring and waited for the bell.

David was well and truly fired up and rushed to the centre of the ring on hearing the strident clanging of the bell. He then began to box as trained to do by Big T. David tried every trick in the book but couldn't knock the champ out. It was touch and go throughout the contest and the fight was to go the full distance of fifteen rounds. To our delight David won on points and he was now the middleweight champion of the South Sea Islands. Wrapping the belt around his waist the referee lifted his hand in victory to a din of cheering. On our way out of the arena we went in the promoter's office where David was paid eighty pounds and I palmed three pound for my debut fight.

Some of the cash went to our trainer and David's belt was for him to take home. We rushed to join the crazy gang of Aussies for a celebration party.

After a long walk past the War Memorial Hospital and towards the small town of Samabula, David and I eventually arrived at the Aussies villa. The bout was playing on my mind and I felt a tinge of guilt for the man I had knocked unconscious. Unquestionably it was barbaric of me to punch the face of a beaten man and I wasn't comfortable with that. David on the other hand was exhilarated by his winning the middleweight championship of the South Seas.

On arriving at the villa we knocked back a few beers and relaxed. As we became high we danced and sang and enjoyed a great party until the early hours of the morning. An early morning swim in their villa's swimming pool helped to wake me up and almost back to our old selves we made our way back to our apartment. I needed to rest; my body was aching from the previous night's fight.

During the next three months I trained even harder and won four fights. David defended his title twice and Tom Hini kept on fighting month after month. Within 12 months he had beaten several Fijian heavyweights and after four more bouts I also remained undefeated.

*   *   *

Back at Bish Limited there was a farewell party being held for our Australian friends as their secondment to Suva had finally run its course. I took their addresses and promised to keep in touch. I was still hoping that by some miracle David and I would eventually find a way out of Fiji and cross that vast ocean; perhaps to meet up with them again.

After the crazy gang left it left me with more time to train and familiarise myself more with Suva. I took the opportunity to visit the museum and sure enough, Rev Thomas Baker's bible and the battleaxe used to murder him were there on display. These were kept under glass and were well preserved Along with other utensils that had been used in ceremonial sacrifices I also saw war canoes, spears and bush knives used in the days of cannibalism.

When I mentioned Ratu Udre Udre's tomb that was situated close to my home village one of the museum's curators explained that soon those boulders would be recovered and would join the other artefacts; a cement tomb was to be built over the grave as a tourist attraction.

Twelve months passed but still there was no sign of my finding a way to leave the islands. During those months grandfather Chand died and again I returned to my village for his funeral. He was cremated on the same spot as was his adored wife. After evening prayers father took me aside and spoke quietly to me. "You can't go back to Suva again, Krishna."

"Why not," I countered. "I love being there. My friends and my work are there. I have to return and besides, David and I have plans to box in other countries."

"No Krishna, I have been offered work at the gold mines. My van is now too old and dilapidated to drive around the islands as a mobile shop."

"What will you do at the gold mines?"

"Driving. There is a welding shop there where you could work."

"So, it's all arranged is it?"

"Yes! We will live together. Soon we have to find Sabita a husband and we shall need hard cash for her dowry."

I didn't at all fancy the idea of leaving Suva behind as yet another dream turned to dust but I did concede that the thought of being at the gold mines held a certain appeal. I had heard that they were paying three pounds a week and there was a good boxing club there too. The club was run by the current Fijian light heavyweight champion Naliva Filimoni. Reluctantly I was forced to agree with dad and my travel plans with David were put on hold.

The next day both dad and I drove to the Emperor Gold Mines of Vatukola. There, after being interviewed and put on the payroll we ventured out into the street in search of somewhere to live. It was as we strolled that we spotted a rusty old refrigerator with a "Coca Cola" logo on it. It was half hidden behind some shrubs in an overgrown garden. "Come on," father said; "That looks like sly grog. Let's have a beer and they might know somewhere available to rent."

As soon as the Indian owner of the bar saw our approach he opened the dingy wooden door and the beer appeared as quickly. Father and son sat cross legged on the floor and touched glasses to our new venture as we sipped the beer slowly.

"Are you new at the gold mines?" the man smiled.

"Yes we are. Do you know of any flats for rent in this area?"

"Well, I know a man who works at the mines too. He has a small house to rent around the corner from here. It is not far from the Catholic Convent College."

When we asked him how we would find it he told us to walk past the church and the college until we came to the Public Works Department. "Rajendra lives there on the right," he added helpfully.

Before we left the shop's owner scribbled the name and address of the man he called Rajendra on an old cigarette packet and handed it to father. After another goodwill beer we thanked him and drove towards the church.

"What was his name again?" I asked father.

"Rajendra."

"Rajendra what?"

"Rajendra Prasad."

After knocking on a few doors and asking we eventually found the house we wanted. It was nicely built on stilts and had corrugated tin walls and a tin roof. Greeted by barking dogs' father climbed up the steps leading to the veranda and tapped quietly on the wooden door then waited on the open veranda as I nervously watched from the window of the van. Shortly afterwards I heard the door creak open and a tall young Indian woman greeted father. Dressed in a bright green sari and carrying a small baby in her arms she was breathtakingly beautiful.

I heard father hesitate and mumble at the unexpectedness of the greeting when she asked how she might help him.

"We are looking for Rajendra."

"He is at work. Perhaps I can help you?"

"Yes, we are told that there is a house that might be for rent."

"Yes, we do," she smiled "I can show you that."

I overheard the conversation and seeing how it was going I stepped out of the van to join them both. The lady's gaze held mine and we both smiled. She was making quite an impression on me; perhaps it was mutual? "By the way; my name is Nirmala and I am Rajendra's wife."

Father and I looked at each other and waited as the attractive Nirmala stepped inside her home and placed her child in the hammock. Picking up some keys we walked back down the steps and across the overgrown lawn past low hanging branches of a mango tree. There we found a house similar to her home. The difference was that this one was on the ground rather than propped on stilts. Nirmala opened the unpainted wooden door and ushered dad and I inside.

Following her we entered a small lounge and then found two small bedrooms. There was also a shower room with cement walls and floor but no tiles or paint.

"What rent are you asking," father asked. I could see he wanted it. She told him the rent was four pounds a calendar month.

Without hesitation father said he would take it and unbuttoning his shirt pocket took out the money and handed it to her. "We'll move in sometime tomorrow if that is okay?"

Nirmala smiling handed the key to father and invited us to join her for tea which we were happy to do. On the drive way home I sat with my own thoughts. My mind kept drifting towards the beautiful sari-clad young lady called Nirmala. I wondered if father had been as impressed by her natural beauty as I was. When he broke the news of our moving to my mother she was happy that at last we are able to get away from the old tomb and its horrific past. My sisters meanwhile ran around the other huts excitedly as they gave everyone the good news.

That evening we packed what belongings we had in old soapboxes and met the rest of the extended family in the big house. There we said our goodbyes and after a restless night's sleep set off for the small town of Tavua; the gold mines of Vatukola and what was to be our new home.

CHAPTER 3

As the towering palm trees and dust clouds fell behind our family sat quietly in the van and wondered what the future held. Within two hours later we had passed through Tavua and had pulled in at the small petrol pump of the Morris Headstrom shop. Having filled the tank dad bought us each an ice cream treat with jelly before continuing our journey. From the centre of the town we took a left to get on the Vatukola road and forty minutes later arrived at our new home. Manoeuvring the car carefully father pulled up as close to the house as he could.

Looking forward to seeing the very friendly and pretty lady I was first to go up to the veranda where I knocked on the door. Almost as if she was expecting us it swung open immediately and there she was; dressed in an ankle length white pleated skirt with a short Indian curta (blouse). This fell just short of her slim waist and her small button naval. I couldn't help but notice her fingers and toe nails were painted red. Like most comfortably off Indian women Nirmala was wearing several layers of gold necklaces and her hands were festooned with gold bangles. As soon as I set eyes on her my jaw involuntarily dropped: I tried to speak but the words wouldn't come. Perhaps she noticed she had made an impression on me and helped me out: "Hello Krishna."

Still tongue tied I pointed towards the van at the bottom of the flight of steps where my family were expectantly waiting. "Yes," she smiled. "I heard you coming but I couldn't rush out as I was feeding my child."

Stepping lightly down the veranda steps Nirmala welcomed our little family and taking us to our new home showed mother and my sisters where everything was while father and I unloaded the van. Before she left us to get on with settling in she asked us to join her as soon as we had finished unloading. There would be tea and refreshments on the veranda. "Rajendra will be home soon and it will be good to get to know each other," she added with that bewitching smile of hers.

Once inside the house it was decided that my parents share one bedroom and my sisters the other. I was to sleep on a single fold-up bed in the lounge. The house was small but was an improvement over the bamboo and grass hut we had finally vacated. After showers and a change of clothing we went across to Nirmala and Rajendra's home and were soon seated on the veranda's coconut matting. Within a few moments

Rajendra arrived. Shaking hands as we greeted and introduced each other we opened a few bottles of beer and enjoyed the banter and the evening sun as it was beginning its descent behind the Queen Victoria Mountains.

Rajendra interrupted our chatter: "Water and electricity is free here. It's supplied by the gold mines."

"Wonderful! What sort of work do you do at the mines?"

"I am foreman in the fitting shop," he replied proudly as he set his glass down. "And you? Where will you be working?"

Father grinned: "I am hired as a truck driver and Krishna as a welder in the boilermakers section."

"It's all shift work you know, except for sportsmen: They are exempt from night work if they are serious and good at what they do."

Grinning widely I told them that I was a professional boxer and I outlined my boxing career to date. "Then you'll be working days only," Rajendra said with a light-hearted smile.

As we chatted I could hear Nirmala's gold bangles tinkling and guessed she was somewhere inside making something; preparing food maybe. My sisters Sabita and Malti were also in there and helping her. Judging from their giggles they seemed to be getting along fine. Within minutes delicious Indian food was served on genuine china plates. There were also drinks in proper glass tumblers and tea in china cups.

As we enjoyed our meal I couldn't keep my eyes off Nirmala and it seemed to me that she had the same problem with me. There was chemistry, magnetism, an attraction that for me went far beyond appreciation of her beauty. I tried of course not to make it too obvious but failed miserably. On occasion it was as if we two were there alone.

Our landlord's wife revealed a fine gold ankle chain clearly on view as she sat down on the floor next to my sisters. My imagination ran wild as we spoke and flirted with our eyes. Was she playing games with me? I was so much younger and she was far more sophisticated than was I. Our glances soon changed to eye-holding and at that stage I had no idea if others had noticed but I no longer cared too much about that. I was enchanted. I felt I had to get to know her better. When we finally said our thanks and farewells Nirmala smiled wickedly and holding my gaze said in a low voice: "It's nice to meet you, Krishna."

My voice was unnaturally husky: "Yes, I feel the same way; it is nice meeting you too."

That night I fell asleep dreaming about her. All I could think of was what a lucky man Rajendra was to have such a stunning wife. Early the next morning father and I reported for work. First of all I was tested on various types of welding before being taken to the boilermakers shop and given work to do. Father was sent back home: It was suggested he get some sleep and told to report back for the night shift at nine thirty that evening. There was a shortage of drivers on the night shift.

After finishing my day's work I signed up at the boxing club. After sparring for a few rounds with Naliva, my new trainer I sparred with Leweni Waqa. He was the guy

I had been listed to meet on my first fight as a professional boxer. He looked extremely strong and super fit and I was pleased we had met and would be working out together. Naliva kept on encouraging me as I worked out on the heavy punch bag and when finishing we talked about his previous fights. "I saw you win the light heavyweight title when you beat Semi Tavolia. It was a fantastic fight."

"Yes, thanks but I need many more wins like that one. I would love to go overseas and try my luck over there. I believe they pay a bundle there."

"Me too, I would love to go to England. By the way I had the privilege to train with Kitone Lave and Johnny Halafifi when I lived in Suva. We became good friends."

He smiled as he recognised the two names. "I saw them box in Windsor Park in Lautoka. They are both magnificent fighters. I am sure they both deserve to be fighting for the world crown. Especially how Lave destroyed Don Cockell in just two rounds and Marciano took nine rounds to knock him out."

We parted on a friendly high with him telling me how glad he was to meet me and how much he looked forward to training with me. He closed by asking if I was fit enough for another fight. I grinned and told him I was looking forward to a few bouts too and learning more about my boxing career. My name, he said, would be put forward with Grants Boxing Promotions to see if he could get me a fight soon.

The small track I took when strolling home took me right past Nirmala's veranda and I couldn't help but notice her standing there as if she was waiting for me. "Hi Krishna," she called.

I think she guessed at how pleased I was to see her from my broad smile. Joining her I told her my name was actually James. I added that I had been baptised in the Catholic faith and suggested to her that she call me Jamie. Nirmala giggled for a while before she spoke. "And what made you give up your Hindu faith, Jamie?"

"It's a long story. Someday I will explain," I laughed.

"Please tell me now. I have no plans and I was a little bored before you came."

"I have been working and sparring. I can't be good company: I really need a shower before I settle down, Nirmala."

"Please stay and have a beer before you go."

I hesitated but sprawled in a chair she had offered me and took the beer when she offered it. "Thanks, I really need this,"

As I sipped the beer straight from the bottle I told her how it was that I was baptised into the Catholic Faith. "That means you must have eaten cow meat?"

I told her I had but not since leaving school I could make my own lifestyle choices and had reverted mostly to my old way of doing things. She said she didn't mind at all and commented that these days more and more Hindus were eating meat.

"Is Rajendra working tonight," I asked her.

"He hasn't long left. I am surprised you didn't meet each other. His night shift starts today and it alternates every two weeks. He has two weeks of nights and two weeks of days."

I told Nirmala that my father was working nights too and added that I was pleased that my boxing interests meant I didn't have to do shift work.

"How old are you, Jamie?"

"I am seventeen." As I spoke I hoped my youth wouldn't have a negative effect on our friendship. I suppose I could have lied and told her I was older but there was no need. She smiled and revealed the most beautiful teeth I had ever set my eyes on. "You're in your prime then. You will stay fit for some time but you will never be fitter than you are now."

I felt my skin glow at what I took to be innuendo and unsure of the situation there and then I thanked her for her beer and stood up to leave.

"Please, what is your hurry? Do stay a little longer, Jamie. I like talking with you."

Shyly I was becoming aware of something I couldn't define but instinctively knew it was more than mere neighbourliness. "I like talking to you too, Nirmala, but mother has made dinner. She will be soon out here looking out for me."

Regretfully I bid my neighbour's wife goodnight but in bed that night, whilst I was still thoughtful and regretful about Susan, I found I couldn't get Nirmala out of my mind. Questions kept running through my mind. I was perplexed. Why was she so nice and so friendly towards me? She is married with a new baby; her husband looks young and fit and he has a good job. I felt sure she couldn't possibly be unhappy with her life and I felt at the same time that I was equally sure she wasn't promiscuous. Perhaps she was just a sociable sort of person and lonely or insecure on her own at night while her husband was on night shifts.

Nirmala was to be found on her veranda each evening as I arrived home from my sparring sessions. It became something of a nice habit and one I looked forward to and after the usual small talk and a beer we would joke as we got to know each other better.

It was a Friday evening after a good workout at the gym that I bumped into my father and Rajendra when walking home in the rain. They were on their way to work. We did not have much to say; the rain was after all coming down heavily and we were in all a hurry. As I neared Nirmala's home I saw her waiting for me and apart from not much else she was wearing a smile that was as inviting as a smile gets. The veranda being soaking wet we did the sensible thing and went on through into her lounge. Handing me a towel she helped me dry my hair and somehow we ended up in each other's arms kissing passionately. The smell of a perfume I later learned was called Evening de Paris. I had never before been so closely entwined with a woman wearing perfume and my head was swimming as brushing her soft brown skin with my lips and tongue tip I mumbled: "Where's the baby?"

"He is sleeping in the hammock," she sighed as she draped her arms around my neck.

"Rajendra will kill us both if he finds out."

"He won't find out. Don't worry," she smiled. We were both breathing heavily in anticipation of whatever was to come.

"But why would he not; you are so young and beautiful . . . he . . ."

Nirmala clearly wasn't interested in discussing her marriage or her fidelity and was by now pulling me towards the bedroom. There was no bashfulness about her; without preamble she quickly began to undress and soon we were passionately in each other's arms; revelling in our raw passion for each other. This was only my second occasion as a lover and I was well out of my depth with this over sexed femme fatale. I think that had I been more experienced this would have been the most exciting experience of my life. I was overwhelmed by the magnitude of what had just happened between us I was prepared to bolt out of the door. Not so nervous was a very relaxed and languorous Nirmala who still stretched out on the marital bed whispered fervently; "My prayers have been answered."

I asked her what she meant and she simply said I had answered her prayers. This was a puzzle to me and she went on to explain that she had weakened at the knees as soon as she had set eyes. She reminded me that it was the time I had climbed down out of our van during the first visit.

"I looked at you. You looked so young, tall and handsome. I knew you were God sent."

"But Rajendra your husband, he too is young and so handsome? And you have a child?"

"No, Jamie. Virendra is adopted. I am childless. Nirmala went on to explain that her husband's family were derisive and she was getting the blame for being barren.

"Please look at me, Jamie," she murmured softly as she took my face in her hands: "I am nearly twenty years old and have been married for five years. It's high time I became pregnant. Indian families expect a child during the first year of their marriage, hopefully a boy; everyone expects a boy. They mock Rajendra too for not producing one.

"I am known as the barren one. Just look around the village: all the Indian girls between the 15 and 18 are married and have children. Imagine what it is like for us? I am the only one who has been married for five years and still without child.

"The wives of Rajendra's brothers had babies within nine of ten months of being married; they have baby boys and I don't. Rajendra's mother is always having a dig at me for not producing a grandchild for her. I'm sure they are planning something bad for me as they've done to other women. They are capable of it."

Nirmala looked unhappy. "They brought this barbaric custom from India. I know it. They'll damage my face with acid and banish me from my home. You are the only one who can perhaps save me from being humiliated by these primitive minded people. Please, Jamie, help me and I promise to do anything in return to help you. It is so important."

I went numb for a while after hearing such a passionate appeal and then thoughtfully I asked her what the consequences would be if I did succeed in making her pregnant.

"It would save my marriage and most probably my life; no one will ever know that you are the father."

RETURNED TO DEVIL'S ISLAND

I thought about it for awhile and took a more considered look at her. She was without question very beautiful; no man could ever walk away from her. What had happened was the most stimulating experience that I ever had and I felt I couldn't betray her even though I felt compromised. I had fallen for her and could never retreat regardless of my first love.

I might never see Susan again. She has been indoctrinated and with the passage of time she had surrendered to her fate at the convent and adapted as do many prisoners; they become institutionalised. I knew in my heart she would never be free for St Mary's was her only home; the nuns her only family. I looked at Nirmala before gently kissing her on her full lips. As though I was her saviour and in her eyes I probably was she held me tightly and kissed my face, mouth and neck before I had a chance to speak to her again.

"I'm sure Rajendra will eventfully find out about us."

She placed her finger on my lips as though to calm me: "Yes he will but we have his blessing for he wants a boy so badly that he's willing to turn a blind eye and let us produce one for us."

"There's no certainty that it will be a boy. What happens if the child, presuming we have one, is a girl?"

"Then we'll have to try again and again until I produce a boy."

Nirmala was much more relaxed about things than I was after having explained the situation to me. I was for my part happy enough to go along with it. Heaven sent indeed? I knew where she was coming from now.

Reaching under the bed Nirmala pulled out a Hindu book entitled Koka Shastra Hindu Book of Love. Flipping through its pages she drew my curious attention to some of the illustrated sexual positions. She was convinced that certain of them were more likely to produce a boy child. "Look here on this page. It says a boy child is conceived by making love in these positions."

Looking over her shoulder I felt a little embarrassed on seeing the graphics. It was the first time I had seen depictions of lovemaking outside of my imagination; I remember wondering how on earth people achieved some of the positions suggested. "That's surely just an old wives tales," I scoffed.

"You might be right," she conceded before adding that there was no harm in finding out and anyway it all looked like fun. Before I had time to answer her she began to kiss me again. I was as quickly aroused this time and we again surrendered to passion.

In a moment of clarity I took a quick look at the clock on Nirmala's dressing table and saw I was now very late. Mother would be looking out for me. Quickly dressing I climbed back into my wet clothes and kissing my lover goodbye and with a hurried assurance that I would be with her again soon I rushed home.

It being a Friday night I stayed up late helping my sisters prepare for their new school. Mother had enrolled them into an Indian primary school around the corner. They were both excited and looking forward to going there.

The following morning I took a stroll to the river that meandered gently behind our new home; I was looking for a good spot from where I could swim. On arriving there I was horrified to see the murky rust coloured water. It was a reminder of the beach at the river's mouth behind St. Mary's. The lush green foliage on its banks had turned brown, the natural fish stock and amphibians, frogs for instance, had disappeared. I later discovered that the waste discharged from the gold mines up river contained mercury used to separate gold from the earth and was consistently poisoning the fresh mountain waters. The true price of gold was in the badly polluted river and the sea into which it flowed. It was ebbing poison. I was horrified to think there were several gold and sugar refinery mills around the islands. They were all built on river banks and this was the price of progress.

Despondently I walked back to the house and as I arrived I could see Nirmala hanging her washing on a line strung from one palm to another. "Hi Jamie, aren't you going to the football tournament?"

"What football tournament?"

"Today is the Fijian Cup Final day."

On asking her where it was being held she told me it was at the Valabala Football Ground. She added that teams from all over Fiji would be playing each other. Rajendra, she told me had just left. "If you rush you'll catch the bus outside the Public Works Department building."

I wasn't in truth a football fan but the thought of going to Valabala excited me as Susan, who was still preying on my mind, was in the nearby convent. Taking Nirmala's advice to heart I hastily put on a pair of jeans and shoes and rushed off. As I flew past her veranda I could see her leaning against the doorframe with a bottle of beer; there was little interpretation of that devilish knowing smile that spread across her loveliest of faces.

Any idea of going to the football match instantly evaporated. Smiling I walked to the veranda and straight into her front room as casually as her husband might. As I did so I could hear her sliding the door bolt behind me and mad moments later we were in each other's arms kissing as passionately as we had the previous evening. Taking me again by the hand she led me to her bedroom where Virendra the adopted baby lay quietly in its hammock. The beer was down my neck in a single gulp. Hurriedly I stripped off and was clearly ready for anything. There was no need for me to have memorised the various positions; Nirmala had already done her homework and was well ahead of me.

I was still very edgy about what we were doing but being in experienced hands I just went with the flow and enjoyed the experiences of her lovemaking. It was at moments like this that Nirmala was extremely vocal but half the time I didn't understand what she was on about as she whispered endearments. What I did understand was that she was overjoyed at her good fortune; our family having arrived and their bringing me with them to her. I gathered that I was the answer to all of her often repeated prayers, which she repeatedly mentioned.

RETURNED TO DEVIL'S ISLAND

Nirmala had fallen into our relationship with both passion and commitment. There was an endearing transparency when we chatted together. She told me how she knew instinctively that I was inexperienced when she first set eyes on me. She had planned to seduce me over a period of time but events had got out of hand. She purred like a kitten: "You are a very handsome young man and it does make me wonder why you don't have girlfriends. Perhaps you did but never made love to any of them."

I told her that my feelings for her, from the moment I first set eyes on her, had been the same. I did confess that she was not quite the first woman I had made love to. I told her I had made love only the once and at a time when my lover and I were both fifteen years old.

"Who was she and where is she now?"

"She was in my boarding school and is still there. Nuns watched us like hawks and didn't even allow us to talk together."

"But did you ever tell her that you loved her?"

"Yes, several times and she told me that she loved me too."

"But why is she still there? Hasn't she a home to go too?"

I told Nirmala that it was a long and emotional story and I wasn't even sure where to start. She was eager to hear all about it. Telling me we had the entire afternoon together there was plenty of time for me to tell her.

"Her name is Susan," I told her: "She is so beautiful I can't begin to tell you how much."

"She is Indian?"

"No, she is white and speaks with a very strong Australian accent. You could never miss her even in a crowd, Nirmala. I wish you could see her eyes; a tawny light brown, one with a fleck in it. Apparently her parents are Australian and live there in Australia somewhere."

Nirmala was dismayed at the poignancy of the convent exile and asked how her parents could be as heartless as to leave her there to rot. I explained that it apparently had been an acrimonious divorce. They had left her at the mercy of the nuns when they had returned to Australia. That was how it had been explained to me but rumour had it that Susan is the illegitimate daughter of an Australian nun who had an affair with a priest. Her, father the priest had returned to Australia after he was excommunicated by the church and she, the nun and mother of Susan had been banished to the Leprosy Hospital on the island of Makogai. All contact between mother and daughter had been forbidden by the church.

The story saddened Nirmala but I was more prosaic and suggested that she switch the radio on. Father would wish to know the football scores; otherwise he would be curious as to how I had been spending my time.

Afterwards I read the Hindu Book of Love whilst Nirmala changed the baby, fed and then returned him to his hammock. We made love once more before I crept silently from her home and into my own. There I was asked had I enjoyed the match.

I lied; I had little choice and told father that it had been a wonderful game; a record turnout and of course I was able to tell him the scores. He asked had I seen

Rajendra there and I told him I had not. I was cheekily tempted to tell him I had seen his wife but resisted the temptation.

Later that evening I was filled with remorse for my behaviour. I had been so true to Susan and now I had betrayed her just as her parents had let her down. I doubted if she would ever wish to see me again had she known what had occurred between me and Nirmala. I was increasingly anxious and wondering as to what the consequences might be of Nirmala becoming pregnant? I was apprehensive about the possibility of becoming a father at such an early age. It was for awhile my fervent wish that I stop having sex with her. I was also worried that becoming a father and being involved in a relationship might interfere with my plans of going abroad. On the other hand the opportunity to make love to such a beautiful and enchanting woman, several years older and much more experienced that I was an opportunity that might never cross my path again. It was a difficult balancing act.

On the Sunday morning I awoke to the sound of lashing rain, thunder and forked lightning. On the table beside me the radio crackled and whistled and the small ceiling light flickered. Lying quietly in my bed I listened as mother and my sisters prepared breakfast of hot chapattis and eggs fried in garlic and onion. Afterwards, we sat around the small table eating and listening to a pundit warbling a few Hindu prayers on the old radio. Much later that morning domestic routine was stopped in its tracks by a rapping on the door. For some reason I was nervous about answering it and when it was opened my instincts had clearly served me well. There on the doorstep was Rajendra and he was smiling sheepishly.

"Good morning, Jamie"

Bidding him good morning I felt a sinking feeling in the pit of my stomach and little knew what to expect. I need not have concerned myself too much. He told me that Nirmala would love to have our family over to lunch and urged us to come on over as soon as we were ready. The invitation was a relief. If Nirmala had been a little indiscreet or intimated she might be with child by someone other than him then there could easily have been a confrontation or worse still our eviction. I showered, changed and then rushed up there. The others followed.

Not surprisingly the veranda was soaking wet due to the downpour and so we gathered in their front room and sitting traditionally whilst leaning against the timber walls watched as Rajendra opened bottles of beer. My father was rolling marijuana. No one batted an eye-lid as he did so but I stuck to the beer; smoking hashish was normal in Hindu homes.

There were jokes told and much merriment as the women prepared the food and waited on us hand and foot. This was so typical of Indian homes. The men do not help in the household. The women cook, clean not only the dirty clothes but the men's shoes too; it is the ultimate man's world.

After several different curries, chapattis, pilau rice and Indian sweets the men retired to their beds while mother helped Nirmala with the dishes. For my part I decided to take my sisters for a long walk and on our return I prepared them for their new school the next day.

On the Monday I wished both my sisters good luck before leaving for my own work place. On the way I passed Nirmala's veranda and saw her waiting for me. She called out to remind me to be early and be back soon after work.

I was amazed to see school children in uniforms rushing to the college situated across the road. After passing the Public Works Department I passed the same college. Its surroundings were crowded with teenage girls of every ethnicity imaginable. Most were gathered around the statues of Jesus Christ. So all new to me, school was back after the mid-term holiday. The quiet road I was used to was now turned into a thriving thoroughfare; the noise drowning out the sounds of the tropical birds in the fauna that surrounded us.

As I rushed past the convent's gate I couldn't resist glancing at the groups of mostly attractive schoolgirls. On seeing me pass there was a chorus of voices calling out: "I die there."

It was true; the girls were worse than the boys. I never thought that I would be embarrassed but I was on that occasion. Things got worse. I rushed on with my head down only to walk straight into a wooden telegraph pole. The shock unbalanced me and I sprawled on the ground; my humiliation was complete. The girls cheered and jeered as I steadied myself and ran on towards the goldmines. I remembered my young Fijian school mates called out the same expression to all the girls they fancied. It is a Fijian way to let someone know that you fancy them. Loosely interpreted it meant; I will die there either in his or her arms or between their legs if they had a chance. I knew from my past experience that the girls were just letting off steam. That is what young people in Fiji do especially, when in a group and showing off.

That evening after work and training I sauntered home past the convent which by then was closed. With my head down I walked steadily on. I was tired after the long day but still looking forward to seeing Nirmala. Suddenly I heard a voice that stopped me in my tracks and then again I heard those all too familiar words: I die there. Looking up I found I was face to face with two schoolgirls, both smiling nervously.

"Hi stranger!"

I smiled and said greeted them in like manner; holding out my hand to greet them in the traditional fashion.

"I am Sara and this is my friend, Lisa."

I introduced myself and explained that I had just moved there with my family, and that I was working at the mines. They told me they knew all that; they had seen me that morning passing the school and the unfortunate accident too. They wanted to know if I was alright. I was quite taken aback by their kindness but was again a little tongue tied. I told them I was late because I use the gym after work.

Looking more closely at them it was clear they were both very appealing. Both were wearing their school outfits of white top, grey pleated skirt, black shoes and white socks.

"You're from the convent, yes?"

"Yes, it's our last term before we go to college."

On asking them which college they would be attending they told me it was to be St. Joseph's. I knew it of course. "Have you been there?"

"Yes, several times." I told them. "We used to go there regularly on picnics or help the priests with gardening and clearing the rubbish before the college opened."

"Oh, that is great. You must tell us all about the place."

I told them I would someday and as I carried on my way to Nirmala's home I heard the both of them giggling and reciting those words again: "I die there!"

When I arrived at Nirmala's her mother-in-law, Indra, was just stepping through the herbaceous bushes and out on to the road that skirted her home. She nodded in my direction and then scurried away towards her own home over the hill. I presumed she had called on a visit and had probably given Nirmala a critical talking to about her failing to produce a grandson for her.

I stood behind the hedge and made sure she was well out of sight before stepping up to Nirmala's veranda and into her lounge. As I went in I saw she was sitting on a settee feeding the baby. Clearly she had been weeping. Sitting myself beside her I embraced and gently kissed her. Then, without saying a word she stood up, left the baby in the hammock and bolted the front door.

Grabbing my hand she pulled me towards her bedroom. "I'll bloody well show them that I'm not barren. It is their son, who has the problem, not me, so why should I be the one who is criticised?" Within minutes we had both stripped off and were as nature intended; Adam and Eve. Afterwards I rushed on home.

Over the next few days my lifestyle continued much the same way; work, gym; meeting and making love on the way home. The only thing that separated the uniformity of life was my growing friendship with Sara and Lisa. They looked young but then I was a teenager too; we were all young and it was with a quickening pulse that I began to look forward to meeting up with them. Each morning they greeted me with the same chorus, giggling and laughing and pushing one another towards me. Then one Friday evening after gym I was making my way home when I saw Sara who on this occasion was on her own.

I asked where Lisa was. She told me that she had to help her father out with something that needed doing; in the family laundry.

"You mean Fong's laundry?"

"Yes, Mr Fong is Lisa's father. I wondered if you might fancy coming to the cinema with me tomorrow. There's a movie I am desperate to see and Lisa can't make it."

I told her I would love to but added that she was young and I had no desire to cross swords with her parents. She told me she was close to being sixteen years of age and assured me that her parents wouldn't have a problem with our going to the movies together.

She did look younger but I had little choice but to take her word for it. She swore she was telling the truth about her age and when I seemed comfortable enough with it I asked her what the movie was. It was Jail House Rock starring Elvis Presley.

RETURNED TO DEVIL'S ISLAND

My seven o'clock suggestion was turned down; it had to be the afternoon matinee and then arranged we went our separate ways while I carried on to Nirmala's home. She had just finished feeding the baby and had placed him in his hammock to sleep. As I entered she as usual bolted the door behind her and turned to face me. I took her in my arms and kissed her passionately. "Jamie, I feel so happy. This is the happiest day of my life"

"But you always look happy."

"I mean I am very, very happy," she added with meaning. She was trying to tell me something. I asked her why she was happier than she usually was.

"My period is late. I think I am pregnant." As soon as she had told me she grabbed me in delight, kissing my face, my forehead, my ears and my lips. I was in a sort of shock and found speaking didn't come easy. Excited, she pulled me towards her bed and astride me started to unfasten the front of my pants. Nature ran its natural course that evening but I think it already had.

Such was her mood and excitement she made love to me more passionately than ever before. Over and over again she kept repeating I love you, Jamie. I love you so much." It was as if I had saved her life. Perhaps I had, by producing another life.

Once our passions had subsided she slipped off the bed and handed me a beer. Sipping it quietly I realised I was still in awe at what she had told me. I was it appeared to be the father of her child; furthermore a love child conceived out of wedlock and out of love. I loved Nirmala but I wasn't in love with her, perhaps a bit infatuated but that was all.

It did occur to me however that this could be the end of my career and my plans for travelling abroad. I tried not to dwell too much on such thoughts. Yes, I was very affectionate towards her but was I really in love as I had been with Susan? Was I really just a stud? I didn't really feel that I wanted to talk about her pregnancy. Father I might be but I didn't feel like one and had no wish to. I changed the subject.

"I met a nice young girl today called Sara."

"I know Sara. She is the daughter of the boss of the Emperor Gold Mines. Her father is American and her mother comes from the small island of Bau."

"Bau? Some of my school friends came from Bau."

"Girlfriends?"

"No," I told her: "I only had eyes for Susan and no one else."

"Do you still miss her?"

"Yes I do and feel guilty for being unfaithful to her?"

Nirmala smiled whimsically as though she had thoughts of her own; perhaps a past love in her life: "You'll get over her one day. I am sure of that."

I told her that was unlikely to which she replied that there wasn't much point in my not moving on. The nuns would never set her free to marry and added that by now Susan would almost certain to have forgotten me. Nirmala preferred talking about her own exciting news.

"You being pregnant," I ventured tentatively.

65

"Yes, of course, Jamie. Can't you see how important it is?"

Holding her hand I asked her how she could be so sure. She then revealed that on the following Monday she had an appointment booked to see her doctor. She would then know for certain and added that if the receptionist got to know it would be all over the village within hours. Sensing my timidity she then went on to assure me that no one would know that we were lovers or that the child would be mine. I was still wondering about the consequences and she seemed able to read my thoughts. All I could think of was what now?

Downing my beer I left her home and pondered the dilemma. It was certain that I was infatuated with Nirmala but I was not in love with her. I admired her beauty and her stunning figure; I certainly enjoyed being with her but that was it. I wondered what had made her tell me she loved me. That did bother me as it wasn't any part of the arrangement. That could really complicate matters. As far as I was concerned we had both achieved what we had set out to achieve. That night I drifted off to sleep thinking of not one but three mortal beings; Susan, Nirmala and her perhaps child.

On Saturday morning, after counting the money I had saved, I took my sisters to our nearest town Tavua to shop. They returned beaming happily with new sandals and for me a new bright red Hercules bicycle. I proudly rode home that day with one sister sitting across the cross bar; the other standing on the foot rests of the back wheel holding on to my shoulders. I shall never forget the grins on our parents' faces when we got back home.

Leaving my sisters at home I rode my new toy up and down the road outside the depot, which was what I was doing when Sara spotted me. Coming across she too enjoyed sitting on the cross bar and the riding around until it was time for the matinee.

On our arriving at the shed like theatre Lisa Fong who had in fact got time off was there to meet us both. Once inside we settled down in our seats, close to each other but not exactly together. Inquisitively we glanced at each other and smiles crossed our lips as the lights dimmed and the movie started. After the matinee Lisa did have to leave in a hurry. Something needed taking care of at her father's laundry and after she had left us Sara and I strolled slowly towards her home.

"Jamie, you were at St Mary's so you must be a Catholic; are you?"

"Yes I am but what makes you ask?"

"Because we go to mass every Sunday and I would like you to come to mass tomorrow?"

I told her that I hadn't been to mass for many months but the teenager was insistent that I join her for the service. I asked her if Father O'Leary was still there. She told me he was and asked if I knew him. I told her he was the parish priest at St Mary's before being transferred to St Joseph's. And so it was arranged that I attend mass with her.

I really had other things on my mind right then but as we reached and paused behind the herbaceous shrubs that shielded her home from view our eyes met for an instant and then I took her in my arms, holding her so close I could physically feel our hearts pounding. Lifting her chin gently with my left hand I kissed her fully on the lips; something I was becoming quite experienced at thanks to Nirmala's lovemaking. My head swirled as I experienced Sara's response; her tongue probing between my lips.

"So," she smiled as our clinch relaxed a little. "Now you'll definitely have to come to mass in the morning?"

There was only one answer to that and my feelings were such that all desire for Nirmala faded. I had no longer any wish to see her or her husband Rajendra. They had used me for their own good and now I must get away from them. I was discreetly passing their home trying to keep as low profile as possible fervently hoping I wouldn't be seen when I heard her calling me.

"Jamie, do come up for a beer. I have poured one for you."

This time it was Rajendra and he had indeed at least taken the top off a bottle of beer; this time unusually it was a Fosters beer. He laughed and told me it was from kangaroo land.

Having made love to his wife so often and so passionately I felt a little awkward about sharing his company and couldn't really figure out how to engage in a conversation other than small talk. I did realise that whatever his wife and I did it was with his blessing. His only concern was that I get the both of them off the hook by making Nirmala pregnant. It was essential for him to prove to his family and the world at large that he was virile and very much the tiger. You couldn't put a price on that.

The awkwardness was broken when Nirmala walked into the room with the baby in her arms. She asked me how Sara was and I told her about our going to the matinee.

"It's a start," she replied and for a moment her gaze met mine and held my own gaze. There was curiosity in her smile as though she wanted to delve a little deeper but had decided against doing so. Somehow I got the feeling that she approved. It was then that I noticed father's arrival; he was carrying two large bottles of Fosters and he too was interested about the new flavour. As soon as he had settled down Rajendra turned to him. "Nirmala and I think our prayers have been answered. It seems she is pregnant at last."

Feeling uneasy about the news I gulped the beer fast and grabbed another bottle. Father was clearly delighted. Whether he would have been had he realised he was about to become a grandfather was another matter. Congratulating them both he shook Rajendra's hand warmly: "Well done," he said and then repeated his congratulations. Nirmala's eyes met mine as they often did and a devious smile creased on her face. It would seem that there was not much wrong with her anatomical procreation system. Soon we were joined by others of my family; they were allowed ginger beer but definitely no alcohol.

"When will you know for sure," asked mother.

"I am seeing the doctor on Monday," Nirmala smiled.

It seemed I was the only one who wasn't particularly enthusiastic about Nirmala's supposed pregnancy. The food was plentiful as were the drinks; it must have been near midnight before we said our final good nights.

On the Sunday morning I got myself suitably ready for the mass and set off towards the Church of the Sacred Heart. As I approached Sara's home I saw her leaving with her parents and her small brother, Andy. It seemed a little incongruous as on my own I followed the small family party from just a few steps behind. A little later I lingered as after the call to church we each dipped our fingers into the holy water in the wall-fixed clam shell basin.

Only after I had crossed myself, kneeled and bowed to the altar, did Sara acknowledge my presence with a head turn and a sweet smile. I stayed close to her without making it too obvious to her family who were blissfully unaware of my presence or my purpose. The sermon given was probably the last I wished to hear. Father O'Leary carefully, "Thou shall not steal." I had stolen communion wine and a few shillings off the collection plate.

"Thou shall not covet thy neighbour's wife." There went another broken commandment. And so it continued; Thou shall not commit adultery. This too I had done. Perhaps I wasn't cut out to be a priest.

Once the sermon was over everyone took communion and as I hesitantly got to my feet I could see Sara looking intently at me. Thank goodness she couldn't read my thoughts. Trembling with the fear that a bolt of lightning might strike me down for the gravity of my sinning I joined the line moving towards the communion rail. "Please God; do forgive me for I have sinned." I whispered to Him alone under my breath as I drew closer to the altar.

After receiving the white wafer on my tongue I returned to my seat and felt considerable disquiet. Sara later told me that she thought I was feeling unwell as my face had turned a grey pallor during communion. Before the service had drawn to a close I quietly left and went straight home; I didn't even pause to pass the time of day with Father O'Leary as I should have done. At home I just grabbed a bottle of dad's beer and thought what a fool I had been by agreeing to go to the church that day. Sitting on the edge of my bed and on my own once again I sipped my beer. I now had Susan, Nirmala and Sara to occupy my thoughts.

How beautiful Sara had looked in her white dress. Was that her real reason for wanting me to join her at the church; so I could see her at her most appealing? That morning she had been wearing stylish Cuban heels and on her full red lips a hint of lipstick. There was no doubt about it; she was an incredibly beautiful young lady. It was then I was brought to earth by my thoughts of her father. He was a powerfully built giant of an American. He must have stood head and shoulders over any other men in the community. What he might say if he was to learn that I was about to date his precious and precocious daughter really didn't bear thinking about. Consumed by a mix of curiosity and desire I soon grabbed my bike and set off on the short distance to Sara's home. All was fine with us; her greeting couldn't have been friendlier and we were soon riding up and down the dusty street.

Feeling her fragranced hair blowing up on my face was something of a new and welcome experience. Her perfume was definitely Evening in Paris, though I could only imagine what Paris smelled like in an evening. The perfume was enough; it made my poor head spin. When I saw her small white hands clutching the handlebars I impulsively leaned forward and kissed her hair.

"Why are you so quiet, Jamie?"

"I'm thinking how lucky I am to meet you. You are so young and so beautiful."

"Please don't tell me lies?"

"I'm not lying. You really and truly are beautiful."

She didn't answer but in the soft breeze that accompanied our ride I fancied I heard her sigh as we rode gently down the dusty bumpy road towards the beaches. It wasn't long before we could see sparkling sea and the golden sand in the distance. Once there we dismounted and embracing Sara, we kissed passionately. Then, picking her up, for she was as light as a feather to me, I walked towards the water's edge before laying her gently down and lying beside her before pressing our lips together. As our bodies merged I could feel her slender thighs pressing against my own and as our bare toes playfully touched she abruptly pushed me away and got to her feet. "Jamie, it is a mortal sin to go any further and you know it."

"It's alright, babe; I wouldn't do anything to hurt you." Pulling her towards me and taking her in my arms we again kissed. Sara interrupted our canoodling by asking if I had been to this beach before. I told her I hadn't and asked if it was new to her too.

"No: My father has a motor launch. Sometimes we go out to those islands." She pointed to several small islands a land mile distant. I smiled: "I would love to take you there with me."

"Then, Jamie, you will have to buy or borrow a boat."

"Perhaps I should have bought a boat and not a bike."

Sara ignored that suggestion and instead pointed to an islet a little to the left of where we were lying: "See that one little island on the left, that's the only one with fresh water. It has a small creek with a pool of water."

After a little more petting we walked along the water's edge and chucked a few stones into the sea before pausing for a little more canoodling. Far in the distance we could see a pod of dolphins sporting along the shoreline. Soon they were close enough for us to throw them wild cucumbers we were gathering from the nearby foliage. Leaping high in the water and making their distinctive noises I watched as Sara splashed into the sea to join them. "Come on Jamie, come in the water," she called. "We've been swimming with then since I was a baby. My dad has trained them to swim with us."

I hesitated but reasoned that if she could as easily join them then so could I. Running into the lapping waters we were soon out of our depth but close enough to join the fascinating mammals. They were very playful and more importantly it was comforting to have them there for we knew that dolphins and sharks are mortal enemies; there are no sharks where there are dolphins. Evening seemed to descend too soon but the red glowing tropical sun was already touching the sea's horizon. It was time to go to our homes. Our day was ended by affectionate kisses again behind the shrubbery on the approach to her family home.

Monday morning was the next time I was to see Sara, as usual she was standing by the school gates with Lisa and those I described as the chorus girls. Less confident in the company of more than one girl I waved shyly and putting my head down sped past. This was no time and no place for messing about. I had to keep my mind on my work and this evening there would be another training session. This was something of a diary entry for me; it was the first time I had seen a poster advertising a major boxing tournament with my name on it.

I had moved up from the preliminary four rounds of boxing to the six rounds, under the supporting bouts for the main events. I was to meet local middleweight Tanoa Vunivalu and it would be six three minutes rounds contested at the Valabala Theatre. The location pleased me as it was the same theatre the nuns had taken us to see the religious movies. It was close to the beach and my old school. "You have two weeks to get super fit," advised Naliva "I want to see you every evening at five: Is that clear Jamie?"

I of course told him it was and after a super-charged training session I rode off to tell my family but first there was Sara to boast to. She was waiting for me and after meeting up we hugged and kissed in the shadows of the tall hedge. I think I could count her in as a girlfriend by now.

When I did arrive home a party was in progress. Nirmala and Rajendra were celebrating and their small veranda was heaving with their relatives. "Hi Jamie, over here," a familiar voice called out.

By this time, between the training session and the bike ride home through the tropical heat I was perspiring like a horse.

"I won't be long," I called out as I pedalled past and dashed inside my own home. It was then that I was told the reason for the celebrations at our neighbour's home. It had been confirmed, Nirmala was indeed with child and we were all invited over for a party. By the time I had showered, changed and made my way over there I had to fight my way through all their relatives. There were Nirmala and Rajendra's grandparents, aunts, uncles and numerous cousins; people I had yet to meet were everywhere. Everyone was clearly having a good time, laughing and chit-chatting, stuffing themselves with the food being constantly brought out to the veranda on trays.

When the happy couple saw me they rushed over and told me the news themselves. Nirmala hugged me and Rajendra shook my hand enthusiastically. I didn't know whether I should congratulate them or hold my tongue. I decided on the latter and sitting in the corner of the room deep I was in thought. I was after all going to be a father. My father and Rajendra were both enjoying their marijuana whilst I continued to sip my Fosters in silence.

On the Tuesday morning father and Rajendra, who were on a day shift, left for work before I did. A little later I mounted my bike and as I passed Nirmala's home she called out to me not to be bashful and reminded me that I must remember to join her that night. Did she suspect that I had by this time moved on? During my pause she called that the other two were going fishing and wouldn't return until late. She added breathlessly that she must see me that evening. I was friendly enough but made no direct reply. Sensing my reluctance she persisted. "I will be so disappointed if you don't come."

I wasn't too sure and smiling at her a little sadly I rode off into the distance. In a way I felt that though I was the pivotal part in what was happening I wasn't a part of it at all. I was a spectator and that what had happened was little more than a sport.

As I approached the gates leading up to the convent I could see Sara and Lisa waiting for me and so were about one hundred other pupils. As I smiled a nun came rushing over. Wagging her finger she reprimanded them all. Her white habit reminded me of St Mary's. I smiled and rode on.

That evening I arrived just as father and Rajendra were leaving with a group of Indian friends. "We're going fishing," they shouted. "We will be back late." I took no notice of them. I knew how the Indians fished: they did it the lazy way. All that was needed was a bright Tilly Lamp and a few spears. Once the lamp was lit, fish and other sea life, attracted to the light, would surround their boats. It was a turkey shoot quite honestly. There were no skills needed. Some were trapped in the small fish nets whilst others were speared and bludgeoned by marijuana smoking fishermen. Where was the fun or the sportsmanship in that activity? A little downcast I went into our house to shower and have a little dinner. Afterwards, sitting by the radio I heard the knock on the door. It was gentle but persistent. It was Nirmala.

"Oh Jamie, please can you help. My radio has gone dead. I think the copper aerial on the roof has fallen."

I knew well that this was just a ploy; that there was nothing wrong with the radio but had little choice but to follow her over and into her home. Again I heard the bolt slipping softly home in its casing. My reluctance soon proved to have been locked on the outside of their home too. All thought of attending to her radio evaporated as her scent filled my sensations. Turning towards her I was consumed by wanting her and taking her in my arms we entwined. The old lust we had for each other, the sexual chemistry kicked in and neither of us paused as our clothes descended in a heap on the rattan covered floor.

Afterwards I lay holding her tightly but my thoughts were now on Sara and I felt sad and shamefaced. It was becoming difficult to exclude Nirmala from my life.

"Why have you gone so quite, Jamie?"

"Oh. I am just thinking, Nirmala: Everything has happened to me so fast. I really don't know what to do for the best. One minute I think of Susan and Sara and then I am thinking of you and the baby. What am I going to do?"

"Just be your normal self," she smiled: "You are young and good looking. Of course the girls are going to be attracted to you. But remember Susan is a million miles away from you and it is unlikely you will ever see her again. It is life. You enjoy life and move on. Follow your boxing career and do go on seeing Sara."

This was followed by a brief pause before she added: "And me of course. At least we two are here and Susan is not."

I thought deeply for a moment as something else was beginning to bother me. "What happens if I get seriously involved with Sara; it could affect the travelling plans I have?"

She gave my question some thought as my hands stroked her breasts and midriff; I was still a little infatuated with Nirmala.

"I think Sara is the best thing that has happened to you so you must go all out to make her your proper girlfriend. She is so pretty; you would make the loveliest of couples." I noticed she had pointedly ignored the concerns I had for travelling.

"Her father is American and he will have my guts for garters if he finds out that I'm seeing his daughter."

Nirmala smiled and in a strange way she was like an older sister offering the advice of someone more mature: "You just cross that bridge when you come to it. In the meantime you must date her. Once you have made love to her you will find that everything falls neatly into place."

Nirmala's suggestion heartened me. Maybe I could have my cake and eat it; anyway, her saying she loved me might have been either a slip of a tongue or not necessarily a deep abiding committed love. My neighbour's wife was willing to help me through my troubles and dilemmas. Nirmala could be good for me.

I was kissing her and thinking it was time to go when she softly spoke almost as a whisper: "Just a word of advice, Jamie. Sara could be a virgin. Please, be gentle with her when you take her and remember to withdraw before you orgasm otherwise you could get her pregnant too".

I smiled: "Yes, mother; I do."

My light-hearted response reminded me of my own mother: two hours to fix a radio? I quickly dressed and left Nirmala still naked on her marital bed. Such was life.

On the Wednesday evening after a good session at the gym I was hoping to get past Nirmala's veranda without being seen when she nabbed me. "How is Sara?"

"She is well but not allowed out except Saturday evenings."

"Are you seeing her this Saturday?"

"Yes, we plan on going to the movies."

"Why don't you bring her here and baby sit for us?"

Her invitation puzzled me a little. "Here, Nirmala? And where will you go?"

"Rajendra and I are going to the movies."

I told her I was seeing Sara the next day and would let her know. Nirmala smiled wickedly as she stepped back inside her lounge. Later I waited until my dad had finished his evening prayers before asking him if they would like to go to the movies that Saturday evening and take my sisters along with them. Mother asked what the film was. "It is a Hindi film called Chandrasekhar."

"I saw a poster," said Sabita and my sisters delighted at the prospect of an unexpected night at the movies nodded enthusiastically. Mother did ask if I would be going too. I told her I couldn't much as I would like to be as I was babysitting due to Nirmala and Rajenda going to the movies too.

The next morning as I was on the way to work I met Sara outside the convent gates and told her the exciting news. Her smile was as wicked as had been Nirmala's. "I'll have to lie and tell my parents that I'm going to visit Lisa Fong."

The beam on my face told her everything she needed to know about my enthusiasm: Sara and I couldn't wait to be together alone and as adults; as a bonus uninterrupted privacy. Her face turned crimson but Sara was as excited as was I. Cocking my leg over the cycle's seat I again mounted my cycle and continued on my way to work. The following days couldn't pass quickly enough and I salivated at the thought of being alone with Sara in Nirmala's love-home.

That Saturday after I had showered I put on a light top and my boxer shorts and soon afterwards was tapping on Nirmala's front door. Rajendra was there of course as his wife; my lover showed me how to prepare the baby's bottle in case he woke up hungry. Then with a knowing look and a wink she left for the cinema with her husband. "Help yourself to the beer," she called. "And do have a nice time."

Soon my family would be on their way to the theatre too and beginning to relax a little yet still with a mixture of apprehension and excitement I tuned the radio in to Radio Rotorua, transmitting love songs from New Zealand. Finally I settled down with a Fosters before going out on the veranda to wait for Sara. When she arrived I hugged her.

"You smell of beer, Jamie."

"I do?"

"Yes, I can smell beer all over you."

I told her that Nirmala had given me a Fosters while we were waiting for Rajendra to get ready. Sara laughed and called me a naughty boy and raising her hand as though to give me a friendly slap I grabbed and kissed her slender fingers. Then, hand in hand we walked up the steps of Nirmala's veranda and into the front room. This time it was my turn to ritually bolt the door behind us. I asked her if she would like a little beer but she would accept just the smallest of sips. She was more enthusiastic about our kissing, which was to my way of thinking a pretty good start to an evening filled with promise.

We both felt quite grown up as the rims of our glasses touched and we saluted each other. Coincidentally, in the background the radio was blaring the Slim Whitman favourite; Please Help Me, I'm Falling. I hoped it was the beer and not the record that caused Sara's face to screw up in disgust.

After I had put my glass aside I took her in my arms and we kissed passionately. I was really quite shy for pre-nuptial formalities and hesitated before I picked her up and carried her to the bedroom where I lay her on the bed.

Sara was heartbreaking lovely to me and as we kissed again and again my hands were beginning to wander; to explore and marvel at her youthful curves. I needed to sense her response and I knew I was pushing the boundaries. Sara went through a ritual of protestations as my hand gently stroked her bare thighs. "No, Jamie; it is a sin. We mustn't."

It wasn't apparently a mortal sin to kiss and fondle each other and nor was persistence a sin either for it wasn't long before my hands were fondling her breasts, sadly still hidden underneath her top. This activity made her giggle and it was perhaps the first time her breasts had ever been touched by a man. Other than mild protestations her undulating movements only served to encourage me further and she grasped my head in both hands as I covered her body with kisses.

I was becoming bolder and was fondling her lower belly and feeling her warm thighs through the thin fabric of her dress that had by now ridden high up her thighs. It was somewhere around there that resistance became futile. Without meaning to be I suddenly became too demanding and she was as much in need as I was. By the time I hooked my fingers in her panties I knew that soon we will be lovers and I was to later learn, the first for her. Nirmala's advice was well appreciated. Sod's Law being what it is the baby began to cry but it was not likely to interrupt what we were doing; our chance might never arrive again. She had now gripped me with both arms and began to kiss me long and hard. I gently straddled on top of her and felt penetration. We were now one, our groins were grinding and throbbing gently.

"Jamie! I am hurting inside; please, please take it out of me."

"It is all right, baby; just stay there in that position for a while and don't move; I know what I am doing."

"But, Jamie . . . ?

I covered her lips with mine to stop her talking whilst behind me I could hear the baby still crying for attention.

"The baby; we had better see to him," cried Sara.

I told her that he was safe; he couldn't fall from the hammock and only wanted attention.

"It's my first time I have ever done anything like this before, Jamie. Please don't get me pregnant. I will be severely punished; think of me, Jamie; please, please!"

Ignoring her protestations I continued to thrust gently whilst revelling in her expressions that showed a mix of all consuming passion mixed with fear.

"Jamie. I am committing a mortal sin and how can I ever confess to Father O'Leary on Sunday?"

"Please Sara," I whispered reassuringly. There was no need for her to have to confess to anyone. I added that the nuns would be wild with jealousy if they could see us now. I was thinking in particular of Sister Magdalene, which might not have been the best idea when we were making love.

"Please, you mustn't worry, Sara," I whispered soothingly as I felt myself submerged sufficiently deep for our groins to grind together. "I really know what I am doing."

"How, how is it you know what you are doing," she mumbles: "Have you done this with other girls?"

It was hardly the time to start telling her about the passionate lovemaking that Nirmala and I had experienced on this very same bed; the same bedclothes. "I read a Hindu book of lovemaking techniques once."

We both remained in that position for a while with Sara's thighs on either side of me I relaxed a little as I concentrated on bring me if not Sara towards the cataclysmic climax I knew would soon be mine. It was then that I began to experience sensations already familiar. Remembering Nirmala's advice I waited until the last possible moment and quickly withdrew. I was just in time, hopefully.

Sara had other than lovemaking on her mind as she leapt from the bed and standing there at the bedside looked aghast at the bloodstains that now spotted the clean bedding. It was then that the enormity of what we had done began to penetrate as deeply as I had earlier done; Sara was now trembling and sobbing. In despair she fled to the bathroom and locked herself inside. My tapping on the door brought no response except the sound of her sobbing. It brought back memories of Susan and how she too had run to the refuge of the bathroom after we had made love for the first time and the fear of her being pregnant. Then suddenly it dawned on me, what if Susan had conceived a child? How was I supposed to know? I had left her at the mercy of the nuns when I boarded the Royal Mail Bus. My mind was in turmoil.

Sadly, I sat on the side of bed thinking of Susan and now here was Sara, what am I suppose to do? I was in deep thought waiting for Sara to emerge from the bathroom. When she did so, there was just the slightest of wistful smiles on her beautiful but noticeably ashen face. I begged her forgiveness as I held her tightly. Sara smiled sadly but told me that if it had to happen she was glad it had been with me. She added that it was because she was in love with me. It was why she had allowed me to make love to her.

My words echoed hers and I expressed my love for her as endearingly as I could; telling her how beautiful and yet so young she was. Growing in confidence she said in return that she was glad that I had come to live here. It had previously been boring but since meeting me she knew she wanted me just as we had experienced.

I reminded her that she had been with Lisa the first time we had set eyes on each other and that early on Lisa had accompanied her when we met. Sara reminded me that it had been dark and she was a little afraid, especially as I was older. Like a dog at a bone she then expressed her concern at the bloodstains still clearly evident on the bed sheet. I told her I would fix it; I would think of an explanation. Would there be a need I thought to myself as picking up the bed sheet I went in the bathroom and washed the tell-tale stains before lighting up the benzene fuelled iron and drying the wet spots.

Seeing she was still a little unsure of things I offered her the bottle of Fosters and was a little taken aback to see her take deep gulps of the beer she had earlier claimed not to like very much. Afterwards we lay back on the bed listening to the sounds of the hits of the time; Elvis Presley, Petula Clark and Hank Williams that blared from the bedside radio. The baby had by that time realised it wasn't going to get the attention it had cried for and had gone back to sleep.

"I love you so much, Jamie," she whispered as we quietly enjoyed the samosas that Nirmala had left for us. She told me how happy she was that we had met.

"Me too," I whispered endearingly: "I love you, Sara. It was fate that brought us here together."

As I spoke I looked at the clock: It was almost 11pm and urging her to tidy herself quickly I followed my own advice. Seeing Sara off I was sad that I couldn't take her home; that would have meant abandoning the baby in its hammock. We were there of course to baby-sit. "See you tomorrow in church," she called.

See you in church? The very thought of mass terrified me. Oh no, not again, I thought to myself for I had committed yet another mortal sin. How could I face communion? I wondered if she would take communion and felt sorry if she was to have little choice in the matter. It was my fault and perhaps I was the devil incarnate. It was hardly a series of Christian acts I had so far been involved in. With such thoughts I sat back on the veranda and hurriedly downed another bottle of beer before Nirmala and Rajendra showed up. I went to bed thinking of my Susan and had to go back and see her somehow? Then I thought of Nirmala and Sara before falling fast asleep.

With the arrival at church on the Sunday we both took communion and immediately after mass Father O'Leary came out in a great hurry to meet me outside the church. I bid him good morning as smiling benignly he reminded me that on the previous Sunday it seemed that I couldn't leave the church quickly enough. He wanted to know if I had a problem. I reminded him that our family had just moved in and there was plenty that needed doing until we had properly settled in.

"Never mind," he smiled graciously. You are forgiven. It is so good to see you again. How tall and splendid you have grown, James. You must put a little time aside to join me in serving mass."

Assuring him I would give it some thought I told him also that I would soon come to confession and I was reminded of the times available for me to do so. As I walked away from that place of worship I wondered why the devil I had to mention confession. It was then that Sara came out of church and walked past me. I think she had held back until Father O'Leary had finished chatting with me. "I'll see you after lunch," she whispered before catching up with her parents.

When we did meet up we again made for the beach which we now called ours but on this occasion dark clouds appeared on the horizon before long heavy drops of tropical rain began to fall. I took it as an omen for as there was no fear of thunder and lightning it was a chance to shelter with her on an almost deserted beach in our small bower under the canopy provided by the trees. Uppermost in my mind was my desperate need to see her naked. I anticipated the epitome of nubile beauty and I was not to be disappointed.

Sara had been too self conscious to fully undress the previous night but today we had the beach and the foliage to ourselves. Strangely, we both undressed but did so separately to then emerge as God intended. Well maybe the way He intended. Again we ran towards the waters as the warm raindrops spattered on our bare skins.

As we surfaced laughing and spluttering we took hold of each other and kissed before realising we had company. We were surrounded by Sara's friends, the dolphins. I counted thirteen of these amazing sea creatures but Sara told me that sometimes there were as many as twenty of the creatures. We played with them like children until later we stepped back on to the beach and enjoyed the sight of each other's nakedness.

"Jamie!" she confided in me: "I am still hurting but I'm not going to stop you from making love to me but please be gentle."

"We could go into the bushes," I suggested. This time I was less impatient and thoughtful for our passion had since changed into that of mutual love. Later we picked wild cucumbers for the dolphins and returned to the water's edge to play. Fortunately, the Fijian rain is warm and not at all unpleasant and Sunday is the best time for such excursions as ours as church-going natives spend the day cooking and eating.

"Why are you so quiet, Jamie?"

I smiled as her words broke into my thoughts: "Because I am thinking how much I love you. I'll miss you once you go to college."

"I have to pass my entrance exam first."

She told me that she wasn't too confident about passing them but brightened up when I told her I would help her. It was something we could do when baby-sitting.

Goodness knows what her parents must have thought when I dropped Sara off at her home. Her wet clothes were clinging to her leaving very little to the imagination. Fijian girls of her age rarely wore bras.

My next five evenings were spent training. My trainer massaged me daily and put me on a native diet of taro, tapioca, yams, fish cooked in coconut milk and lots of fresh oysters. As the date in which I would be fighting drew closer I was beginning to feel superbly fit and confident.

On the afternoon of the fight we both travelled by bus to the town of Valabala. After the medical and weigh-in I was allowed a light meal and a little time to relax beneath palm trees. Changing into boxing shorts on my return I was to say the least a little apprehensive as I waited back stage until I heard my name called.

Leading me to the ring my trainer and I came face to face with Tanoa, my opponent He glared at me but I felt no need to return the glare and smiled. The referee called us to the ring's centre to give the usual reminders before we returned to our respective corners.

As the bell rang I closed the gap between me and my opponent and immediately subjected him to a barrage of blows. He blinked a few times, perhaps due to the unexpected ferocity for I look mild mannered and hide my hardness well. This time I hit him with a right cross to his chin and watched as he fell heavily. On this occasion he was saved by the bell's clanging. Back at my corner Naliva advised me to go after him with heavy right hand punches aimed at his jaw.

"Don't box him, fight him toe to toe; let him have your heavy right hand to the chin, Jamie."

As round two progressed I ducked several times and then caught my rival with a heavy right counter punch to his chin. Down he went again. This time the bell couldn't save him. At the count of ten the referee raised my hand and declared me the winner.

Naliva and I stayed back to see the main bout of the evening. This was between heavyweight champion Miliano and Laitia Vakaduadua the chalenger. As the fight progressed a scuffle broke out. Laitia was irritated by the Indian referee's continuous interference. At the start of the round seven the goaded Laitia took a vicious swipe at Patrick Rahman the referee, a blow that knocked him out for dead. There was pandemonium as all hell let loose. The crowd were on their feet and police rushed to the ring to stop the fiasco. The referee was stretchered off to the hospital but there was a happy ending when he was later pronounced fit. Laitia wasn't so lucky: He was found guilty and banned from boxing for three years.

* * *

The following morning the news had already got around. I was woken by mother begging me never to box again. "Please Krishna, you can play football, rugby or tennis but why box and have your good looks ruined?"

She was right but I had to win the middleweight title. Only by doing so could I hope to save some cash and travel abroad. After breakfast I rode to Naliva's village hoping to find him as I needed a massage to get rid of the few aches and pains I received during the fight. Arriving at his grass cottage I realised no one was there. Wandering through his village the dogs barked and pigs squealed but otherwise it was deserted. It was then I remembered it was Sunday. Everyone would be in church. I hung around till the sound of lali drums indicated the service over and soon people dressed in white converged carrying bibles under their arms.

As soon as he spotted me Naliva approached. Shaking hands he introduced me to his wife and two small sons and together we strolled to his home where I received my massage and later joined them to a light breakfast. When leaving I noticed an overturned canoe beneath a nearby palm. Naliva told me it was never used and invited me to take it.

Offering the use of my bicycle in return but he wouldn't hear of it, telling me his children were too young to use the canoe anyway. Thanking him profusely I got my bike home and then jogged back. That day I was likely the most excited teenager in the community as I carried the canoe with its paddle to the river and rowed it to my home. Wait until Sara sees this I thought to myself. We'll be able to explore those small islands on the mouth of the river.

After Sunday lunch I waited for Sara and as soon as she arrived we fell into each other's arms. "Congratulations for winning the fight. I heard it on the radio last night."

There is something else you can congratulate me about," I smiled. "I have a surprise for you, baby."

RETURNED TO DEVIL'S ISLAND

Leading her to the river's estuary I pointed to the nearest bank that was half hidden behind rows of sugar cane. "Wait for me. I will meet you right there in fifteen minutes."

As she walked towards the river I ran home and after carrying the canoe to the river I rowed the several hundred metres to our pre-arranged rendezvous. Sara was tickled pink when she saw me. "Going native are we? You should be able to handle this like a toy."

I grinned: "I believe your mother's ancestors from the island of Bau were the finest canoe handlers in the land?"

She took no offence and pointed out that they would have been massive war canoes whilst this was hardly bigger than a dinghy. I ignored her comment. In this instance size wasn't important. All that mattered was the beckoning sea. "Never mind with all that stuff," I said: "Just get in here and let's go and explore those islands out there."

After helping her in I paddled excitedly down river as she laughed and joked about the hollowed out wood trunk I was rowing. "Row, row, row your boat," she sang and teased me all the way to our intended destination.

On our arrival at the river's wider estuary I paddled on towards the place where we had made love on the beach before heading in the direction of the third island on the left.

"Why didn't you come to mass this morning?"

"I had to see a friend. It was important."

"You are a heathen, Jamie."

I grinned at the beauty straddling the thwarts of the canoe. "After I have finished with you today you will not be calling me a heathen, you will be calling me a cannibal."

Sara getting my drift blushed at my bravado whilst I continued to paddle until we arrived in the shallow water surrounding the tropical islet. It was the sort of idyll one sees so often on Fijian postcards. It was our lifestyle but we would never take it for granted. As I pulled the canoe up the beach I was aware of Sara disappearing from view into the lush green vegetation. "Come and find me," she called gaily."

I looked behind the boulders and among the banana plants, searched through the tall reeds and canes but there was not a sign of her. As keenly as a hunter I silently crept under hanging branches and it was I who was suddenly pounced upon by Sara. Pushing me back onto the soft sand she sat bestride me, pinning me down and kissing me.

It was an uneven struggle. I picked her up like a doll and carried her into the sea until knee deep in the warm waters I casually tossed her into the lagoon, which wasn't too deep. There we kissed to our hearts' content and it was long before our presence attracted the school of dolphins. This time they were a distraction from our own performances but we couldn't ignore them.

On this islet there were no cucumbers and so we collected fallen coconuts. Slicing them open with my machete I fed the pulp to the creatures. Soon afterwards, Sara took me by my hand and showed me around the tiny island and the small water pond at the source of the fresh water creek. There the water gushed from beneath the black rocks. "This is where father brings us for picnics but don't worry, he has gone native today and won't leave the comfort of his home with it being a Sunday."

The two of us spent the rest of the afternoon making love and chatting. I asked her about her father and told her I understood him to be American. I was curious as to how he ended up working in the mines. She explained that he had first arrived here during the war as a young soldier. At some stage he had needed treatment at the local hospital. It was there that he had met Sara's mother who was a nurse at the same hospital. Not surprisingly he presumably thought the islands were superior to the lifestyle back home in the United States and after a courtship they had married.

Sara's mother interested me more or at least her background did. "I believe the history of Bau is most horrific, during the cannibalism years that is."

"Yes, I know," Sara said thoughtfully: "Sometimes mother tells me some real horror stories about her predecessors."

This only served to arouse my interest more and I pressed her to tell me some of the truths about the island and its peoples. She laughed lightly and said that might not be such a good thing; they were not nice things that happened back then. Anyway they were long stories. Laughing I reminded her that we had all afternoon. Sara asked if I had seen her mother. I had of course. I had seen her at the church. Sara told me that though her mother is a native Fijian she looks almost European.

"She is a descendant of Europeans?"

"Yes, how did you know?"

Pausing during my silence my new girlfriend went on: "In the days of my great great grandfather, Spanish and British adventurers' ships came to Bau in search of sandalwood and other treasures around our shores. Many of these craft foundered on reefs barely hidden beneath the approach waters. Rumours flew around the world that some of these vessels had cargoes of gold and silver. Following on the deserters, mutineers and bounty hunters from other ships soon arrived at Bau. They introduced rum, whisky and gunpowder. At one time there were as many as twenty or more Europeans living on the island of Bau. Some attempted to integrate by dressing in masi cloth and painting their faces as did the natives. Many took part in ceremonial sacrifices and cannibalism and because they were different they lived like kings among the Fijian kings. The leader of these Europeans was a man called Charlie Savage, who, despite his English sounding name came from Sweden. He was given the title of a chief. In inter-tribal wars Europeans were hired as mercenaries to kill, pillage and rape. It was because they had and could use guns and gunpowder that few dared to question their authority.

Young women from defeated villages were dragged before the kings of Bau and raped in orgies. Charlie Savage would often beg for their freedom and when successful keep them as wives for himself and his fellow Europeans. He once boasted of having a hundred wives.

The Europeans only worked when ships arrived to collect sandalwood. They didn't need money as wages but by assisting trade they received much rum and gunpowder for their guns. One day Savage and eleven of his white companions had gone to load a sandalwood ship nearby. The village chief told the men that he wanted neither their assistance nor the ship's interest. There was no more sandalwood left on the island.

The ship's captain had other ideas and anyway he had received instructions to load sandalwood and that was what he intended to do. The wood was to be transported to Australia.

There was a village assemblage by the irate chiefs and they stuck to their demands; there would be no more sandalwood taken. As the captain negotiated with them he became heated and used abusive language; calling them bastards, savages and cannibals.

Not surprisingly the chiefs couldn't lose face nor ignore such insults to their way of life. A fight broke out and under Savage's orders the men began to burn the village huts and 'kill the bloody natives.' At the first sounds of gunfire hundreds of natives came out of hidden locations and surrounding the Europeans they began to attack them with spears and battleaxes. Four of the Europeans were clubbed to death during the fracas. Their deaths and their victory aroused the bloodlust and confidence of the natives further and after smearing themselves with the fallen men's blood they attacked repeatedly and ferociously.

Sara paused and might have finished the story there but I urged her to go on. I was anxious to hear more of her story. "One of the Europeans, a man called Norman fell to the ground with a spear piercing his body. Savage and the remaining white men fought back but they were no match for the savagery of cannibals who were well used to fighting anyway.

Another of the Europeans fell with a spear piercing his skull. The only survivors were Savage and five of his compatriots: Their names were Martin Bushart, Thomas Daphne, Peter Dillon, William Wilson and Paddy Connell. Realising they were staring at defeat they attempted to escape by climbing a high rock nearby."

"How do you remember all these names?"

Sara laughed sweetly: "I've been listening to the same old stories since my childhood. I will write a book about them some day."

"Did they escape?"

"Don't be impatient Jamie. Just wait until I finish my story?"

She went on to explain that the five men reached to the top of a high rock as they dodged arrows and spears. It was a futile attempt to flee. Soon they were surrounded by hundreds of natives who encouraged by the booming sound of death drums were intent on their blood.

Four arrows went through Daphne but he didn't go down; he kept re-loading the muskets as his comrades fought for their lives. Then a spear sliced through his shoulder but he still kept on re-loading. Finally the fierceness of the natives proved too much for the remaining Europeans. Daphne jumped down from the rock as arrows continued to strike him. He was clubbed to the ground and dragged away. Savage and Paddy decided to climb down and beg for their lives. Someone stepped forward and clubbed Paddy to death but Savage was taken hold of and taken alive. With his hands secured he was carried to the ovens. From the top of the rock the remaining three; Bushart, Dillon and Wilson watched as the Fijians tortured Savage by slicing off his nose, ears, penis and balls whilst he was still alive. His screams were drowned by the sound of the death drums and kava drinking clapping natives."

I was horrified by Sara's account of the battle but fascinated I urged her to finish the story. Goodness knows how I was going to sleep that night.

"Well," said Sara. "The two bodies were dissected with bush knives and wrapped in banana leaves were placed in earthen ovens. The natives sat around drinking kava as they awaited their dinner. The three remaining Europeans trembled with fear as they took this in. They knew they were to be the next day's meal.

After the feasting ended the sound of death drums resumed and shortly before nightfall the three were taken alive and brought down to the ovens. Their hands and feet were bound by rope and each was laid flat on the ground for the next morning's feast. Fortunately for them the heavens opened up that night and the Fijians took to sheltering in the nearby caves. During the heavy rainfall Dillon wriggled free and liberated his mates. They got out of harms way and lived to tell the story and this is why you are hearing it now."

"Wow! That is some story." Sara was a beautiful story teller and I was totally absorbed by the scenes her words conjured up in my mind. "Yes, me too: My mind boggles at times when I hear mother's stories."

"Did the battle take place on your great great grandfather's land?"

"No, it took place on the island of Vanua Levu but close to my great grandfather's land. The high rocks are now visited my hundreds of tourists from all around the world."

I asked her where her mother fitted into this unravelling story. It was then she revealed that her mother was one of the descendents of one of the beleaguered Europeans. She herself being so European in looks was something called a throwback. Although not pure white she was clearly a racial fingerprint of one of those castaways.

She went on to say that after the feasting was over the skulls of the dead men were used as cups for serving kava. It was then that the natives started to kill the offspring of the Europeans who lived on the island of Bau. The Europeans and their progeny had turned the racial mix into a caste system with those children most European in appearance being the most favoured. Some of them, including pregnant girls, had successfully escaped by canoes across the straits to the main island. They were fortunate for this not so narrow strip of water was renowned for being shark infested. Sara told me that her grandmother was one of the girls who had escaped; her mother had been born to her.

After listening to her story I was horrified and too unsettled to kiss or make love to her. We quietly dressed, pulled the canoe into the water and paddled back. During our little trip I told her the story of my old bamboo village and its nearby tomb; of how three hundred and fifty men, women and children were murdered in ceremonial sacrifices and sex orgies. There wasn't much in the islands history that matched the paradisiacal notions of Western man.

On Monday morning, when passing Nirmala's veranda, she insisted that I see her that evening. "Please Jamie. I need you to be with me whenever it is possible."

I told her that I couldn't do so as I was training hard for my next fight and that was important to me too. She then reminded me that I was the father of her child. It was if though this placed me under some sort of an obligation. I smiled shyly but didn't commit myself. A little further down the dusty road I bumped into Sara and Lisa. "It's a long time since I saw you, Lisa," I smiled.

"Tell me about it," she said. "I have to help my father out in the laundry. We are just about to open up a small bakery and café behind the theatre."

"So more work for you?"

That was where we left it; there was work to be done. My trainer wasn't too pleased to hear that I wouldn't be training that week. "Jamie, you could become the next middleweight champion if you work hard at it."

"Thank you, my good friend. I will think about it."

When I arrived behind the hedge outside Sara's the welcome was as warm as always but she couldn't go off somewhere with me. One of the family's rules was that Saturday night was for studying. I told her I would help her if she were to baby-sit with me at Nirmala's. Sara smiled deviously at the thought. I think she too doubted there would be much studying done there.

There was no avoiding Nirmala when I reached her home. The beer was opened and so was her bedroom door shortly afterwards. It seemed she had the hots for me despite my going cool on her. I wasn't inclined to linger afterwards though. There was my sisters' homework to be completed.

It became something of a pattern; my seeing Sara whilst and trying to avoid Nirmala but I wasn't very successful. Nirmala is very beautiful, seductive and I was if nothing else a normal hot-blooded male. I was beginning to have a love-hate relationship due to the seductress's power over me. She could use her looks and skills of persuasion as few others could and I was easy prey.

Saturday was soon on us and my family went to the movies as did Nirmala and Rajendra whilst Sara and I did the baby-sitting. When Sara arrived she had brought her text books. They were placed on the table and then ignored as we stripped off, headed for the bed and lost ourselves in lovemaking.

Afterwards I retrieved the Hindu Book of Love from under the mattress and gave it to Sara before opening a Fosters and tuning the radio. On my return my girlfriend's eyes were popping out their sockets as she studied the many sexual positions. "Can people really do these things?"

"We could soon find out," I cheekily suggested.

She giggled: "So this is where you have learned the things you do to me or would like to do to me?"

Asking me how I had come by the book I told her Rajendra had given it to me. Sara was curious and then wanted to know if Nirmala really was pregnant. I told her she was, that it had been confirmed by the doctor and the whole village was gossiping about it. I was momentarily worried that Nirmala might have been loose-lipped but my thoughts were broken by Sara whose passion for lovemaking was fast becoming insatiable. She told me that the girls thought of me as some sort of Adonis; which did wonders for my ego. I also learned that she had narrowly beaten Lisa Fong to linking up with me.

Telling her that she was more appealing I added that Lisa too was very attractive. I was warned off. She also revealed that Lisa's father had arranged her marriage in Hong Kong and she is expected to follow his orders and travel there very soon. I asked her if Lisa realised who the lucky guy was to be.

"No but she has shown me a photograph of him. He's much older than she is and he really should be seeing a dentist with his teeth. The Chinese are like your own people; they arrange their daughter's marriage when they are very young and bundle them off to their husband's home."

My own two sisters were typical of the culture. They were not allowed to go anywhere alone or to meet anyone. My mother chaperoned them to school and back. Sara thought that a pity; especially their being so attractive. She thought it remarkable that they were even prohibited from speaking to men and contrasted it with the freedoms enjoyed by the male members of a family.

"Yes, sons have all the freedom in the world."

"Do your parents know about us?" Sara asked with a quizzical look on her slightly freckled face.

"I don't think so but I don't care if they do," I shrugged.

Flicking through the pages we were soon aroused by the graphic nature of the pictures and only later did it occur to us that we hadn't given a thought to Sara's homework. She was happy enough, telling me she enjoyed the alternative homework more and was enthusiastic about learning every position in the book. As she later went on her way she reminded me that there was mass in the morning.

I told her I couldn't get to it but I had promised Father O'Leary that I would be going to confession. Wagging her finger at me she again reminded me that there was confession at 7am. I told her I would be there but clearly I wasn't enthusiastic.

Sunday morning I did however keep my promise and whilst at the church took the opportunity to ask the father if Father John was still at St Mary's. He told me he was and added that Sister Magdalene had to return to Ireland to attend her father's funeral but would soon be back. The thought of her spiteful face sent shivers down my spine and the condolences weren't heartfelt; I was just being conventional. I would have loved to ask him how Susan was but held my tongue.

Following lunch was the much looked forward to playing on the river with Sara. She had earlier asked me what was on my mind when I had been staring at her bare legs at the church. Bending the truth a little I told her I had been thinking of how lucky I was to be in love with such a beautiful girl.

"Liar," she teased. "I know very well what you were thinking, you horny devil."

"If that is what you think then wait until we get to the islet."

"Don't you even think about it," she sniggered before abruptly changing the subject. She wanted me to tell her more about St Joseph's. I gave her a rough verbal diagram of the place and the restrictions imposed upon us. Even visits to the beach were forbidden lest the young ladies see the Fijian fishermen as the good Lord had made them. "Will you visit me; at the weekends?"

"There's not much chance of that. Catholic missionaries don't allow friendship between boys and girls. It's taboo to even write letters to each other." I told her a friend of mine had been expelled from St Mary's for writing love letters to a girlfriend. All the students' mail is read by their teachers. I was going to tell her about Susan and me getting punished after the Easter parade but I held my tongue. Being inquisitive she would have asked me a million questions.

Sara was sitting provocatively at front of our canoe and each time she crossed her legs I couldn't help but see her panties. I felt sure she was being provocative as she smiled wickedly; there was little doubt that she was enjoying the effect it was having on me. After passing a cluster of houses on the banks of the river I gave the paddling a rest and let the current allow the boat to drift. Despite the canoe wobbling dangerously I was able to join Sara and to embrace her. At first she was apprehensive about the boat's movement but soon relaxed. That was until she saw the canoe's drifting had brought it to the river's bank.

Regaining the situation we made it to where her father moored the family boat. There I was able to wade to the shoreline and pull the canoe in behind me. It was deserted and so stripping off we spent a little time diving in the lagoon. Only later did we run to the freshwater pool to wash the salt from our bodies and to freshen ourselves up after again making love. It seemed we were both insatiable and a good couple to be in love.

It left me in a relaxed frame of mind for when I later joined Nirmala's family and my own on the veranda. I was a little concerned that amidst all the gaiety my sister Sabita was looking depressed. I asked her what was bothering her but she wouldn't open up. Woman stuff I thought to myself and dropped the matter. I still had my mind on Sara anyway so finishing off my beer I called it a day. It was much later before everyone returned but again I couldn't help but notice Sabita's wretchedness. It preyed a little on my mind as I drifted off to sleep.

She was as sad the following day; mother thought it was depression and I could identify with that as I rushed off to work and passing Nirmala's home pretended not to have heard her calling my name. Work that day was pretty much routine until I heard my father's screams as he came into our workshop. "Krishna! Krishna! Sabita is dead."

Bewildered and immediately sick to the pits of my stomach I rushed past him as he broke down weeping. Grabbing my bicycle I was home in minutes. As I had passed Nirmala's home I could see the gathering crowd of curious and concerned onlookers.

As I rushed into our home I saw a figure covered with an old blanket. "What is it?" I screamed.

"It's Sabita. She's taken her own life," mother was howling piteously. Horrified and trembling I knelt down and lifted the blanket away from Sabita's sweet little face. It was very much as if she were sleeping other than there being a blue pallor and there was blood trickling from the sides of her sweet shaped lips and noticeable the deep scouring marks caused by the rope having been around her slim swan-like neck.

"Why? Why?" I bawled before breaking down and weeping uncontrollably. I was still breaking my heart when father, gasping for air and weeping uncontrollably, arrived home. From somewhere outside I could hear the police Land Rover's sirens and moments later our anguished family and concerned neighbours were joined by the two uniformed police officers. Carefully picking up the small corpse they gently deposited her tiny form on the long seat inside the police vehicle.

"Please come with us?"

Their instruction was aimed at my father but he was in no fit state to accompany them and besides he was obliged to comfort my mother who was weeping copiously. Insisting that a member of the family accompany them I climbed up into the vehicle and I sat beside my little sister's body. She had been with us for such a short time. It was then that I saw my other sister Malti. She had run all the way from the school on hearing the news. I jumped out of the police jeep, cuddled her and kissed her distraught face before getting back in the jeep and driven away. I sat in the back seat cuddling and sobbing as with sirens screaming it bounced along the dusty roads of our town.

The police were thoughtful and kind to me as they explained that the body had to be taken to Lautoka General Hospital for a post mortem. The Land Rover swept along the Kings Road as I held Sabita's little body and sobbed. I kept on repeating my question that couldn't as yet be answered: Why had she done this most terrible of things?

There were so many happy and shared memories going back to when she was born. We had so often played together; laughed, fought, cried, helped each other and confided our thoughts. Now she was sleeping and wouldn't ever wake or return. My world had turned upside down and there was a sick feeling in my stomach and an aching void in my heart. The previous Saturday she had been to the matinee with us and seemed perfectly happy.

In shock; I was distraught and weeping. I remember passing through Valabala and along the beach and as we did so I thought bleakly of the plantation where I once had a fight with Francis, the school bully. Then, thanks to Father John's boxing lessons, I had knocked him out cold with a right hand punch to his chin. My mind deflected to Susan and I wondered how she was and did she still remember me. What if she had become pregnant? The nuns would be giving her and our little baby hell. Or she could have been banished to join her mother on the island of Mokagai. Somehow I have to get back to St. Mary's and try to see her but how?

An hour later we passed St Joseph's College and a depressing three hours later, arrived at the hospital. The policemen carried the blanket covered body of my sister into the mortuary and placing it on the slab said their goodbyes and left me to it.

Neither had thought to ask us if I had the means to return home. I was ill prepared for being stranded two hundred miles away with my small dead sister. Not knowing any one in a strange town and not having money to pay someone to take us both back home after the post mortem I had no idea what to do. There was no telephone in our home and how could I let father know that we were stranded.

Troubled, I sat miserably on the steps of the mortuary and wept. Through my tears I made out an Indian nurse who I recognised. Her brother Vinod had attended the boarding school with me and I remembered her from her visits. Rushing over to her I called her by her name, Urmila?

She looked at me carefully and seemed apprehensive: "Yes; we know each other?"

"I was in St Mary's boarding school with your brother. I remember you from your visits to him." I then began to sob and as recognition came to her she placed her arms around my shoulders. "What on earth is the matter?"

I told her that my sister Sabita had taken her own life and her body was now in the mortuary. Urmila cuddled me and then leading me into the hospital canteen she ordered cups of tea for us both. Explaining my dilemma she took me into town on the hospital bus and found a driver of a small van willing to return us to our home. Thanking the lady I boarded the truck and from there went to the mortuary and knocked on the wooden door. A nurse came out and told us that it was now alright to collect her little body. "Please enter."

Following her into the mortuary I saw Sabita's blood soaked body on the cement slab. I screamed and ran out. "I can't do it," I screamed. "The bastards have left her sliced up body on the slab without covering or wrapping her." I was violently sick behind some shrubs.

The truck driver gently wrapped my small sister's body in white hospital paper before carrying her out and placing her inside the van. I was near hysterical but somehow I managed to climb inside the truck and sit next to her body before we drove home. In just a short while she was reduced to a bundle wrapped in white hospital paper that I was cradling in the back seat of the van.

The memory of seeing her body after the post-mortem had been carried out on her haunts me to this day. They had slit her body open from her tonsils to her vagina and removed something from the crown of her head as well. Her beautiful jet-black hair was awash with blood. Later, friends and neighbours collected the necessary money to buy a cheap coffin before we buried her in the cemetery close to home.

It wasn't until weeks later that we learned the true reason why she had killed herself. Father was forcing her into an arranged marriage to a much older man. She had refused but couldn't reason with father. Finally, she had no choice and as she couldn't defy father she took the only alternative way out as she saw it. I had not the slightest idea of what was going on behind my back otherwise I would have helped her. I had been too involved in my own life and failed to recognise her needs. Rarely was there a time when a brother was more needed. I confronted father but he confessed that he was only trying to do what he thought best for his children.

It was on the third day of mourning that I returned to work. As I passed the convent I saw Sara, Lisa Fong and their school mates quietly watching me. No one said a word; they just stood by the school gates and watched silently as I went on by. After work was finished for the day I returned to the gym and took out all my frustration and anger on the heavy punch bag. I was determined to fight anyone to hide the pain of losing my small sister. When I did see Sara that evening she hugged and kissed me.

"What happened, Jamie and why did she do such a thing?"

I told her that Sabita had fastened a rope to the rafter over my bed before fashioning a noose. Then, placing it around her neck she had jumped from the bed. By the time mother missed her and searched for her it was too late; my sister was hanging there motionless, all life having left her. Mother had quickly cut the rope and managed to drag her outside the house but it was too late. Sabita had died from strangulation. Sara just hugged and kissed me gently.

I was devastated at the loss of my sister; especially the poignant and tragic unnecessary end of her life. No one should go out of their life under such circumstances, least of all a child. As a consequence my father and I became increasingly estranged. In my frustration and anger I worked out every evening; boxing, skipping, punching the heavy bag, lifting weights and jogging each morning before work. By then the convent had closed for the summer holidays and Sara had finished her final year and was expected to attend St Joseph's. In the meantime I had beaten the number four-rated middleweight named James Chandra by knocking him out in the fourth round.

It was only after the passage of weeks that the pain became less sharp. I wished I could say the same for Malti, my surviving sister and my parents. They were inconsolable and they each suffered in silence. I tried to cheer Malti and took her to the matinee. The summer rain soaked us both as we made our way to the dilapidated theatre. When we arrived we spotted Sara and Lisa Fong. The girls were helping out in Mr Fong's new bakery and the small café attached to it by selling soft drinks and ice cream. Going in we asked for coffee and took our seats at a little table next to the counter. Sara served us and we made arrangements to meet the following morning on the riverbank.

Malti and I watched what was to be her first Elvis Presley film: Wild in the Country and it was good to see her good humour return again. On the Sunday I met Sara as arranged and after a little cuddling we took the canoe for a boat trip down river. She told me how much she had missed me as we held each other tightly. It was a release of sorts; a return to real life and out of the dark tunnel. After a marathon of kisses and at Sara's suggestion I lay in the middle of the canoe so that she could straddle and make love to me. It was obviously a position in Nirmala's book and it had caught her imagination. I did as she wanted but the straddling me was difficult; the boat's narrowness and wobbling had its limitations.

RETURNED TO DEVIL'S ISLAND

Afterwards we noticed we had drifted past the three islands and were about to strike protruding rocks barely visible under the blue waters of the reef. Taking my paddle I expertly manoeuvred to one side of them as Sara, lying in the middle of the boat, recited her Hail Mary. A much relieved girlfriend later crawled towards me, kissed my feet and held on tightly as I rowed back to the island. It had been a close encounter with fate.

We were aware that where we had been the dark blue area of sea was exceptionally deep and the coral reefs problematic for swimmers. Being again naked together caused our normal high spirits to return as in the excitement of the encounter with the deep we had forgotten naked state. Picking Sara up I carried her to the freshwater pool where we again made love. At the critical moment I was about to withdraw when Sara stopped me from doing so. "It's alright, Jamie. According to Nirmala's book it is safe right after a period."

"But you started your period the last time we were here?"

"Yes, I did but that was over five weeks ago and now I am just finishing my next lot."

We chatted about the speedy passage of time when she reminded me that she would be going to St Joseph's the following week having learned that she had passed her entrance exams. She was however reluctant to go though and said she preferred to stay with me.

I impressed upon her the importance of her education and the opportunities that would be there on her graduation. She couldn't quite see it that way and had already thought her life through. We would marry; I had a job. We would have children; everything perfect. I looked at her innocent face and took her in my arms and kissed her. "You said that you would like to go to California and meet your grandparents."

"I would love to meet them but then return here; this is home."

"On what date do you leave for St Joseph's?"

Telling me her father was taking her the following Sunday I suggested we return here to the beach on the following Saturday. This would mean her telling lies to her parents again. When the Saturday arrived Nirmala came to our aid and persuaded Rajendra to see a movie. It was because of Nirmala's understanding and tact that Sara and I managed to enjoy our final evening together. Most of that evening we held each other tenderly and affectionately and it was only after many tears that we parted company. I watched Sara go as the darkness of the tropical evening absorbed her slight figure. Under a distant street lamp in the far distance she tuned to wave and then was swallowed by the night.

After mass the following morning I hung around the church till I saw her step into her father's car and again watched sadly as the distance and dust parted her from me. It was a very dejected Jamie who on the Sunday afternoon paddled out to the islet of love to lose himself in his loss. The following day however Nirmala was in the best of moods. "Jamie, please come up and feel my stomach, the baby is moving and kicking."

She told me she hadn't been able to sleep; such was the excitement of her pregnancy. She told me the mite had made its presence known through the night and repeatedly kissed and thanked me for bringing about the change in her fortunes.

When I finally left Nirmala I was feeling very apprehensive. The convent's pupils had returned following their summer break. Many had gone on to college but were replaced by new students. It seemed to me that it might make something of a personal harem as I heard once again those words: 'I die there!'

Besides the theatre, the gym and church there was little opportunity to make new friends. I stuck to the gym but my interest in boxing by this time was waning. The gym had now become merely my refuge from Nirmala's attention seeking demands. It occurred to me too that now the reason for her husband turning a blind eye had been overtaken by events I could be treading on dangerous ground. My job was done. Surely it was time for an exit with dignity?

I received occasional letters from Sara. She was happy there and had met some of my old school friends from St Mary's. There was precious little written of an intimate nature and her letters were more along the lines of a sister writing to a brother. I knew the nuns read the incoming and outgoing letters and that love to them was just another four letter word. My replies were also platonic and as time went by the letters between us became fewer and I did wonder why? I was soon to find out. It happened as I was riding home that I saw Lisa by the roadside. "Hey Jamie I've been waiting for you."

"Lisa, have you heard from Sara?"

"Yes, I have one letter, that's why I waited to tell you about it."

I must have looked puzzled: "Why? What is it?"

"Here take it home and read it," was all she said. Thanking her I rushed home and as I read its contents I learned she had smuggled the letter out and handed it to Fatty, the Royal Mail driver, before the nuns had a chance to read it.

Sara written words told of a wonderful boy she had met called Biren. A millionaire's son, she had fallen in love with him. I remembered Biren. He had been impoverished when in boarding school with me. Happily for him and his family, manganese had been found on the island and they had become rich overnight. Naturally I was jealous, disappointed, sad and angry. There was nothing I could do but pine but my pity was more for me than for her.

One thing after another it was on the morning after that bombshell that when listening to the births and deaths programme we learned that my paternal grandfather, Lal had died. Family and friends were advised about the time and location of the funeral. Father, mother and sister Malti took the bus to our old village to attend the ceremony. I left for work and saw Lisa by the convent. I gave her back Sara's letter. I had no wish to keep it.

That evening after finishing work I went direct to the gym and had a long hard on myself workout. By the time I finished it was dark and I wasn't happy about returning to my dark and empty home. It was still just a short while since my sister had taken her life by hanging. She had chosen to use my bed to do so and I found it difficult to face the prospect of sleeping right there in the emptiness of the house. Even though I loved Sabita I was superstitious and constantly tried to read her mind during those last moments as if the answer might still be somewhere in the bedroom.

I rode home but as I passed Sara's home I bump into Lisa; she was it seemed waiting to see me. I told her about my parent's leaving for grandfather's funeral and she said softly that she was so sorry I was having such a tough time of it. It was then I recalled Sara telling me that her friend was crazy about me. I needed some distraction: I plucked the courage to ask her if I could see her later. Lisa coloured and chewed her lips before thoughtfully answering:" Sure; why not? I will call at your home but first I have to go to the bakery and make my excuses."

As I rushed home I heard Nirmala's voice calling sweetly but pretending to neither see nor hear her I scurried past. Despite the hiss of the shower I heard a knock on my door. Wrapping my small towel around my waist I opened the door to come face to face with Lisa. Her eyes opened wide at my near nakedness and then smiling she pushed past me as she assured me that all was right at the bakery.

Uncertain, I wondered should I return to the shower or stay as I was, just gazing at Lisa's beautiful face. Our eyes met and the chemistry did the rest. Simultaneously we embraced and then gently I lifted her chin up closer to my lips and kissed her. As I picked her up and lay her on my bed my towel fell to the ground. Again her eyes opened wide; she covered her mouth in surprise and then started to nervously giggle. By the time I was making love to her the giggles had been replaced by sighs.

"Sara told me your father is very tough on you, Lisa, and expects you to work hard twenty four hours a day?"

"Yes," she muttered: "My Chinese upbringing dominates the old values but to hell with Chinese traditions. I hope father rots in hell." I told her that Sara had also revealed that an arranged marriage was soon to be her fate. "Yes, bundled up like a package and posted to Hong Kong and then married to a complete stranger much older than I am; old enough to be my father."

I told her that it was her choice; she couldn't be forced to go but she said arrangements were already in hand. The paperwork arranged and the dates set in stone. She told me of her regret that Sara had got to me first this was in her view because her father was more liberal than was her own and so had greater freedom. She told me how she had been consumed with jealousy when Sara had revealed that she and I were lovers. Finally she said she wished she could run away with me; as far away as possible from her father and his twisted cultural traditions.

I felt it best to hold my tongue. I really wanted to help her escape but feared that the Chinese being a vengeful lot they would put a reward on our heads; we would be likely hunted down and slain; an honour killing. Such a fate didn't bear thinking about. The white net curtain was now shimmering in the breeze causing the poorly fitted lamps over my bed to flicker and cast their dark shadows against the wall. After twenty minutes of lovemaking I came to a stop. It was excruciatingly clear that Lisa had other things on her mind and anyway didn't appear to have the enthusiasm for lovemaking that I thought she might have. It was all a bit routine; mechanical and lacking passion. Her indifference spurred me on and if I wasn't going to experience her feelings then I would satiate my lust for her.

I later apologised and excused myself by telling her I had been carried away by the heat of the moment. She told me I was forgiven; it was alright. Sara had told her that the pain is only during the first penetration and is more than compensated for by the sensations that follow. She then told me she had fantasised about losing her virginity to me. Afterwards she spoke aloud: "Jamie, I knew you were in total control but tell me; was that safe or can I become pregnant?"

I realised I had forgotten to withdraw and felt the panic rising in me. Grabbing her hand I pulled the teen into the bathroom and washed her thoroughly under the strong jet of the shower. But I knew dam well that washing hygienically wouldn't do much good if she became pregnant; it would be too late for that then.

"Sara told me everything that you two did."

"Everything?"

Lisa grinned cheekily: "Yes: She left nothing out. Remember she is my best friend so it is natural that we talk. I know all about your love island and the positions you learned from Rajendra's book."

I guessed at what she was hinting at and asked her if she would like to come to the islet of love on the following day. Lisa was agreeable but again reminded me that she had very little freedom and was expected to work long hours at her father's business premises. All I could reply was with my parents being away this was a once in a lifetime chance for us to be both together. "I have friends who live behind Sara's house. I'll go there first and then sneak in here," she replied as she told me it was past time she was gone. As we strolled past Nirmala's home she emphasised her need to accompany me to the islet where Sara and I had gone so often. She told me she would do whatever was necessary to escape her work routine.

On the walk back I was pretty focused and under no illusions as to the likely outcome if Lisa's father was to realise what was going on. I was messing with a horrible death. The Chinese are notorious for their vengeful murders. We would likely both be killed. Recently a mob made up of Chinese parents had attacked a native youngster for messing with a Chinese girl in the nearby town. He was hospitalised. The thought of them coming after me with meat cleavers terrified me. With such thoughts I was nervous about sleeping in the empty house and knocked on Nirmala's door instead. She was as pleased as ever to see me. "Your dinner has gone cold," she mock scolded me: "Your mother asked me to make sure you ate well and that I keep an eye on you. I saw the Chinese girl sneaking into your house earlier. Please be careful, Jamie: You don't mess with the Chinese. I don't have to remind you about that case in the newspapers."

I told her I recalled the near murder and told her Lisa was dreading her impending fate and suffering in silence. The teenager wanted me to help her before she was bundled off to Hong Kong. "Yes she's under pressure to go there and marry a middle aged man. She is vulnerable and someone must help her." I was reminded of my own sister's death.

"The Chinese are not known for killing themselves. They kill others but never commit suicide. Be extra vigilant, Jamie. She is so beautiful and it will be difficult to keep away from her but is she worth being beaten up for or worse?"

Knowing Rajendra was on nights and convincing myself that he might be appreciative enough to show thanks by turning a blind eye to my sleeping with his wife I asked Nirmala if I might stay the night with her. She laughed lightly: "You know you don't need to ask me: I had no intention of letting you go to an empty home. I need you and need you now; the baby can't be far off. About six weeks."

As I sat on the bed's edge I watched as she undressed. Her lithesome beauty she had enchanted me with had been replaced by her swollen Buddha-like tummy. Strangely I found this arousing; it emphasised further her femininity and as we relaxed she asked me had I had sex with the Chinese girl earlier. I told her of how I had been showering when she arrived and things just sort of went from there.

"What will Sara say?"

I laughed lightly: "The same thing if she ever found out about you and my baby."

"I hope it is a boy with your handsome looks."

"It might be a girl with your looks."

"I wouldn't mind but Rajendra and his family have made their minds up that it's to be a boy and, according to the book it should be a boy."

I was cynical: "It's all a load of Hindu mumbo-jumbo. I don't believe everything written in the book. If those positions really worked then all babies born in India and China would be boys and here in Fiji too."

Girls aren't popular throughout these regions and they are often just given away to people who don't have kids of their own; they are disposable children. Others are rescued, if you can use the term, by Catholic missionaries and brain-washed into the faith. Not much of a choice for children; abandoned and starved or institutionalised. I had seen so many instances at the boarding school and it was horrendous how they were programmed and beaten repeatedly until they conformed. This isn't religion; it is the plunder of people's minds and souls. There were some nuns who were well meaning and friendly. They would give us sweets and greeting cards that had been sent for them from abroad.

"Did you suffer a lot when you were in boarding school, Jamie?"

Nirmala had broken into my thoughts. "Not only me; other children too and most of all the older boys. Our head sister, Sister Magdalene had a thing about what she described as the sins of the flesh. Each morning the boys' bed linen was carefully checked for evidence that they had been masturbating. If anything was found then they received a real bad beating. One poor boy was beaten to pulp twice a week. He told me that he had wet dreams and couldn't do anything to prevent them from happening."

The next morning I left Nirmala's home quietly; she and her child were fast asleep and there didn't seem much point in waking them. With a day's work behind me I might have been excused for feeling jaded but seeing Lisa waiting at the roadside brought me to fighting fitness again. "I can't walk with you, Jamie; we might be seen but keep your door open and I will be there soon."

When she arrived at my home as promised we went straight into a clinch. She told me that I smelled of fire and welding fumes. Unsure of whether that was a good or bad thing I told her I would shower and suggested she joins me in it. It sounded like being a lot of fun. She declined and was more concerned about being home late. She watched transfixed as I stripped off and stepped into the shower. Seeing a guy undressed and have a shower wasn't something she was used to. Her hand went to her mouth at the unexpectedness and I supposed my boldness. She was alright with it though and as soon as I dried we went to my bed and we made love.

Lisa was as enthusiastic as was I but looked pensive afterwards. Lifting her chin I kissed her and told her that everything would be fine; there was no need for her to concern herself. There was something else on her mind. "Sara told me that Sabita had hanged herself from that beam over your bed. Is that right?"

I pointed to the roof beam and there was a morbid fascination as she pictured the scene as she imagined it. A few minutes later she quickly dressed and told me she had to go. Telling me she was sorry she added that we could only meet on brief encounters; the family business was always pressing.

She told me that so far I had given her the most wonderful days of her life; that she had no regrets and then we left the house in darkness. As we walked hand in hand I asked her if things were really hard for her and if she thought the marriage in Hong Kong unavoidable.

She told me that she didn't have any say in the matter. She had a choice: Go through with it or run away; she could also go the same way as did my sister. She didn't think she was brave enough for that. It was a horrifying thought and brought home again the wickedness of forced marriages. How could women be sold off as chattels by their own families?

Lisa squeezed my hand tightly. "My marriage has been planned since I was in nappies. That is why father wouldn't allow me to take the entrance exam for St Joseph's. I had set my mind on going with Sara and the other girls. Father wouldn't hear of it." I left Lisa as close to her home and strolled back to Nirmala's.

Nearly a week later my parents returned from my grandfather's funeral and the strain on their faces was obvious; it had been a rough time for them both. I learned that after they had cremated grandfather and were preparing to return home my grandmother Rani suffered a massive stroke and she had died too. Another cremation; another delay and I was now without grandparents.

November 1957 marked an eight and a half month passage of time since Nirmala and I had first made love. She was rushed to Tavua General Hospital and to the delight of everyone a seven pound baby boy was born.

RETURNED TO DEVIL'S ISLAND

There was much jubilation and it was decided that the newborn would be named Surendra. In the company of my parents and Malti I nervously made my way to the hospital. On seeing the exhausted mother I kissed her on her cheeks and saw for the first time the baby. Inwardly I was weeping; his perfect little face and head full of jet-black hair made the perfect picture. As I touched his tiny fingers he gripped my finger as babies do and held it tightly. Bending forward I kissed the child and could smell the baby aromas. I asked God what I had done. Later in bed I was overwhelmed by emotions and cried myself to sleep. He was mine but never would be.

Life otherwise returned to normal or at least moved on. Lisa told me that Sara was due home for the Christmas holidays. Que Sera was my only thought. What will be will be. Nirmala also returned to normal and obviously having enjoyed the new baby experience left me in no doubt that an action replay was expected. I was admittedly a little reticent but my feelings were no match for her beauty and her powers of seduction.

Rajendra was very happy too and looked the cock o' the walk. He had after all produced a child and a boy child at that. Life couldn't get much better. Not quite the same could be said for me. I was the father but someone else was doing the fathering and taking the credit. Sara did arrive home but I avoided her; I felt replaced and wasn't too happy about that. Besides, there were so many memories that I couldn't help but stay in love with her.

Lisa did keep me informed of Sara's whereabouts. She also told me that as soon as Sara had set eyes on Biren she had fallen hopelessly in love with him. Yes, but he was a millionaire's son; he owned a new Morris Oxford and being a generous soul showered gifts upon her. Who was I to complain? I was no saint either and could hardly take the moral high ground. I had been enjoying sexual liaisons with Sara and Nirmala simultaneously and Sara had hardly been out of sight when I was lasciviously taking Lisa's virginity. It wasn't until Christmas Eve that I saw Sara. I was drawn like a magnet to the church and watched her from several pews behind before making my way out before she was aware of my being there.

Seeing Lisa at my home on Christmas morning wasn't something I expected but she was there for good reason. She had brought a delightful hand-made Christmas card for our family. This made me feel mean for I had not bothered to buy one for her. Father and mother, Malti too were overwhelmed at the gesture, especially when I invited Lisa in to meet them. This was a much hurried introduction for as always Lisa had much to do back at the family business. My parents were absolutely terrified about my friendship with a Chinese girl. My father angrily reminded me about the unfortunate young Indian who was almost murdered by the group of Chinese men. "For god's sake please keep away from that Chinese girl," he told me. I smiled and let it be.

Just before Christmas dinner we gathered on Nirmala's veranda where there were many free spirits; alcohol and guests. There was something of a pall over our family's celebrations though as it was occasions like these that Sabita's absence was most notable. I quietly sat and nursed my own child as I wondered what the future might bring. I knew that Nirmala and Rajendra would worship and spoil him but what would my relationship be with him? Would he look like me? Questions raced through my mind such as what if I was to leave to live abroad; this would mean I would never see Surendra again. My thoughts were absorbing me and were broken only by my father's sobbing; the whisky had got to him and so we took him home.

When we returned I saw mother and my sister making a fuss of Surendra and couldn't help thinking what a pity that my mother couldn't know that the child she was making such a fuss of was her own grandchild. Had I been Nirmala's husband, Surendra would have been Malti's nephew.

Boxing Day brought an unexpected surprise when Lisa called by again. She told us that the businesses were closed for the day and she had told her father she was off to visit Sara. Well, she was doing that alright. I was over the moon at seeing her but nevertheless apprehensive. She seemed however perfectly comfortable with the visit and seemed as one of the family. I sometimes wished she was. I hated seeing her go. Later walking over to the canoe she waved to me with its paddle. "Come on; aren't you going to take me for a river cruise then?"

My parents' eyebrows shot up at her forwardness but grabbing the machete and throwing the small craft over my shoulders we two set off for the river banks. When we heard mother calling for us to take Malti with us we pretended not to hear her and rushed away. Lisa was thrilled at the experience; it was a first for her.

The day was typical of the South Sea Islands and far too warm for clothing other than that needed to keep one's modesty. Throwing my t-shirt and flip-flops off I bedded my feet in and set out for the islet of love. Lisa was excitedly looking at all of the places and experiences Sara had told her so much about.; the powdery white sand, the multi-coloured tropical birds and the sun scorched islets breaking up the blue ocean's horizon.

As soon as we beached the boat I took Lisa's hand and headed for the fresh water creek. This was hardly a new experience for me but it was a milestone of sorts. After cooling off for a while we began to kiss and make love on the water's edge. "So this is what you and Sara were doing then."

I resisted the temptation to say anything as she pulled me in the direction of the beach. I grabbed Lisa's hand and we stepped in the water but she pulled away from me and sat on the water's edge. "Stop, Jamie; stop! I can't swim."

"Of course you can," I laughed. "All islanders can swim."

She was an exception to the rule; her father never allowed her near the water and so as I sported in deep waters Lisa contended herself with wading in the surf up to her navel. The dolphins soon joined us. I think Lisa had thought I was joking and seeing them so close she dashed from the water in fear. "It's alright," I called to her: "I was nervous at first but they are very gentle creatures. They don't hurt you. They love playing."

Holding my hand tightly she took one step at a time into the deeper water where she could still touch the sand with her toes she got playfully used to the idea of stroking the sea creatures and feeling the silk-like texture of their skin. Soon she was enjoying herself as much as I was. Our idyll was soon to be spoiled by the sound of an approaching motorboat. Rushing from the water before we could be seen we dashed for the fresh water creek and dressed.

My first thought was that of Sara. She had once told me that her father used to bring them here for picnics. Then I remembered it was Boxing Day and traditionally the natives would be eating whilst the Indians would be getting inebriated and maybe fighting between themselves. Climbing up a palm I looked around me and could see several white Europeans on their way to one of the other two islands in the cluster. Lisa thought they might be the directors and managers of the Emperor Goldmines on their way to do a little fishing.

Sitting with Lisa nestling in my arms I found myself wondering why Hindus celebrated Christmas. None believed Jesus of Nazareth or the virgin birth yet they celebrated the tradition by consuming copious amounts of alcohol. Any excuse?

Lisa was feeling peckish so I shinned up a palm and selected a couple of coconuts for our lunch; hence the need for the machete. The rest of the afternoon went idly by and before returning to the land of prying eyes we once again joined our bodies to become one beneath the swaying palms and with the sun on our backs, whichever of us decided to play the dominant role in our lovemaking. It was a beautiful experience to the sunset's backdrop.

The following day left me little choice but to resume working at the foundry though the convent remained closed for the holiday and the students were still enjoying their vacation. Not so happy for me for when I turned up the welding shop's foreman called me into his office. His wagging finger suggested I was in some kind of trouble. "Jamie. Have you given up on boxing? If you have then you will have to report for night shift as do the rest of the men here. You can't have it both ways."

I told him that wasn't my intention; it was just that I had a few personal problems to sort out and reminded him of the tragic circumstances of my sister's death. I reminded him too that this tragedy had been followed shortly afterwards by the deaths of my grandparents. He understood and sympathised but didn't miss the opportunity to tell me that I was pushing my luck; it was either boxing or shifts; deal with it.

The mere thought of night shifts in that smoke filled depressing workshop wasn't something I relished. I did return to the gym but it was a half-hearted gesture. I had finally decided that a boxing career wasn't for me as there were many other pleasures of life. These too might be curtailed if, as mother had warned me, my looks were to be altered. The lure of life abroad strengthened my resolve and I was still mindful that boxing was my get out of Fiji ticket.

On the way home that evening I stopped at Lisa's bakery and could see her serving at the tables of the small café next to it. She lost her plot when she saw me looking at her and quickly disappeared into the kitchens. It was her mother who served me and when Lisa finally emerged from the kitchen she was obviously edgy at my presence. We couldn't chat and even as she welcomed me she did so as she would a casual diner.

Her parents were watching us both like hawks. Did they suspect anything? I felt a little uncomfortable and went quickly on my way.

As I passed Sara's home I could see her washing her father's car. Slowing down in my bike I looked across her but to Sara I was the invisible man. That wasn't such a nice feeling either and so I pedalled off on my way to Nirmala's where there might be a better welcome waiting for me.

I wasn't disappointed; there was and they were all there, Nirmala, Rajendra and the two children. Rajendra was soothingly holding Surendra and I gratefully took the beer offered by Nirmala. She asked how Sara and Lisa were doing with that knowing corner smile of hers that suggested it was our secret. I was reticent; there wasn't much to tell her anyway and I was still hurt by Sara's rebuff. Rajendra wanted to know who Lisa was and when told he commented on her looks and called me a lucky bastard. He wanted to know if it was serious. Nirmala frowned. "It better hadn't be. One minute those Chinese are being nice to you but they would slice you in two for treading on their territory, which includes getting fresh with their daughters."

Rajendra winked: "You are young and good looking, Jamie," Make the most of your good fortune. There are so many beautiful girls at the convent and they are all gagging for it. You know what I mean, they talk of little else. You go and give them what they want, my friend. I wondered if there was a double meaning as I coolly sipped my beer and dwelled on his words; Nirmala was reading my mind and no doubt picturing me making love to the girls from the convent as I had done to her.

"You are in a real man's world Jamie, make the most of it before you marry and settled down with children?" said Rajendra.

"Well, I am a real man alright but getting married is the last thing on my mind." I laughed with good humour and left for home.

It was after dining that we switched the radio on to learn that the Fijian government had started repatriating Indians to India. Not everyone would be eligible but just one child per family of original indentured labourers brought to Fiji by the British government. Father could hardly contain his excitement. "I must enquire about that information. I really should go to India and discover our family roots."

We didn't give the matter much thought but he was serious and within weeks he had obtained a passport and registered for repatriation. It was an unexpected and a sad parting. We all wished him all the luck in the world as we watched him boarding the Tasman airline at Nadi Airport. He was at least returning to his native India in far better style than his forebears had arrived in Fiji.

Before dad left us he promised to return to us within two years to find Malti a husband and for me a beautiful wife. We were sad to see him go but within our hearts we considered it a blessing that Malti and I were not being pressured into marriage with strangers.

After father had left us for his mother country I encouraged Malti to go on her own to the shops and pictures. A little independence would do her good. She did in fact meet a local young Indian boy whose name was Ramesh. Their love blossomed and they were to later get married. She was only fifteen years of age at the time, which was a little sad but it is the way things are and we have little choice but to accept them.

After the happy couple's marriage and departure I retired to bed and was a little concerned about their marriage. There could be many twists and turns to Indian marriages. Most thankfully were on equal terms with their husband's families but other young brides found themselves as little better off as slaves working for their husband's family. Malti might even become a baby gro-bag and I could never figure out why Indian mother-in-laws felt it necessary to dominate the girls who marry their sons.

It happens not only in Fiji but in Indian communities all over the world. I had a much troubled sleep thinking about my little sister. I was only three years old when she was born yet I still had vivid memories of her birth. It had been late at night when father rushed out of the house to alert my auntie to come and help my mother during the birth. I could still recall cuddling Sabita as we looked in on the proceedings from behind a flimsy mosquito net that separated us from mother lying on a mat on the floor. I was wondering why my mother was in so much pain.

Beside her was a small hurricane lamp that was casting giant shadows on the overhead bamboo rafters. Next to the lamp was a bowl of water and I saw someone's hand pick up an open blade shaving razor and wondered what it could be for. It looked like the person holding the razor was cutting something, followed immediately by a baby's cry. Within minutes mother was sitting with a newborn child in her arms. I must have then slept as the next thing I remember it was daylight. When I used the toilet I could see father digging a hole behind our home from where I was relieving myself. He told me to keep away but not before I had seen something that looked to me like a piece of flesh being buried. With his spade he shooed the two curious dogs and a pet piglet away until the hole was completely filled.

I was much older when I learned that the flesh being buried was the afterbirth following the cutting of the umbilical cord. I was often to try and figure out how children survived such primitive introductions to the world.

It wasn't long after my father's departure that I met Lisa on my way home from work but on this occasion the poor girl was very distressed. I was horrified to see her as she was obviously in a state of shock. Grabbing her arm I asked her what the matter was. She told me that the forced marriage was on and her ticket to Hong Kong purchased. She had literally been sold; such was the value of Chinese and Indian women.

She begged me to help her as her bags were already being packed and she was due to leave the following morning. Her school friends were standing around and expectantly waiting for my response.

"He cannot force you, Lisa."

Plucking up enough courage I followed her to her little shop and as I was about to enter Mr. Fong slammed the door shut in my face and bolted the door. Suddenly I was surrounded by a group of Lisa's friends. This gave me enough confidence to presume that Mr. Fong wouldn't do anything rash in front of witnesses. I banged the door till it finally opened and heard Mr. Fong's excited voice.

"Go away, you Indian man," he called: "You bring shame on our family. We never want to see you in our shop again. If we do you will be killed." I ignored him and forced myself in the shop, followed by the group of girls.

I could see the meat cleaver lying on the table but held my ground and begged Mr Fong to listen to me. Turning bright red with anger he was clearly furious at my interference and rushing towards me jabbed his finger repeatedly in my chest: "Everyone in the community is talking about you. You have brought shame to my family. Please, for your own good go away otherwise I have no choice but to kill you today."

There was no reasoning with the Fongs; the Chinese are obstinate as are our own people. I couldn't change tradition or challenge a father's position. I watched aghast as he grabbed Lisa's hand and roughly dragged her into their home. Hearing her pitiful cries I left in disgust.

We were all deeply saddened about the abruptness of Lisa's fate being decided. On the following morning, as I walked to the bus stop, I encountered her school friends who were standing in small anxious groups. I nodded in their direction and waited.

As soon as I saw Lisa's parents approach I trembled with unease and had no idea what might happen. It was then we heard the voice of a nun calling the pupils into the school yard. Her shrill demands were ignored by the students as we waited until Lisa and her family drew closer. The tears were streaming down Lisa's lovely face as she clutched her mother's hand. Her friends were the first to kiss her on each of her tear-stained cheeks. Bidding her goodbye and then with their own thoughts rushing back into the school's yard to deal with their sorrows in their own way.

This left me on my own and terrified but I instinctively went up to Lisa who freed herself from her mother's grasp. Clutching me around my waist she begged and wailed for me not to abandon her. "Please help me, Jamie. You are the only one who can help me. I don't want to go to Hong Kong."

Mr Fong dropped the suitcase he was clutching; rushed over and separated us. After slapping Lisa several times across her face he spun on his heel to face me. His eyes were bulging and he was clearly furious. His punches came thick and fast but used to such parries I ducked and weaved avoiding each of them. His missing me did little to cool him down and I finally had to grab him by one of his wrists when one of his punches did catch me over my eye and brought a flow of blood.

Lisa's mother and her two younger sisters were screaming in Chinese and I couldn't figure out if they were encouraging or discouraging him. We were separated only by the arrival of the bus. The driver seeing the melée used his bus to frighten us apart.

Lisa ran headlong towards me but her father got to her first and roughly pushed her up the steps and into the bus. Breathing heavily he then loaded the suitcase and turning towards me said something in Chinese and spat into the dust. The bus's engine kicked in and I ran to follow it until it disappeared in a cloud of dust.

RETURNED TO DEVIL'S ISLAND

With Lisa gone and Sara involved with her new love I was feeling miserable and unsettled. It was then that my thoughts became consumed by a wish to put distance between this heaven and hell place. There was an air of unreality about the township.

All I wanted to do now was leave as quickly as possible and find work back in Suva; to maybe fight every bout that came my way. I would then put enough cash aside to travel further afield. But how was I going to leave mother alone in what had been our home for quite some time? What of Surendra? He was my own flesh and blood? How could I turn my back on such ties?

It was then I thought of a plan. If mother were to live with Malti and her new husband Ramesh then I could leave with a clear conscience. An inducement would be my sending them money from my earnings. Mother was not as enthusiastic; in fact far from it. "First your father and now you want to leave. If you go we might never see you again, Krishna."

"Ma, please just let me go to Suva and try my luck again at Bish Limited. They might need welders at their engineering department in Australia."

"Australia? No Krishna. If you go to Australia then we definitely will never see you again."

"Please ma," I begged. "Let me just try. I believe the wages in Australia are much higher than they are here. Once I have earned enough I will return. I also reminded her that Malti would welcome her presence; a balancing hand. With much persuasion and promises she conceded and I was given my get out of gaol card.

A few days later I moved mother to my sister's home, which was local. I then packed my bags and said my goodbyes to Nirmala but wept as I kissed my son Surendra for the last time. It was then my turn to stand at the bus stop outside the convent gate. There to the chorus of the convent girls I hugged my family and waved to the girls before boarding the bus. As I took my seat I felt mean and heartless for running away from so many people who thought so much of me.

I was still tearful as the bus sped past the Tavua River from where I could see our love islet glistening in the sun. Had it been the last goodbye of fate? We passed our old village by the tomb and several hours later the bus came to a stop at the main Suva Bus Station. Was I two hundred miles away from home or was this now home?

Strolling with my luggage banging on my legs I took a route through the city centre to the Tongan part of town for it was there that my old school friend, David, had a small bed-sitter. Fortunately he was home and pleased to see me. His place was moderately furnished. There was a small shower area with a toilet and after sprucing myself up and getting a few beers down me we boiled tavioka and fried fish on the apartment's primus stove. After a chat about our shared dreams of leaving Fiji I slept on a mat on the floor with David taking up the one single bed.

Routine for David meant his going to work whilst I walked to the city centre to open a bank account before visiting the immigration department to apply for a passport. Next day thanks to David pulling strings I was re-employed at Bish Limited.

CHRIS NAND

As soon as I felt settled I penned a few postcards to loved ones back home; letting them know my whereabouts. My mailing included a letter to Susan. Whatever adventures befell me I couldn't get my first and truest love off my mind.

At Tom Hini's boxing club I met up with my old friend Tom who by this time was heavyweight champion of Fiji. Having just defeated a heavyweight called Henry Bray on points he was preparing for his next contest against the Australian heavyweight champion Allen Williams.

Tom introduced David and me to a new guy at the club. Manoca Pau was middleweight championship of Tonga and was visiting Fiji. He had just beaten a Fijian Indian named Daniel Nadan on points and had his sights set on fighting David for the middleweight championship of the South Sea Islands.

As soon as David discovered what Pau had in mind we both left and joined forces with Daniel Nadan at a different boxing club. Once we left Tom Hini's club Pau officially challenged David for the title via the Fiji Times newspaper; from that the fight was arranged. It was not to take place in Fiji but in Pau's home town in Tonga. We liked the idea and it was our only chance to leave the islands. Within weeks we had collected our passports and applied for visas to enter Tonga and Samoa.

On the following Monday morning on arriving at work I was introduced to a new foreman. He was an Englishman named Bill Bailey and was originally from Birkenhead in Cheshire. As we chatted he told me that after serving his apprenticeship at Cammel Laird's shipbuilders in Birkenhead he decided to come to the South Sea Islands of Fiji.

From that day on I became firm friends with Bill. He helped me to obtain my beer drinkers permit so that instead of sneaking into sly grogs I was now free to use the local pubs. I became a regular visitor at his villa, the same one once the home of the old Australian crazy gang. Together with Bill and his South African born wife, Vera, we had some great times together. It was Bill and Vera who introduced me to the music of Bing Crosby, Perry Como, Frank Sinatra, Dean Martin and Pat Boone. We often had barbecues at their home where I swam in the pool and enjoyed cool beers.

It was a Sunday afternoon as Bill and I were splashing around in the pool whilst Vera prepared lunch. As we relaxed we heard the doorbell and in walked Mr Bish as large as life. He was not only the boss; he owned the villa. He was surprised at seeing me there and told Bill that he shouldn't be inviting natives into his home again. On hearing this Bill was outraged and told Mr Bish to leave and to leave us alone. As the boss left I dressed and left them too it, thanking both for their kindness and hospitality.

Vera was adamant that I should stay but I was equally unbending: I wouldn't be the cause of problems being visited upon their home or place at work. When we reported at work on the following morning a row broke out in Mr Bish's office; the outcome of which Bill handed in his notice, left the job and presumably lost the villa too. I was sacked on the spot.

Bill and Vera moved into a hotel and we met there for a drink and a chat. A few weeks later they travelled to Auckland. He had prospects with Mason Brothers Engineers in Auckland. He told me his brother worked there and that I should write to his brother as he would pass my letters on. Not long afterwards they boarded the liner the Southern Cross and once again I seemed to follow a pattern of waving to friends as they disappeared over distant horizons.

CHAPTER 4

David and I jogged mornings and worked our butts off skipping, punching the heavy bag and sparring. The hottest months; October, November and December had flown by and been replaced by monsoons, hurricanes and tropical downpours. It was 1958 and there was much else happening too.

Early in March a local man, James Anthony, distributed pamphlets about the town. He planned to form a Workers Union similar to those in other countries. A meeting was called and held on wasteland outside the Century Theatre. Having nothing better to do David and I joined the small crowd and we listened to what Mr Anthony had to say. He reminded us that the European workers in Fiji were much better paid than were the island's native workers. Yet the same work was being expected of them it was only right that we formed a workers union and so bring justice to all. As the meeting progressed the Fijian police arrived. They ordered everyone to abandon the meeting and leave immediately. The officers were ignored. No one moved.

Sensing civil disobedience the police began to fire tear gas canisters to disperse the crowd. Panicking, we ran for our lives with our eyes burning as if someone had squeezed lemon juice directly into them. As we fled we were caught by the police and still struggling roughly thrown into a Land rover and transported to the police station where we were interrogated and locked up for the night. We stood upright all night as the small cell was crammed with a few hundred people and there was no room to lie down and sleep.

The next morning a small crowd gathered outside the prison and demonstrated for our release. It seemed to work and we two were soon set free. It was only when walking home that we realised the extent of the disorder. The shop windows of Indian and Chinese businesses had all been broken and the goods looted. According to the Fiji Times the riot was recorded by the BBC and was making the news across the world. A few days later our visas were granted and David and I concentrated on planning our journey to Tonga.

Two days before departure we settled the outstanding rent and moved into a small hostel called Ismail's Lodge. This was situated close to the banks of the Waimanu River, Suva Wharf and the boats. Out of the blue, as so often, Fiji was hit by a catastrophic rain storm followed by a hurricane. The city was hit badly and the important bridge spanning the river washed way.

From where I was standing at my window I could see there was no way shipping would be allowed to sail anywhere that day; let alone Tonga. I remained in my room feeling hungry and disappointed at this unexpected delay. It was gone noon before the weather improved and I could finally leave my room. As I was descending the stairway I couldn't help but notice the landlord in conversation with a young European woman dressed in a long brown raincoat and with her head covered and protected by its hood.

She looked vaguely familiar and drawing closer heard her voice which I immediately recognised: It was Susan. Ecstatic at the prospect of finding my first love again I rushed down the last few steps towards her. My unexpected appearance caused the waif-like figure to turn and as soon as she set eyes on me she swept out of the door and out into the street. There she began to run as fast as her feet could carry her, sweeping in her raincoat as she did so whilst hanging on to her caped hood. Such was her haste to put distance between us she was very nearly struck by a passing truck. Overwhelmed by mixed emotions; love and rejection, I rushed after her and kept my eyes glued to the running figure as she crossed the road to Burns Philip's stores. Trying to keep her in view I had no choice but to pause to allow a bus to pass and after it had chugged slowly by the fleeing Susan had disappeared into the throngs.

With my eyes searched madly through the mass of people going about their business and I briefly caught sight of her hurrying across a plaza towards the market. I called but it was futile; my voice was lost in the melee of street noises. Susan disappeared into the crowds and running in the direction she had taken my eyes were scanning heads trying vainly to catch sight of her. Because of the poor weather conditions most people were carrying unfurled umbrellas and they too were dressed in raincoats, many in hoods. This added further to my woes.

I crossed the road once again at the bus station; I must have been distracted as I did so and my carelessness nearly cost me my life. A bus screeched to a halt and the driver yelled out in Hindi: "Sala pagla rasta dek lo" (Watch the road, mad arse). His warning caused me to come to my senses and as I shouted my apology he glared and put the bus into gear again.

I looked desperately everywhere for her but finally had little choice but to realise the futility of my search. Suva is a big place and home to countless numbers of people. It was time to dry out and get something warm down my neck at the Suva Lodge on Cumming Street. This was the place where I had enjoyed dinner with father when Queen Elizabeth and her husband, Prince Phillip were visiting the island. That was in the past and my thoughts were dominated by the present.

The storm had not in fact abated by very much and the rain was still coming down in windblown sheets, whipped up by high winds causing the afternoon to turn unimaginably bleak. Doubts set in and by this time I was beginning to wonder if my mind had been playing tricks on me; that the lady had not in fact been Susan; instead, alarmed at my eagerness, a stranger, to get to her a lady resembling Susan had taken to her heels to escape unwanted attention.

To be certain and to put my doubts at rest I obsessively continued my search for her. Scanning passers-by I also checked shops and doorways. It was then that I came across her. She was sat huddled and protecting herself from the storm swept streets in a store's doorway. Delighted at having again found her, but disturbed by her situation, I called her by her name. Susan glanced upwards in my direction, our eyes met momentarily and she then spun her head around as I took hold of her and tried to hug her to me. For some reason unknown to me; perhaps my perceived betrayal, she pushed me away from her.

"Susan! I have been going out of my mind searching for you; why did you run away when I saw you? You knew it was me."

The slightly built girl stayed quiet with her head turned and ignored my question. "Susan; Please: You are breaking my heart. What is the matter with you Susan? It's me, Jamie. Please don't do this to me? I love you Susan and you have never been out of my thoughts. Don't ignore me like this. Please talk to me."

Reluctantly and slowly she turned towards me and spoke; her voice was quiet and controlled. "James, please leave me alone. I never wanted to see you ever again. Do you understand that?"

"Well that is a start, Susan. At least you remember my name."

"Don't be funny, James. There is nothing at all amusing about us meeting like this and during a storm."

"Please, Susan! Return to the hostel with me. If you were going somewhere today I can tell you that according to Fiji Radio there won't be any boats leaving at all today. I too was going on from here. Do come back with me; it is a warm shelter; an opportunity to dry out."

She was stoic and her head was held down and looking to one side. "I can't come back with you: Not today, tomorrow or ever. Please leave me alone, James."

By now I was desperate and I was finding it difficult to figure out the reason for her being so stubborn. I was at a loss as to her obvious antipathy. "Susan; this is not the nicest places for a young woman to be. There are many drunken sailors in town. It isn't safe for you. I beg you, darling, please come back. I promise that there will be no demands made of you. All I am interested in is your welfare; to see you warm, dry and safe. You shouldn't be out at all in this appalling weather."

At that moment a sharp gust of wind swept down the road fronting the store we were sheltering in and took with it the wooden window blinds, which missed us both by inches. Several yards away the Waimanu River was beginning to spill over its banks and with heavy rains in the hills surrounding the city adding to the torrent it was inevitable that where we were now standing would soon be a raging river.

Susan desperately looked up at me and we again had brief eye contact. Her tired face was pallid but despite the conditions she looked as beautiful and alluring as she ever did; hers was a natural beauty and with it came an enchanting charm. I was mesmerised by what I could only describe as the perfect of angels in this most bizarre of situations. As I gazed down at her my heart pounded and swelled with longing for her.

It was then that a police car appeared at the junction of Cumming Street and Thomson Street; its public address system was warning everyone to seek shelter. The hurricane was returning and would likely pass again and more powerfully so. "Get inside please! Go inside; keep out of the storm. Go inside."

I looked at Susan and begged her again and again until finally the gathering storm seemed to make her mind up for her. Taking up her small suitcase she fell behind me followed in my footsteps a few feet behind. What chance I wondered had brought her here, and to my hostel doorway. Could it be fate?

Susan was clutching her rain swept coat to her as we quickly went on our way and by the time we reached the top of Thomson Street there was relief that the water levels weren't as high as I had expected. I reached out to take her hand as we tried to cross the still busy and windswept street but she was having none of it; no physical contact. She was determined to follow up behind and still plainly reluctant to do so as we crossed and picked our way through the debris thrown up by the storm.

As I opened the hostel's door I noticed hesitancy as I held it open for her to come into the welcoming shelter. Looking around her she nervously stepped inside and slamming closed the main door to keep the worst of the weather outside we made our way up the steps to the small room I was renting. My attempts to help her remove her raincoat were repulsed. "I have a chill," she said. "It is best that I leave it on. May I use the bathroom?"

I pointed to the bathroom door and watched as she slipped inside before closing the door carefully behind her; I heard the bolt being drawn. Twenty minutes of consternation passed before she joined me again. The years had perfected her but one thing had never changed; there was still the fascinating dark brown speckle in her eye, which I in my innocence thought of as representing me.

When she finally emerged from the bathroom she was still wearing the raincoat and hood. "I am sorry, Susan. I have been sitting here with my own thoughts far away. I should have prepared some tea. I'll go to the kitchen and bring us some or perhaps you would prefer a glass of hot milk to get you warm?"

Her only concern was that the hostel's manager would not be too happy if a young woman was taking refuge in a guest's room. I told her to relax and to not concern herself. I added that I knew the owner well and of course he wouldn't mind. She thanked me for my kindness "I am very grateful to you but . . ."

I stopped her right there: "No buts about anything, Susan. You have no idea how thrilled I am to see you and hear your voice again. You can't imagine how I have missed you; I deluged you with letters. Couldn't you have replied to at least one of them? You could have smuggled some message out; Ram was always so obliging, you know that. He lives here in Suva."

"Drop it, James. That was all a long time ago. We were children then and it was just puppy love, we aren't kids anymore."

"How can we drop it, Susan, we grew up together; we shared so much at St Mary's. How can you forget so easily, or dismiss what we had together. It was so important to me; it or rather you were so much a part of my life; a part that mattered above all else. You can't be unaware of that?"

"You made your choice, Jamie. That choice was to leave me to fend for myself. Have you so easily forgotten that part; is it convenient for you to do so?"

"Susan! Where's that bright, cheerful and optimistic girl I used to know disappeared to? It was the most awful of dilemmas for me and I am not proud of what I did. I have tussled with it ever since; felt nothing but remorse. No matter how I tried to justify it I felt I was fooling myself. You were the only good thing to come out of that awful place."

I paused in my protestations but again she wasn't making eye contact. After a long pause she spoke again. "I've travelled a long way; a bus with square wheels and you know what these road are like. I am tired and I have to get some sleep."

It was obvious that Susan was certainly carrying a lot of baggage and that upset me, especially if I had placed the burden on her slim shoulders. I asked her if she had since married and told her that whatever had happened to her in the time since I had left I would understand perfectly; after all, we had endured much together. I had noticed a ring on her wedding finger but Susan had tried to hide it by pulling her raincoat closer to her body.

"Please Jamie; stop this nonsense, I shouldn't have come here with you." With that she picked up her bag and went to the door. I stood in her path and begged her not to go. All I deserved was an explanation; it was the least she could do. At that point she held my gaze for a few seconds before speaking: "You want an explanation? Jamie. Open your eyes and look at me."

With that she took off her raincoat and threw it on the floor, revealing a pure white nun's habit. My jaw dropped and I tried to say something but I couldn't; the words I was trying to formulate in my mind wouldn't come.

"Are you happy now? Why didn't you let me go when you saw me in town?"

"But, Susan!"

"No discussions, Jamie. I am a nun and a fully qualified medical doctor. I am on my way to the Leprosy Hospital on the island of Mokagai."

"I know of it; it is hell on earth there. Ordinary people don't go there. There are many more graves than there are living souls."

"I will never break my vows. I accept my destiny. I am not the coward that you are, James."

"Whatever you may think of me I am no coward, Susan," I told her firmly. "I can't tell you how glad I was to escape the mind-numbing control freaks of the Church. Jesus Christ himself would have distanced himself from it. What kind of Christians beat small children as they do? That place was God-forsaken and taken over by bigoted charlatans. Had it been as the scriptures demand and wasn't woven through with hypocrisy and cruelty; if it practiced what it preached I would likely have been a priest by now."

Unheeding of what may have been blasphemous words to her she turned again towards the door. I was desperate for her safety and besides I couldn't see her disappear into anonymity; I felt too much for her for that, nun or no nun. "It's getting dark out there, Susan. Listen to the weather; it is appalling. I can't allow you to go from sanctuary into such danger."

Exasperated at being foiled by the state of the weather she sat on the edge of the bed before taking a good look around the room and then returned her gaze to me. "Why are you in a twin-bed room when you are single, on your own?"

"I'm not alone but you might like to know who is joining me later this evening. I will though keep it as a surprise; a pleasant one I assured you."

"I think you had better tell me, James. You must know that there is no way I can be in a room with two men."

"How do you know my surprise is to be a man?" I tried to laugh as I felt the pressure between us easing. It seemed the weather outside that had brought so much misery to others had brought me only good fortune. I still couldn't believe that after six whole years I had found Susan again. She insisted that I tell her who I was sharing the room with and relenting I asked her if she remembered little David who shared our class at St Mary's. She too brightened up at hearing his name. "Of course I do. He was such an imp and despite it he was the nuns' pet; he got away with murder."

I laughed. "I wouldn't say he went that far but he is the current middleweight boxing champion of the South Seas Islands."

"Boxing? You are still boxing?"

"Yes, I'm rated number one challenger for his title but our being friends since we were kids makes fighting him problematic. We have refused to fight each other. If we did so there would be no winners. We just couldn't do it. Anyway, we have been selected to represent Fiji in Tonga and Samoa. That is where we are headed when David has gone to his parents' home in Nausori. He is visiting his mother and father before we leave."

Susan thought about my revelations and it was pleasing to see her visibly relaxing. It had been an upsetting day for the both of us. "You have grown tall and you appear to be in the best of health yet you earn a living by allowing other men to punch you senseless?"

"No, I earn a living by punching them senseless," I retorted but not too unkindly: "If all goes to plan then Tonga and Samoa will serve as stepping stones; From there it is our intention to go to New Zealand and then to England. We need to make the money first; the only way we can do that is by fighting."

Whilst Susan was in a more relaxed frame of mind I was totally drained by the emotion of the day's events. Evening was drawing in and anyway the skies were overcast; night would be on us soon. I tried switching the lights on but the power was disrupted. That wasn't unusual at the best of times but the islands were more prone to power failings during storms. "The tea: I am sorry; I forgot all about it."

"It doesn't matter. I will survive until morning."

"The kitchen here is closed but we can go to the Lodge afterwards, they have their own generator so the power cut will not affect them. "

"You haven't told me why you're still single. Most Indian men of your age are well settled down at your age, usually with children."

I thought it best not to ask her if she had conceived after our love making in her bed or tell her I was already a father if not a husband. If she had become a mother she would have let me know by now. A heavy weight has been lifted from my shoulders and I was much relieved. "You made that a difficult thing for me to do, Susan. How could I be a husband to another woman when the images I held in my mind were all of you?" I paused thoughtfully: "There were opportunities but I always met this emotional brick wall. I often fantasised about meeting you again and there being a happy ending to the story. In truth you were the only woman that was ever in my mind to marry."

"Surely a handsome hunk like you had at least plenty of girlfriends. I doubt I was the only one." It occurred to me that she might be mocking me but there was no trace of it in her voice. I told her I had dated several girls but the relationships had been no more than skin deep. She replied that it was a pity I felt that way and added: "Don't waste your time waiting for me. I am married, to the Church. My life ahead is well mapped out and I have every intention of keeping to the path."

I told her that was a shame as she was far too beautiful to give her life to the Church based on unfortunate occurrences in her early childhood that were not of her doing. The Church couldn't possibly be her natural habitat. I pleaded with her to join us; to come with David and me to Tonga and from there to New Zealand and then England. The future was no place for regrets.

"You don't get it do you, James," she smiled as she raised her hand. "It is a ring, it is a wedding ring," she said sincerely. "I am a bride of Christ and he takes good care of me. Not you, nor your daydreams about life in England."

I told her I thought she had been brain-washed and institutionalised by frustrated nuns. I fervently told her that I thought Sister Magdalene rather than God was behind her being posted to such an awful notorious island. Turning to her and holding her face directly before me I told her: "She never did like you or anyone else. She no doubt relishes the thought of sending you to hell on earth."

Susan responded with a glare. "How dare you speak to me like that? I recall that you were once as passionate about becoming a priest and you had no difficulty in devoting the rest of your life to Jesus Christ and His works."

"Yes," I told her. "When I did I was an impressionable and naive twelve-year old. I saw the light alright and it was outside the Church; God doesn't just shine his light inside churches; he shines it everywhere."

"Jamie, you're not thinking. What if those nuns, who you describe as false, had not been there to take us in when we were both helpless infants and in my case had no sanctuary. Imagine what my life would have been. I simply wouldn't have had a life of any kind. They saved me."

"But, Susan darling; sorry I mean sister or whatever you wish me to call you. If you go to Mokagai I will be in hell for the rest of my life just as you will. I still feel for you and the cross I will bear will be constantly thinking of you on the island of lepers; the island of death. I can picture it so well. I wouldn't wish the place on my worst enemy yet you are going there?"

"I am a nun, a sister so calling me darling is a little inappropriate. And how precisely will you suffer might I ask?"

"You will be very vulnerable there; those diseases are contagious and I couldn't bear to think of you suffering."

"Don't be childish, James."

"And don't you be naive; being a nun and praying morning, noon and night doesn't make you immune."

"My faith in God's love helps me a great deal. Whatever fate has in store for me it is His will and there will be a purpose to it even if it is beyond our understanding."

"Susan, I am not trying to scare you but my mother used to tell us stories when I was little about my father's married sister named Ram Kali. At the age of twenty she caught leprosy and was banished from her home. My uncles and aunties forced her out of the village as though she were a dog. She was forcefully separated from her two children who were barely four years old and she was not allowed near them ever again.

She took refuge in an abandoned hut before the Catholic missionaries discovered her and they took her to Mokagai where she lived for 30 years before she was cured. Returning to our village her two children had by then grown up and had children of their own.

I was five years old when I first saw her and remember the deep scars on her face and mutilated hands. I used to sit on her knee and listen to her stories about the island. It was she who first told us that the patients there had named the island devil's island.

She told us that she was horrified on arrival on the island as over five hundred people with decaying limbs and faces were her companions in blood and flesh covered dormitories. On her return she tried hard to be part of the family again but my family treated as an untouchable. Devastated by not being wanted by the family she eventually returned to Devil's Island for her own good and perhaps died or still lives there."

"Then I now I have another mission to find her too and let you know how she is or was," mumbled Susan.

"Huh! It's like talking to a brick wall, you are stubborn and will never listen to me, whatever advice I give you. It doesn't suit you; being a nun and praying all the time."

Going over to the window I looked outside. The winds had abated and the rain had stopped. "It's calmed down a great deal. Perhaps we should go out for something to eat. I haven't eaten since before I saw you at reception."

"It is the same for me. I haven't eaten anything since this morning either and I could do with something but it isn't really the done thing for me to be strolling along with a man."

"No one knows you here so you are unlikely to be recognised. I shall limp; it will look as though you have taken pity on me. Let's get tidied up."

Susan remained thoughtful and her response constantly problematic. "There's a convent here in Suva; expecting me, they will be wondering where I am."

So, whatever her reason for calling in at the hostel she hadn't been looking for accommodation. I pointed out to her that both of the town's bridges were under water and there being no ferry service those expecting her were hardly likely to question her non arrival. "They will expect you to have sought sanctuary; this you did."

Without a great deal of enthusiasm she got herself ready and moments later we were on Thomson Street. The rain had started falling again but it was much lighter and at least the wind had dropped and the town was returning to normality. Perhaps the waiter at the lodge thought it a little strange that Susan didn't allow him to remove her raincoat but she told him she had a chill. He didn't press the invitation.

She now seemed much more relaxed and self-controlled and smiled as I told her there weren't any menus here; you order what you want and they sort it. Her choice was goat curry, which hardly surprised me but not too hot. As we waited she explained that she had been in Ireland for five years studying medicine and of course settling in to the Order.

"I listened attentively but I couldn't take my eyes off her as we ate. It was then I noticed the whites of her veil discreetly revealed beneath her hood. Our eyes met several times but there was no connection as such. The Order had done their work well and as far as I was concerned the results were not to their credit. They had vacuumed Susan's psyche and remodelled it as they thought it should be; it must have been a thoroughly dehumanising process. I supposed the Susan I had once known had disappeared as if she had died. She had in a way for she was now a semi robotic programmed flesh-mechanised tool of the Church. I knew it would be futile to try to separate her from the Order. "So what was Ireland like, Susan? Did you like it there?"

She smiled as she dabbed lips I had sometimes kissed and always yearned for. "Yes, it was very pleasant. It is a very strict regime but they're friendly enough."

"Outside such a cloistered existence how did the country itself strike you; the people and the culture?"

She smiled at her recollections: "Surprisingly very little as there was little opportunity for that. Life largely revolved around the university and the ecclesiastical buildings. But I must tell you I saw quite a lot on my way back my flight took me to Liverpool and London before I carried on to Singapore, Australia and finally Fiji."

"It sounds great if you like flying!"

"Yes but I had other things on my mind." I hardly needed to guess at her thoughts as her airliner had touched down on Australian soil. "Your parents were Australian."

She nodded. "So I am led to believe but it is impossible trying to get anything from the Order. They are unbelievably secretive. It is as though they don't want me to know you had a life before the Order."

"Precisely: They have no wish for you to know. The truth seeks the light, it doesn't shun it." I hesitated before adding: "Do you think the rumour about your mother being banished to the leprosy isle, where you are heading, is true? Do you think she could still be there?"

Susan sat quietly and thoughtfully before answering: "She could well be."

"Be candid, Susan," I pressed her: "Is that the real draw; the real reason why you are so focused on Mokagai?"

"Yes, between you and I, I begged Sister Magdalene for the posting. I needed to find out. I still do. It is something of a mission in itself. As if I can do the Lord's work; there is a price to be paid but a reward too. I don't feel as though I am in control; it is as if my feet are being directed by an unknown force."

"Your parents behaviour probably then influenced your life far more than if you had a conventional upbringing. How strange? They could have told you. They would know if she was there or not. Sister Mary who brought you up must know the truth."

"You don't understand their thinking and nor do I. The Order would never reveal anything; it would be against all they had been taught but they don't see anything wrong; there is no betrayal of their faith in allowing one to find out for oneself. I must know the truth. Not just about my mother but about my beginnings. I have no roots and I am not a new species; I belong. Everyone should belong."

I was both pleased and surprised that she had started to unload her thoughts and I was the grateful recipient of them. I felt genuinely sorry for her plight and my heart still ached for her beauty and protectively I was smitten by her vulnerability. I wished so much to take her in my arms and comfort her. My thoughts were taken up by figuring out ways by which I could help her; I owed her that much after I had so badly betrayed her.

"You're quiet. I am boring you?" she said quietly almost thinking to herself.

"On the contrary; I'm glad you feel able to talk candidly. We all speculated at school about how you ended up in school with Indians and native Fijians. You were the only European child there. I'll never forget the day you pushed a candy into my mouth after I was forced to eat beef. It was love at first sight and," I hesitated to say it but I added it anyway: "I am still in love with you, Susan."

There was no response from her and I could hardly know what was going on in her mind, what emotions were colouring her thoughts. "Has it occurred to you, Susan, that the storm that has struck Suva might well have been divine intervention? Have you considered how coincidental it is that it brought together all the loose ends to make the impossible achievable? Things like that don't happen by chance. It is surely a blessing disguised?"

I thought about what I had just said; a blessing in disguise and laughed. "What are you laughing at James?"

"The expression I used; a blessing in disguise and you being disguised under your raincoat. It all fits. You are a blessing in disguise and surely it is symbolic." She thought it trite but attempted a weak smile and shortly afterwards we made our way back to the hostel after purchasing several scented candles. As soon as I opened the hostel's hall door I noticed several others in the hallway but there was no sign of David or the hostel owner.

Going straight up to the room I had rented I illuminated the interior with the candles; the electricity there was still down. It was at my suggestion that Susan changed into a pair of my jeans and a shirt; her habit really needed to dry out; such garments are not at all suitable for wet weather conditions. Susan now looked so slim and shy; a changed persona entirely; the authority of the nun had been replaced by a timid slightly-built waif of incredible heart-wrenching prettiness. It was difficult for me to take my eyes off her. She needed her sleep and for that matter so did I. As I climbed into David's bed, for it was clear he wasn't going to show up this evening I had a vague recollection of Susan snuggling down before I too lost myself in the night's sleep. It was a deeply flawed night, spent by dreams and punctuated by images I could make little sense of.

I thought I was still dreaming when I woke in daylight to see my guest standing at the window; something outside had caught her attention. "It looks like the storm has cleared and we'll be on our way today."

"Yes," I said quietly. For some reason my enthusiasm had waned. Going on our way was going on our separate ways. "And, I don't know whether to be happy or sad, Susan. To have met you under such extraordinary circumstances and then for you to disappear back into the void is one of life's most incredible acts of give and take."

"Oh, it was a chance meeting; that is all, James. Don't read so much into it. You will do so well in your boxing career. I know it. You will of course have that handsome face of yours misshapen by fists. Come and see me at the hospital when you do: I shall see what I can do to fix you up again."

"I smiled at her breeziness and it seemed she didn't quite feel as strongly as did I about our imminent parting. She was likely excited at the prospect of finding her mother on what I had described as the Island of Death. I smiled: "If anything our getting together only proved I was right in cherishing and keeping hold of the love I had. I still have the same longings for you."

"James. You're not being fair on yourself. You're not only a good looking guy in a job; you have one that has a certain celebrity status. You will meet the most attractive girls and quickly forget about your drab nun."

I assured her that in my eyes she was far prettier than any Hollywood enchantress and that I would never forget the images of which I had plenty. Impulsively I took her hand and felt some surprise when she didn't withdraw her own as we gazed out of the window together. We were both pensive and deep in our own thoughts, which were perhaps not matching up as harmoniously as our hands were. Even touching her was as endearing as was looking at her. I was seeing her with my hands and my heart was going into overload.

Outside the rising sun brought just enough warmth for the mist to evaporate almost as we were watching it doing so. Around us were such beautiful landscapes; a natural marriage between nature and the myriad ways of humanity. From somewhere distant we could hear the bells and Vedic chants of a Hindu sadu. Pushing our heads through the window could see him in the far distance. The priest was gazing fervently at the heavens above him and offering a brass cup full of water to the sun, which they believe is one of the gods.

As Susan turned away from the window our eyes met and on this occasion there was the light of times past in them; a recognition and dare I think it, a warmth. My attempt to pull her towards me was however thwarted and as she pulled away we both heard the tapping on the door. It was Mr Ismail, the hostel's proprietor who had come to let me know that all river traffic was back to normal; the ships were preparing to set sail that afternoon.

Before he quietly closed the door behind him he told me he had received a message from David. He was to meet me on the boat. Susan was still standing motionless at the window but transfixed by her habit spread out on the chair. As I quietly went about packing my stuff I was becoming aware that she was upset, her shoulders occasionally convulsed and she was wiping away a tear or two. Feeling the need to comfort her but unsure as to how to go about it I could sense she was torn by conflicting emotions. Would we both experience a hell on earth at a wrong decision made at this most fundamental to our lives?

"Susan; you know that any decision made now will either bless or curse the rest of our lives. Come with me; leave all this behind you. Don't live with regret in your heart every minute of what remains of your life and mine; I don't want that. There will be other ways to find your roots without your suffering too much from them."

She thoughtfully looked again at the habit lying draped across the seating; it was annoyingly neutral. What wouldn't I have given for it to have fallen to the floor at that very moment? It seemed that the decisions made were to be without divine intervention. The robes ecclesiastical symbolism was achingly meditative. Her eyes seemed intrinsically sad when they met my own. Taking her hand on a whim I raised it to my lips and kissed her fingers. There was no resistance; that occurred only when I attempted to take her in my arms and kiss her lips. Had I so soon forgotten that this was God's wife I was holding so delicately?

"Please, Jamie. This is why I ran away from you. I don't know how to handle it anymore. It is all so painful; how can fate be so unkind to me? All of this is so tormenting; it is a test that I am finding quite unbearable; of how you have come into my life on two occasions and with such meaning. It is all too much. As if that is not enough there is my father in Australia and my mother almost certainly on the island and it is all because of me. There is such torment in my heart; only the Church and the Order can help me."

"Susan, I am so sorry for all your dilemmas for they are mine too. Follow your instincts. The order has no more rights to you than do I. You can still belong to God; most people are without making the personal sacrifices you are bent on making. Duty is the instincts of others. What of your own?"

She was inwardly looking but this was balanced by pragmatism: "My parents may already be dead. I have to find them and discover my roots; I cannot go to my grave without knowing. I am in torment you cannot believe how I am tortured."

I reminded her that it was they who had abandoned her and surely they should be looking for their lost lamb of a daughter. I reminded her too of the awful life they had abandoned her to; the tutelage of power-crazed mind-bending Sisters of the Order whose duty seems to be not service to their God but service to their Church, which was hardly the same thing. I was angry and confused and could tell she was torn. I needed at least fifty one per-cent of her answers. Gently and persistently I tried to persuade her to leave with me; for us to live as God truly intended and that we would marry and have children in His likeness; the reason for our being on earth. Only by doing so could we return order to her fractured earlier life as an abandoned child; to ensure that her children, the grandchildren of her wayward parents were loved and cared for as she never had. The extent of her agitation was self evident. "Jamie, please help me!"

What I would do next would settle the matter as to whether her God existed or not. With a snort of exasperation fuelled by frustration I walked to the bed and took that omnipotent icon of her slavery and hurled it through the open window. "I have wanted to do that ever since I set eyes on it," I cried tears of frustration as I did so.

Susan ran to the window just in time to see the cape and garments gently floating in the still swollen waters of the river; she watched in disbelief, her eyes opened wide as she watched the turbulent waters embraced the religious apparel as their own. Soon the dress code disappeared from her view; absorbed by distance and saturation.

I was quite unprepared for the stinging slap but catching it on the rebound my attempt to kiss it, to beg forgiveness was only encountered by her protestations. Susan struggled and spoke passionately about the sin I had committed as she tussled with me in her vain attempt to repeat the slap. Finally her struggles became weaker and her protestations turned into whimpering of surrender followed by endearments, and so it remained until after we had consummated our love for each other. Yet another sacred symbol had disappeared as effectively as had the first. We lay there in disbelief at the enormity of the events that had so completely changed our lives.

"I am so sorry Susan. I wanted you so badly that I was completely consumed by my love for you. The memories of our first love affair never left me. Her reply was to kiss me gently on my lips.

"I missed you so much, James." she smiled whimsically as her memories all flooded back to that fateful days. "All I lacked was the courage to dash after you and climb on that Royal Mail bus too. Do you want to know what happened to me after the bus had taken you away; after I had helped you with your spilled bag?"

I didn't reply; there was no need for me to. She was going to tell me anyway but I wasn't too sure I wanted to hear. It could not have been a happy occasion for her or for the Church. Where was her god then?

"Once the bus pulled away, Sister Magdalene, Sister Chang and Sister Mary dragged me into the washhouse. There they pinned me to the floor and rubbed carbolic soap on my tongue. They let go of me only when I began to splutter and choke but they weren't finished with me. They cut all my hair off; they shaved me completely bald and as they did so they told me that no dirty boys will ever wish to kiss me again.

"It didn't matter to me; whatever they did I didn't care at all; it was nothing compared with my missing you. That was the most painful part of all. I so much regretted not joining you on the bus, James. I was paraded once again in front of everyone at the school. She sent Father John looking for you but the bus had long gone by then. I was hoping that he would find you and bring you back but was very disappointed when he returned without you. I always hoped and prayed that one day you would come and rescue me but you never did. I prayed every night but you never did return for me. Why didn't you?

The pretty Sister of the Order was visibly upset as was I as I listened to her recount the details of the unfolding tragedy.

She sat with her shoulders hunched and her head down and her eyes looking at where her order's garments had been before they had been hurled out of the window. "I hated being at St Mary's even when you were there. I always longed to be somewhere else so imagine what a sheer hell being at St. Mary's without you was. I looked out for you every time the red bus arrived; I cried myself to sleep every night."

"Susan, my darling, I was boxing every two or three weeks and saving every penny and with it carrying the dreams that I would make enough money for us to come together again and marry. I was under no illusions; with me gone and the nuns, doubly on their guard, I knew that rescuing you couldn't be easy or even possible. They wouldn't let you go as easily as they allowed my escape. I had a family to run to and to protect me. But the culture of my family meant our living together with an escapee was out of the question.

"You could at least have tried."

"I sent you so many letters and post cards and you did not reply. I had no idea of your circumstances. For all I knew you might have settled down quite comfortably; you may have ignored my letters simply because you wished to have nothing to do with me. How could I know otherwise? I couldn't. Had I attempted to see you or rescue you I ran the risk of making your life hell. I may have placed you at great risk at a time when you would not have welcomed my attempt? I might easily have made matters much worse rather than better for you. The church has a lot of influence with the government, they could have had me arrested and put in prison."

I added that it was all in the past now and that was the best place for it. What goes round comes round. I was still kissing her face when she looked with horror at her watch. "It's almost one o'clock, James!"

I told her to get herself ready; we had just enough time for a hurried breakfast and we could discuss what lay ahead on the ship. The jeans looked a little baggy on her slim butt but her appeal was still there and if anything she looked boyish in them and the bright red hula-hula shirt that was too garish for me to wear. I must have had one too many when I had bought it. Tying her hair in a pony tail restored her to the epitome of sweet femininity: In my view she was ready to take the Miss World competition by storm.

As we strolled hand in hand with my suitcase in the other I still couldn't believe I had won her heart again. My unfrocked nun was catching the ship with me; we were going to Tonga and from the sequence of yesterday's coincidences surely it was God's will that we did so. Such was the confusion of thought as we stood on the quayside. I couldn't take my eyes off her, neither that nor the silly grin on my face.

Don't fall into the dock," she laughed impishly. "It could ruin your boxing career."

I was ecstatic at the turn of events and laid out my plans; the intention to box my way into the money needed to get to England and build a new life where the opportunities were far better than they were here. "Well if I do I won't be looking for your nun's habit," I laughed happily.

"Have you given any thought of what you intend to do with your life when you are in England, James?"

"David's uncle is there already; he is a London bus driver and he will make the necessary introductions."

"You can drive?"

"No, not yet but I will soon learn. I understand that after a period as a bus conductor they teach you and get you through your test if you wish to."

"You; we will have to have somewhere to live."

She then told me of what a great dreamer I was. Like everyone else I was buffeted through life by fate and I just went along with it, trying to make sense of life's mysteries even if often being frustrated and failing to alter the direction life was taking. I explained that there was a pretty good social care system in place in the United Kingdom and those looking for work were supported. This was the reason why so many people from all over the Empire were flooding to England. "Some," I explained, "claimed handouts for years before finding work."

"You don't want us to live on hand-outs? Don't forget too; there is my fare to England to be thinking about unless you are thinking of me helping me to stowaway on a ship."

As she spoke they saw nearby an approaching Hindu priest offering flowers and rice to calm the sea god by planting a lotus leaf burdened with rice on the waters. He chanted and we two watched as soon the leaf was overwhelmed by a wavelet and sank destined for its eventual watery destination. I hoped that we wouldn't be joining it. Taking Susan by the hand I squeezed through the milling crowds. There was quite a noisy multitude as there were three ships now loading not only today's passengers but yesterday's too. Suddenly we could see David; his distinctive features standing out from the sea of anxious and excited faces. His expression was something not to be missed; he gaped incredulously as he recognised Susan and realised we were a

RETURNED TO DEVIL'S ISLAND

reunited couple. He was clearly delighted: "Is this the same Susan from hell? Sorry, I mean St Mary's. I can't believe it is really you; you look even more beautiful than when I last saw you. Perhaps life has sprinkled character over your lovely features. Are you coming to London with us?"

Susan laughed at his greeting then looked at us both quizzically. "So you two dreamers are still together? I guess you are off to conquer the British Empire?"

We were both as swaggering as young men are; nothing was there that couldn't be achieved. "Come on," I called. "There will be time enough for chatting and catching up when we are on the boat."

"Not that one," David pointed to a rusty old boat. "It is going to the Leprosy Island, Mokagai before it goes on to Tonga. The whole island stinks like hell and the boat smells even worse."

I glanced at Susan but she looked away as we took our steps up the ship's gangway to find ourselves on the ship's decks. The SS Matua was filling fast; hundreds of Tongan and Samoan tourists were returning home. Pau was already onboard and as soon as he saw us came over to greet us. "Maloleilei" He laughed; his greeting could be translated into good day. As he rejoined his merry compatriots drinking their kava, clapping and singing we took in our surroundings and looked around our fellow passengers.

It looked more like Noah's Ark for we were surrounded by livestock. There were pigs, goats, small calves, poultry and bags full of shopping the visitors had bought while on holiday in Fiji. Before long we heard the rumble of the anchor of the adjacent boat being hauled up and the seaman standing onshore calls out: "Please hurry! This is the last call for Mokagai."

I could hardly have asked for more, such was my personal happiness but I wondered at Susan's feelings. "Are you alright?"

Susan didn't look at me or answer me direct but instead vacantly gazed towards the throngs scattered along the wharfs. I am not sure she heard me and at that moment I was distracted by seeing Pau walking towards us with beer and refreshments for us both. "Last call for Mokagai!"

Suddenly Susan rose to her feet and without a glance at any of us she sprinted towards our ship's gangway. I was horrified and could hardly believe what I was seeing: "Susan," I screamed. "Don't go; don't give your life away. Don't throw mine away; I cannot live without you. Come back! Come back," I screamed. "I love you."

I watched in shock as she forced her way through the confused mass of people and made her frantic way towards the second ferry, pushing past other boarders, knocking them aside. I dashed after her barely aware of the barrage of muttered oaths as I blindly chased her down the gang plank and across the pier. Finally catching her I caught hold of her wrist. Twisting towards me I could see her eyes were desperate and tormented; she was like a woman possessed and perhaps she was; her life experiences had deeply wounded her. She piteously screamed, "You're hurting me James. You are chasing dreams. It will never work. Let me go."

CHRIS NAND

Around us onlookers were perplexed by our behaviour and anxious to be on their way. Now the dilemma was mine to deal with. Should I continue to hold her I could easily dislocate her wrist. Other passengers were looking at me angrily. The police might at any time arrive for they were always present at times and places like this. Time wasn't any longer on my side. If I were arrested that would be a mess. On the other hand if I relaxed my grip she would slip free and she would be gone from my life forever. Whatever powers dictate our fates there would be no action replay on this one.

I loosened my grip enough for her to free herself and as soon as she realised she was free she tossed her bag over the ship's taff rail to land on the deck. Beneath the ship's stern the waters were already churning from the thrust of its propellers. A few metres away the stevedores were removing the holding ropes and the ship was edging away from the wharf. Hands reached over to clasp her hands and with legs stretched she clambered on board just as the distance between the ship's hull and the quay made recovery impossible. From that quay I watched in dumb despair as having clambered aboard she looked mournfully back at me. "You'll always be in my thoughts and prayers . . . please take good care of yourself . . ."

Tears were streaming down my face and hers too as I turned to make my way back to the ferry we had first boarded. Totally devastated I stood at the edge of the boat and watched Susan's boat gather speed. After the passengers had finished boarding I looked across the bay once more and caught the last image of the ferry Susan was travelling on being absorbed by the heat mist and distance. I was disconsolate.

Our own ferry departed shortly afterwards. Thankfully David and the others left me to myself; I was inconsolable as I watched Suva too disappear over the horizon. All enthusiasm for my journey had now faded and I was left with a sick sensation in the pits of my very being. To have heaven so unpredictably placed in my hands only to see it snatched away as suddenly and unexpectedly as it had arrived. I felt fate was taunting me. I wept and sobbed not just for the cruelty of losing Susan but for all I was leaving behind; my mother, sister, Nirmala and my newborn son Surendra. What was it that was driving me away from paradise? All my earlier nostalgia and homesickness had been brushed aside by the promise of spending the rest of my life with Susan. In my mind I had already lived the future with her yet now it had all the finality of death upon it. As I wondered if I might see any of them again the thought that it was unlikely filled me with dread for the future. I must have looked a very forlorn figure.

When I looked at my watch I noted that it was 5pm; the date being April 28, 1958. The first leg of my journey lay ahead, towards countries situated on the far side of the world and the horizon ahead of the plunging ship's prow. This was the first stage of that long voyage; the 500 mile sea passage to Nuku'alofa the capital of Tonga.

The day was pleasant enough following the stormy intrusion the day earlier. The sun's warmth penetrated my skin and the sea sweeping underneath the vessel was as smooth as a millpond. Our fellow passengers were all in a good mood; one of them was strumming a ukulele and a chorus of voices were singing in chorus the Fijian farewell song: Isalei.

RETURNED TO DEVIL'S ISLAND

My misery was complete but I was hardly dying though that would have been a release. It did have its comparison in my mind being flooded with memories and the feeling of devastation; the heartache spread throughout me until my entire body ached with wanting, longing and uncertainties.

The singing did something to put balm on my depression. The other passengers were using the boat trip as an excuse to party. It was too early for alcohol but when Pau handed me a Fosters I dropped its contents down my throat without realising the potential fall-out. "Come on, Jamie," he said. "Drink up. You will feel better for it."

Later we were invited to lunch by new friends we had made acquaintance with and clearly there was much good dining yet to be enjoyed by my newly found friends. My eyes followed as Pau suggested to where I could see several ladies carving slices from a whole suckling pig. David was starving; more so than I was, but it would have been impolite to refuse hospitality so hesitantly I took what was offered and tried to tucked in, but could not bring myself to eat. The beer was more appropriate to me than the food that came freely and without limits. David ate as if it was his first meal in a week and as soon as the meal was over the ukuleles were produced and the singing began.

As the melodies poured as did the blouses of the younger women until sadly did the ship's dipping and rolling increase. Now, without warning as is common to the region the weather deteriorated at the onset of evening. If the ship and its progress were unsettled it unsettled the passengers too and I noticed that the songs had now turned into hymns; travellers were already feeling queasy and apprehensive. Many had laid out their coconut matting and had decided to lie down and see the storm out that way.

I was to pay the price for my over indulgences of Fosters though it must be said that it was David who was first to the ship's rails. I followed but by that time I was hardly alone; it was unwise to stand at the rail downwind of other passengers. The hurricane that had brought so much destruction a day earlier was still prowling the South Seas and we were sailing right into its path.

The ferry was by now plunging and rolling and with what seemed to us difficulty holding its own against the fury of the storm. As it pitched and tossed we began to hear screams and then the crashing of loose tables and chairs as they slid down the pitching decks to fetch up against bulwarks and rails. People were grabbing at anything to prevent themselves from being flung about the decks. As they did so the ship threatened to capsize as sweeping green waves, speckled with foam, reared and swept towards the ferry as though determined to pound it into a watery grave.

Other poor souls had jammed themselves into corners but for some the security was short-lived. Every so often a wave would burst high enough against the ship's heaving sides to cascade spray and heavier water across the decks. Soon everyone was soaking and alarmed whilst many a prayer was being mouthed. Others among us huddled together for fellow creature comforts whilst coping with the nausea caused by the ship's violent movements as its bows reared before plunging again and again to meet the next green backed challenger. Overhead the skies were threatening and the low cloud was being swept through the heavens by the fury of the tempest. If we thought that things could hardly get worse we were to be disappointed and those who were somehow managing to avoid the cascades of seawater and spray were soaked through by the relentless rain that came down from the heavens.

How we made it through the night I have little idea and little reason to wish to recall it. When a ship passes through a storm at night the fears of the unknown are magnified a hundredfold and the dawn brought little relief other than the ability to see better the cause of all our miseries. There was no lunch to be had that day.

On arrival at our Tongan port there was exultation of a kind drive by the relief of reaching a port many feared we would never see. My miseries had been compounded by my fears for Susan whose ferry would have been tracing a similar route across the sea charts. As we docked I could hear someone shouting: "Look! There's the Royal Palace of Her Majesty Queen Salote of Tonga."

Making our way to the rail David and I peered across the bay to the white wooden edifice surrounded by the tallest of royal palm trees lining the escarpments of the palace. Moments later the brave ferry that had so proved its seaworthiness and craftsmanship of its builders squeaked and jarred along the huge wooden tyre fenders lining the Queen Salote port's quayside. Locating our luggage I was in such a weakened state it was difficult for me to grasp and carry my own. My legs were wobbly having got used to the ship's movement and now the comparative steadiness unsettled me. I did catch up with the others and followed them through immigration where our documents were being looked over.

"Welcome to the Kingdom of Tonga." The man who welcomed us was a giant of a fellow and dressed in a white sulu with matching jacket; a cap and canoe-sized open-toed sandals. Another called out: "Have a nice stay in our kingdom." We couldn't help but grin. After making our way out into the streets of the capital, Pau who was familiar with everything gave us a running commentary of where everything was. He pointed out the Post Office and Royal Palace before guiding us along the Taufa'ahau Road dotted with many Chinese and Indian retailers; the Methodist Church and further along the convent before we finally reached our destination, Moala's Place restaurant. Welcome home," Pau grinned. "This is where you will be staying."

"You too?" I asked him.

He explained that his village was some twenty miles inland but he was staying with his sister who lived close to the royal cemetery further up the road. But now we were to meet the Moala family. It was then that the unpainted door of the restaurant flung opened and a well built man smiled and greeted us warmly. "Malolelei fefehake."

"Good morning. How are you?" answered the widely grinning Pau as we were led inside to the restaurant's tables that had been placed ready for us. As we took our seats, ladies who were well proportioned to say the least, warmly greeted us. One of them we were introduced to; she was Josefina; the patron's wife.

We learned that Moala is the village chief as well as being the island's chief boxing promoter. He is also a manager and trainer; three for the price of one someone grinned. Pau was obviously proud of his acquaintance with the illustrious islander and told us Moala had trained many of the truly great Tongan fighters including Kitone Lave and Johnny Halafifi.

We were quite rightly impressed but far too tired to show the level of enthusiasm the occasion merited but when told of the rough passage we had experienced they sympathised. There would be time yet to become better acquainted. As though reading our minds he took each of us off to inspect our rooms. Following him along the restaurant's garden paths we made our way to a large hut with its bamboo walls and its grass thatched roof. It was similar to the one that was the centre piece of our own village but much larger and it did enjoy a supply of electricity.

Inside there was a large radiogram standing in its lounge area and the walls were adorned with family photographs. They were obviously very proud of their establishment which well they might be. I counted six bedrooms each of which was separated by bamboo canes but lacking doors. Threads of beads hung as curtains over the door frames and the floors were carpeted by homemade coconut matting.

"This is our home; you have met my wife and we share with my son Tevita and my daughters Monica and Isabel. You'll meet them all a little later. In the meantime do feel free to rest." Pointing to the two rooms situated at the rear he told us his wife had prepared them for us. "The shower room and the toilet are in the back garden," He called as he returned to the garden patios. My eyes were already closing through lack of sleep and mental exhaustion and we were soon asleep.

* * *

When I awoke I had slept the entire night through and could hear roosters crowing, birds singing their hearts out and the barking of dogs. Dressing quickly I rushed into the gardens and found what I needed; the grass hut toilet. From there I could see a light on in the restaurant. As soon as Mrs Moala and her children set eyes on me they burst out laughing; it was a strange welcome which I failed to understand but just then Mr Moala walked in and laughing handed me a mirror. "Take a look." I peered at my reflection and saw my face was covered in multi-coloured paint daubs like the mask of a native god. I hesitated and was at first a little peeved but soon saw the joke that had been played on me and laughed.

"These are my children. Monica, Isabel and little Tevita" Mr Moala said proudly as he made the introductions. The greetings exchanged the girls told me they were attending the Mormon University. Whatever they were learning it had done much for their sense of humour. Monica explained that the earlier evening they had looked into my room and saw us both fast asleep. "Isabel, Tevita and I painted your face," she laughed mischievously.

"Did you paint David's face?"

"He was sleeping on his side so just painted one side of his face."

Sensing I was a little put out at being picked on she told me I mustn't feel angry. It is a well known practical joke in these parts and no offence is ever intended. It is a fun thing. Smiling, I looked at Monica and Isabel. They were both typical Tongan teenagers; tall and carrying a little extra weight; pretty with pearl-like teeth and frizzy Afro-style hair. They seemed a happy-go-lucky pair and any unease I had felt was replaced by good humour. In fact I was delighted that I seemed to have been so readily accepted by the family. Monica was still giggling as she sat me on a chair and cleaned the paint off my face with soft masi cloth. "We have painted your stomach too but it will come off with a good scrub when you're in the shower," she said and sniggered nervously. Shyly I looked up to see her face and smiled.

"I was dead as a dodo last night and didn't feel a thing," I told her. The hurricane had taken its toll but I was now feeling my old self again and would likely feel on top form after breakfast. I did wonder how David was and thought I must call him.

"Yes, do so," she said. "We can have breakfast together before we go to school. Take a shower and meet up with us in the restaurant."

When I did strip off and saw where they had painted my body I was a little surprised at their daring and a little uncertain as to the likely reception when coming face to face with the young ladies at the breakfast table. But it was it seems par for the course, no big deal and we just giggled. There was no hint of innuendo or anything risqué. David arrived and greeting us with a nod and a maloleilei joined us. We laughed to see the paint on his face and explained to him the events of the night. He took it all in good form too.

After breakfast the girls showered; put on their school uniforms; white blouse with brown skirt and brown sandals. We waved them off as they piled into a Morris Minor and sped off waving happily through its back windows. Chatting with the youngest child, the boy named Tevita, he proudly told me that he was seven years old and went to the Mormon Primary School situated just around the corner. "Jamie, will you and David walk with me to my school? The boys at my school want to see you both."

We were a little flattered to learn that they were interested is us and to them we were celebrities. David and I accompanied the child across the Taufa'ahau Road to the tiny Mormon school next to the Church of the Latter Day Saints. There we were surrounded by children between the ages of six and twelve who called us fungatua (fighters).

David play sparred with the good natured kids and after seeing Tevita through the school gates walked on to the post office where we picked up some post cards and stamps. As soon as we could find a park bench we settled down to scribbling our messages that were soon to be sent on their way to my family and to Susan too. On our way back to our digs we met several Indian shopkeepers who recognised us from the Times of Tonga news paper and radio talks where we have been mentioned. As a friendly gesture we stopped to chat with them. Word was certainly getting around about our presence there. It was a small and narrow town with a village mentality; just perfect.

I asked where we might find a pub. A man laughed. "There are no pubs here, mister. Tongans are very religious but you can have a beer with us in our homes anytime you want to." We thanked them all very much and walked along the road.

Back at Moala's Restaurant we found Pau waiting for us and eager to show us around his town. "Malolelei, fefehake?" Pau was good humoured when I told him about our painted face baptism to the friendly island. When I asked him if it might be a good idea to show us around the town he told us this was it: "There are no pubs, clubs or bars with dancing girls as there are in Fiji," he laughed. "These people are Mormons. Alcohol is off the menu and so might I add is coffee. Only cocoa is served in restaurants but don't concern yourselves too much as there's always one and I shall take you to a pub a little later. But first I must show you the gym where we are all going to work out. Don't forget why we are here."

Strolling to the rugby club we entered a shed like building. "Training starts at three in the afternoon so be here around 2.30pm; change and get ready for sparring."

There was a clubhouse adjacent where we made for the small bar and ordered beer. "This Fosters beer seems to be available everywhere," I commented. "The Australians have cornered the market and making a fortune."

"Keep quiet about this facility," Pau advised us. "It is best the Moalas don't know we drink alcohol."

Later, after a Tongan sized lunch of fresh fish, yams, sweet potatoes, oysters and cocoa, we rested until it was time for our work out at the gym. Pau and his training partners had finished their workout and were leaving just as David and I entered the gym. Mr Moala put us through a rigorous workout, skipping, sparring, punching heavy bags, and lifting weights.

With training completed we paused at the rugby field for a while and watched some of the biggest men I ever set eyes on before walking back to Moala's Place. I couldn't believe the sheer bulk and size of the Tongan people. Some were on bicycles; others were walking but all seemed in a good to be alive mood. Many seemed to know we were visitors: "Have a good stay in our kingdom," they called out to us as they cycled by.

Back at the restaurant Monica and Isabel were there with a group of girls they had brought home from their university; they were excited at the thought of meeting us. Coming from my humble background I felt reserved but Monica insisted that I must say hello to her friends. One by one we shook hands and kissed each on the cheeks to the chorus of offa attu after which we showered before joining the family for the evening meal. As we sat around the restaurant's largest table we enjoyed suckling pig, beef, fish and chicken as it was brought from an earthen oven called an emu. Afterwards, Monica insisted in driving us around Nuku'alofa to show us around her town.

"Tell me what offa attu means?" I asked Monica as she drove us about the locality.

The young lady threw her head back and laughed at my question. "It means I love you. Why do you ask?"

"It is because the teenage girls shout offa attu when they see us. I suppose it's a bit like the teenagers in Fiji who call out 'I die there' isn't it?"

"Yes, that's exactly what it is, we all do it. Do you have girlfriends in Fiji?"

"No, we don't piped up David: "And how about you. Do you have a boyfriend?"

"My guy had to go to Salt Lake City in the U.S. to be educated there; he is to become a Mormon minister."

"Sounds a bit like us", said David. "We could have become priests if we had been brainwashed by the nuns at our school."

"How about Isabel? Does she have a boyfriend?" I asked.

She replied that it was the same story. Her boyfriend and many of our young men are in the States for their education. At the beach close to the Royal Palace, Monica brought the car to a stop as we gazed silently at the horizon. The golden South Seas sun was about to set and we watched it until the dusk turned into tropical darkness before taking the route back to our new home. During the drive Monica asked us a million questions.

"How old are you Jamie?"

"I'm twenty two and you?"

"I'm eighteen; two years older than Isabel."

"But you and Isabel both look over twenty" which I wasn't sure was the right thing to say. Maybe at their age it was a compliment.

"Yes, all Tongan girls do. We become women at sixteen."

"What are you studying at the university?"

"I'm on a teachers training course. Once I qualify I also go to Salt Lake City for further education."

I asked her if she had ever been off the island. She told me only the once, that was during the Queen Elizabeth's visit to Suva. David told her it was a small world for we had been at the event too. "A pity we didn't meet up then," she laughed playfully.

After our evening meal David spoke warmly about the Moala family, their kindness and the good food. Mr Moala reminded us that we had to watch our weight or we would end up as heavyweights. Everyone here was well built and that included the women. It was just as well they were friendly. Once outside the restaurant David quietly whispered: "I like Monica and might ask her for a date, and you can date Isabel, Jamie: She's your type."

I knew he meant well but after being reunited with my Susan I remained married, body and soul to her. I told him how I felt and added that when I had earned enough I would return for her.

"Jamie, you really do have to come to terms with reality. Forget Susan. She'll never leave the church for you or anyone else. She has well and truly been brainwashed by the nuns."

As we chatted the owner of an Indian shop where we were browsing at introduced himself, He had heard about us: "I know who you are," he smiled: "There's talk on

Tongan radio that two young Indian boxers are here to fight. Everyone thinks that Pau will knock out David the champion and take the title away from him. Which one of you is David, the champion?"

As soon as I pointed David out to him he took my friend's hand and beaming with pride said: "You Indians make us proud but please be warned. These Tongans are big, strong and heavy punchers. I've seen Pau fight and in the ring he turns into a killer. He has knocked all of his opponents out. His emphasis was on the word, all. David and I smiled and were walking off when other Indians arrived and invited us for a beer. Shrugging, we went with them into room at the rear of the shop.

We found Monica leaning against the window looking out for us when we arrived back at Moala's Place. There was no questioning the family's friendliness and when after the meal we retired to our rooms and slipped beneath the bed sheets I heard the two girls entering their own bedrooms. They were chatting happily away in their own language and giggling between themselves.

On the following morning Mr Moala took the two of us to meet a man named Tofu Kivalu. He, we were told, represented the Tongan Boxing Association and had asked to meet us. After a chat during which there were a few forms to be completed we set our feet in the direction of the beach. We hadn't been walking the sands for long when David was violently sick and we had no choice but to return home. The change in our diets was affecting him. He was used to eating his mother's home cooking. Fortunately I was exposed to rich Tongan food well before I came to the island.

As I was enjoying a chat and breakfast with Monica and Isabel the following morning a young man arrived; he was carrying a small poster advertising the fight night. The main event was between Pau and David. It was billed as a 15 round contest for the middleweight championship of the South Seas. Mine was a supporting ten-round bout with a Tongan middleweight named Jimson Viliami Luis. This was billed as the final eliminator to fight the winner between Pau and David. The thought crossed my mind: Would I have to fight David after all?

After breakfast I went to David's room and gave him the news but he preferred his sleep; he didn't want to talk about what might never happen. Later when jogging I was pleasantly surprised to see the same posters placed around shops, palm trees and car windscreens. By the time I returned David was up and looking much better than he had the previous night. "It's good to see you up. We've only fifteen days of training; do you think you can make it?" He assured me that he was fine with everything.

Following dinner Mr and Mrs Moala retired to their beds leaving us in the restaurant with their two daughters, Monica and Isabel. We four sat around listening to the radio and chatting. The girls were chatty, teasing and flirtatious and at some point one of them asked me if we two went to the Catholic Church on Sundays.

"We used to when we were in school together but I don't fancy going anymore," I replied truthfully. "We prefer staying at home and listening to the radio, or to go for an early morning walk"

"Everyone goes to church in Tonga," we were told: "Only the very old and the sick stay at home and if you don't want to go to your own church than please come to ours. The Catholic Mass starts at eight in the morning and ours starts at ten so you can come to ours after your Mass," suggested Isabel.

I wasn't inclined to start going again to church but felt I didn't have much choice. I looked at David and he didn't look too enthusiastic about going back to the Catholic Church either but after seeing the disappointed looks on the girls' faces we both finally agreed. Going to church was easier than disappointing them.

Whilst at the Moalas' we were invited to tour their farm in Kolovai Village a place called the Village of the Bats. We would be there to meet their stepmothers; their stepmothers being in the plural. The girls reminded us that theirs was a Mormon family and multiple wives were encouraged. "Will you two marry a man with several wives?" David wanted to know.

"Why not? We can all be happy together under one roof and bring up children together."

I hurriedly changed the subject and asked why they called the community the Village of the Bats? Monica told us it was because the local trees are covered with fruit bats. Interesting but because of our training regime we both decided that preparing for the fights was more important than touring a farm.

But we did settle on a Saturday visit and after breakfast Mr.Moala suggested that his daughters take me in the Morris Minor; he would follow with his wife and son in his Bedford pick-up. He first had a little shopping to do for his wives in the countryside. David was staying behind as he still wasn't feeling too good.

Monica and Isabel were both dressed in ankle length flowery dresses their mother had designed and made for them. Pulling on a pair of boxer shorts, tee-shirt and flip-flops I sat beside Monica as she drove off and before long we were cruising a long dusty track bordered on either side by idyllic countryside; palm groves, banana plantations and lush green trees laden with tropical fruit.

It reminded me so much of my old grass and bamboo home by the old tomb and I felt a little home sick. Before we had driven far the palm groves thinned and the road descended in winding curves towards the ocean. Scattered about us were rusty shacks, some of which had colourful curtains strung across the doorway similar to those at the Moalas' home. None had glass windows but the more solidly constructed buildings had louvered shutters.

Animals grazed while children played rugby with coconuts on sandy patches nearby. Women were gracefully carrying baskets filled with clothes or produce on their heads, often with babies neatly strapped behind their backs. The dirt track branched off towards the far side of the island and Monica pulled the car to a stop outside a large grass hut. "Your country is very beautiful but I didn't see mountains or rivers."

"Our main island Tongatapu is flat; there are no mountains or rivers but the surrounding islands have many hills and they do have mountains and rivers. Look over there, Jamie. Those trees are covered with fruit bats," said Monica.

RETURNED TO DEVIL'S ISLAND

After stepping from the car I approached the tall trees and looked up. "Don't stand underneath them," called out Isabel. "Your head will be covered in bird shit."

I was amazed to see every branch of these trees was covered with fruit bats, each of them hanging upside down. "Over here," called a big shirtless man. I could see steam seeping out of the ground with a small group of villagers standing in a circle around it. It reminded me of the first time I had seen earthen ovens in the mountain village and knew exactly what was there beneath the ground. As we approached them Isabel introduced me to two attractive women, both of whom again were well proportioned. "These are my two step mothers Malisa and Esita," Isabel announced proudly.

I shook hands with the two women who looked not much older than Monica and Isabel. Giggling excitedly they invited us inside the big house where we sat cross-legged on the mats. By the time the girls' parents had arrived we had eaten a bellyful of freshly cut melons. Later we feasted on suckling pig; yams, taro and tapioca; all the home-grown produce of their own farm. We were waited on hand and foot and after wiping our mouths we thanked them all and slipped out of the house followed by Monica, Isabel and Tevita. "Where's the beach?" I asked.

They pointed to an area behind the nearby coconut grove," as I gathered up my swimming trunks and towel from the car. "You won't need that stuff," grinned Isabel. "We all swim naked here."

"You do?"

Tevita by now was dashing from hut to hut inviting their friends to join us. Before long a group of about twenty, mostly young people joined us on the beach. I had already seen the thick shrubbery around the coconut grove; the powder white sand and blue ocean waters lapping the beach. Someone called out and this was followed by a sudden rush to be the first to dive into the ocean. Flimsy sulus, boxer shorts and tee-shirts were all discarded and left on the beach.

I was stunned to see the unashamed nakedness of my hostesses as they too ran in front of me to dive into the ocean. This was no time to be shy; anyway, Monica and Isabel must have checked me out when they had painted my face and stomach on the night on my arrival.

When in Rome, thought I. Stripping off before chasing after them I dived headlong into the water where we wrestled in the water, pushing each other and tickling. Some went out of the water to playfully dig holes and make animal shapes in the wet sand; others were playing tag. The Moala sisters chased me through the shallow waters until I tripped and fell on the beach. They were on me in an instant, pinning me to the ground. I felt embarrassed at being wrestled to the ground by two naked girls but the others cheered and clapped at the spectacle. Managing to free myself I dashed for the water's edge and they were as quickly behind me where we enjoyed a good swim before dressing and returning to the big house. There, once we finished eating we had a tour of the Moala farm during with time two small squealing piglets were selected from the farm, tied up and placed in the rear of Mr Moala's pick-up.

On the way back we were drained and tongue tied following the day's experiences and the journey was completed in silence. Images of the naked bodies of my companions paraded through my thoughts and I reasoned that I too had no longer any secrets from them. It was certainly back to nature here. Group nakedness being a new experience to me I was both shy and a little embarrassed. Perhaps their living so close to nature made it less of a big deal to them than it was to me. I also found myself thinking of the relationship between Mr Moala and his three wives. I hadn't noticed any affection between them. Why had such pretty young girls married him? Was it love or lust or had they married for status and security?

As we parked the car the two servant guys took the piglets to the rear of the house and tied them to a post near the shower hut. Going straight to David's room to see how he was I looked in vain; there was no sign of him. After checking the showers I joined the family in the restaurant. "Is David alright?" asked Isabel.

"He's not in his room? Perhaps he's gone for a walk." I told her as we sat around the table listened to the radio. The girls' parents liked their early nights and taking Tevita with them they left us to it. As we chatted my mind was constantly distracted by the day's events at the beach. Being your typical male I couldn't get over the voluptuousness of the girls; their breasts were almost as big as watermelons and they fascinated me. It had been an amazing day. I had taken in the lush green countryside of the beautiful island and was impressed with the natural friendliness of the Moala's. My thoughts were interrupted with thoughts of Susan and my mood abruptly changed to sombre.

Even though I was in the company of two beautiful young women I was overwhelmed by sadness and thoughts of what might have been. I was getting to my feet to take my leave of them when a waiter walked in carrying hot chocolate drinks. Monica protesting at my imminent departure pulled me back to my seat and holding my hand continued to ensure I forgot any plans or an early night. She was smiling shyly. Isabel also took hold of my hand and as natural as you could imagine we carried on chatting together.

At that point in strolled David large as life. He told us he had walked and met by chance a Mr Patel who had invited him for a beer and a meal. It was pleasing to see David looking much better than when I had last seen him. He didn't hang around; he said he needed his sleep.

As bedtime approached the three of us left the restaurant and we entered the dormitory section of the house. While I disappeared into the shower the girls selected some records and placing them on the automatic record player's turntable the modern music soon permeated the otherwise tropical stillness of night. A little later I sighed as slipping beneath the clean bed linen I lay awake listening to the music. I recall the melodies played that night, they included Love me Tender and Wild in the Country by Elvis; Pat Boone's April Love and Nat King Cole: When you Fall in Love and similar melodies.

Not long afterwards I heard the girls returning from their shower and as they passed my room they were sniggering and giggling. "Good night and sweet dreams Jamie."

They had both retired but the records played on and my nostrils caught the aromas of frangipani wafting coming from their bedrooms. It didn't take much imagination to picture them rubbing the oil over their nakedness as was common to the South Seas Island women. Frangipani petals are crushed, mixed in coconut oil and used as a sweet smelling perfume.

As the lights were extinguished the room was bathed in the brightest moonlight imaginable; it shimmied through the slats of the bamboo walls and gave me a romantic lullaby of sorts as my thoughts returned to Susan.

At first light I awoke to the raucous sound of squealing pigs. Alarmed, I pulled my boxers on and sprinted to the bathhouse to see what all the mayhem was about. There I came face to face with two men who, armed with heavy wooden sticks, were beating shit out of the two piglets. As soon as they saw me they grinned broadly showing a row of yellow-white teeth. Glancing at their hands I could see they were covered in blood and I involuntarily gasped with horror. To one side there was a fire now burning fiercely in the earthen oven and I then looked back at the injured piglets. Close to death their limbs were smashed and both were covered in their own blood. I was sick with revulsion at the sight I had seen and running back inside the house I nearly fell over Monica. "What's the matter, Jamie?"

"Those two men are beating the pigs to pulp; please can't you stop them."

At this she began to laugh: "That is how we prepare them before cooking them. It is called umu. If we didn't beat their bodies to pulp then the meat wouldn't be tender enough to eat, silly."

Her soothing explanation did little to settle me; it had been an appalling sight for anyone to see. I returned to bed and after the noise had died down went quietly into the bathhouse and looked sadly at the blood-drenched soil. By then I could see flumes of smoke seeping out from beneath the mounds of soil. My hands were trembling as I shaved and showered before dressing. Much of the island's natural charms had deserted me. Leaving the house I heard Isabel shouting: "See you before ten, Jamie, and don't be late"

As I crossed and then strolled down Taufa'ahau Road I could hear squealing piglets as house after house prepared for their Sunday feasts. My stomach was still churning when I stopped outside a Hindu shop called Sita Ram's. I needed to steady my nerves and stomach before crossing to the church gates.

The church bells began to chime and my heart began to thump with the fear I now had of God. Perhaps it was paradise but the scenes I had taken in reminded me that heaven was too close to visions of hell. The white painted timber walls of the church and the brightly painted red corrugated tin roof somehow reminded me of my old boarding school. Smartly dressed Tongan families with crunchy mats wrapped around their bulky waists walked pass and as they did so they smiled across at me. Some greeted me with malolelei as they made their way through the gates of the church.

At first hesitating I then felt I had little choice but to follow and as I entered I dipped my fingers in the clam shell filled with holy water before making the sign of the cross and then taking my place kneeling in a pew. The prayers and the hymns were familiar to me; they had all been learned by heart at St Mary's, which was to me dedicated to the martyr St Susan. When it was time for Communion I knew it was wrong of me to receive it without having attended to confession but I had done so many times in Fiji and was now a little blasé about doing so. I joined those receiving the white wafers on tongues and afterwards quietly retreated before bumping into the young priest. "Hello Young man! It's nice to see new faces in our church."

He smiled broadly as I greeted him: "Hello Father; I have just arrived in Tonga from Fiji."

"You must be one of the young boxers they're talking about on the radio."

"Yes, father, my name is Jamie."

Telling me again he was pleased to make my acquaintance he told me his name was Francis, Father Francis. And where is this David I have been hearing about?" he asked.

I told him my friend was feeling unwell as we turned to chat with a European family who had joined us. The father of the small family was a tall slim man of about thirty-five of age. His wife looked much younger and they had their daughter with them. Introducing himself as Robert he then turned to his wife, Ruth and daughter, Claire. "You must be the young boxer?"

As I nodded he said, "Yes, I know all about you and David. Where is David? I told them that he wasn't feeling well and had confined himself to the house where we were staying. Ruth smiled: "My husband is a boxing referee. He officiates at major bouts held throughout the islands."

I was a bit taken aback to meet the islands boxing referee. Turning to Claire they told me she attended the Catholic college right next to the church; they all nodded in its direction. What a beautiful young lady, I thought to myself.

As I was leaving the small party Robert called out to invite us both to visit anytime we were free. They explained that their detached villa was close to the beach just past the Royal Palace on the right. As I turned I saw Claire thoughtfully weighing me up and smiling. I again waved but this time it was directed mostly to her before crossing to Moala's. I later joined their family on a stroll to the Mormon Church. "Why does everyone wear those odd crunchy mats tied around their waists?" I asked.

"It's our custom here," I was told. "It is a custom that has been observed since life started on these islands, even our queen wears it," explained Isabel.

Tevita looked up at me to ask if I had seen their queen. Only when she attended the coronation of Queen Elizabeth in London I told him; it had been broadcast on cinema screens around the world.

In no time at all we reached the tall narrow tower of the Church and entered through its main doors. One by one we shuffled along the narrow pews until we found a seat close to the pulpit. Monica and Isabel looked as pure as angels in their long white dresses as we waited for the pastor to begin the service. The sermon was filled with drama and a few worshipers were in tears as the minister yelled and screamed at them. I did not understand Tongan very well so didn't get the gist of the sermon. Maybe it was just as well!

"Let's hurry to the Methodist Church," said Tevita.

I couldn't imagine why the urgency: I had two lots of communion already and couldn't take more of that. "We are going to see Her Majesty Queen Salote," the youngster said breathlessly. "She will be coming out of the Methodist Church and will be walking towards her palace."

With that we rushed ahead and sure enough saw the queen leaving her church with her family and walking slowly towards the Royal Palace. She did look the part and was quite magnificent. A tall and very beautiful woman she was in fact one of the tallest women I had ever seen. She towered over everyone as she walked gracefully towards her palace, smiling and waving at the crowds as she did so.

Walking on to Moala's I felt that I wasn't in the mood for dinner. The image of those piglets being clubbed to death weighed heavily on my mind. A beer or two suited me far better. Unfortunately the club was closed; no alcohol is served on Sundays in Tonga.

David later joined us and was looking much better as we gathered to eat although I grimaced at seeing the flesh of the two piglets and after grace was said we tucked in. I watched in silence as everyone enjoyed their meal. I selected instead sweet potatoes and fish cooked in coconut milk and finished on freshly cut watermelon. Afterwards David and I went for a walk. He was now fit enough to jog, shadow box and carry out light exercises and on our way back we swam in the ocean before taking an afternoon nap.

That evening after dinner David and I strolled towards the church and again bumped into Robert, Ruth and Claire. Benedictine out of the way Robert asked if we would like a beer at their villa. That was something we couldn't pass up. As we turned right at the Royal Palace and reached the promenade I told them the horror story about the piglets: "It puts me off suckling pigs," said Claire; Ruth was quick in agreeing.

After ten minutes drive in which we passed many elegant homes we arrived at their detached villa. It was surrounded by tropical vegetation and was clearly silhouetted by the moonlight. Parking the car beneath a giant breadfruit tree I stepped out and opened the doors for the two ladies. We then took the moment to appreciate our surroundings. The moon could hardly have been more resplendent; its reflection silvered the ocean as far as the horizon and the soft sound of the surf breaking was hauntingly beautiful; an imagery one never forgets.

We told them how fortunate they were but I guess they knew that. As we stepped inside the hallway we could see a delightful oil painting of Claire. There were several more of Robert and a few of the Tongan Queen Salote. He sure had had good taste and connections. Pausing at each one I muttered: "They are so beautiful and such a true likeness of the subjects."

It was then that we learned that Ruth was the artist. One respects such talent when visiting art galleries but seeing that standard of painting in a private home and meeting the actual artist was a privilege indeed. Robert smiled: "We studied art at Leeds University but I leave the painting to Ruth nowadays."

His wife opened the beer, handed them to us and had clearly overheard me complimenting her paintings. She thanked me for my kindness as we walked through to the lounge. I was impressed and showed it. I asked if Queen Salote had visited and sat here for the portrait.

Ruth smiled. "No, she didn't sit here. Every so often I would be summoned to the palace and I would proceed from there."

"It sounds thrilling. You must have felt very honoured."

"She is a very beautiful person, sweet natured and intelligent. It isn't at all surprising that she is very popular. It was a pleasure for me too; she is very graceful and good company."

Changing the subject Robert began to chat about our reason for visiting Tonga and again mentioned that he might be officiating; it would be him or a Mr Moulder, a police inspector. As the conversation swung to David my eyes were glued on mother and daughter; they were both stunningly beautiful. Robert got my attention back again: "So this is just a port of call on your travels! What are your plans for after the bout?"

"There are three events arranged; two here in Nuku'alofa and then there is one on the island of Va'vau. After that we travel to Samoa and possibly New Zealand and England."

"New Zealand? We are from Auckland," Claire said brightly to which her mother added that they were all native Auckland citizens having been born there.

"If you chaps do go to New Zealand then you must let me know," said Robert. "I have a friend at New Zealand's consulate and he'll help you to obtain a visa."

We thanked him profusely; you don't often get an offer like that. As we thanked him he turned to his wife: "Show Jamie and David your studio, Ruth," He was obviously very proud of her accomplishments.

We two followed Ruth and Claire into a large lean-to attached to the rear of their home. I was the first in and we were both taken aback to see oil paintings of locals lining the walls of her studio. "All these are soon to be shipped to Auckland," the artist explained. "My father has an art shop on Queen Street."

To say we two were impressed would be an understatement and for once I felt that my compliments fell short of expressing my genuine pleasure on seeing such skill. As I moved from painting to painting Claire walked close beside me and she was enjoying herself as much as I was for she was seemingly as attracted to me as I was to her. There was chemistry between us. Like her mother, who she obviously took after, the teenager was tall and slim with long jet-black hair and light brown eyes. She would have made the perfect glossy magazine model. Our hands brushed momentarily and it was no accident that they did so.

I found the fragrance of the women's perfume intoxicating. I had never encountered it before. Afterwards returning to the lounge for another beer Robert took us back to Moala's Place. As soon as we stepped inside the restaurant we could see the family gathered around a table that was bending under the weight of the food placed on it. As always they were all eating and talking in loud voices and desperate to know where we had been. We told them and they chorused that they knew the palangi family. "We saw you in Robert's car and guessed you were going to their home."

"Palangi? What does palangi mean?" I asked.

"In our language it means white European. Did you see Claire?"

Stop chattering so much," laughed Mrs Moala. "Do take a seat and have supper with us. You must both have lots of meat and oysters every day to keep you strong and fit for the fight."

We two ate grudgingly and after the long tiring day were not the best of guests. After the traditional hot chocolate drink I made the first move by bidding them all goodnight. Alone in the privacy of my room I stripped off and after wrapping a sulu around my waist went to the well to clean my teeth and shower.

Not long afterwards, as I was lying on my bed, I heard someone placing records on the radiogram and this was followed by light footsteps approaching my room. Tilting my head I could see Monica's smiling face looking in at me. Without invitation she sat on the edge of my bed and placed a kiss full on my lips. "I missed you, Jamie. Did you know that? I bet you did not," she pouted. "I thought about you all the time when you weren't here."

The thought of returning her kisses didn't appeal to me very much. The taste of pork repulsed me and it was in the middle of that dilemma that her sister Isabel came in. Flinging her arms around my neck she kissed me too. When they heard their parents down the hallways they both rushed out to clean their teeth; shower and rub oil into their skins.

My thoughts instead turned to Claire. I guessed her to be maybe sixteen years old. Her mother Ruth would have been in her early thirties. It was remarkable how talented and attractive she really was. I couldn't help but wonder if Ruth might be planning for David or me to sit for her. She had seemed to be sizing us both up.

The next morning following our morning jog along the roads and beaches, and with breakfast behind us both, we walked with Monica and Isabel to their car. Again I was taken aback at their displays of affection; both flung their arms around us and kissed us both on the lips before climbing into the car to drive to their university. As so often my thoughts had been elsewhere and I was going to protest but thought better of it. Back in the restaurant David had a fit of giggles at the thought of us being ambushed by the two girls. He pulled my leg about the incident. "It's nothing," I laughed; "They are young and having fun with us, that's all."

"Not from where I see it, Jamie. You're going to have your work cut out fending those two off."

"David," I said earnestly: "We can't get involved. They might well be two beautiful babes but we are here to fight, earn some money and move on."

"You have Susan on your mind don't you. It's bothering you?"

I told him that it was true; I was still gutted by her unexpected departure and I didn't expect my feelings to change. I repeated my intention of making a comfortable living and returning for her. She was the only one I truly loved and I knew that getting over her would never be possible.

"Don't be a Saint James, Jamie. You were humping Nirmala not long after splitting with Susan and you got her, your landlord's wife pregnant. Just enjoy yourself when the opportunity arises. If you don't I bloody well will. Those two sisters are gagging for it."

"Have you forgotten, David? They both have boyfriends in the States; future husbands. Oh what's the point of talking: I'll tell them that you fancy them and perhaps they'll turn their attention on you, they did kiss you as well?"

"Yes, they did kiss me only because I was standing next to you but I think, Jamie, their hearts and much else is set on you. Nothing changes; you could always pull the girls better than I could. I wish I had whatever it is. Why did Susan fall for you and not me or for that matter the other boys at St Mary's?"

"Leave it alone, David. Maybe it'll be your turn to be raped tonight." As I spoke Mr. Moala stepped in with The Times of Tonga newspaper in his hand. I could see our names and photographs but couldn't make head nor tail at what was written about us. I was still gazing at my name on the boxing advert when Pau walked in. He went to shake David's hand but my friend refused.

"I'm here to beat you, retain my title and move on. I'm going to knock you out. Do you understand?"

Pau just smiled; said maloleilei and turning on his heel left the room. We chatted until lunch after which we rested for a few hours before strolling to the boxing club for training. A small crowd gathered outside peeped from the slats in between the timber walls of the clap down building. As we completed training and stepped from the gym we were greeted by several schoolgirls. Judging from their uniforms some were from the convent and others from the Methodist and Mormons schools. David and I shook hands with some of them and I looked around to see if Claire was there. I spotted her standing next to a bicycle that was lying on the ground. As I did so I caught her smile and soon joined her.

"Hey Claire! Good to see you again."

"Hello Jamie! I guessed you and David would be training and brought some of my friends to meet you both."

I glanced across at the group of giggling schoolgirls and turned my attention to Claire again. I asked her if I could ride with her back to her home. She smiled and thought it was a brilliant idea. Handing my boxing kit-bag to David to take back to Moala's I smiled as he shook his head in exasperation and walked off. Picking up the bike I positioned Claire on its cross bar and set off. "This is my father's bike; he sometimes lets me use it."

"I am glad it isn't a ladies bike," I laughed as we jauntily wobbled along the dusty highway. "Otherwise I might have had to run alongside you."

She threw her head back and laughed at the thought of my doing so as my thoughts returned to Vatukola where so often Sara and I had shared a bike ride just like this one. In a reflective mood I couldn't help but wonder at how her love affair with my friend Biren was coming along.

"You've gone very quiet, Jamie. Why aren't you talking to me?"

"I was just admiring the ocean, perhaps we could stop at the beach," I laughed as my thoughts returned to the present: "That was what I was thinking of unless of course you have to be home early?"

She told me that she wasn't expected home before sunset which was still a couple of hours off, and so we continued to a secluded inlet at the nearby beach. As I lay the bike down on the sand at the water's edge we slipped our shoes off and began to paddle in the shallow wavelets as they gently rolled up the white sands. Claire reminded me very much of Susan. It must have been her demeanour because Claire was a brunette whilst Susan is a blonde. In appearance they weren't that alike; again, Claire was slim and tall. Susan too was slim but petite and not so tall.

I couldn't take my eyes off the classical beauty that Claire symbolised. The tropical sunshine had turned her fair skin into a golden suntan and strands of her jet black were turning blonde; the epitome of womanhood at its most nubile perfection. After standing there mesmerised and staring at her for a few minutes I eventually took her hand and on impulse I kissed it. My flirtatious move was unexpected and perhaps premature but her expression told me it wasn't unwelcome. Her lips parted in anticipation and taking her in my arms we kissed longingly and passionately, each giving as good as we got.

As we broke our embrace I was conscious of the need to refresh myself after the gym workout so pulling my tee-shirt over my head I dived into the water and then spun to watch Claire as she readied herself to join me: "Mind your school uniform," I called from the depth of the water.

"I have others."

After swimming towards me our bodies touched again and this time our kisses were again extremely passionate, lingering and sweet; we were exploring with feeling and pushing boundaries. "I was longing for that," I said gently as I came up for air.

"Me too."

"The swim or the kissing?"

"The kissing, silly."

I told her the feelings were mutual as we languished in the waist deep waters of the lagoon. "They're Japanese trawlers fishing for tuna," she said as she saw me looking towards the distant fishing boats. The sun was setting before we mounted the bike again to complete the ride to her home.

"I am glad you found me, Jamie," she said, her voice floating on the zephyr-like breeze as we ambled happily along the dusty lane towards her home. "I had been thinking how nice it would be if a tall dark stranger could come and find me here."

"You must have a boyfriend, Claire? You are very beautiful and irresistible."

She turned her head back towards me and smiled shyly: "No, I do not have a boy friend, Jamie. You're the very first. There isn't a lot of choice here. There are lots of very handsome young boys but none I fancy. Anyway, the Tongan young men are very nice and friendly but too big and fat. I'll never be able to wrap my arms around one of them." She began to giggle before she spoke. "Have you seen them?"

I shrugged and asked her how long she had lived in Tonga.

"We came here five years ago; I was getting on for eleven back then. Mum and dad hadn't originally thought about staying here but mum loved it; it suited her painting ambitions. It definitely was a good idea cause she sends them to my grandfather; who has an Art Gallery in Auckland and he can get good prices for them. Then dad got a job offer he couldn't refuse. They needed an advisor for the tourist department. Tourism is really taking off here. Sometimes I travel around the islands with him to seek out new travel destinations but when I finish at the convent next year I hope to go to university in Auckland."

"Your parents will remain in Tonga?"

"No. Their plan is to tour other South Sea Islands."

"Are there many Europeans here; I mean young European, men?"

She laughed broadly. "No. Not at all! This is God's waiting room. There are many here who are retired; it is an elderly population mostly. All they want to do is talk about the past when all I want to do is talk about the future.

Not sure of my reception at the villa in the company of their daughter I decided to drop Claire off short of her home and walk back to Moala's but as I turned to go she persuaded me to come with her and say hello to her parents. She told me they had taken a liking to me so there wouldn't be a problem. I didn't share her confidence. I was dripping wet still and she looked bedraggled. I decided to stay outside on the porch but they both came out to greet me, her father bringing a beer with him.

On the way back I fell to thinking about where I might entertain Claire on our first date. There wasn't much for young people to do in Tonga. At least Suva had pubs and clubs to go to, here there was nothing. No wonder they flock to the churches for a sing-along and a bit of socialising with other likeminded people. Fortunately my days were more or less full that brought intensive training, jogging and walking with David. We were planning our fights and looking beyond them to pastures new. I was also aware that I was beginning to fall in love with Claire; our affections ran deep and again she reminded me of the substance of the love Susan and I had for each other. Because of this I didn't feel as though I were betraying my first love.

As days went by I met Clair daily after each afternoon's workout at the gym. We cycled to the beach and swam in the ocean, having a beer with Robert and Ruth before returning to Moala's for dinner and bed. Overnight David and I had become celebrities. We had already been told that the Crown Prince of Tonga, His Royal Highness Prince Sia'osi Taufa would be at a ringside seat on the big night. There was to be a highly level of security at the event. This was not so much to protect the prince as to prevent gatecrashers from getting in.

RETURNED TO DEVIL'S ISLAND

Suddenly fight afternoon had arrived and David and I followed our manager on foot to the rugby ground that was now partitioned with bamboo walls and a boxing ring set in the centre. Inside there were already about 2,000 spectators sitting cross-legged on the grass enjoying the preliminary bouts. I was wearing black shorts with white stripes and black ankle length boxing boots. David wore navy blue shorts, white socks and black boxing boots. We listened carefully to Mr Moala's preparatory talk:

"As you climb into the ring, look to your left. You can't miss his Royal Highness. That is where the prince will be sat. You must remember to bow your heads in his direction before climbing into the ring. Do the same when you are leaving it. We jogged on the spot. We were both impatient for the action to begin. After the fourth preliminary contest, followed by a supporting bout between George Mahoney and Sacopo Kete for the vacant heavyweight championship of Tonga, Mr Moala came running to fetch me.

As I entered the ring I bowed to the Crown Prince and smiled. I then glanced over at Robert who was the night's referee and a smiled curled my lips as I made my way to my corner. Looking around nervously I could see Claire and her mother sitting cross-legged on the grass in the company of a small group of girl students. Sat just behind them were Monica, Isabel and Tevita. I smiled in their direction too as I rubbed the soles of my boots into a tray of grit to stop me slipping during the contest. A few minutes later I saw Jimson Luis enter the ring and bow towards the Crown Prince. He looked cocky and was grinning from ear to ear. Clearly he thought he had the fight in the bag.

After the usual pre-fight instructions, a mantra we had heard many times before, we waited for the bell to clang. Suddenly, the crowd began to cheer and the voices of Claire and Ruth rang loud and clear in my ears. As the bell sounded I stepped forward, touched the gloves of my opponent with my own and tested the water by jabbing him in the face with fast left jabs.

He was strong but short for a Tongan. I took full advantage of this by jabbing and keeping my distance. Moving light-footed around the ring I began to box with stinging quick punches to his head and body. I had already decided that I was going to win this one. There was no way I was going to lose and return to Fiji beaten. I needed the win for the next leg of my journey to New Zealand and finally to England. I went after Jimson Luis; I was playing cat and mouse and setting his head up for the killer punch. If I didn't win this fight I was not going to secure a fight with the champion and with it the chance of winning the title.

By the fourth round my opponent wasn't quite as confident; in fact he was looking unsure of himself and his skill was less measured. He was no longer fighting; he was now defending himself as he tried to put off the inevitable and maybe win on points; salvage something from what I already knew was to be a debacle, for him.

Not that I was feeling much better. I was totally fatigued and hoping it wouldn't be too obvious. I was starting to regret burning the candle at both ends recently. I remembered what my trainer in Fiji used to tell me: "You have a heavy punch Jamie, don't box him, better to fight him."

During round five I went after him. I was determined to finish him. I had little choice and as we stood toe to toe trading punches I got lucky; I caught him with a heavy right cross to the jaw. Jimson slumped to the canvas and I sensed victory. Robert counted to ten and the fighter remained on the canvas as the referee raised my arm. I was excited but not so much as to forget protocol. Turning, I bowed towards his Royal Highness and then towards the frenzied crowd before leaving for my dressing room.

Mr. Moala was already leading David to the ring and so I quickly dressed and rushed back to the ringside to give my support to my friend. It was then that the public address system burst into life:

"Your Royal Highness; my lords, ladies and gentleman! We now come to the main event of the afternoon. This is for the middleweight championship of the South Sea Islands. In the red corner weighing 72 kg and wearing red trunks is the challenger the middleweight champion of Tonga Manoca Pau. He waited for a pause before he began the announcement. 'In the blue corner weighing 69 kg and wearing blue trunks is the middleweight champion of the South Seas David Raja Singh from Fiji. The contest is for fifteen three minute rounds. Your referee is Mr. Robert Taylor of New Zealand."

The announcer then left the ring to the referee and the two combatants. Robert called the two boxers in the centre of the ring and gave instructions. After touching gloves the two boxers stepped back in their corners and waited. As the bell clanged David began to jab but kept his distance from Pau's heavier punches. His adversary tried to draw closer but David's short sharp jabs kept him at arm's length and as round one ended I put David ahead on points.

The first round set the pattern for the following six rounds. David's superior boxing technique kept him ahead on points but by the end of the twelfth round he wasn't looking too good. He was being worn down and set up. The Tongan crowd was baying for blood, David's blood.

A group of local Indians and our own small group were cheering David on whilst I watched grimly and in silence. Pau is now cutting through David's jabs and clearly he has the upper hand. He is choosing where and when to strike David. It was clear that victory was going to be his and finally Mr Moala threw in the towel and the fight was stopped. As Robert lifted Pau's arm David stormed towards the referee to give him a tongue lashing. "What the fuck was that for? I was ahead on points and was going to knock him out soon." Ripping his gloves off he pointed a jabbing finger at Mr. Moala. "This is because he is bloody Tongan."

I tried to calm David but he told me to fuck off and stormed out from the ring. He was as disinclined to listen when we joined him in the dressing room but he wouldn't listen to sweet reason. He took it all very badly. I followed him back to our rooms and looked bleakly on as he stuffed his belongings into his suitcase and stormed out. My promises to train with him and get a re-match had no effect on him. He told me he was taking the first boat back to Fiji.

RETURNED TO DEVIL'S ISLAND

I reminded him of our future plans and that they had included the both of us; that this was a heat of the moment thing. He wasn't having any of it. He just told me he would see me in England one day. He added that he wouldn't let those Tongan bastards get away with it. It was sad to see him go as he dejectedly disappeared and made his way to the wharf and the ferry boats.

We had experienced so much as friends that had begun so long ago at St. Mary's. How could he just walk away from all we had planned after a brief feeling of injustice? There will always be fights in which the result is contested hotly. I determined to carry on, train even harder so as to by necessity win my next two fights and continue on my quest with or without my best friend. I was still bemused when Monica and Isabel arrived home. They kissed and congratulated me for winning my fight. I told them about David and we were soon joined by Mr and Mrs Moala. They chatted excitedly in Tongan but the only thing that registered with me was David's name cropping up several times.

They were disappointed at David's departure but they tried not to show it. Mr. Moala told me to cheer up and let it be known that we were off to the Village of the Bats for a relaxing weekend. As the two daughters and Tavita dashed off to prepare my thoughts were on Claire. I told Mr Moala thanks but no thanks; I had a lot of catching up to do; letter writing and to chill out after what had been my biggest fight so far. I was now the official challenger for Pau's title. It was my only chance to fight him and revenge David's defeat. Mr. Moala was disappointed he really wanted me to go with them to the village of the bats but he understood.

I was resting on my bed when Monica came in and kissed me again. "You have to come, Jamie. Our stepmothers have arranged a feast in your honour. You are the star of the show. All father's boxers go there after their fights. Please Jamie, come on get up."

She tried to pull me out of my bed but I was stubborn and cursing me in Tongan she left the room. As soon as she had done so I dressed and set off at a jog to Claire's home. On arriving I could see her wistfully sitting on the steps of the porch with her chin resting in her hands and gazing vacantly at the beach. As soon as she saw me she lit up and rushed towards me. I was glad of my decision not to go to the Village of the Bats. Placing her arms around my neck and kissing me, Claire whispered sweet nothings about her pride in me for winning the fight. I sure knew I had made the right decision.

"Congratulations, but Jamie, I was so nervous watching you box. I must have said a dozen Hail Mary's for you to win."

I laughed and told her that her prayers had been answered and I added with meaning that my prayers had been answered too. I told her we could do as we wished as training was off for the following three days. It was then that I saw Robert and Ruth on the porch and went over to join them. After congratulating me they suggested we celebrate with a clubhouse drink. Robert drove us to the clubhouse and parked on the road outside. Once inside the club I was immediately surrounded by well wishers, one of whom introduced himself as Daniel Forester. Handing me his business card he suggested that I call and visit him soon. I looked at his card and was amazed to see his home address.

"You are from Tahiti?"

"Papeete," he smiled. "It is the capital. Do come if you can make it. I think you would find it well worth your while". His broad smile was followed by a knowing wink. I was intrigued and kept him in sight. He was clearly in good spirits as he asked the barmen for the best champagne of the house.

"Where's David?" Forester asked. "I had him ahead on points when the towel was thrown in."

Robert was in agreement: "The same for me too but his legs were letting him down and I could understand when Moala threw in the towel. He wasn't going to give him much longer before he stopped the fight. I told them about the horrendous trip to their island but in truth David had plenty of time to recover. I didn't mention his returning to Fiji. What would have been the point?

After Forester departed he again invited me to visit him. Robert explained to me that Daniel was a successful entrepreneur who commuted regularly between Tonga, Samoa and Tahiti. I was also told that Radio New Zealand had reported that my Tongan boxer friends, Kitone Lave and Johnny Halafifi had won their fights in New Zealand and were now on their way back to London. Lave was now nicknamed 'The Tongan Torpedo' cause he was knocking out his opponents left right and centre. Their success concentrated my thoughts. I hoped to follow in their footsteps soon.

As we later headed for the car I could hear Claire asking if instead of joining her mother and father if it would be alright if we two strolled for awhile. Her parents didn't have a problem with it. I certainly didn't. All we got was a reminder not to be late for dinner.

Dusk was just setting in as we headed for Moala's Place and when finally we arrived I let us both in and turned on the lights before taking Claire into my arms. Tonight we had the place to ourselves; the family having gone to the Village of the Bats. Carefully choosing what I thought were records she would like I stacked them on the turntable and locked the main door behind us. Then, picking her up in my arms I carried her to my bed and lay her down before joining her. It was her first time and my thoughts went to Nirmala's book of love and her motherly advice. This time I spread my towel over my bed to take precaution. What seemed like eternity of cuddling and kissing, we finally made love. She afterwards told me that she knew our lovemaking had been inevitable from the first moments she had set eyes on me. It was an opportunity for me to tell her that I had felt the exact same way, ever since we had kissed each other on the beach. We kissed for a few seconds before I helped her to dress. It was a long tiring walk to her home but of regrets I had none. As we did so she told me she was in some discomfit and asked if she would be alright. I reassured her but how could I know? She then wanted to know why there weren't any doors in rooms where I was living.

"I don't know. It's a family house I suppose and there weren't any doors where I was living back in Fiji."

"Do Monica and Isabel come to your room?"

"No, I go to bed long before they do and anyway they both have boyfriends."

"It must be very lonely for you?"

I told her it was but I passed the time one way or another. I went on to tell her that I passed the night more pleasantly by thinking of her. Tonight had made that something to better look forward to. We kissed long and hard as we walked and then whiled away a few precious minutes deep in our own thoughts on the moonlit beach before I finally walked with her to her front door. Ruth insisted that I must have dinner with them. It wasn't difficult to be persuaded though I felt a little shamefaced at having so recently seduced their daughter.

"When is the next fight, Jamie?" Ruth asked as she prepared a light snack. I told her it would be soon. "It is to take place at the same rugby ground and afterwards we go to the island of Vav'au. Do you know anything about Vav'au, Robert?"

Claire's father settled back into his seat: "The Governor is a good friend of mine. A man called Simon Broomfield."

When I asked if he was English he replied: "No, he is a Tongan with an English name. He was at the fight today. He was sitting behind the Prince. I would like you to meet him before he returns home. There is a chance I might be asked to referee over there. If I am we can travel together."

"Are they as religious as they are here in Nuku'alofa?"

"Very much so but they are more Wesleyan than Methodist. The Mormons are just settling in over there."

"Wesleyans?" I could hardly keep up with these different Christian religions. Why so many I thought.

"The story goes that the first Christian missionaries to arrive here in Tonga were the Wesleyans about a hundred years or so ago. The advance party were two Englishmen; David Cargill and William Cross."

"I remember the names; someone once mentioned them while I was at school. I believe they were in Fiji as well."

Claire and Ruth joined me on the settee. As I looked at both and more especially Claire I could never have imagined that I would ever have the chance to love someone so young and so beautiful.

"Va'vau was their first home but after converting the islanders they went to Fiji well before the Reverend Thomas Baker did."

I told them I knew the Baker story.

"What happened in Fiji?" This time the question came from Claire.

"When the two missionaries arrived in Fiji they were accompanied by their wives. The natives thought that they were gods as no one had ever seen white faces before. The Fijians were naturally apprehensive. Cross and Cargill tried to convert the natives to Christianity and attempted to stop cannibalism. Why shouldn't they? Encouraged by their success in Tonga they had decided to try their luck in Fiji. At first they had a great conversion rate on an island called Lakeba. They then moved to the larger island of Viti Levu and set up camp close to the island of Bau."

"Bau?"

"Do you know Bau?" Robert asked: I told him that one of my friend's mothers had come from the notorious island and had told us horror stories about her ancestors.

Our host continued: "Cargill reported that one day, as he entered a village to preach, he saw blood soak corpses of men, women and children carried into the village where they were presented to the High Chiefs as presents. Cargill noticed that grass huts were decorated by human bones and skulls. He was appalled but to have interfered would have been suicidal as there was a feast being prepared.

Clutching his bible with both hands he ran to his home and on the way there saw bodies of children being mutilated. He was still running for his life as the death drums were booming around him. Eventually, he made it to the safety to his own hut. The next morning he found heads, hands, feet and other human remains outside his home, presumably as a gift but who knows; a threat?.

Together with his wife and two small children Cargill was living in primitive conditions with no sanitation or tap water. A few weeks after that awful incident the family were to become ill. First the two children died and then his wife died also. He buried them in the fields nearby and wandered about from there on; he was a lonely and thoroughly dispirited man. New missionaries in the meantime had arrived and helped the Reverend Cargill to return to England. Later, when he was returned to good health he re-married and caught a ship back here to Va'vau again.

Ruth and Claire were fascinated by the account of the missionaries and their families as in terms of generation these things had happened not so long ago. "Then what happened?" asked Ruth.

"He lived here on the island with his new wife but he was still a shadow of the bible thumping evangelist who had once determined on Christianising the islands. He eventually took his own life by drinking laudanum. He is buried on the island.

"And the new missionaries who landed in Fiji?" The question came from me.

"A Reverend Calvert and Reverend Lyth took over where Cargill and Cross had left off. The two were visiting remote villages and spreading the word of Christ. They had as usual left their wives alone in the mission house. When told that fourteen girls were to be put to death in a nearby village the two white ladies raced to Bau in canoes where the death drums were already throbbing. This meant the rape and slaughter of the youngsters had already begun. As soon as these two missionaries' wives reached the Bau house of worship they stormed into the sacred temple. This place was taboo; it was the one place in which no female had ever dared to set foot. Stunned by their sudden appearance the High Chiefs halted the rape and slaughter. Unfortunately they were a little too late for some of the unfortunate kids; nine of the girls had already been raped and killed and their bodies were lying there, ready to be dissected before being cooked and eaten. The white ladies of the cloth managed to free five women and take them back to their home where they nursed them to health and kept them as housemaids.

After listening to Robert's story we were stunned into silence. "How bloody awful," said Ruth? Claire didn't speak but looked towards me. Our eyes met and it felt like a sharp object had just pierced my heart. The momentary silence was broken by Robert asking if I would like another beer. I thought why not, it is Sunday tomorrow.

"You'll be going to mass," asked Ruth.

I had to think about that one. Mass means confession and Father Francis would wonder why if I missed. I had been guided by nature and instinct when taking Claire's innocence; now I had my conscience and spiritual side of my life to consider. It seemed everything has a price. I told Ruth I would be there but I didn't add I would prefer being elsewhere.

By that time the night was getting late and I was now beginning to ache from the earlier punishing bout in the ring. Ruth wouldn't hear of me going back to the empty house so I was happy enough to take up the kind offer. It was difficult trying to get to sleep after my shower; I was painfully aware of Claire lying possibly awake as I was in the adjacent bedroom. I think thought transference must have been working for the both of us; I was soon pleasantly surprised by her warm nakedness as she silently slipped under the sheet to join me.

Just after dawn I awoke her and as soon as she slipped back into her own bedroom I dressed and made my way to Moala's for a shower and change for there were matters ecclesiastical to deal with. Father Francis took my confession, fabricated sins taking the place of less tenuous ones. I did feel guilty about this additional sin but at the same time I wondered why I bothered with the Catholic Church at all. It seemed to me that it was pretty pointless given the life I was leading and the sins I was committing. I didn't believe in it but somewhere inside there was a thin spiritual strand holding me to the faith. Only time would tell if the strand would snap; the faith had already guided me and seemingly was reluctant to let this lamb go.

After mass I met up with Claire first and then met up with her family. She looked so pretty in her white dress; I longed to take her in my arms but that would hardly have been the done thing so we both resisted the temptation and stuck with convention. Her parents were soon beside us. "Goodness, you left early this morning," Ruth said with concern in her voice.

"Yes, I hope I didn't disturb you both. I needed to get back and shower, change for church."

"Are the Moala family back then?"

I told them they weren't. Claire smiled deviously as Ruth invited me to dinner. "No squealing pigs, I promise." We all laughed. I asked if Claire and I could go to the beach first, to which they were perfectly in agreement. When we finally arrived for dinner Robert was already uncorking the wine and the meal that followed was one of the most delicious I had ever experienced. I certainly seemed to have discovered my idyll and could only hope the rest of my life was as fortunate. Once I was alone with

Claire it was then the question was popped with: "Mother wishes to paint your picture you know, Jamie?"

I looked surprised and was pleased at the invitation: "She does?"

"She thinks your physique and good bone structure ideal; in fact she thinks you're an artist's dream subject."

I was pleasantly intrigued and must admit it gave my ego a boost. The thought of being painted by such an attractive woman excited me and I asked Claire if she would be there too as the painting progressed. She told me she could pop in from time to time but added that her mum likes to be left alone when painting. "By the way," she added: "My birthday is on Thursday. I have invited friends over. They want to know if you are coming."

"From school and all sweet sixteen no doubt," I laughed with a raised eyebrow. "Huh? I don't think so."

Claire ignored my light-hearted jibe that they were younger than they claimed but I pressed the point home. "You said you were nearly eleven years old when you arrived here, five years ago. That means you'll be sixteen yes?"

She grinned impishly and she made a mock salute: "Yes, sir!"

Later strolling the length of the beach we held hands and occasionally pausing to kiss we mingled with others likeminded. My thoughts as always were confused. I was one minute thinking of Susan and what I saw was her predicament; the next I was absorbed by Claire's youth, charm, personality and incredible beauty.

A little later when back at my temporary home there was still no sign of the Moala's. I undressed and from the comfort of my bed listened to the radio. I could still breathe in the essence of Claire's perfume even in her absence. The silence was broken by the sound of Monica's car pulling up outside. Pulling my shorts on I looked outside and was surprised to see just the two girls and no sign of their parents.

Greeting them both I asked where the others were; their small brother wasn't with them either. "Would you believe it, Jamie? They have decided to stay there an extra few days." Said Monica.

Both girls had knowing smiles on their pretty faces. This should have told me all I needed to know or rather, didn't want to know. "They thought you might need this."

Taking the bundle of banknotes from Monica I flipped through them to discover I was richer by a respectable £150 Tongan pounds. "It is your share of the purse."

My fare to New Zealand was seventy pounds and this would be more than enough to cover other expenses. Feeling pleased with myself I placed the cash in my suitcase and lay on my bed. The girls were full of themselves; singing, laughing and teasing each other as they showered and rubbed the ever-present oils into their soft brown skins.

I might have expected it and I suppose I half did so; the girls then entered my room and pounced on me. I found it unnerving and laughed like a nervous idiot. Both teenagers were in the highest of spirits and quite unfazed by their own nakedness and mine. We play wrestled together and in no time at all nature took its course after which we relaxed and sat around enjoying the freedom and intimacy of the adult free atmosphere. Both girls were jealous of my liaisons with Claire for my dating her was now common knowledge. I was full of remorse having given in to their demands and thought of Clair and my dearest Susan.

"I don't know why you bother with that white bitch," said a clearly disgruntled Monica. "We can have a lots of fun together and why don't we get married and be like this all the time?"

"Mother and father would love us to marry," added Isabel who was warming to the theme. In my innocence I was caught off guard: "Me getting married! Which one of you," I grinned good naturedly. I couldn't be sure if they were serious or not.

The two girls rolled their eyes as thought to say, heaven help us. "Both of us, Jamie; you could marry the both of us. Where's your problem with that?"

"Where is the problem with that? You both have boyfriends in the United States who think you are going to marry them. How is that for just one problem?"

"Oh fuck them; they can both go to hell. We're not interested in them anymore are we Monica? We both like you and we can make you very happy here in Tonga."

"You seem to have forgotten something," I smiled: I am just travelling on, passing through. You know I have to travel on to New Zealand and then England."

There was a pause and a puzzled frown on each of their adorable faces as their minds debated the dilemma: "You really do love that white bitch, don't you?" Monica said gloomily. I could see her whimsical smile was genuine.

There seemed to be little point in beating about the bush: "I am in love with Claire if that is who you mean."

"Okay," she flounced with a shrug of dismissal: "There's no problem with that. Here's the deal. You can marry the three of us. Father has three wives too so it isn't an issue. We can live with it and so can you and that way you get three girls and you can take your choice whenever you want."

Isabel was thoughtful and perhaps bearing in mind the relationship we now had asked if I was as intimately involved with Claire. "I suppose you are. Otherwise you couldn't be in love with her could you?"

I had to think quickly to try and keep some sort of balance. I reasoned that the best way was to lie my way out of the fix. I was cute enough to know a strategy of entrapment and commitment. The last thing I needed was acceptance of what they had in mind for it isn't easy to do a runner on an island. "No, she is too young and you know it." I lied.

"Bullshit! This is Tonga there and lots of young girls of our age get married here, it's no big deal." She then went on to tell me, as if I was interested, that she and Isabel had been lovemaking since they were fourteen-year olds. It was the way of life in these parts; no one questioned it; couples were often married at that young age.

It was difficult to grasp how these girls could talk in such a matter of fact way about something that was to me so intensely personal. It was as if they were discussing their first solo visits to restaurants or shops.

I didn't have a lot to say but my mind ran riot as I thought of all those sportsmen Moala had managed. Clearly his daughters had managed them pretty well too. I think I had been a little naïve when on arriving on the island and at the Moala's home I had thought they were gaol-bait.

I have very little recollection of my later falling asleep but I knew I had been set up, not just by the girls but by their parents. They fully expected to return to find their two daughters engaged to be married; a boxing champion a member of the family.

* * *

At first light on the Monday morning we heard a commotion on the street and learned that a beached whale had been discovered on the beach near the Royal Palace. As we arrived we could see a gathering crowd around a massive grey whale. The fitter men and the youngsters too were vainly trying to push the massive creature back into the sea but every time we made some progress the passive creature was pushed back up by the incoming surf. Our attempts were proving fruitless.

The police finally arrived and we were ordered to stand back as the officers took aim with their .303 rifles. There was a burst of gunfire and bullets slammed into the mammal's head. As the water around it turned red I felt nauseated by the spectacle and went quickly home. I was told later that Tongans hacked chunks of meat off the corpse and carried it back for their dinner tables.

As soon as the sisters left for college I crept back into bed and slept until noon before making for the clubhouse. I was a bit surprised to find the Tahitian businessman there. I grinned widely: "Mr Forester, it's good to see you again."

"Jamie; hey, cut the shit and call me Dan."

We sat on the barstools and ordered large beers as engagingly he asked me when the next fight was going to be. I said it would take place within the next three weeks and I would be fighting Pau for the middleweight title of the South Sea Islands. I added that I had good reason to look forward to it; I wanted revenge for David's ignominious defeat. I asked Dan if he would be at the encounter.

"Sadly I won't as I have to visit American Samoa but I will be back before I fly out to Tahiti and perhaps see you before I go."

"I will love to see you before you return to Tahiti. I am heading for Va'vau for my last fight, and then on to Samoa and American Samoa," I told him.

He grinned as he lifted the beer to his lips. "You will have to come to Tahiti, Jamie; you'll love it there. I have a hotel on the outskirts called Le Village. I have something in mind for you and I think you are going to like it."

I was happy to run with that but I did remind him that my plans were to carry on to England via New Zealand. "You come to Tahiti, man. You can always fly from there to Auckland but once you're in Tahiti you'll never want to leave I can assure you of that. New Zealand and England don't hold a candle to that place. Ask the people there where they would prefer to be."

"Is it better than Tonga?"

"Tonga? There is nothing in bloody Tonga. Look at this clubhouse, it's a fucking dump. This is Hicksville. You will realise that better when you see my place. Our clients come from all over the world; and they keep coming back for more. And it isn't because my prices are low; they are not."

"By the way," he added: "I have contracts with airline companies whose aircrew use my place. Just wait until you see the air hostesses, my friend. They are breathtakingly lovely. Tahiti didn't get its Island of Love sobriquet without good reason."

"I was told there is a surplus of women. Most of the young guys have gone to the either France or the States to find work."

"You heard right but those air hostesses are so hot you really do need to wear your asbestos gloves when you are handling them. You like the girls don't you, Jamie?"

I shyly smiled and looked at Dan. He looked like the cat that just had the cream. I told him that after Samoa I will try my uttermost to visit him in Tahiti. He told me to go to the Tahitian consulate in Taufa'ahau Road and mention his name. There wouldn't be a visa problem.

I headed back to Moala's for a light lunch and rest before reporting for training. When I arrived other boxers were already in training. Moala wasn't there of course, which was a blessing in disguise. Thanks to his daughters my get up and go had by now got up and gone. A little later I met up with Claire and we cycled to her home. It seemed her mother wanted to see me about something. I had already guessed what it might be and I wasn't wrong. Not long after we had reached her home, Ruth turned to me: "Did Claire tell you that you would make a good subject?" she smiled sweetly as she handed me a coffee.

I told her she had and I felt honoured to be having my portrait painted by the artist responsible for painting also the Tongan queen. She laughed and told me that to any artist whoever was sitting was just a subject. She bucked my spirits up by telling me that my looks and physique as a top sportsman was something the queen could never have. I was thankful for her remarks. I liked the compliment or was she just being subjectively professional?

It was arranged that I would arrive the following morning at 9 o'clock; there was the promise of breakfast, which I think was to ensure I wasn't going to be late. I didn't pay too much attention to the curling smile on her lip but it suggested to me some sort of satisfaction. I was just happy to get the chance to experience something I had never done before.

CHAPTER 5

Monica and Isabel were setting the table for dinner as I walked in and excitedly told me they had good news for me. "You and Pau have been invited to the Royal Palace on Friday; the Crown Prince wants to meet you."

I stared at them. "You are pulling my leg?"

They giggled as they confronted me. "We are not, Jamie! The prince is a boxing enthusiast and he likes to meet all visiting sportsmen and he encourages them to do well. I would have been surprised had he not wanted to meet you," Isabel smiled with self-satisfaction.

My wardrobe left much to be desired; that was going to be a problem. They assured me that I didn't need a suit; smart casual was alright but the essential piece of attire was the raffa mat fastened around my waist, which is traditional. I was also expected to show respect but that went without saying. I did try on Moala's waist mat but it was about four times too big for me. On seeing me the sisters were in hysterics and in the end we settled on Tevita's mat. It fitted my slim waist perfectly.

I was less playful and more anticipatory the next morning as I made my way to Ruth and Robert's home. Posing for a painting was something new to me. I was sociable enough in the company of the family but realised that with Robert at work and Claire in school I was going to be alone with Ruth. Silly though it may sound I felt a little vulnerable being in such intimate surroundings and situation with such an attractive woman. She was also very friendly and tactile.

Unlike me, Ruth was very relaxed but then this was my first time as a sitter but how many had she painted and drawn in her life? Not long after I arrived she casually pointed me in the direction of the studio and told me she would join me shortly; the implication being that I make myself comfortable. The idea was that I pose in my boxing gear and while I was waiting I warmed up with some of the usual exercises. When she did appear she was carrying a jar of coconut oil. She invited me to rub it on myself; it would give my body gleam, she told me. I was also to adopt a classic fighting pose.

I did as she asked and watched as she sauntered over to the easel. The artist was wearing a light top and baggy shorts; perfect for both the climate and the setting. So were her long tanned and bare legs I thought to myself. Could the swaying of her hips have been deliberate I wondered.

Like her daughter Ruth was a superbly proportioned woman. Nervously I licked my dry lips when I saw that she wasn't wearing a bra.

Apart from the age difference she was clearly Claire's mother. Ruth smiled as she sketched and as her right hand dabbed and stroked at the sketch her left hand would occasionally brush back the careless strands of hair as they floated over her high cheekbones.

I tried to move my thoughts to other interests: "That's fine, Jamie," she said. "I need to get this right and you're being a sportsman I need to catch the nuances of your muscular ripple. Can you flex your abdominals for me? I need to paint every curvature of your stomach muscles."

I exhaled and flexed myself for her and held it for several seconds for which I was rewarded with a beer. Taking a break I straddled a stool to take the weight off my legs as the artist offered me a beer. She was standing so close my senses were overwhelmed by the scent of her perfume; was she deliberately provoking me I wondered. "I'll have a taste of that beer," she said with a light laugh as bending over her lips brushed my own shortly after I took a swig of the bottle's contents.

"Tasty, very tasty."

"Me or the beer?" I said impishly with a shy laugh.

"How do both sound?"

I took a chance that I wasn't reading too much into a little light-hearted teasing "Are you really going to complete the picture today? I have to run along, meeting Clair after training."

She smiled sweetly as her finger tips with the long nails stroked a curve across my abdominal muscles. She suddenly grabbed me and began to kiss passionately. Her hands gently peeled my boxer shorts downwards and she pushed me onto the hard chair. Pulling her skimpy clothes off her she straddled my thighs and made love to me in the seated position. I resisted at first but after a while I gripped her in strong arms and gave in to her demands. It was a typical hot day and soon we were drenched in sweat but well and truly satiated before we stopped.

Heck! Was this some sort of competition between mother and daughter I wondered? I was thinking of Robert and was a bit ashamed as the thought of Claire also crossed my mind. Only afterwards and after a little thought did Ruth seem to be reading my mind.

"Nothing to be sorry about, Jamie; it happened, no regrets. I planned this to happen the first time I saw you outside the church.

"Isn't it a bit awkward? You know I am in love with Claire."

"Jamie; a few more weeks and you will be gone out of our lives forever and leaving behind only the memories. This talk of love is bullshit; don't mess with it. Just enjoy the good times when the opportunity arises. Claire will be going to university soon. She's young; she will meet others."

The next hour was spent with Ruth touching up the pictures and as I no longer needed to pose I got dressed; showered and changed. By the time Robert arrived for lunch we were the picture of urban convention, taking tea and looking as fresh as the tropical weather allowed.

The artist hardly looked at me as she kissed her cuckolded husband but gave me a knowing wink as she set the dining table. After lunch I strolled down to Moala's place full of remorse. I thought carefully about her advice too: she was much worldlier than I was and it was true that I was falling in love every five minutes. Maybe I was confusing infatuation or lust with love. I couldn't tell the difference. I decided to take my girlfriend's mothers advice and try not to confuse the two; talking of which, just who was my girlfriend? Was it Claire or was it her mother? Oh well. I had better think of the training that needed doing; maybe I should be thinking more of that.

I wasn't feeling too good about my behaviour that morning and by the time I met Claire after school, she remarked on my being quieter than usual as we shared the bike ride. We were passing a lush green banana plantations. "How did you get on with mum this morning, did you enjoy sitting for her?"

I hesitated for a few seconds before I answered her. "It was a new experience for me but I liked it; your mum's nice; very easy to get on with."

"I am looking forward to seeing the paintings," Claire smiled as the first raindrops splattered around us as we parked the bicycle in the banana vegetation and sought shelter. "There's something about the rain," she said quietly as she leaned into me; my back was against thick foliage.

"It gets your clothes wet?"

The teenager laughed; she had a good sense of humour and she laughed a little more as she pressed herself closer on to me: "I will keep you dry."

My head swam as I felt her hands. They were just like her mother's had felt earlier, tracing their way down my midriff; tickling me to the beat of the raindrops. "It's better here than on the beach," she gasped. The grass was wet so we clumsily made love leaning against the thickness of a banana plant. Well it was Clair making love to me as I was still in a daze and full of remorse.

Dusk was falling as we afterwards made ourselves respectable and headed for her home. As soon as I dropped her off I headed for Moala's Place. After dinner there was the usual shower and a catch up with Isabel and Monica. Nothing else; I think I had enough for one day and I headed out the door hoping to meet Dan at the clubhouse.

The barman told me the business man had been waiting for me but had since caught a flight to Samoa. He wasn't expected back until the Friday evening. The following Wednesday I received letters; one was from my sister Malti and the other from Nirmala.

There was good news from Malti as she had her first baby, a little boy. Mother was well and happy but missing me. Nirmala's letter was a bombshell. As soon as I opened it a photograph of three little boys fell out. I recognised Virendra her adopted son and Surendra my own son but wondered who the other child was. My eyes quickly scanned the letter's scrawled contents. In it I read: "This is your other son Narendra. Before you left for Suva I became pregnant again. I wrote several letters to your address in Suva but they all were returned back to me.

"Little Narendra was born on May 7, 1958. Thank you, Jamie for giving us two lovely and healthy boys. We are grateful to you and will always remember you."

I looked at the black and white photograph and read the letter over and over again. I was feeling emotional. I longed to go back and see them, hold, smell and love them but what good would that do? In law Rajendra and Nirmala were the registered and natural parents. I wasn't even a spectator.

I hid the letters and photographs in my suitcase and walked to Ruth's villa. I wasn't expected but I was welcome all the same. She had a more mature sense of proportion than I did and any expectations of extras were dashed. We sat and chatted awhile and I questioned her Catholicism. She conceded that whilst they went to church she cherry picked the bits of the faith that suited her. She told me that it was largely customary and for appearances sake.

"You go to confession?"

"Jamie, don't be bloody naïve. Of course we do but we don't have to tell the priest everything. You have to use your own discretion what you think is a sin and what is not a sin. "

"But you believe in some of it?"

"You're young and gauche, Jamie. It will pass. Let's not talk about religion."

"I was just wondering if you believed in God."

"No, I do not actually. I used to be a devout Catholic and that summed up the school I went to but after I met Robert at university I began to have my doubts."

I asked her if Robert was a non-believer too. Without answering my question directly she told me they had entered many student debates on theology. It was clear that the peoples of the Third World were devout in their faiths but the West to their own religion paid lip service rather than church service. It was done for appearances or there was an ulterior motive, like opening up trading opportunities.

"Just look around the South Sea Islands," Ruth said. The islands are riddled with bible thumping evangelists, here it is the Mormons. Do you know why, Jamie? Because winning hearts and minds is followed by the church building. This leads to schools being built, then universities and finally entire communities. They are all Mormon. They have captured a colony by the force of the bible rather than through arms. There is more than one way to skin a cat, Jamie. In the West people are sick and tired with religion and the churches are empty so the soul saving missionaries come to the South Sea islands. The Methodists and the Catholics did the same in Fiji. It was open season for missionaries spreading the gospel. They converted all the poor and destitute in these island. People go to church and spend their entire life praying but you know jolly well that prayers don't work. Let me tell you a story," she went on. She was certainly a woman of broad intellect; a university graduate as and when she preferred.

"It is about a young man from Pakistan who attended university with us. Although he was a keen boxer he never won a fight. He prayed five times a day but he still never won a fight. He was pretty useless and even Robert knocked him out. The advice he gave to him was stop praying and start training because prayers do not work Jamie, end of story."

"Robert? He is a boxer?"

"Yes and a bloody good one too."

I laughed at the revelation. Being a referee doesn't necessarily mean you are a practiced player at any sport. "I have a story that is similar, Ruth. It is about a pundit in Fiji. His lifelong ambition was to swim in the holy waters of the Ganges. Learning of his heartfelt wish the people of Fiji collected enough money to pay for his pilgrimage. He got there eventually and he swam daily in the filth of the holy river. It seems his sins were forgiven just as he had fervently wished but he did die of cholera and dysentery as a result of swimming in the filthy river. Yes, I too have doubts about prayers, his prayers did not help him did they?"

The story tickled Ruth who threw back her head and laughed but then getting to her feet she said: "Come on Jamie, we have much work to do."

After an hour of sketching and painting she wanted to know more about me. "All I know about you is what I read about you in the newspaper or hear on the radio."

I told her I was born in Fiji and given the name of Krishna by a Holy Man who predicted I would travel the world and always be surrounded by beautiful young women; a bit similar to the Lord Krishna.

"It didn't need a Holy Man to tell you that," Ruth smiled: "I can tell you that women will find you appealing wherever you go. Claire tells me that the girls at the convent talk salaciously about you; you are a good looking guy with personality; you treat women the right way. You have it made."

I knew where she was coming from but like similar young men, and women too, I had used my appeal to get my own way often. Even so I asked her if that was what she really thought.

"There's so much choice it's hard to concentrate on boxing and training twice a day. I don't have what it takes to box professionally anymore. It is true that I am distracted by the girls. Perhaps I should forget about boxing. It has served its purpose. It has brought me this far.

"You see! That is why you would not be a good long term partner for Claire. All you want to do is sow your oats."

I realised I had said the wrong thing and hesitated before I spoke again. "I didn't mean it that way, Ruth. Maybe the Holy Man was right when he predicted that I will be surrounded by beautiful women, which isn't quite the same."

Ruth reminded me: "As atheists we do not believe in that bullshit, Jamie."

I thought about what she had said: "I have a Hindu back ground and its very confusing what to believe?"

Ruth was a little agitated: "So go out there and surround yourself with women and don't box anymore."

Fortunately the awkwardness was broken by the sound of Robert's car in the driveway. Over a beer I told him that I had been invited to the Royal Palace on the following Friday. I would be personally meeting the Crown Prince. "That sounds like fun. Do you have a crunchy mat to wear around your waist?" Asked Robert.

I explained that I had and it was then they reminded me that I mustn't be expecting a beer there. "They are staunch Methodists and alcohol is really unthinkable. It is best not to even talk about it. Stick to boxing, Jamie."

"To be honest," I said: "I am a bit apprehensive about going and will likely have a few before I go."

"You will spoil the event if you do," Robert warned. "If he smells alcohol on you, and he will, you will be treated very coldly and quickly shown the door. Just act your normal natural self. He doesn't bite. He is genuinely a really nice guy and there is nothing at all pretentious about him."

I was a little cynical about the prince's attitude towards alcohol. Having learned something of English society I suggested that whilst training at Sandhurst he must have had a few recollections of visiting the local hostelries with his fellow cadet officers.

It had been a long day and after lunch I didn't hang around. I needed my sleep. I needed to build my strength for more working out and I hadn't forgotten I was to meet Claire early that evening. I found her to be a little downcast when we were on the beach together. I hoped that she hadn't learned of the small trysts I had enjoyed with her mother. I was barking up the wrong tree. "Jamie," she said quietly. "I feel very sad that soon you will be gone and I will be left alone in Tonga again."

I smiled at her forlorn sincerity. "But, baby; have you forgotten? You will be going to university soon. It's not so much me leaving you as you leaving me."

"It's true," she sighed: "They want me to go but I don't really know what's best for me. I suppose New Zealand will be more fun than Tonga."

In an attempt to brighten her up I told her that her dad had borrowed my passport. "He is sending its details on to a friend at the consulate in Auckland. They're arranging a visa for me. We can meet up there."

She smiled winsomely. "Please promise to look me up as soon as you arrive there?"

I told her I would find her wherever in the world she was which seemed to console her. That day we just held each other tightly as we thought our own thoughts. There was little reason for her to be down unless it was the passage of time and the changes to her life this implied. Her sixteenth birthday was imminent.

Personally I hate shopping and admittedly did so with poor grace. Perhaps it was because the capital city wasn't the best place for anyone to shop, there being so much cheap stuff on display. As I examined a necklace of some yellow metal an Indian shopkeeper reassured me that it looked the part. It was he said a genuine gold string imported from India. How would I know? To me, one yellow metal was much the same as any other. It could have been a brass necklace and the coral plastic for all I knew. I trusted him and bought it for my young conquest. The man was still chuckling to himself as I left his shop. Perhaps I had in my naivety made his day. Such shopkeepers are common elsewhere, Fiji included.

Skipping gym that day I put on blue jeans and the dark red hula-shirt similar to the one Susan had worn when she had come to my bed-sitter in the hurricane. I had a good look at myself in Monica's full-length mirror before strolling to Claire's party. As I approached her villa I could hear the band playing. The door of the villa had been left ajar but I lightly pressed the bell button anyway before pushing the door open. Better that than to take liberties. I think I had taken enough of them already. As I walked down the hallway I came face to face with Ruth. Obviously in high spirits she leaned upwards and pecked me on my cheek as she complimented me on my appearance.

I was enjoying the proffered beer when Claire slipped in; looking out of this world in a flowery sulu that was clinging to her thighs before reaching down to her slim ankles. This was complemented by her white sandals, a chemise top that clung to the contours of her breasts; all of which was set off South Sea Islands style with a hibiscus flower pinned over her right ear.

Embracing her I congratulated her on both her appearance and her birthday as I kissed each of her cheeks. Her perfectly shaped lips curled into a smile. She had obviously paid attention to her appearance and again I complimented her as I presented her with the gift I had bought earlier. The fact that Claire wanted for very little hadn't made the choosing of it any easier.

As luck would have it she was genuinely thrilled and the gift might easily have been an expensive pearly necklace. It meant a lot to her; not the least when tenderly I took it from her and placed it around her slender neck and throat. It was perfect for her. "A real native beauty," I mused.

She smiled broadly. "Yes, my girlfriends are all dressed the same. You must come and meet some of them"

Taking me by the hand the excited sixteen-year old led me out across the expansive patio and into the villa's lush gardens. Smiling, I met each of her friends and as tradition required kissed their cheeks as the trio on the stage strummed their Hawaiian guitars. We watched enchanted as the small circle of maidens swayed to the light airs of traditional hula dancing.

I swallowed hard. The girls were at their most beautiful and in such a setting I might easily have been in paradise itself. Claire's eyes glanced across and caught my own and she smiled sweetly. I was hoping the impression I made on her was similar to the one she made on me. If so, she was very much in love as I was.

As the appreciative audience clapped approvingly the small band began to play Vaya con Dios. It was the most popular song of the islands at that time. Taking Claire in my arms we did a slow dance until we were interrupted by a great deal of humour. This was directed at the lead singer who obviously hadn't learned the lyrics and was mumbling his way through it. He was fortunate that the humour was light-hearted. To his credit he and his band made it to the early hours of the morning without further embarrassment. The dawn was breaking when I bid goodnight to Claire, Ruth, Robert and the other guests. It had been a long day and a short night. I was showing the strain when I turned up at the clubhouse to see if Dan was there as had previously been arranged. He was stopping over on his way to Tahiti.

"Malolelei Jamie!"

"Malolelei, Dan! You had a good trip to Samoa?"

"You could say so," he said with a self-satisfied grin. "We're building a hotel complex on Pago Pago. It's been a bit of a pain getting it through the various stages but the plans have finally been approved. It is good timing. The American's are pouring in like never before and the numbers are predicted to be rising further. Every hotel bed will be pre-booked the way things are going."

"So I know where to find you when I need a job?"

Looking at me thoughtfully he placed his glass on the bar and chose his words carefully. "Please do, Jamie. There'll be a job for you. I know you're as bright as a button and I can rely on you."

"I have applied for my visa for Tahiti and then it is New Zealand for me."

"It will be good to see you there, Jamie. I don't think you will regret your visit and it might just make you think twice about going to New Zealand," he added with a wink.

I smiled and looked at the clock on the wall. "Hey! I have to rush. You would never guess it. I have to be at the Royal Palace; a guest no less and I have to be there at two o'clock or it will be the Tongan Tower for me or worse."

Making my way back to my room I prepared myself for the Royal Palace. I am sure I looked the business in my natty white tropical suit but the girls were in stitches when I started to wrap the crunchy mat around my waist. I wasn't as amused as they obviously were but looked on the bright side of things; there aren't many who get an invitation to meet royalty.

When Pau arrived we took it easy and approaching towards the palace gates I was conscious of my ridiculous attire. It might have been traditional but if ever an outfit was designed to make one look ridiculous this was it. The mat wobbled as I walked, much to the amusement of gawping traders. It was a relief to reach the palace gates without being entangled in my mat and falling over. The massively built palace guard had studied us as we approached; perhaps forewarned of our arrival, and nodded us to one side: "Wait here, someone from the palace is coming to meet you."

Moments later we were met by a boy of perhaps twelve-years of age. As we carried on under his guidance we asked him if he was a royal guard too. He told us that he wasn't but his mother was one of the household's cooks. He told us he was visiting when someone asked him to meet us and take us to the palace library.

Pau and the youngster chatted in their own language before we crossed the lawns and reached the long and narrow veranda fronting the palace. Once there he tapped the wooden floor of the veranda very gently with the palm of his hand. We two waited anxiously until a very tall well-built man appeared through one of the doors and shook us warmly by the hand. Chatting amiably he guided us to a huge room that was part library and part games room. My eyes took in my surroundings as we entered and I could see the shelves were stacked with volumes of every title going from The Encyclopaedia Britannica to dictionaries in various languages. We were led to a massive settee situated next to a snooker table: "Make yourselves comfortable," he smiled: "His Royal Highness will be here to see you soon."

By the time ten minutes had passed my heart was racing as I had never met a person of any real importance before. It was then that I heard approaching footsteps and four large men entered the room. They were followed by an equally tall and well built man. Suddenly, Pau fell to his knees. I hesitated to do so but thought better of being discourteous and joined him. "Do stand up please," we were invited.

We rose to our feet as His Royal Highness, Prince Taufa'ahau Topu walked towards us holding his hand out as a greeting. Grabbing his hand Pau again fell to his knees in supplication. This seemed to me to be a little over the top. Turning to me the prince extended his hand. "Pleased to meet you, your Royal Highness," I mumbled.

There was no need for nervousness. He was perfectly at ease "Sit, sit," he urged still grinning from ear to ear.

We settled into a massive settee whilst the prince did likewise on the settee opposite to our own. His first question was to know what we thought of Tonga. I told him that it was a most beautiful island and added that the friendliness of the people made it the perfect place to visit or to live in. I meant what I said. I wasn't in to flattery. These were my true impressions.

Turning to Pau, who he addressed in Tongan, the ensuing conversation was interspersed with names that I recognised; Kitone Lave, Johnny Halafifi and George Mahoney. Drinks were brought. It was as well that Robert had reminded me not to expect alcohol but I would have killed His Royal Highness at that moment for a cold beer. Instead freshly squeezed fruit juice arrived and touching our glasses we toasted each other's health and success in the arenas of sportsmanship. "Are you returning to Fiji?" asked the Prince.

"No, you're Royal Highness. I am heading for Samoa and hopefully will travel on to Tahiti, New Zealand and England."

The prince smiled and looked a little distant for a few moments. Perhaps he remembered far different pastures and climate in that place on the opposite side of the earth. "You will like England. I was at Sandhurst for three years. It is a very cold country compared to here but it is in its own way very beautiful and quite different to the South Sea Islands." He then looked straight at me and asked: "Do you know that Kitone Lave was our palace gardener before he won the heavyweight championship of Tonga?"

"No you're Royal Highness, I do not."

The prince smiled proudly and after chatting for a few minutes he rose to his feet, smiled again and after shaking our hands and wishing us both well he left the room. It had been a surrealistic experience. Was I dreaming?

Pau and I waited in the room and it wasn't long before we were approached by a grey haired middle aged Indian gentleman. Smiling, he introduced himself as Billy but told us the locals called him Billy India for obvious reasons. The main reason for his being there at the palace was his expertise in preparing exotic Indian hot dishes of a kind which particularly pleased the prince and his family. He informed us that on the prince's behalf he was inviting us both to a feast at his home.

I was surprised but pleased with the thought of Indian food and as we followed Billy through the rear gates of the palace and on to where he had parked his car we passed a large pool of water. "Is this a palace swimming pool?" I asked.

Billy laughed at the suggestion: "The royal pool is very luxurious. Far more luxurious than this pond. This swimming pool belongs to the royal turtle."

"The Royal turtle? You are pulling my leg?" I was incredulous.

"No, not at all," he countered. "The English explorer Captain James Cook presented it to the Kingdom of Tonga in 1776. The captain had bought it from a Dutch merchant in Cape Town in South Africa. It was the voyage in which the great sea captain had embarked on his third and final voyage to Tonga. I suddenly remembered reading at school about it but I told him I thought this had occurred about two hundred years previous.

"Yes, that's right," he smiled: "Turtles live very long lives and it isn't unknown for their lifespan to reach three hundred years." With that, Billy led us to a magnificent tropical garden and sure enough, there was the very same turtle gifted to the kingdom to centuries earlier.

When we arrived at Billy's home I saw the same musical trio that had played at Claire's birthday party had just arrived. They recognised me from the previous night's event before Billy introduced us to his Tongan wife, his two teenage daughters and son named Raj. "Please don't worry yourselves: I am not a Methodist and my home is booze friendly. Here there is a wide choice of drinks; whisky, beer, kava, the lot." As he chatted and made us welcome he opened a couple of cans of Fosters.

We both followed our host to the rear of the house to find that it opened on to a lagoon fronting a beautiful white sandy beach. The smell of Indian curries mingling with the natural tropical fragrances reminded me that I was starving and for some strange reason I was now wistful for home. I found myself thinking of Susan having dinner with me at Suva Lodge before she left for the island of Mokagai. Such memories often imposed on me; they wouldn't let me go. I now wanted to cut short my visit and I made excuses about having to visit friends. However, when Robert and Ruth's name came up Billy brightened. He knew them both, and Claire of course.

He beamed: "I know Robert and Ruth very well. A good idea! I will ask Raj to drive to their home and hopefully return with them."

Despite my weak protestations at the trouble young Raj's car was soon disappearing in a small cloud of dust. He must have caught the family at the right time for we were soon joined by the three of them. I was glad to see Claire with her mother and father too. Claire was on top form again after having had a dodgy tummy. It was the early hours again before I made it to where I now called home and it was clear that neither Monica nor Isabel were amused at my appearance.

"You stink of alcohol."

"I had a beer. What's the big deal?"

"Where? At the Royal Palace?"

I told them I have been invited to a private party at Billy's India's home which invited the tart remark that it was supposed then that it wouldn't be long before Billy's daughters would be niches in my bedpost. "Don't be like that Monica," I grimaced: "It was nice of Billy to invite Pau and me to his home."

Neither of the girls replied and after a visit to the bathroom I was relieved to slip under the bed sheets. Thankfully; neither visited me that night. I sure had a lot of catching up to do and it was gone eight in the morning when I heard Isabel's voice calling me. "Come on, Jamie get up. It's Saturday and we are going to my step-mothers."

They may have been but I was in no mood for such a visit. Again I managed to wriggle out of the invitation and it was with relief that I heard the car disappearing in the distance after they had put breakfast behind them. I had other ideas; all I wanted to do was spend the day with Claire if it was possible.

When I arrived at her villa Ruth was there to greet me and their late breakfast included me. Claire's suggestion that we go for a long bike ride might well have been music to the ears of her parents but Claire had other ideas. I had already mentioned that the Moala family was absent. As we passed the Royal Palace we changed direction and headed towards my place.

Perhaps we were already behaving as a couple for the next half hour lying on the bed was spent discussing the dilemmas and the need for my training to recommence. I had a pretty tough fight ahead of me. It was fortunate that Claire, through her father, knew some of the issues that were causing me anxiety; she even knew the fighters I was talking about. Naturally she was horrified at the possibility that I might be beaten and I did what I could to allay her fears. She agreed with me that the sooner I began to train the less likely the chance I would be beaten.

After making love, Claire expressed a mild curiosity about my past girlfriends. There are times when a man has to do what a man has to do; tell lies. I told her that she was my first and that I had learned the techniques from a manual on sex. Producing a couple of Fosters from under the bed she reminded me that Moalas wouldn't be happy to find booze in their home. Thinking about what had gone on in this very bed, not to mention Moala's three wives I reminded Claire in turn that Mormons have a few sins of their own.

"Like? What sort of things? "

I hesitated before telling her that Mormons have multiple wives and group sex isn't unknown in their homes. As I spoke I was wondering how she might react if she ever discovered that her mother and I were lovers. I was consumed by guilt as I kissed her.

RETURNED TO DEVIL'S ISLAND

"You . . . you're just so beautiful Claire," I told her.

"And you're quite a guy yourself," she giggled playfully and then with a touch of seriousness: "You're kind hearted and thoughtful too and I am going to die if we don't meet up in Auckland. Promise that you will keep me posted from where ever you are."

I fervently promised undying fidelity and added that she must let me have her grandmother's address in Auckland first. I didn't say much else for obvious reasons but I had a feeling that Ruth would want to have access to me when her daughter was in New Zealand. I was playing with fire and I knew it.

Sure enough, I was right; Ruth was delighted to hear that I was staying in Tonga for the time being. After lunch at Claire's home we two went to the beach and swam for a while before making my way back. I was reminded about Sunday Mass and the Monday morning's modelling assignment arranged with Ruth.

Back at Moala's place he and his wife were back from their country home and a match was now arranged with Pau. This bout was to be for the middleweight championship of the South Sea Islands, David's old title. In preparation for the fight I jogged for five miles each day; swam in the ocean and sparred eight to ten rounds with the other boxers at the club.

After sparing at the gym I would meet Claire and we would either go to the beach or seek the privacy of the banana plantations. During the evenings leading up to the contest Mr.Moala massaged me and supervised a Tongan style of diet. I invariably finished up with fresh oysters and a mug of cocoa before retiring. Fortunately his daughters kept their distance and I wondered if their father had warned them to keep well away from me and my room. Each morning at dawn, my trainer would wake me and I worked hard at building my stamina up. This involved running fast uphill behind the Royal Palace. Only when I had endured each work out could I expect breakfast and a rest. From ten onwards my time was my own and those happy hours were often spent in Ruth's studio.

Finally the night of the big fight arrived. Mr.Moala, I and a group of boxers had lunch together before strolling to the playing fields where the fight was to take place. As on the previous occasion the arena was partitioned. I changed to being fight ready and then began the warm up. As soon as the supporting bouts were concluded I climbed into the ring ahead of Mr Moala and from my corner I could hear amidst the clamour the voices of Ruth and Claire who were in the company of scores of young women from my girlfriend's school.

Bowing in the direction of the Crown Prince I waited patiently in the blue corner. Minutes later the crowd erupted as their idol Pau entered the ring. He too solemnly bowed towards the prince and took his place in the red corner. Robert who was refereeing the bout called us both to the ring centre and gave the usual pre-fight instructions following which I touched the gloves of my opponent and we both returned to await the bell.

As soon as Mr Moala slipped the dressing gown away from my shoulder the bell sounded and I was finally face to face with Pau. I wondered at what his strategy might be. He had a wide smile on his face and was clearly confident of victory. Coming in with left jabs and right blows I skipped, ducked and weaved. I managed to stay away from him; I was happy to see him use up his energy as I wanted my reserves to be stronger than was his. It was my way of doing things. I jabbed fast to his ducking head, managing to catch him several times on the nasal and the point of his chin.

As the bell signalled the end of round one Mr. Moala observed that Pau looked heavier and more sluggish than he had been when he fought my friend, David. Mr Moala's advice was to send persistent flurries of blows to Pau's head to unnerve him; shake his confidence. I took his advice to heart and by the seventh round Pau's left eyebrow was cut and bleeding. At the close of round eight Moala told me that in his opinion I was ahead on points. Reminding me that this didn't mean I had the bout in the bag he suggested an attempt at knocking him out. My coach pointed out that the three judges were Tongan and the decision could go against me if it was too close a fight.

By this time I was feeling zippy and knew I had plenty of reserves; the hard training and balanced diet was paying off. In the ninth round I went after Pau with the same vigour and determination as I had in the previous fight against Luis. Pau was clearly looking rattled and his confidence had drained away. As he parried my blows and made a few attacks he was muttering something in the Tongan tongue, which I of course couldn't understand. For all I knew he could have been praying or cursing me to drop dead, I didn't care.

Two more rounds came and went during which I kept the upper hand and then at the beginning of round twelve I went for it. Catching him with a vicious right hook to the solar plexus his knees buckled and my opponent slumped to the canvas. Robert counted to ten before lifting my hand in victory. Mr. Moala for his part retrieved the belt from Pau's corner and wrapping it around my waist grunted, "Congratulations! You are the new Middleweight Champion of the South Seas."

Proudly I waved to the sullen and silent Tongan spectators; their disappointment was clearly evident. Bowing again in the direction of His Royal Highness I left for my dressing room. I hadn't been there long when I was embraced by Ruth, Claire, Monica and her sister, Isabel. Also cheerleaders, the Tongan school students. After shaking hands with as many well wishers as I could I rushed home to shower before meeting up again with Claire.

Later, as we relaxed on the beach she implored me not to fight again and to remain in Tonga until she was ready to travel with me. My destiny however was already mapped out. I was now only 500 miles into my odyssey and I fully intended taking the remaining 11,500 miles that separated me from my final destination. I had no intention of returning to Fiji a broken and dispirited failure.

As August approached Claire finished her final year at the convent and after a heart wrenching separation she was bundled off to Auckland earlier than she expected. I was certain her mother played a big role in her sudden departure.

Now I was in Ruth's domain and she was totally free to manipulate me in every which way she pleased to do. Fortunately she had some spare time left to finish her oil

RETURNED TO DEVIL'S ISLAND

paintings of me and the selected ones were now adorning the walls of her studio. This time the captions carried my impressive boxing title.

On August 26th, after a farewell to the Moala family, Ruth and Robert I sailed from the Tongan capital. It was the same banana boat, the SS Matua, that had brought David and myself to a region known throughout the world as the Friendly Islands.

We were bound for the island of Va'vau and on the way stopped at the small island of Tofua. I remembered this island from the book Mutiny on the Bounty. It was here that Captain William Bligh and the twenty-five loyal men who had stayed with him rested for the night after the shipboard uprising; it was after they were cast out to sea in a small launch. The Tongan natives had killed John Norton, one of the crew members as he tried to make friends with them. From here Captain Bligh and his men rowed across the seas, including the Tongan Trench and then on past Fiji before being eventually rescued in Java.

After loading in Tofua our ship sailed into Neiafa Harbour and docked at Va'vau. Here there was more copra and bananas to be loaded so I decided to take the opportunity and perhaps find a bar close by. After admiring an amazing sunset beyond Mt. Tabau I stepped of the boat and strolled towards a ramshackle corrugated tin houses known as the town. Certainly I was downhearted at leaving Tonga. This was my last night's stay on this beautiful group of islands and I was missing Susan, Claire, Ruth, and my family home in Fiji. Unfortunately there was an absence of bars on the island where they took their religion very seriously. I passed several churches of different denominations; these stood back a little from well groomed gardens and tarmac streets.

It was long before I chanced upon a small group of shirtless old men sitting around a large bowl; they were chatting away and in high spirits as they sipped their heady brew. Looking friendly they waved cheerily in my direction and beckoning me over where they offered me a coconut shell full of freshly mixed kava. Taking it from the one who had called over to me I thanked him before gulping it straight down. Knowing their customs well I didn't offend them by offering payment and after several drinks and a sandwich at a small tea outlet I wandered back to the ship and found a small space on deck for a few hours of sleep. I was pleased that I did not have to box here in Va'vau as it was cancelled due to a row with my opponent Manoca Pau. He was angry that I had knocked him out and had taken revenge for taking the title from my best friend David.

It was while trying to sleep on the deck that I reflected on Robert's story about the Wesleyan Missionary Rev David Cargill. This was the island where the man of the cloth had committed suicide by drinking a full bottle of laudanum. Somewhere in an unmarked grave on the island were laid his bones. Before dawn broke we sailed onwards across perfect calm seas towards American Samoa. Looking back towards the land I saw the friendly islands gradually dropping below the horizon. All those exciting months with the nicest of all people and my love with the fairest of them all was just a memory. My life at this point seemed unreal and I wondered if what had happened had been other than a dream. I put it down to the effect of the open seas where days could pass when a ship and time might stand still, poised between the blue cloudless skies and the deeper blue of the greatest ocean on earth. I was sailing into the unknown once again.

During the voyage a crew member told me we are now crossing the Tongan Trench. At over six miles deep it is the second deepest ocean trench in the world. I again reflected on the story I had read about the journeys of Captain William Bligh and of Captain James Cook. In 1776 he had crossed the Tongan Trench several times on his ship Endeavour during his visits to the Kingdom of Tonga. There the explorer was worshiped by the Tongan natives who showed their appreciation by giving him hundreds of suckling pigs, yams, sweet potato and freshly caught fish. It was he who had named the islands the Friendly Islands. Some Tongans still joke that the Kingdom of Tonga gave him lots of food to fatten him up like a pig ready for the ovens.

Twenty four hours later we could make out the flickering lights of Pago Pago in the distance. Several hours later we berthed at the small harbour at Atuu. It was by this time too late for wandering ashore and so I dozed on the ship's deck until morning. I would have a month ashore to discover whatever needed to be discovered.

When I awoke it was light and there was much commotion from a steady stream of trucks, forklift trucks and the ship's crew busying themselves with various tasks. From where I sat I could see the Rainmaker Mountains in the distance and when I peeped at the wharf below I saw shirtless men with tattoo covered torsos were loading tons of green bananas and pine apples on the vessel. Tidying myself up I picked up my suitcase and making my way down the gangway I sauntered through passport control and customs. Once safely ashore I was immediately surrounded by anxious Samoan women all trying to sell me something. I smiled and listened to their American accents. "Please mister, can I help you? Do you want a taxi or a hotel sir?"

"No," I replied: "But I need a small room to rent."

There was a chorus of voices each imploring me to stay with them. I smiled and looked at the young lady standing nearest to me. She was an appealing looking young woman and perhaps the eye contact did it for me.

"Do you have a room to rent?"

Lowering her eyes modestly she told me she had and I followed her into a dilapidated old building known as the Rainmaker Hotel. I was astonished to see there the new inventions that I had heard about but never set eyes on before. It was in here that I first set eyes on a television set. I remembered what my father had once said about the radio that could show moving pictures. Transfixed I stood in front of the small black and white television set and watched a Mickey Mouse cartoon.

"Sir! Do you want the room or not?"

Brought back to what I knew as reality I trotted, suitcase in hand, behind my petite guide through the bar's rear door and out into the blinding sunlight again. Here there was a tropical garden and bamboo huts overlooking a white sandy beach. The young woman accompanying me opened the door of one of the huts and invited me to take a look inside. There I discovered a wooden floor and looking around was pleased to see that it had all the amenities one could wish for including a primus stove for cooking facilities.

"Everything is here except the toilet and bathroom is outside and it is shared with others," she explained as I took in my more than satisfactory surroundings. "It is nice. How much?"

"Its $50 a month but you have to pay at the reception."

"How much is that in Tongan pounds?"

"The receptionist is a friend of mine and she will calculate the best price in town."

I followed her to reception and handed eighty Tongan pounds to the receptionist and thanked the young lady before heading back to the cabin. Perhaps it was the sea voyage, maybe the relief at having so quickly found myself a pleasant berth at a price well within my means; I lay back on the bed and literally passed out. The journey on the ship upon which I had been deprived of a proper bed had sure taken its toll.

It was late in the afternoon when I awoke. Showering, I dressed before entering the bar through the back entrance where I set eyes on a machine with flashing lights that played records. Around it young women were dancing and drinking beer straight from the bottle. I watched with curiosity as a young lady selected records on what I was to learn was a jukebox. Moving closer to have a better look, I wanted to see how it was done. As I did so she smiled and glanced towards me.

"Amazing," I grinned. "Please can you show me how to use this?"

Her smile was welcoming. "You're new to our islands, yes?"

"Yes. I haven't seen one of these machines before."

"It's called a jukebox. Here I will show you how to operate it."

She showed me how to select the records and pay by using the slot before rejoining her friends near the bar. They chatted between themselves in Samoan and laughed continuously as they did so. Strolling over to the barman I ordered a Fosters and asked if I might pay for it with Tongan money. "Sure you can," he laughed. "But we only serve American beer here and I'll have to give you change in dollars."

I told him not to apologise; I needed the change in local currency to get to grips with the jukebox. Tasting the new beer called Budweiser I studied the logo on the bottle. "It's good," I agreed.

The ballads I chose were those of Elvis Presley: Wild in the Country, Love Me Tender and Jail House Rock. Then, sipping the beer from the bottle I sat at the bar feeling a little pessimistic. I was missing Claire and was longing for everything I was leaving behind. Half of me wanted to return and the other half wanted to explore further into the unknown world. After a bite to eat I returned to my hut and scribbled a few letters to Claire and another to my sister Malti. It was good to feel them so close to me as my pen scribbled away. I then wrote another but more heartfelt one to Susan before falling asleep. It had been a long day.

Next morning I slept till noon before I had brunch in the bar and later strolled around the shops, bought some cocoa and milk before returning back to my cabin for another afternoon nap. It was dark when I woke up and after a shower and change of clothes I went back to the clubhouse. The place was packed with young Samoan girls, many of whom were dancing to the music blaring from the jukebox. As I sat on the barstool and took in my surroundings I recognised the face of the young lady who had showed me to my hut. Again the eye contact was enough; smiling she approached me.

I learned that her name was Mari-Lou and queried that her name seemed American. She laughed: "Of course it is American. We are Americans here. She told me she had never been to the U.S. but her father and two brothers lived and worked in Los Angeles. She added that she hoped to join them one day.

"I believe most of your men here work in the United States.'

"Yes, that's where the money is and so the men won't stay here. Look around you; there are approximately eight women to a man."

I looked around at the smiling group of reasonably attractive women and somehow thought of Monica and Isabel. Here they were very much like the Tongan women and the ethnic relationship was plain to see: They were pretty and each seemed to have brilliant white teeth and very dark often frizzy hair. After some more small talk, we danced. "I can cook for you if you want; just pay me for the food that I buy."

I was of course agreeable to her suggestion but told her my taste was for seafood rather than red meat. We settled on oysters and as we dined she suggested we use the next day up by going to the rocky part of the beach to look for oysters.

As we danced, Mari-Lou introduced me to many of the others in the bar-restaurant. It wasn't long before I was made welcome. Not unusually, due to the hospitable nature of the island's people, we all ended up in my cabin. Chattering away it was clear that I was something of a visiting celebrity; they were always eager to welcome friends and gossip from someone who was better travelled in the South Seas than were they. The following day I took in the locality and did a little catching up; it seemed my body and mind was determined to take a holiday. Again I was pushed in this direction by the friendliness of the locals and bar and beach life became for me the norm.

Mari-Lou became a good friend of mine and I learned much about her. She wasn't short of money and made her living from selling artefacts to tourists. She also received a little money from her father in Los Angeles. She was sixteen as were most of her friends and for whatever reason; the rich diet and the over indulgence common to the islands, she was a big girl; they all were.

As seemed typical of my lifestyle or was it a distraction to heal the past, it wasn't long before we were sharing more than pleasantries. Such involvement soon moved on to sharing lives or at least that was Mari-Lou's intention. She told me her father could soon acquire the necessary paperwork that would open up a new life on America's western seaboard. She did however understand my desire to travel to New Zealand and then on to England; the nation that held an attraction far greater than did anywhere else.

By this time we had become very good friends and were the subject of gossip in the bar; it seemed I had been hooked and Mari-Lou had wasted no time in telling everyone of her conquest. They are worse than the men when it comes to gossip.

RETURNED TO DEVIL'S ISLAND

The rest of my four week stay in Pago Pago continued idyllically; the bonus being that I no longer had to keep to a punishing daily fitness regime. I was a competent boxer and had the awards to show for it; I was not however a driven one. My career had fuelled and financed my burning desire to get to England and this was still a long way away. At the end of September several British and U.S. naval frigates arrived. They had been in the South Seas since Britain's nuclear test on Christmas Island a year earlier. The girls made a beeline for the visiting European sailors who looked the part in their tropical whites. They must have thought they were in heaven; I suppose they were. It sort of left me out in the cold and there was less room for me, less fun to be had in the bars and so I kept mostly my own company as I figured out a way to get to West Samoa. I wanted to like yesterday.

There were the goodbye hugs and kisses when my day of departure arrived; it was always sad to leave behind friends one has made and places were memories are collected. I was advised to go on down to the port where there were always ships available to cross the next link in my voyage. Sure enough, at the wharf of the small port I saw several schooners. They were from different ports of call; the Cayman Islands; some were from Fiji but New Zealand and Nuku'alofa registrations and flags could be seen too. I asked around but they were all going in the opposite direction to the one I wished to take. It was then that I noticed a small fishing smack preparing to leave the port. Speaking to the guy who was clearly in charge I asked him if by any chance he was bound for Western Samoa.

My luck was in. Furthermore the vessel's departure was imminent and the fare a reasonable twenty U.S. dollars. Within hours I was settled on board watching the island of Pago Pago absorbed by the sea mist behind our ship. As quickly as my isle for a month disappeared from view we set our eyes on a land mass ahead. "It's a place called Apia," I was told. He added that we would be there in less than eight hours.

Everything around these parts pivots around making your friendliness and your intentions known. Ask questions and a lot of advice comes your way. "Do you know anywhere there where I can rent a small room or something?" I asked the skipper.

"No, I don't," he replied: "Just walk past the harbour wall through town to the village of Lalovaea, you are bound to find something there. They are all signed up. You won't have a problem."

As soon as we tied up I pulled my stuff together and headed for what was obviously the main road leading into and through the town. Again I got lucky and when several joggers approached me in attire which reminded me of my not too distant past I asked them if they were boxers. It was a good guess; they were and they asked me if I boxed."

"Do I box?" I beamed at the group of guys; maybe my luck was in. "I have just arrived from Tonga where I have been boxing. I had intended boxing here in Samoa but it didn't quite work out that way."

"My name is Gabriel Stevenson," the biggest of the group said by way of introduction. He was a giant of a man and undoubtedly a heavyweight. They told me where their boxing club was situated and there was of course an invitation to visit them. Jogging and unencumbered by a heavy suitcase they got to the villa which served as their club before I did. My knocking on the door was answered by an elderly man who directed me to a shed at the rear of the building. Soon, Gabriel and I were again chatting amicably as were the rest of the group's athletes. We talked for a while before I produced the belt I had won in Tonga after my fight with Pau.

They were impressed and wanted a sparring bout there and then but I was at pretty much low ebb after my month's relaxation and travelling. I declined the offer telling them I needed a little time to myself. First I had to find somewhere to stay. "No problem, you can stay with me at my mother's."

That was my accommodation sorted and all done within an hour of docking. Not bad I thought to myself as I watched those guys in training. It was then that I felt that my heart had gone out of boxing and until I figured out some other way of earning a living and adding to my meagre savings I wasn't going to be going anywhere.

When the training came to an end I strolled with the boys to their nearby village of Lalavaea. I suppose I must have hinted that I needed some kind of employment as one of the group asked me if I was familiar with massage. I was of course; it is part of boxing life and culture. I told them that I knew masseurs in Fiji and had learned my skills from them.

"I am defending my heavyweight title in ten days," grinned Gabriel. "If you can help me out with sparring and massaging then you could stay at my mother's home free of charge; I will pay you a few bucks for your services as well."

That was a perfectly agreeable arrangement for me; the afternoon fight was to take place at the Apia Park situated close to the Robert Luis Stevenson Museum. I told him that I needed to get back into shape myself as I had been burning the candle at both ends during my travels.

Gabriel laughed. "It's the same when I go to American Samoa."

"Have you been in the Rainmaker?"

"Many times," he grinned broadly: "It's a favourite of mine and I have many young lady friends out there. All their men are in the States and they're gagging for it. You know what I mean?"

I thought of this grotesque monster-sized pugilist making love to Mari Lou and shivered at the thought. Later, as we were seated in his home; a house that was built from timber walls with a corrugated tin roof, he told me his mother wouldn't be long. He told me she was shopping and the beers were produced. "Are you a relative of Robert Luis Stevenson?" I asked him.

"Yes, most of us in this village are. I must have hundreds of cousins, nephews and nieces. He was a randy old bastard you know," he muttered thoughtfully.

"He is buried near here isn't he?"

"Yes, just behind there." Gabriel pointed in the direction of a steep mountain side in the distance. "That's Mount Vaea. I go up to the summit most mornings and I will take you in the morning, it is good exercise for my legs and builds up the stamina."

RETURNED TO DEVIL'S ISLAND

When Gabriel's mother returned we were introduced and she showed me to a small room. Gabriel's room was situated next to it, when he wasn't on his travels; usually to Tonga, Fiji and New Caledonia.

"Boxing?"

"Yes, I lost on points to Tom Hini the Fijian Champion."

"Tom's is a good friend of mine," I told him. "He helped me out after we were hit by a tidal wave."

"Did you know his last opponent died after the fight?"

The news shocked me. "No, it's news to me. What the hell happened?"

"Tom knocked him out and as he fell his head hit the canvas. He was taken to the Suva War Memorial Hospital but the damage was done. He died shortly after admission."

The news distressed me. As a boxer you live with the bruises and the scuffs, the blows you couldn't avoid but you never think of the blow that can cause brain damage or worse.

There's no dusk as such in these parts; darkness comes rapidly and as we sat at the small dining table we ate to a cricket chorus backdrop. That evening we watched a 35mm recording of the world heavyweight championship fight between the holding champion Rocky Marciano and Jersey Joe Walcott on a small canvas screen. It was a remarkable improvement on listening to a match on the radio but the commentator was still needed for his spin on the bouts.

Early next morning after breakfast we dressed appropriately and set off for Robert Luis Stevenson's tomb somewhere up the steep forested mountain. After walking through a steep and lush green forest track for almost an hour we arrived at the summit of Mount Vaea and approached the great writer's tomb. Gabriel and the other boxers sat down to admire the amazing views from the summit. I for my part was fascinated by the tomb and sat beside it as a flood of memories came back to me. I had read his novels during my boarding school days in Fiji. Afterwards we descended and took a different route that was known as 'the road of loving hearts' and stopped at a mountain village. As we approached the villagers came out to greet us.

"These are all my relatives," Gabriel proudly laughed as he introduced me to each of them in turn. Those milling about us included bare-breasted girls and equally bare-chested men. A source of wonder was Gabriel's massive biceps. As they chatted the less timid squeezed his massive arms and talked excitedly in the Samoan tongue. As so often it was an idyllic setting as we sat beneath the palms chatting amicably whilst the nubile village girls plied us with beer.

"Don't people drink kava here?"

"They used to but they now prefer beer. We have to go back now; mother is expecting us for lunch."

As we were leaving the village Gabriel reached into a plastic bag he was carrying and speaking in Samoan took out a handful of fight tickets and handed them to the small group waving us off. On the way back to Gabriel's home we bumped into several American tourists on their way to visit the tomb; they were accompanied by tour guides.

"Do you have a manager?" I asked Gabriel as I massaged his tattoo covered shoulders.

"I had one but he stayed back in Fiji when we were there."

"What will you do after this fight, Gabriel?"

"I am planning to go to New Zealand and try my luck over there."

I told him that was what I had in mind but in a candid frame of mind I confessed that my heart had gone out of the sport. He shrugged; it wasn't the first time he had heard of an early retirement. He told me that he knew someone at the wharfs who was able to fix up cheap travel by boat. It was decided that we would look him up after the big fight; maybe we could go to New Zealand together.

After several days training the much looked forward fight arrived. Crowds of spectators were coming into town, many from outlying villages. They would make a day of it, feasting and partying, all of which added to the exciting atmosphere. As the day progressed many farm animals were slaughtered. Their remains were cooked in earthen ovens similar to those used at Fiji and Tonga but here it was called Poi Poi. Not for the first time did I dwell on earlier cooked offerings that hadn't necessarily been of animal origin.

After lunch Gabriel and the rest of us reported for duty so to speak. There was the routine medical and weigh-in followed by a warm up exercise and good natured sparring between the team members. I took my opportunity and nipped into the ring side to see the other fights taking place that afternoon. As soon as the last preliminary bout finished I rushed to the dressing room area and swapped my shirt for a white T-shirt that had the name Gabriel Stevenson printed on it. Then together with three others we accompanied Gabriel to the ring and through the cheering crowd. Gabriel dressed in blood red boxing shorts, black boots and white socks looked very much the magnificent gladiator.

The clamour was ear-splitting as I raised the middle rope of the ring with both hands and simultaneously pressed the lower rope with my right foot. This created a gap big enough, just, to allow Gabriel to enter the ring. As I looked at him I was glad that I wasn't his adversary.

Glancing across the ring I could see his opponent was already standing in the blue corner. He was head and shoulders higher than the top rope and his three hundred pounds body weight looked menacing. Gabriel was a big man but his opponent by comparison reduced his massive form to that of a more or less ordinary individual. He was clearly up for it and filled with confidence. His loathing and contempt for our corner was apparent as he spat in his bucket and glared across. This was what the excited crowd expected to see; hatred meant a good fight.

After the referee's instructions we stepped out of the ring as the bell rang for round one. Immediately the two boxers leapt from of their stools, touched gloves and without preamble launched themselves at each other. Those of us at the ringside saw and felt the blood and saliva spraying as the two protagonists beat shit out of each other. There was a real hatred and determination to win by both adversaries.

At the end of the round I wiped the sweat from Gabriel's face and passed him the water necessary for cleaning his mouth. He gargled to clear the blood from his mouth before he spat into a bucket. "Go for his solar plexus, Gabriel. Hurt him until he crouches down and then go for his head with powerful knockout punches." I suggested. The others agreed that the quick kill strategy was good.

In the second round that was exactly what he did do. We watched in awe as the giant slumped like a felled ox to the canvas. The referee counted him out and after lifting Gabriel's hand high in victory he wrapped the leather belt around his waist. Gabriel's family and friends jumped into the ring. They bodily picked him up and carried him around the ring in jubilation. Those of the opponent's party half carried the dazed hero from the ringside.

Later we all made our way to our hero's mother's home for the celebration. The news had quickly got around the entire community and before long the small family home was surrounded by a crowd of well-wishers. "Don't eat and drink too much," Gabriel advised me: "Tomorrow we are going up to the mountain village for another celebration."

"The two of us?"

"No," he smiled as he pointed in the direction of a party of young women relaxing nearby. "They are coming with us."

The girls might have overheard or at least picked up the gist of his intentions; they smiled and waved across at us. I conceded that they were seemingly the brides of paradise. "Tell me about it," he said with a curl of his lips. "I missed out on much during the weeks of training. It is now time to do a little catching up. I am aching for it. It is about time you were rewarded too, Jamie. We need some relaxation after that don't we?"

"Are everyone on the team coming with us?" I asked.

He smiled and winked. "No, the rest are returning to the village right now."

"But it is pitch black out there?"

"They have hurricane lamps; they do it all the time. Only the two girls will stay behind with us." He gave me a wink and you know what that means look.

Sure enough, a little later the main body of the visiting group lit their kerosene lamps and departed for their mountain village. As soon as they disappeared from view Gabriel took one of the girls by the hand and took her to his bedroom. He noticed my hesitation: I asked him where his mother was. He casually told me that she was fast asleep and uncaring. "Have fun. We'll catch up in the morning," were his parting words.

As soon as I heard his rooms door's bolt slide into place I gazed across at the remaining young woman and it was her who broke the ice. "My name is Rosemary but you can call me Rosa and my cousin is called Marisa."

"Do you have a boyfriend?"

"No but my cousin Marisa is Gabriel's girlfriend."

"Does Gabriel have other girlfriends or is Marisa the only one?"

"Yes, he has several girlfriends in the village," she smiled sweetly and evidently couldn't see there being a problem in that. I must have been losing my will to live. I was desperate to leave for Tahiti, New Zealand and finally England and there was nothing more on my mind except my past life. We just sat and chatted the night hours away; downed a few beers, retired to bed and slept easily together but without what would have once been once an essential prerequisite to sleep.

After breakfast we slowly made for their great grandfather's tomb. There was no rush and I was glad of that as my knees were knocking together with fatigue. When we finally arrived at the hallowed spot it was already surrounded by tourists whose cameras were much in evidence. Some were posing on the top of the tomb and I thought I heard Australian accents and this reminded me of Susan. As I drew closer to them I caught their attention. For the next few minutes we exchanged pleasantries and I learned that they were on an excursion around the South Sea Islands.

The travellers told me of some of the places they had visited, which included Fiji, Tonga, Pago Pago and New Caledonia. After leaving here they were scheduled to visit the Cook Islands, Tahiti, and Auckland before returning to Brisbane."

This was to me quite fascinating to the family group I was chatting mostly to and I told them a little about myself. They mirrored my friendliness. His name was Peter, his wife was Sylvia and they were accompanied by their twelve-year old daughter, Laura. She was a delightful child wearing both her freckles and baseball hat with considerable appeal. Peter it would appear had little to complain about but he did rue the fact that he had expected to see more bare breasted South Sea islanders. I told him there were plenty of those; sadly most of them were men.

Gabriel had overheard our confidentialities and finger clicking our young companions that a photo opportunity was to be had, they laughed naughtily and posed bared breasted with the writer's tomb as a backdrop and afterwards encouraging us to join them for more snapshots.

"Come to our village, we have many more girls for you to photograph," said Gabriel invitingly. Our new friends were incredulous and excited by the prospect of being introduced to authentic Samoan village life. It was an opportunity not to be missed.

"All of us?" they chorused.

"Sure, why not? We are about to have a feast and you are more than welcome. It could likely be the highlight of your tour."

Eager for the experience they gathered their kit together. It was to be an experience for us too as today there was to be a feast in celebration of Gabriel's victory in the ring. I took a quick head count. There were eleven tourists now in our party; a mixed bag of men, women and children.

On arriving at our village we found the villagers were as excited as the tourists and were honoured by their presence. Then we were neatly arranged beneath the palms where we were assured of maximum shade. It was needed it being such a hot day.

RETURNED TO DEVIL'S ISLAND

Shortly afterwards the village lovelies brought beer from a tub that had previously been filled with water to cool the beer bottles down. It had served as a fridge but hardly an efficient one. These were handed out to the unexpected but very welcome visitors. We touched bottles with the visitors and drank the slightly warm beer before steaming hot poi poi was laid out on banana leaves. This was a dinner party Samoan style and the visitors were thrilled at the chance to go native. The cameras were clicking all around us. "Bloody fantastic," declared Peter. "What are we celebrating?"

"He has just retained the heavyweight championship of Western Samoa," I replied as I nodded in the direction of Gabriel.

"I can't believe it. We are dining with the heavyweight champion of Samoa?" echoed Silvia.

"Are you a boxer too, Jamie?" asked the couple's daughter who had likely guessed as much by my athletic build. I told her I was but I was considering career options. Such was the visitors' gratitude that when it was finally time to take their leave we were invited to visit them on their schooner. It was they said a fine craft, named the Barracuda; it was moored in the in the Apia port and would be moored there for several days before they leave for the Cook Islands. After the feast the Australian visitors thanked Gabriel for his hospitality and left before dark. I was by this time giving some thought to carrying on to Tahiti but thought mention of a sea lift to Peter might be a little premature; I bit my tongue and bided my time.

Before sunrise I left Rosa fast asleep in bed and made my way to the moorings where the Barracuda was moored. If you don't ask you don't get: I really needed that lift to Tahiti and Peter could only say no. Once there on the quays I could see that all was quiet on the sleek yacht and I reflected that it was still early in the day. It was mid morning before I spotted Laura on the boat's deck.

As soon as she saw me she greeted me warmly and when I asked about her father she went below decks to call him up. Moments later I had joined them for a breakfast on the ship's stern. It was then that I plucked up the courage to ask of him a big favour. Peter looked at me questioningly: "What's on your mind, Jamie?"

I told him I had a friend and a job waiting for me in Tahiti and was wondering if a place on board might be found for me. I was willing to pay or work my passage. Sylvia and Peter glanced at each other and then, something passed between them and then turning to me he smiled. "Sure, Jamie. Can you handle a boat?"

I was honest enough to tell them that I had no experience as such but I was willing to learn and wouldn't be picky about any tasks they might give me to do. "You will need a visa; the bloody French won't allow you to land without one."

I assured them that all my paperwork including a visa was in order and that I wouldn't be a burden to them. They were happy with that and the trip was arranged for the next days. I declined their invitation to go all the way to Brisbane with them. That was too big a leap of faith at the time; first I had to see Tahiti and Auckland.

Back at Gabriel's home I showered with a self satisfied smile on my face. I had grasped the nettle; it hadn't stung. That evening I once again walked the 3km walk to the Barracuda. The lights were on when I reached it; it was truly a magnificent looking craft. I had never thought to ask Peter what business he was in but he had obviously been a success in whatever he was involved in. On this occasion I didn't have the balls to disturb them. I might have been pushing my luck. As I strolled unseen past the sloop I saw cartons of bananas destined for Great Britain. How I envied that fruit. It would be there in England before I was.

There was within me nostalgia; much mixed feelings I supposed. My gaze wandered across to the shimmering lights of American Samoa. Mari-Lou would be there, with her memories too, and the rest of her friends too. But my feet and heart were itchy; I needed to be on the move to new places and experiences.

It was much later that I arrived at my lodgings and was a little taken aback to see Rosa there, and in my bed too. She told me she had been lonely without me. For some reason I desperately wanted my own space and again in the morning I left her where she was slumbering peacefully and ambled down to the not too distant beach. The swim had the opposite effect to that intended. Afterwards I simply lay on the sand and slept the sleep of the dead. It was something of a stupid thing to do. When I did wake my unprotected skin was blistering from the effects of the direct sunlight.

Back at Gabriel's it was suggested that I take a cold shower; I was assured that it would bring me relief but though the spray was tepid it still hurt like hell and only seemed to make matters worse. "Where is Rosa," I asked.

I was told she had gone looking for me. I was still sitting on my bed when she arrived back. "I have been looking for you, Jamie, where have you been?"

I admitted my failing before telling her that I was leaving for Tahiti and hardly for the first time in my life I made then and the following morning my thanks and commiserations about my having to say goodbye. All I seemed to do was make and break friendship moulds but I was driven. There was no future in the past.

At first light I slipped painfully out of my bed and showering carefully to avoid aggravating further my scorched back I hurriedly packed my small and by now battered suitcase and headed towards the wharfs. There was a price to be paid for my impatience; I arrived there long before the family were up and about.

When they finally did see me sitting eagerly on a box awaiting their presence Peter asked me the question that hardly needed answering: "You're early, Jamie. Are you sure you want to come along? This isn't just a flight of fancy?"

I managed a wide grin as I beamed back at him, "You bet it is no flight of fancy; I just can't wait to get going."

He laughed as his brow furrowed: "You haven't robbed a bank have you, Jamie? You're not a fugitive from justice are you?"

"No," I assured him. "Just wandering feet; I am on a mission," I laughed as I joined them on the Barracuda's deck. From there on I was shown my cabin and given a running commentary as to where everything was and introduced to the shipboard way of doing things their way.

RETURNED TO DEVIL'S ISLAND

As I was shown around the craft I was dumfounded. I had hardly expected a cabin of my own and would have been more than happy sleeping on a long seat or in a hammock. There was far more room inside the boat than there appeared to be when looking at it from the quays.

A little later and after slipping the lines the ship's motor was used to exit the harbour. This was no place to be dependent upon the vagaries of the breezes that wafted across our bows. But once clear of the harbour and headed for the open seas the sails were hauled aloft and they took over from the now silent ship's engine.

I watched with mixed feelings as Western and American Samoa sank into the seas in our ship's wake. Soon there was nothing but the vast ocean all around us. Our journey towards the Cook Islands had begun. Again I found myself thinking of Susan somewhere beyond the horizon; I thought of my family too and the memories of a life that had already seemed lived twice over flooded over me. I missed them all and I was in a world of my own when I head Peter calling me. "All right, mate?"

"Sure," I replied. "I just have a lot of thoughts. You are leaving just another island whereas I am leaving my life."

The boat was now rocking to the gentle movement of what had appeared to be placid seas and from the prow I could hear the bow waters breaking at the slice of the craft's apron before swishing on its way past us.

"In that frame of mind are you, young lad. Well, there's no point in staying on deck, let's go down below and have a beer. I'll put the boat on auto pilot."

Stepping down the small ladder into the small lounge I joined Peter at a small dining table where he passed me a bottle of beer. As I took it I recalled the first leg of my journey from Fiji to Tonga in the hurricane. I hadn't forgotten the seasickness the beer had then caused me. "A toast to good sailing," he said cheerily as we clinked our salute to the weather gods.

Sylvia looked across at me: "Go easy on the beer if you are not used to sailing, Jamie. It might make you seasick."

When I told them I had survived a crossing of the Tongan Trench during hurricane conditions, Laura chipped in to tell us that at six and a half miles deep it was the second deepest sea in the world. When I asked her at which sea one could find the deepest she told me it was the Mariana Trench which is half a mile deeper still. "It's very clever of you Laura. Are you interested in geographical stuff?"

"Yes, I read books and maps and like to know where everything is," she smiled winsomely as she tucked her hair into a ponytail. I wasn't however much in the frame of mind for small talk and also knew that I needed to make myself useful. It was better that I did so without having to be asked. By this time I had noticed a stack of dishes that needed washing before being stowed away. It was while I was getting that task done that I spotted curry powder and a bag of rice. My mouth was watering at the thought of my mother's curries. "Sylvia," I said as I turned to the first mate: "I am a dab hand in the kitchen you know. Can I cook us some rice and curry?"

"Sure, there is some fish in the freezer. Help yourself."

Peeking inside the ship's fridge I found fish that I guessed was tuna. If it looks like a duck, walks like a duck and quacks like a duck, it is a duck. That evening I delighted them all, myself included, with tuna curry. It must have been good tasting for Peter suggested I teach Sylvia how to prepare and cook it as I had done.

We learned much about each other that first evening; that I had been a spectator at the Royal visit to Fiji. I learned that they were there too and had been wandering around the South Sea Islands for the last three years and that Laura's education was being taken care of by her mother.

The days passed pleasurably enough as we crossed endless blue seas of slightly darker hue than the skies above; at night the skies presented a dazzling array of twinkling stars and moonlight to die for. I was thankful that on this occasion I wasn't affected sea sickness. It was four days of plain sailing before we came upon the small island of Manuae in the Cook Islands and approached. Pretty soon afterwards we were carefully and slowly picking our way through the port's cluttered marina before docking at the quayside and taking on fuel. I volunteered to pay for it but Peter refused to take any cash from me.

After a day of shopping and sightseeing in the tiny town we set off for our next destination, Tahiti, which is in the French Polynesian Territories. Peter said we would be in the Capital, Papeete, within twenty-four hours. This was to be the end of my leg of the long journey. The obliging family I had spent several days with were travelling on to Auckland en route for Australia.

"It's a pity you can't come with us," smiled Peter as he busied himself with the ship's tackle and scanned the horizon. I welcomed his offer but couldn't take him up on it because I had already committed myself. "My friend is in Papeete and has offered me employment. I will be seeing him before you sail. If it falls through for any reason then you could find yourself with a very appreciative and hard working crew member."

Tidying up the ship's lines and getting the fenders ready he swivelled to face me and laughed lightly. "Jamie, you are welcome, mate. I can't see the French giving you a work permit in Tahiti. Sorry to rain on your parade but they run a pretty tight ship in these parts."

I said nothing. I was pretty sure that all would be just as we had planned it. By the time we approached Papeete our ship's skipper was on the radio engrossed in conversation with several officials. As we drew closer still a small motor launch carrying a couple of customs officers approached the Barracuda and climbed on board. It was to be my moment of truth. I was a little apprehensive as they made more than a cursory look at my papers and passport. I was pointedly asked what my purpose was in visiting Tahiti.

I was good natured enough about their officiousness: "A good friend of mine, Mr Daniel Forester, sir." I showed the two officials Dan's business card. The rest of the interview was rudimentary. They merely wished to know how long I intended to stay and where I would be going on to. The others weren't interrogated as their flight plan so to speak was well sorted.

CHAPTER 6

There was more official palaver after we had moored the sloop but by noon we were off the quays and greeted by an attractive Tahitian girl who placed garlands of frangipani over our heads in greeting. "Welcome to Tahiti."

After making our way down Waterfront Road and into Boulevard Pomare we were absorbed into the hustle and bustle of Papeete life. After a celebratory few beers we marked what looked like the end of a relationship that had begun at the tomb of Robert Louis Stevenson. It was a melancholy parting for I had grown very fond of them. Once again I was painfully aware that moving on meant severing relationships of a kind of which the memories last forever. Such were my feelings as I boarded a battered old Citroen taxi, some of which moving parts were apparently strung together in a makeshift fashion. Dan's card was all I needed for the short trip I needed to make.

As I stepped out of the cab and paid my fare I found myself deposited at the imposing Le Village gates where I took in my surroundings. It was an amazing place and certainly exceeded my expectations. The hotel and leisure facilities were styled in such a way as to reflect Tahitian life. There were reproduction grass huts dotted slap-dash about; no doubt all with modern facilities. Central to everything there was an expansive white complex that blended well into its lush green setting. Tropical flowers were in abundance; the horticulturists seemed to know their onions I thought.

Against this backdrop the ever-present small sign directing the foot weary towards reception where I was met by several welcoming Tahitian ladies. Ever the dishevelled wanderer they clearly pondered as to what my business was to be with upmarket and very luxurious Le Village. I felt comfortable enough about my surroundings, which I guessed would soon be far more familiar to me on a daily basis. When they asked my name I produced Dan's card. "Just tell him that Jamie from Fiji is here. He is expecting me."

One of the girls tittered cheekily as her colleague made a telephone call. "Excuse me bothering you, Mr. Forrester. I have at reception a gentleman named Jamie from Fiji."

Whatever he said caused her to smile and as she looked at me she winked as though to reassure me. "Mr Forester will be here shortly."

Without taking the offered seat I waited awhile and then suddenly glass doors were thrown open and the impressively built Dan strode towards me. The bear hug was followed by exclamations as to how well I looked, which was hardly surprising considering the life I had been living.

"Your reception ladies are a real shop window for this place, Dan," I said. "I am impressed."

"You haven't seen the best yet. The caliph of Baghdad would exchange his harem for this place. And, just you wait until you see the air hostesses who use Le Village for their stopovers: Then you will know what good looking dames look like."

As we strode into the club house he watched my expression change and he grinned almost to his ears. "Yes, a real club house, Jamie; not at all like the fucking shed in Tonga."

I gazed in awe around the exotic setting and then towards the beach and the palm groves. Despite their ugliness the Tahitian masks adorning the walls looked magnificent and provided the right ethnic character to the swish location. As I took in my surroundings a slim grass skirted waitress rushed towards Dan. She was in bare feet.

"You don't pay them very well, Dan. Don't they get shoes to wear?"

He laughed at the topless babe, her bead necklace bobbing between her generous breasts, she approached us. The red hibiscus flower worn behind her ear reminded me of Claire and the night of her birthday party. There were so many memories; mostly good except for one. How much baggage can a guy carry? Talking of which I must have been a sight carrying that battered old travel worn suitcase in my hand.

Dan ordered a couple of large beers from the youngster and thoughtfully asked if I had eaten. By this time I was starved of food and starved of sleep after the voyage. At the bar there were several young European girls engaged in conversation. "The air hostesses, Dan?"

"Yes, and I warn you, my friend; they are insatiable man-eaters and I suggest you catch up on your sleep before you even think of approaching them. You might think you're God's gift. To them you're tonight's supper. They are employed by various airlines; there's a steady stream of flights coming in from Australia, New Zealand and the South Sea Islands. Tahiti is quite a draw and a good place to invest.

All I needed to invest in was sleep and after being shown to my cabin, and it being hinted at that exciting plans had been arranged for my stay, I was left on my own to familiarise myself with the cabin's layout.

When I looked around me I was stunned to see its contents; it lacked nothing in terms of mod cons. The highly polished teak floor was ablaze with coloured ethnic rugs; the ceilings were varnished natural woods and so complementary to the Tahitian style. There was an overhead fan to keep the humidity and heat at a comfortable level; fridge, tiled bathroom, toilet; shower unit and electricity. The huge double bed underneath the bay window and its panoramic views added up to what promised to be the perfect sleep. Smiling to myself I scratched my head and couldn't believe my good fortune.

RETURNED TO DEVIL'S ISLAND

When I awoke night had fallen and it was obviously late. Looking through the cabin's windows at night revealed much more enchantment. The clubhouse was beautifully illuminated and the tropical trees; shrubbery and palms laden with fruits, were lit by spotlights. The entire village complex looked truly magnificent. I had showered and dressed smart casual. I was inquisitive as to what was going on and sauntered on over to the clubhouse. The music and general clamour greeting me suggested everyone in there was having a good time. Men, dressed in hula skirts were dancing with grass skirted women to a backdrop of Hawaiian guitar melodies. As I picked up my beer at the bar, for which I wasn't charged, I gathered that I was both expected and recognised. "Is Dan around," I asked.

The barmaid smiled: "He is at the far table on your right. You must join him. He wants you over there, sir."

I grinned at her. She was as attractive as were my surroundings: "Jamie if it's all the same to you. I haven't yet been knighted."

Feeling buoyant after my first evening at the holiday complex I glanced over to better see Dan. If I had difficulty picking him out I could be excused. My new boss was surrounded by a group of attractive European ladies; presumably the airline hostesses he had been going on about. Calling me over I joined them at their table. I confess to feeling a little gauche in such sophisticated and glamorous company.

"Hey Jamie I am glad you're awake. Some of our residents are dying to meet you so join us and say hello."

Nervously I looked around me and took in the smiles that said much about the welcome. I would be the first to own up that they weren't the kind of ladies I was used to partying with. Their elegance and sophistication, not to mention their dress style, suggested to me that I might be a little out of my depth.

"Jamie is from Fiji. He will be staying with us for awhile."

"Hey, Jamie; I was in Fiji last week," beamed a tall blonde. "I am Yvonne and we ladies work for Tasman Airlines." Another introduced herself as Carla. I smiled as my eyes went from one lovely face to another. In those introductory minutes I learned a lot about the destinations covered by the airline. They sure had a glamorous job and they also looked the part. Flying on one of those aircraft and being attended to by one of these cabin crew and you knew you had made it in life.

My timing that evening had turned out right. It was just as well I had not slept on. We were all heading into town and the minibus was already waiting and with several impatient cabs behind it wanted to get going. In our party there were Dan and myself; four French and two Australian air hostesses. Dan winked at me as I climbed into the passenger seat: "We are going to the wildest clubhouse in the world."

"Not the bloody Marquee," screamed the girls.

"And your problem is?"

"It's full of sailors who can't hold their drink but they want to hold us," Yvonne said rolling her eyes and expressing her disapproval.

"Not tonight they won't," he grinned: "They will have to get past Jamie and me. We're going to be your minders tonight."

The girls in the rear seats looked sceptical: Half turning in his seat, Dan looked directly at Yvonne. "I've seen Jamie knock a man out in Tonga twice his size so you have nothing to worry about."

I held my tongue until we got to the night spot and once there helped each of the ladies alight. Across the road was the over-illuminated Marquee. Inside was a tourist bedlam and after we had picked our way through the crowded dance floors we were shown our table. "This is the dog's bollocks of a place," I said directly in to Dan's ear; normal conversation being impractical.

"This placed was featured in Readers Digest as being the world's wildest nightclub.

"I can believe it," I said as I watched several inebriated sailors being shown the door by club security.

We booked eight table places but gradually the girls had paired off and by the time the meals were brought to us we were down to four settings. Talking of pairing off, Yvonne seemed to have taken a shine to me; she had at least taken my arm. Dan for his part was draping himself over the beautiful Carla. Taking our places at the table we were situated just a few feet away from the languorous waters of the scenic bay and it was difficult to imagine a more romantic setting.

"Did you know, Jamie; this is the very beach where Fletcher Christian and the other Bounty mutineers stayed. No kidding. You're part of history."

I was familiar with the Bounty story and was impressed. "Sure, they were right here screwing beautiful young Tahitian girls. They were having the time of their lives and must have thought they were on the holiday of a lifetime. Wouldn't you be mutinous when Captain Bligh ordered them back to work? They were told to collect the breadfruits for the West Indian plantations where the niggers would be doing the planting and the harvesting. They mutinied and the rest is history."

I felt a little uncomfortable at his remark and racist undertones but the two girls were smiling self indulgently; perhaps because their merry host was ordering even more champagne. I could see now why he hadn't been over excited by the clubhouse in Tonga where we had first met after that great fight I had had.

"What's the champagne for," Yvonne said.

"Because my friend Jamie has finally made his way here and he is not your average guy. He is the middleweight champion of the South Sea Islands. Bottoms up; an appropriate salutation seeing as this is the land of love and I love shapely bottoms, especially raised high." Dan threw his head and laughed at his own joke.

The meals were of fresh barracuda. Cooked Tahitian style they were wrapped in taro leaves and had simmered in coconut milk and garlic. This was accompanied by yams and sweet potatoes. The dessert was also delicious; slices of succulent fresh pineapple with homemade ice cream. By the time we decided to make our way back to Dan's place he was well and truly inebriated.

In the cab I listened to my employer who had by now become increasingly belligerent with the objects of his scorn now being the French.

I cared? Not me as by this time I was trying hard to control Yvonne's demands in the cab's rear seat. She was a tiger alright. All too soon we were back where the night had begun and as Carla heaved Dan out of the cab my mind drifted to remarks a once sober Dan had made about the promiscuity of the air hostesses.

Was I shortly to find out? Yvonne was already asking if I was looking forward to our nightcap as we strolled towards her cabin rather than mine. Her intentions were quite clear and in a word or two she was predatory and promiscuous. I had a bit of baggage in my mind due to the lovemaking I had enjoyed in the past. This episode was different in that it was without romance; it was pleasurable but mechanical. Instead of giving it was taking from each other's plates. She had what she wanted and was relaxed about things. To her that was the nightcap.

"And you're how old, Jamie?"

"I was twenty two last birthday."

"Oh, I won't guess at your birth sign. Go on tell me."

It told her it was August and wondered where she was coming from as I wasn't really into star signs. "Ah, a Virgo: A bloody stallion; I might have known."

"I box and weight lift to built my strength and stamina. It keeps me fit for everything, not just for the boxing ring. I am curious too, Yvonne. I know it is impolite to ask a lady her age but I am not sure why."

A could see the minefield when she told me I would have to guess. Get it wrong and you're in deep shit. I had to guess younger without over doing it; and even then you can get it wrong. Shriek! "Twenty, perhaps twenty-two?"

"Wrong, Jamie. I am twenty-seven this Christmas. I am the fairy that fell off the Christmas tree you know."

Afterwards she said: "Why don't you stay the night? Otherwise I might have to cross the lawns to your cabin should I need a dessert. You wouldn't have a naked girl do that would you?"

Such was my first night in Tahiti, which clearly was much in line with the promises and boasts made by my friend, Dan. Yvonne was up and on her way to the airport by seven o'clock. "See you in three days, Jamie."

The clubhouse was busy by the time I had pulled myself together and single seats being at a premium I found myself in the company of a bunch of cheerful Aussies. The word had got around as one of them asked me if I was the young fighter Dan had been speaking about. Because of their accents they reminded me of Peter and his wife and daughter. I felt I had to see the lovely family before they left these shores. Gulping my breakfast down I headed for the wharf and on the way tried to send a money order to my sister back home. It was futile.

Better luck followed when I spotted the Barracuda but I was lucky for it was moored in a different place from where I had left it. I was made welcome and even invited to join them for the last leg but I felt I was in debt to Dan. It would have been discourteous of me to have left so early. Anyway I was still curious as to what he had in mind for me. I was soon to find out. On my return to Le Village I found Dan waiting for me and the first words out of his mouth was what he had in mind. "Are you up to the minute with fast moving events, Jamie?"

He didn't wait for my answer but told me that health farms and gymnasiums; keep fit studios were springing up all over the place. Hotel complexes like Le Village would by now be presumed to have such facilities. There was a need for someone competent to set it up and manage it. Someone who really knew about such things and could set an example.

"When I first saw you in the ring that time in Tonga I knew you were the perfect guy for the undertaking. You'll be the biggest draw; especially for the ladies and they sure have the money these days."

I smiled at the guy's flattery as he assured me that he meant every word of it. Following him over towards the beach I could see a long low roofed building. What he had in mind was already in situ. Inside and still in its packaging the most extraordinary array of body sculpting equipment I had ever set eyes on. I am not sure what amazed me the most; the amount or the modernity of it all.

"I shipped it in from the U.S.," he grinned as he looked at my dumb expression. "It is designed and made to the specifications of Mr Joe Weider, the greatest trainer of all time."

I had heard of the iconic figure. It was hard to avoid pictures of him at sporting events and gyms. In my kind of sports he was as well known as a brand; more or less as is Coca Cola. The equipment though was all new to me and wonderfully different from the old equipment I was used to working out with. If only Susan could see me now? I wonder how she would like this kind of status and lifestyle. There was a lot less austerity here than at any missionary station: Here was another world altogether.

"It'll be a learning curve, Jamie," he said as he took one of several body-building magazines up from a side table and hand it to me. Glancing through them I couldn't see there being much of a problem. The fitness regime necessary to bring out results might be but not the usage of the equipment. I told him it was a walk in the park.

"Maybe but it is an expensive one," he chuckled. "Everything is here. What I have in mind to do is set it up and brochure it big style. This place is going to be marketed across the United States and the better watering hole locations of Europe; the ski and holiday resorts used by the filthy rich."

I told him I liked his take on things. In fact I was flattered to be included in the grand design of it all. He told me that time was in the essence; Hollywood was about to descend on this tropical paradise. "Hollywood? Have I missed something?"

Dan told me that the location was going to be used for the shooting of a movie featuring James Mason and John Mills. The title of the film was to be Tiara Tahiti. The actors names were familiar to me. I had also seen Burt Lancaster when they were filming His Majesty O'Keefe.

RETURNED TO DEVIL'S ISLAND

"Let's talk about my plan Jamie. When the wealthy arrive we have everything they need to give them value for money, the time of their lives. My plan is to spoil them rotten; give them the kind of holiday they will talk about and tell others about. I want them to keep coming back and when they do to bring their friends with them. The best salesman of all is the one we call Mr Word of Mouth.

"All over the world people are becoming more health conscious. The world of medicine is putting the fear of God into folk's minds. The gyms in the U.S. are overbooked with the rich wanting to get back their youthful looks. There's a big market too from the young who think it is cool to look good. Every guy wants to look like a lifeguard. We want a slice of that cake."

I walked slowly around the gym and checked out the silver chromed equipment and as I did so I knew that what I was being offered was the dream job in the most fantastic location on the world's surface. "Would I be able to get a work permit?"

"I can arrange that," he reassured me. "This place generates a lot of taxes, offers training, allure, and it reduces unemployment. I am a hard act to follow. I am one of the best things to happen to Tahiti since the palm tree was invented."

"Or the hula skirts!"

He laughed as he proudly looked across the yet unfinished gym before returning his gaze to me. My being here seemed to be the last piece of his jigsaw.

"Your salary, Jamie, will be $200 a month and that is pocket money for you, my friend. This is an all found job so that is on top of your living style; food and cabin home. In return you will need to be the fitness ambassador for Le Village."

I didn't hesitate. "It's a deal, when can I start?"

"You start today. This is your domain," he said as he grandiosely waved across the gym: "Just don't let me down or take the piss. Let me give you one bit of advice that will stand you in good stead throughout your life: Always exceed your employer's expectations.

"By the way," he said as a parting shot: "Don't forget the perks. You could easily double your earnings by looking after the ladies if you follow my drift. Just keep it legal. I don't want to hear a single complaint. I have two teenage sons and a daughter in Sydney. I would like my boys to come over here, learn the trade, and work out with you at the gym."

"Your wife too?"

"No chance; we divorced years ago. This is all for my kids, it is their inheritance; I think the world of them and they deserve it. I want to give them the father I wish I had. But it is not going to be handed to them on a plate," he added. "They are going to work at it for it if you know what I mean. They'll be serving at the tables; learning the business from the bottom."

He abruptly changed the subject. "You know, Jamie; we need good photographs of you before the brochure's printed. I'll arrange for a photo shoot right away. By the way; how did you get on with Yvonne last night?"

"She is a tigress in bed," I laughed.

"I thought she might be. They all have the hots and compete with each other for the number of lays they get. There's not a romantic one among them. They're all on the pill and to them you're just a work-out."

As we were speaking we were approached by three different girls who cheerily waved across to Dan before joining us. I was introduced to them as the new fitness instructor and found myself in the company of Francine, Heather and Samantha. I asked them where they had come from. One was from Auckland and the other two were Australian. I was invited by Dan to show the girls the gym. It was a good sales strategy; these girls meet the wealthiest people; travellers who are influenced by their insider knowledge.

Dan had business to attend to and would be absent for three days. In the meantime I had my work cut out to manage the gym; set it up and make a good impression. As soon as he had gone I invited the three lovelies to tour the gym with me. They had other things on their mind; like the beach for instance. "The gym sounds like a lot of hard work to me," laughed Samantha. I would rather do something much more exciting to keep my stomach muscles in shape," Her friends giggled at the innuendo.

The workout that morning was at the beach rather than the gym and the three of them being alone together perhaps gave them an impish confidence they might not have shown when on their own. It was certainly a case of the girls being in charge. I wasn't complaining as the girls mixed sunbathing and swimming; playing playfully in bikinis which when wet were so revealing they might not have been wearing anything at all. There was no such thing as modesty here I thought.

Later we all headed back to my cabin; the theory being, why mess up more cabins than one. There was showering and hair drying to be done; maybe cosmetics to be applied. Was there anything else? Well time would tell and it did. I was leaning fast that this location or rather its lure was based on no holds barred Bacchanalia. As I entered the shower section I could see the girls were teasing and messing with each other in what I can only describe as inappropriately. There was much affection between them; the kind of activity I had heard something of but hardly expected to encounter. These girls were bi-sexual.

My first thought was of mild shock; the second was that I was intruding but before I could retreat Francine grabbed my towel and tugged it to the tiles. "Come on, Jamie. Don't be a spoil sport; get with it, you hunk. You're not in Fiji now. This is the real world. Why miss it?"

By the time the afternoon had run its course I was beginning to wonder if I could keep up. If I had prided myself on being a bit of a lady-killer previous to Tahiti, I was finding the boot or rather the high heeled shoe was now on the other foot. If we guys had been behaving as these girls were we would be arrested. The job was going to be a lot more demanding than I had anticipated. Another thing I could forget: It wouldn't be me seducing the women; they were going to get to me and the other men first. It was interesting that for the first time I was the prey, Le Village the lure.

RETURNED TO DEVIL'S ISLAND

It was the setting for a pause in my worldly wanderings for the weeks passed by in a constant routine of teaching others how to weight train and body sculpt whilst earning a little bonus with the ladies as Dan had predicted. I certainly wasn't going short and perks don't come much better.

It was a good experience; a life changing period and a distraction from the memories from my past. I had very little time to dwell on what might have happened if Susan had come along with me. Perhaps we would have been in England by now and perhaps married. I was still in love with her and I would have liked to have settled down and devoted my life to her. Could that have been possible I wondered?

A few weeks passed and Dan's two sons arrived and settled in. The tourist receipts kept on rising as did the girth around their waists, despite my efforts to keep them trim. I knew I couldn't compete with the kitchens. I benefited in more ways than one for my bank account was steadily growing. Dan again had made a wise prediction; the ladies were generous. I also ate correctly and worked out in the gym, putting on a few pounds of solid muscle as I practiced what I preached. If I was again attracted to boxing then it would have to be as a light heavyweight rather than a middleweight. I was heavier but in pretty good shape.

Dan left the islands in January 1959. He had a new project in American Samoa on his mind. As money was difficult to export from Tahiti Dan looked after affairs for me and transferred money and letters to my family in Fiji and elsewhere.

Back at Le Village there was a photo shoot of me working out at the gym. New brochures were printed with a centre spread of me posing with my boxing title. Business was good. David, one of Dan's sons, was acting manager when his father was travelling. Adam hung around with me or rather clung to me. He clearly wasn't his father's favourite and it showed. I just hope he learned to deal with the lack of empathy and fatherly affection. To him I became something of a surrogate father figure and he hung about me most of the day. I did wonder if he was gay and if that was the reason for his dad's antipathy towards him. He was certainly affectionate; a real tactile kind of guy who was always invading my space. If anything he seemed to be around even more when I was in private situations and I was a little embarrassed by his apparent interest in me when I was undressed. It was a bit unnerving at times.

He was at the time sixteen and handsome enough but with delicate feminine features and mannerisms. He wasn't the slightest bit interested in the ladies. I worked out a training program for him; enough to keep him out of mischief. He did in fact take to weight training and body building with an enthusiasm that surprised me. He had simply been a slow starter. As so often is the case he became a little obsessive about his looks and toning and he very soon had a confidence and physique that did him proud. Maybe it helped to bring a new masculinity in him?

Returning to reception one evening I found four letters waiting for me? I hurriedly opened the first, which was from my sister, Malti. She had given birth to a second son and had named him James after me. Mother was well but desperate for me to return home. They had received a few letters from father who was still in Central India. He was living in the village of Faizabad where he had managed to locate some of his long lost relatives; his father's brothers and some of his cousins. They were all unknown to us. My grandparents had left them all behind when 70 years previously they had boarded the Fiji bound labour ships in Calcutta.

The next letter was from Claire. She was now at the University of Auckland. In her letter she told me she was still very much in love with me. I missed her too and her letter was for me something I took very much to heart. That letter would be tucked away where I could read it time after time again. Not for the first time I found myself yearning for her and the past. You don't know what you've got until you lose it, as the song says. The third letter was from Ruth. She missed our passionate lovemaking but was pleased she had the portraits of me to remember me by. The fourth note was from Nirmala. It contained a smiling photograph of my two sons, Surendra and Narendra. My eldest was by now almost two years old and my youngest close to his first birthday. I felt sad and regretful that I couldn't spend time with them. After seeing their pictures and reading Nirmala's letter I longed to hold them in my arms hug and kiss them.

Yes, I had gained much in between leaving them and the great career I now had but I had lost much too. I was under no illusions. I was simply going from one paradise to another. Feeling sad and sentimental I headed for the bar, had a large beer then strolled over to my cabin. There I saw Heather fast asleep on my bed. That was the way things were here.

Next morning after breakfast I was back at the gym; there I had an arrangement with a group of wealthy Australian ladies of a certain age. Before long I spotted Adam strolling nonchalantly towards me and in his wake several seriously overweight women. Adam began his warm-up in the gym while I took the group of women for a power-walk and a muscle-loosening swim in the bay. This was the pre-massage regime. Afterwards it was strenuous work pummelling the fat but someone's got to do it.

It was with some relief that I afterwards undressed and stretched out on my cabin bed; expecting a little me time. Out of the blue and without the courtesy of knocking Adam came in the cabin and sat on the bed next to me. He reminded me that his dad was due back that day. He and David were meeting him at the airport that evening. Thankfully, that was all he had come to tell me and thankfully I was soon alone again. I had felt a little uncomfortable with him sitting on the bed almost touching my nakedness.

We were all glad to see Dan back. He certainly had presence and left a gap in Le Village life when he wasn't around. He told me he had met up with Robert and Ruth while he was in Tonga and that Claire was settling down at the university in Auckland. I told him about the letters I had received before telling him how well his two sons were doing at the gym. He agreed that the results were showing already.

"Did you watch any boxing in Tonga?"

"No, but the Tongan heavyweight champion, Kitone Lave who you will remember went to London is still making a name for himself. He has beaten several more British heavyweights and rumour has it that Rocky Marciano has declined twice to fight him.

The Tongans believe that Lave could beat Marciano and indeed both Dan and I hoped so too. He had been a good friend of mine. My boss went on to say that he had good reports in about me; they had come in along the grapevine. He was pleased that I had settled in and I hoped that I had at least met Dan's expectations if not surpassed them. As an aside he told me he was expecting functionaries from the French immigration service. He would be applying for an extension of my work permit.

CHAPTER 7

In the days that followed my extension visa was granted. I had made many friends in Tahiti and began to love living there. One evening in October Dan told me that my friend Kitone Lave had booked in; he would be staying at Le Village. He is going to fight Sakiusa Cawaru the Fijian champion at the national stadium in Papeete. Both of the outstanding sportsmen were booked to train at the gym.

Within days the two fighters arrived and began training but at alternate times. I sparred with Lave, jogged with him each morning and as in the past massaged him. On October 31, 1959 Dan and I sat by the ringside and saw Kitone Lave beat the Fijian heavyweight champion by a knockout punch in round ten. After the fight we had a party for both of the fighters before they flew back to Fiji on the same flight.

Before I knew it my second Christmas was being spent in Tahiti; time sure goes fast when you're having fun, especially in a part of the world in which seasons, if there are any, are barely noticeable. I was again getting itchy feet; there was restlessness about me and I couldn't shrug it off. Only a fool could leave a job and a place like this; what was driving me ever onwards? Most young men of my age would have looked forward to a lifetime working at Le Village.

Even though I had more than any man could hope for on this island of love I felt trapped and that familiar feeling of wanderlust began to haunt me. It was high time I chased my dreams once again and moved on.

As time passed I began to collect information about New Zealand from the air stewardesses; making notes of addresses of factories and boarding houses. Finally I visited the Tasman Airline's office in Papeete and booked my flight to Auckland. Again it was a sad parting and there were a few who questioned my wisdom.

After a farewell party at the clubhouse, and having collected a handful of references from Dan and other clients, I said my goodbyes to everyone and was off on my travels once again. On January 4th 1960 I boarded a Tasman airlines plane at Faa'a airport in Papeete and headed for Auckland, New Zealand.

* * *

RETURNED TO DEVIL'S ISLAND

Feeling intrigued by venturing once again into unknown territory I sat quietly and nervously daydreaming. I was contemplative as I gazed out of the airliner's window vaguely aware of the comforting hum of its engines. Far below the small cluster of islands; the blue lagoon and tall palm trees were soon to disappear behind me. Closing my eyes I began to doze whilst daydreaming about those I was again leaving ever further behind. Out of the blue a friendly voice opened my eyes again. "Hi Jamie, how are you doing?"

Looking up I saw a smiling face, someone I had no recollection of seeing before. "I don't think we have met have we?"

"True we haven't. I stay in Papeete with my boyfriend when I am in Tahiti but the other girls have mentioned you. Heather told me you would be on our flight," the airline hostess smiled.

"That was kind of her."

"Would you like some refreshments?"

"I would love a beer."

"That won't be a problem. Is this your first ever flight?"

I told her it was; that I had arrived in Tahiti by schooner. There was no need for her to suggest I relax; I was quite laid back by it all. Only when we were preparing to land did I feel apprehensive. For me that was a white knuckle ride. Some eight hours later we arrived at Auckland Airport. A few exchanges followed and Heather's friend, who I now knew as Pauline, reminded me of the hotel used by the cabin crews; she even suggested that I join them on the mini bus that was soon to be taking them there. Save on the taxi fare she told me. During the journey, which included a stop at the Tasman Airline office, I got to know Barbara and Grace, the two other air hostesses as the cabin crew were then called.

Barbara's background was Manchester and as we sipped our drinks in the small bar across the road from the airline's office I was listening into the conversation and by now wondering if and when we would get to the hotel. "Do you know if Heather, Francine or Yvonne are in town?" I asked.

Pauline thought about it for a moment and then said: "Yvonne has flown to Fiji this morning. Heather is in Wellington but Francine should be arriving this evening from Sydney. We'll have a little sleep this afternoon then go out for dinner before going on to see a band called The Kingston Trio in a concert. You fancy coming with us?"

"That's the band that sang, Hang down Your Head, Tom Dooley.'

"Yes. They are touring New Zealand. You can come along and see them if you want, they are really good."

That much arranged the bill was paid and the next stop was our hotel. On the way we went down Queen Street and what is commonplace now was then out of this world to me. Nothing, not even photographs prepare you for the sheer height and splendour of modern buildings of a great many storeys. Add to this the crowds, the busy junctions, traffic lights, the trams and shops; I was wide-eyed amazed. I think there were more people on that street than I had seen in the whole of Fiji. This by comparison was a teeming anthill.

Soon the taxi began to climb slowly uphill and I spotted the Rosana Private Hotel sign and then the hotel. There we were made welcome by a lady called Nora who happily flung open the door of a small room situated at the far end of a first floor corridor. I looked around; there was a small bathroom and a single bed with a window overlooking Ponsonby Road. Within minutes of her closing the door quietly behind her I was fast asleep.

When I awoke it was 6pm but to my surprise still light outside my window. Back in Fiji it would be dark by this time; here the sun was still shining. I checked several clocks before I was finally convinced that here nightfall was considerably later than it was back home and this changed with the seasons.

The road fronting the hotel was again heaving with people. The buses and trams were rushing by as cyclists weaved in and out of the traffic. Why was everyone seemingly in a rush to get to wherever they were going? It was quite a spectacle. I also wondered at the sheer numbers of European faces: It was very much as I might have expected England to be. Mine was one of the few non-European faces there; here I was the minority, not the Europeans. At least mine was a welcome face; especially when a little later I opened my room's door to be confronted by Francine and a friend I was yet to be introduced to. Her name was Camilla. Introductions over the ladies went off to do whatever ladies do behind closed doors and forty minutes later they re-appeared; this time the dress code was smart casual. Soon we were joined by Pauline, Barbara and Grace and they all looked so casual and stunningly beautiful, the aroma of their perfume was tantalising.

The six of us were destined for one of the illegal bars in Collingwood Street the police turned a blind eye to. The girls were a byword for vivaciousness. They told me that my visit to Auckland would be an unforgettable experience. I was intrigued but with their high spirits who could tell?

The show was to be at the Eden Park; I had heard of it in sporting circles and one felt that in the present company it was all very sporting. The cab driver like the bar owner obviously wasn't too worried about his licence; I am sure he would have lost it had a cop noticed his cab being so full that I had to sit Grace on my lap.

It was difficult for me to get to grips with the thought that after all these years I was finally in faraway Auckland. Whatever dreams it had held for me I couldn't have imagined the female introduction to the city. No one in Fiji would have ever believed my good fortune. As the band appeared on the floodlit stage the members of the Kingston Trio took a bow and began their performance with the song that was to become such a memorable hit: Hang Down Your Head, Tom Dooley.

It was a great show and was followed by a visit to a restaurant; a favourite watering hole of the air hostesses. That unfortunately was as memorable as it was going to get but perhaps that wasn't such a bad thing. Apart from my brief siesta I had covered a lot of miles over many hours; I was mentally and physically drained.

Not so for me the next morning; the same couldn't be said for Grace for when she replied to my tapping on her door after it had been daylight for awhile she had obviously just awoken and was still in her dressing gown. She was surprised but pleased at my suggestion that we do town together. As I recovered my work references from my room she pulled herself together and not long afterwards we were making our way down Ponsonby Road to Auckland's Queen Street. In answer to her question; did I have any contacts to call up I told her I intended to find an Englishman by the name of William Bailey and his wife, Vera?"

"They are friends of yours?"

"Yes, Bill was my foreman where I used to work in Suva. I also know some Tongan boxers who are here in Auckland. I will find them all when I have settled."

I did not mention Claire. I was thinking I would take a look at her letter again and find her address. Grace wanted to know what the big deal was for me in London when most Londoners would give their right arm to be where I was.

I reminded her that my passport was British; we Fijians were British subjects. However, New Zealand and Australia don't allow us to stay here more than three months. We have to find sponsors to enter the USA which is problematic. Mother England was the least challenging. Anyway, like Dick Whittington I was sure I was going to find my fame and fortune there. My naivety amused Grace.

"Once you see the back streets of Manchester, Liverpool and London, you will be on the first plane back to the South Seas."

Before long we were outside the Garrick Hotel and conveniently a bank where I exchanged my Tongan pounds and French francs for local currency before entering the hotel. It must be a great place to work I thought to myself as we headed for the small reception area where a suave elegantly dressed man was waiting. I asked him if I could see the manager. "You are looking at him," he told me.

Smiling, I dived into my bag to retrieve my paperwork: "I have just arrived here from Tahiti and I am looking for work."

I handed the sheaf of papers including the gym brochures to him. Looking through them studiously he finally peered up at me. He had a broad smile on his face. "I am impressed, son. You are the middle weight champion of the South Seas then?"

"Yes sir, I won the title in Tonga. Do you have a gymnasium here where I can work perhaps?"

He shook his head. "I am afraid, young man, we don't have a gym at the hotel. We do need a helping hand in the kitchen. If you are still interested I will ask someone to show you around."

I looked at Grace then back at the man, hesitatingly. "Thank you for your offer, sir, but I really need to work in a gym or a health farm," I told him with a shrug.

He grinned as he looked me up and down. "Health farms in New Zealand are called pubs. We like to drink beer, get fat and die happy."

I smiled and headed for the hotel's lounge bar where we sat by the bar and ordered two large coffees. "Why do you address every Tom, Dick and Harry as sir?" asked Grace.

"It is what I was taught in Fiji. Every white man was referred to as, sir."

"Well, you are not in a third world country anymore, Jamie. You are in the real world now. Please don't call anyone sir again. Let them call you sir for a change."

I smiled, lifted her hand to my lips and kissed it. "You are so sweet, Grace, thanks for the advice, I like it. How long have you been in Auckland?"

"Six weeks. Barbara and I came together after spotting an advertisement in the Sunday Times; Tasman Airlines were looking for air hostesses. We thought we had better see the world a bit before we settled down; before we got married and had children.

I smiled and looked into the distance. "I have the same idea. So far I've only done two thousand miles around the islands and I have another ten thousand left before I get to London. Will it ever happen, I don't know"

We had beer after the coffee and sandwiches for lunch. When we were parting company I again kissed her hand. She just looked at me and smiled politely. "Jamie, I like you very much. You are sweet, kind and very handsome. In fact, the girls all talk fondly of you, but . . ."

"But what, Grace?"

"Well, Francine tells everyone stories about you."

"Stories? Thanks for telling me this, Grace."

"Oh, I don't mean to stir anything up. I just want you to know and to be a little careful in the future. The less said the better." She tapped the side of her nose as she smiled. Walking out into the road we hailed a taxi to take us back to our hotel. As we stepped on the veranda there was Nora the landlady. As usual she was sitting in a rocking chair and knitting happily away. Handing the rent over to her I made for my room and as I did so she called after me: "Oh Jamie, I believe that West Field Freezing Works are advertising for casual labour. They pay good money. You should go and see them in the morning. You take the No 9 bus outside here at 7 o'clock. It'll take you right there."

I told her I would take her advice and check it out before walking Grace to her room. My companion took her key from her purse and after a pause invited me inside. As we sat facing each other by the small table close to her bed I sensed empathy and taking her hand in mine again and again kissed it.

"Jamie, I am not ready for this. I am afraid I miss my boyfriend in England and don't feel settled here in New Zealand. I might seem bright enough but these are very sad and lonely times for me."

I stood up and tried to take her in my arms to comfort her.

"No Jamie, please don't. I just want to be left alone."

I dropped her hand and walked reluctantly towards the door. "Thanks for your company, Grace I really enjoyed being with you." She smiled. I detected sadness in her eyes but there was nothing I could do so there was little point in my staying.

Closing the door quietly behind me I followed the corridor to my own room where I lay on top of the bed. I suppose I was feeling similarly isolated. Grace's rejection of me bothered me; surely I thought to myself, there was the opportunity for comforting each other.

This was the first time I had ever been rejected by someone. It was a new experience for me and I didn't like it one bit. I was also thinking how sad and lonely my lady friend was. I could have comforted her and let her have my shoulder to cry on.

My thoughts were broken by a rapping at the door to my room. I hurriedly opened it to be confronted by Heather. Without invitation she came straight in to my room like it was hers; like she was my roommate. I had no wish to get involved with either her, Francine or Yvonne again but making that clear to them wasn't easy. I needed them still. They could have made my short stay in Auckland difficult.

After a few minutes of light-hearted banter during which my attractive visitor teased me and there was much sexual innuendo she got to her feet and began to move like a stripper. The music on my radio was perfect for the occasion. First there was her tunic top and then her smart skirt and their removal was followed by her panties being artfully teased down her shapely thighs. After a few dancing movements she watched my reaction and gently pushed me on to the bed and sat astride me like a dominant man and made love to me. Afterwards we lay beside each other as though nothing out of the ordinary had happened, as though we had just shared a meal. "Have you met Grace and Barbara yet?" she asked.

I told her I had and thought they were both nice girls. Her next question was loaded and obvious. She asked me if I had had them too. I acted stupid, like I didn't know what on earth she was talking about. She put it to me bluntly; she sure had a way with words. I assured her we hadn't but they were both feeling homesick and couldn't wait to get back to Manchester.

"It gets everyone that way," Heather smiled sweetly. "They will adapt. We all do. It isn't home they need; it is a man or a woman lover. Once they are getting it on a regular basis from someone like you or me they will be fine. You know what I mean?" She began to giggle.

"But don't Grace and Barbara like dating girls as well?" I asked.

"No, they don't as it so happens but I wouldn't mind getting my hands all over Grace. I am up for it. I am not sure she is though."

I had thought as much without of course saying so and smiled at her reply. She pushed the point and said she could tell I had noticed. She added that Barbara was very beautiful too and she fancied her as well. Heather told me that she, Francine and Yvonne had a few plans in mind that would include the two air hostesses that had taken their fancy.

I was curious at the turn of conversation and asked her how, if that was the way they were, they were into men too. She replied that she wasn't anti-man or anything like that and until she got into the job she hadn't had a relationship with a female.

She explained; "When I first became an air hostess I was just into men but things began to change after meeting Francine and Yvonne. Anyway, the men in this job are mostly gay and aren't interested in us. We just discovered that it was as much fun being ourselves. We are not really gay," she added with a rueful smile: "I suppose though we are bisexual but it is no big deal. I don't like being stereotyped; I am just me."

There was not a lot I could add to that and I just sort of looked on bleakly as Heather dressed and cheerily went on her way, telling me as she paused at the door that she would see me the following day. I suppose that is what you call casual sex. To her it was no big deal; a visit to the gym. "Are you doing anything tonight?" I called.

She told me she had a few friends to meet up with and as I heard her steps disappearing I couldn't help but wonder if they were friends or whether it was another sexual encounter. For some reason I thought of Grace and it occurred to me that she would be on her own in her room. As soon as the girl down the corridor opened the door it was clear she had been weeping. Pretending not to notice I asked her if I could take her out to dinner that evening. We both needed to get a life.

There was a little time to go and besides she had to get herself ready and so for that matter did I. When I did later reach the hotel lounge where we had arranged to meet up what a transformation there was when she walked in. I swear my heart missed more than a beat. She was dressed in a two piece black leather suit and knee length boots to match. I don't think I had ever seen a head-turner like her. The first button of her white cotton blouse was open and I noticed a gold St Christopher's medal dangling from a thin gold chain around her beautiful contoured neck. Her jet-black hair was still damp and clung to her graceful neck. Tied behind her ponytail was a dark ribbon that contrasted perfectly with her painted lips and fingernails. Grace looked seriously gorgeous.

It was then I became conscious about my own appearance which under the circumstances was hardly appropriate. My faded blue jeans and Fijian style jacket looked absolutely hideous. If she noticed my inappropriate attire she said nothing. Self consciously I walked with her to Martins sly grog situated in Collingwood Street. We used up a few beers before my usual cockiness returned but we must have still looked the odd couple; the catwalk model with the somewhat dressed-down dishevelled sportsman. Despite her appearance she guided us both to a fish and chip restaurant: "I haven't had decent fish and chips since I left England," she smiled. "Do you like fish and chips, Jamie?"

"Please order whatever you fancy," I laughed. "Whatever it is it'll be new to me though I have heard it is something of a national dish. The meal is unknown where I come from. In the islands, we ate fish cooked in curry or coconut milk."

Then I thought of a joke my friend Bill had once told me while he was my foreman in Fiji. I smiled to myself and told Grace that in the South Seas islands we don't eat fish and chips; instead we eat finch and chimps. Grace burst out laughing; the thought clearly tickled her. It was good to see her happy again.

My buddy ordered cod and chips with mushy peas and half a bottle of dry white wine. I watched fascinated as she squeezed blobs of tomato ketchup over the fare on her plate. I can't say that the meal was anything other than tasty; she had gained a new recruit for the English national plate.

RETURNED TO DEVIL'S ISLAND

She chatted happily away. "Back home in England my boyfriend and I were season ticket holders at Manchester United. We went to all the home games at Old Trafford. After the match we ate fish and chips from the local chip shop. It was great fun getting piping hot fish and chips wrapped in newspaper and devouring it with our fingers."

"Manchester United? I remember reading in the Fiji Times about the plane crash that killed some of their most important players. That was a month before I left Fiji for Tonga."

"Yes, you heard about it? It was so utterly tragic. They were known as the Busby Babes because they were mostly so young. We knew nearly all of them and we cried for days after that awful tragedy."

Grace again looked pensive and I thought it best to change the subject. "We better head for the hotel now," I ventured. I hoped she would brighten up a little. It was while we were strolling back towards our hotel we heard loud music blaring from a roadside coffee bar. Deciding to stop for awhile; we thought a coffee sounded good.

Inside we could see a group of teenagers sitting around a jukebox and listening to the current number one hit; it was Save the Last Dance for Me by the Drifters. I was still feeling a little uncomfortable in my James Dean attire. I promised Grace that as soon as I got a job and smartened myself up I would love to parade her at the most elegant restaurant we could find.

We reached our hotel where reception was closed for the night. For some reason it just seemed the natural thing to do, we ended up in my room and sat on the bed. We just sat talking about this and that; nothing special. Just getting to know each other better I suppose. When on this occasion I took her hand in mind she didn't pull it away as she had done earlier. One thing led to another and the light touch of the lips soon became a frenzied bout of kissing and caressing, we were just occasionally coming up for air. Grace had her eyes closed for most of the time. It suited me fine as it gave me opportunity to ogle her beautifully sculptured figure from her toes to the top of her generous breasts without being seen to be doing so.

By this time her leather skirt had ridden up enough for me to really appreciate her slim thighs whilst through the open buttons at the top of her blouse the bulge of her breasts were something to feast my eyes upon. Each was cupped by a black lacy brassiere. Again nature took its course and afterwards I was candid: "I have been gasping for you since the first time I saw you at the airport. You are quite a woman, absolutely gorgeous."

"Thanks Jamie. I thought you were quite dishy too but I wasn't too sure because of the reputation you have. I have heard it said you would screw a mossy grid."

I couldn't help but laugh at the thought of that. "So, what made you change your mind, Grace?"

"To be honest; you're not the first bloke I have got it away with but you're the first from the ethnic minority; as they say in England. I knew you were a boxer and it just seemed like a wow experience. Francine and Heather often talked about you and I wanted to see if you were as good as my imagination suggested you were."

I resisted the temptation to ask her if I had lived up to expectations and she never took it further. "Are you are on the pill, Grace? The others are."

"I stopped taking it when I left England as there seemed to be little point. I wasn't screwing around. It isn't me. But I sneaked one in last night when you weren't looking."

"So you had planned to be with me tonight?"

She giggled out of I suppose embarrassment at her forwardness and to cover her blushes she began to kiss my face. It was during our lovemaking that I had the weirdest sense of being with Susan. It was an uncanny experience. I had to concentrate to stop myself calling out her name at one point. Afterwards we held each other tightly, each with our own thoughts until she whispered: "Jamie I have to go and get some sleep now."

Gently I stroked her hair. "Sleep here; I will set the alarm for six so that we can both get up early."

She agreed but it was difficult to sleep that night and eventually I was glad of the alarm going off as sleep hadn't been anything but irregular lately. What followed was another first; my first taste of Weetabix topped with Demerara sugar and icy cold milk. Finally, when we left the hotel Grace went on her way to the Tasman office and then goodness knows where. I headed for the bus to find myself a job.

After arriving at the West Field Freezing Works the personnel officer took a long hard look at me. "You can work in the abattoir?"

I thought about that. "Doing what, sir?"

"What do you bloody well think you do in an abattoir? You kill the bloody animals of course."

I was a bit taken aback: "Including cows?"

He looked at me with a thoughtful furrow on his brow. "Cows, pigs, calves; sheep. It is a fucking slaughter house; it isn't a bloody holiday camp, lad. Here we kill the animals, cut and then freeze the meat for export."

To be truthful I hadn't any idea what an abattoir actually did and it was only then that I realised. I didn't bother replying; I just shook my head from side to side and turning on my heel took the bus back to Queens Street. Killing animals was not for me whatever the salary. I don't take blood money and the job could hardly be described as otherwise.

Arriving back at the hotel and telling them what I had turned down I was offered a job in the kitchen. It wasn't much money but it was worth it. As the saying goes, I would rather wash sheets in a brothel than work in a slaughter house.

It was on my first weekend off in Auckland that I decided to take a trip to Manukau on the city's outskirts. I wanted to see Claire and meet her grandparents as well. Purchasing a city map I boarded the bus going in that direction and the trip wasn't as difficult as I had thought it might be. Finding the address was easier than I had anticipated.

Knocking on the door I admit I was a little apprehensive as to what kind of reception I might receive. A silver-haired middle-aged lady opened it and looked me up and down with curiosity. "Yes, may I help you?"

"I am sorry to bother you but may I see Claire?"

She looked a little surprised at my appearance and request. "And who may you be, may I ask?"

"Excuse me. My name is Jamie. I met Robert, Ruth and Claire while I was in Tonga and Clair gave me this address and invited me to meet her here."

Her face broke into a smile. "I see. You must be the young man in the portrait. Yes, please come in and sit down. May I get you a tea?"

I told her I would love one and after she had poured it we cheerfully chatted the hour away while she questioned me all about my experiences. She told me that Claire had gone to Auckland with her boyfriend and they would be back a little later on that evening.

I wasn't that surprised to hear that Claire had a boyfriend. Why should I be? I had had several partners since leaving Tonga. It was one of those things that most young lovers endure in their lives. I sipped my tea as I admired the room and the surroundings. It was pretty obvious that Claire's grandparents, for whom Ruth provided paintings, were very well off. I asked if they were in touch with Ruth; a silly question I suppose.

"Yes, often. Do you want to see the portraits?"

I told her I would be delighted to and followed her through corridors to a room at the rear of their detached home. It was almost like coming home again to see so many beautiful paintings in Ruth's style I was even more surprised to see that scattered among the rest were several pictures of me. I couldn't help but wonder what she had done with the more revealing ones. "She paints so well doesn't she." I said appreciatively.

Claire's grandmother agreed that they were beautiful paintings and told me they were soon to be on their way to their art gallery on Queen Street in the city centre. I didn't allow my curiosity to ask how much they would go for; it was none of my business. It had been a great pleasure to sit and I suppose in a way I had been well paid in terms of Ruth's hospitality.

There was no point in hanging around further. I thanked the lady for her kindness and asked her if she would let Claire know I was staying at the Rosanna Private Hotel on the Ponsonby Road. I would be there until I could find a cheap fare to London. She told me she would pass the message on and with a reminder that she says 'Hi' to Ruth for me I went on my way. My thoughts were filled with images of Claire, Ruth and Robert as I retraced my steps to the bus stop.

During the return trip I noticed a road sign pointing towards Rotorua. That brought memories back for me too and I recalled listening to Radio Rotorua when I used to baby-sit for Nirmala. Yes; Auckland might have been quite some distance and time away but there was still plenty to inspire my recollections.

It was a scenic route and my eyes wandered across the languid Pacific Ocean that ran parallel to road. As my thoughts idly drifted back to the past I imagined the old tomb of Ratu Udre Udre where I once played as a small boy. Back then I had gazed across this same mighty ocean and wondered so thoughtfully at what might lie beyond its vast horizons. I had been fortunate enough to cross a small part of that same great sea and observe just some of the large and small nations that broke up its vastness. But it was still not enough and I knew I had to go further. I had to see the faraway places that the nuns had talked about and which had inspired me.

My thoughts were interrupted as the bus pulled to a final stop at the Auckland bus station. As soon as I alighted I bumped into a group of Tongans. They were all smartly dressed in their suits but still wearing their traditional crunchy mats around their waists just below their suit jackets. Strolling over I introduced myself. Tonga is a small place and everyone knows each other. My greeting them with a maloleilei was followed up by a hug from a massive man who smiled and shook my hand enthusiastically.

I told them a little of my background and my relationship with Tonga before asking them if they knew if George Mahoney was in Auckland?"

"Yes, George is here. He has just won the heavyweight championship of New Zealand. We're all very proud of him," I was told.

I asked if they knew where I might find him and was told he trains during the evenings at the Auckland boxing club. I gathered it was situated somewhere near to the docks. "You will find him there during week days," said another as I waved them goodbye. Walking on I came to Queen Street and made my way back to the hotel where I found Yvonne and Francine sprawled albeit lady-like in the hotel lounge.

"Hey Jamie, we've been to your room looking for you."

"I've been checking out some old friends," I grinned.

"Did you find them?"

"No, but I met acquaintances so I am getting closer. I know where they are and I will track them down one evening."

"Ex-girlfriends?"

"No," I laughed: "Some boxer friends from Tonga." I saw Francine nudge Yvonne and smile. "Can we meet them?"

As we were chatting several pilots and cabin staff came in and took seats adjacent to ours. I gazed across at the new faces. The tall and pencil slim hostesses looked fabulous in their tunics. My mind wondered if they were also into girls and as horny as my present companions. Getting to my feet I made my excuses before heading for my room. Ruefully I reminded myself that I must purchase a transistor radio; I missed listening to music and the room radio wasn't up to much; there wasn't a great choice of channels.

On the Monday evening after work had finished I visited the boxing club where I found my friend George Mahoney. Congratulating him on his achievement I looked on as he trained after which we had a beer together and talked about the good times we had in Tonga. He spent a little time encouraging me to take up boxing again; reminding me that it was my ticket to England. There were other ways to do that I thought to myself. "No George, There will be no more boxing for me. Training is so boring and my heart just isn't in it anymore."

He smiled understandingly. "They pay very well here in New Zealand. By the way, Jamie, do you know that Johnny Halafifi is rated as the number seven contender for the world light heavyweight title?"

I told him it was news to me. "Well he is and he is coming to Auckland next month to fight the American Eddie Cotton. Please come and train with me, Jamie. I can arrange a six round contest for you on the same bill as Halafifi and you will be paid much more than you ever received in Fiji or Tonga. We are talking real money."

I smiled. In truth boxing was the last thing on my mind and after another bottle of Stein lager beer I left George and his Tongan friends to walk back to my hotel. When I arrived there I was surprised to see Francine waiting for me in the lounge. She was dressed in casual clothes instead of her usual uniform.

"Hey Francine, how's it going?"

Smiling, she asked if I was going to the sly grog. You bet I was. We sauntered down to Martin's and as we were having a drink when Heather and Camilla arrived and took bar seats next to us two. I ordered some beers for them and then having satiated my thirst left them to it. I felt that I needed some time to myself.

The following evening after I finished work I strolled down to the docks. I wanted to see if I could find Mason Brothers Engineers. There I hoped to find my old friends William Bailey and Vera. They had been so good to me during their short stay in Fiji and it would be nice to see them again I thought. The scruffy old building covered in smoke and steam and surrounded by rusty old ships wasn't too difficult for me to find. As I entered through the swivel doors of the office a young secretary smiled and greeted me. She asked if she could help me: "Yes, please. I am looking for Mr William Bailey. He gave me this address when he was in Fiji and asked me to look him up if I was ever in Auckland."

She smiled. "Yes, Mr Bailey is here but he is at a meeting and will be most of the morning."

I asked her if she had his telephone number so I could save myself another wasted journey: That way I could call him and pick a time that was less awkward. Very helpfully she jotted his number down on a scrap of paper. I told her who I was and retraced my steps to the hotel.

Before long my three months visa expired but I de-memorised it and stayed on illegally for another three months. I would take my chances. Eventually I did meet up with Bill and Vera and he kindly arranged for me to apply for the job; he would nod it through and I could work for Mason Brothers. That was good news but it was the only good news. The application had drawn attention to my illegal status in the country. The New Zealand immigration office refused a work permit and residency so I had no choice but to leave the country. Perhaps my overstaying had blotted my copybook. I had to stay on the move.

One of the questions on the application form was: Are you of wholly European origin? It was a polite way to ask if the applicants were White. Obviously, I was not and I had little choice but to leave. I made one more trip to Claire's grandmother but my ex-girlfriend wasn't at home again. She hadn't left a message either, which was in a way disappointing. It seemed she had moved on and maybe her silence suggested that I do so too. I would have liked to say goodbye to her before leaving for England.

CHAPTER 8

On Monday afternoon the July 7 1960, I said goodbye to the air hostesses and boarded the Dutch liner SS Waterman. It was destined for Southampton. Grace and Barbara had supplied me with various addresses in Manchester where I could perhaps find rooms and once settled find some work. They did warn me of the never ending cold winters of rain, hail, fog and snow. I wasn't put off though I had to admit it sounded grim. Hell or high water, I was determined to go there and find out for myself. Anyway, I had little choice. There was no going back.

Once on board I was given the keys and shown to a cabin that had four bunk beds that were crammed pretty close together. They sure pack them in. After leaving my few belongings on top of a bed I chose as best for me I made my way to the decks above and by this time was feeling a bit down and lonely. I can't imagine there were many on board who were on their own: So many of my fellow passengers were holidaymakers, family and friends. As the ship blew its horn and departed the shores of New Zealand I was again missing my loved ones I was leaving behind in Fiji. This time I was sailing so far away that there was a possibility of there being little likelihood of my return. This was pretty final for England was literally on the far side of the planet earth. There are few places further away from Fiji and then not by much.

I stood thoughtfully on the deck until the sun set below the horizon; only then did I make my way to the ship's lounge. Propping up the bar I nursed a large frothy beer with the intention of finding solace in the drink. It was company of sorts. Within minutes I was surrounded by a group of high spirited Dutch teenagers, all of them girls. They crowded me as they ordered their drinks, smiling and giggling as I tried to figure out what they were saying.

Soon a bell rang and the barman told me it was the signal for dinner. A bit lost and on my own I followed everyone else through to the dining room. As I reached the doors the steward tapped me on my shoulder before I could enter. "Sorry, no jeans allowed in here, sir."

I smiled self consciously and thanked him. Returning to my cabin I changed into a smart pair of slacks before returning to the restaurant. That was better: One of the stewards guided me to an empty chair amidst a group of eight older women. Shyly I sat down with the ladies and saw beaming flashes of expensive dentistry beam back at me. As I glanced across the tables I could also see the smiling faces of the teenagers sitting at a table directly ahead of where I was now sitting.

After the usual small talk with my new companions we were soon chatting away like old friends. One of the ladies told me they were on a world cruise having left Amsterdam five weeks earlier. So far they had visited New York, Panama Cannel, Fiji and Tonga. Another lady interrupted and told me that our ship will be visiting Papeete in Tahiti. This was of course where I had worked prior to leaving for Auckland.

From there, our journey was to continue via the Panama Canal to Havana, New York and Southampton before the ship returned to the Dutch port of Rotterdam. This was all news to me. It had never occurred to me as to enquire as to the route the ship was to take. All I knew was that it was on its way to England. In fact, all I was interested in was getting to England in a hurry. That wasn't going to happen now. I settled down for the long haul.

There were compensations. Returning to Tahiti and the chance to see my old friends at Le Village thrilled me. As we chatted and dined my sad thoughts evaporated and I was beginning to feel my old self again. After dinner I strolled around, discovering some more of the ship before joining the ladies for a drink in the lounge bar. As I talked to them I was approached by one of the Dutch teenagers. "Hey," she asked cheekily. "What's your name?"

I looked up at her young face and smiled. "My name is Jamie and I am on my way to England." I replied proudly.

"Jamie. It is a nice name," she replied in good English. My name is Ingrid. I'm travelling with my parents." As she spoke she pointed towards a couple sitting at a table close by. "We saw you boarding at Auckland this afternoon. All the girls think that you are quite dishy."

I didn't reply to that one but whoever says it is the boys who are most forward? I was trying to work out her age before looking over at her parents table and nervously smiling. They were all watching the introductory teenage performance and smiling good naturedly "Those two friends of mine sitting next to them are my friends, Saskia and Maude.

As we chatted the other two girls joined us, their friend Ingrid having broken the ice. They were echoing my own thoughts as apparently age was an important factor for us all. Ingrid asked how old I was. I kept it to myself as I knew it can be tricky. I hoped I looked a little younger; not that I was much more than a teenager myself. "His name is Jamie and he's going to England," said Ingrid proudly to her friends, talking as though we two were old friends. I shrugged and kept on talking to the youngsters.

It was when later I was chatting to the ladies of a certain age that I noticed the very expensive jewellery they were each wearing. Glancing at their gold and silver earrings, necklaces and wads of Dutch Guilders placed in piles on the table in front of them I was impressed. There was some flaunting of the wealth going on or the spectacle of ostentatious wealth didn't faze them. "We enjoyed ourselves in Fiji," said one of ladies. "It was unbelievable and the men are so strong and handsome."

"Tonga and Samoa was great as well," squealed another.

"Don't your husbands ever come along with you?" I asked.

"I would have to dig mine up before I could bring him along," said one. Everyone roared with laughter at her remark. One of the girl's parents said something in Dutch and the teenagers left us alone and went back to sit next to them. They kept on smiling and looking in our direction.

"Those teenagers have their eye on you, Jamie. I think they fancy you," said one of the women with a wink and a nod.

I told them they were a bit on the young side and they reminded me that I too was young. I suppose I felt older than I was. I had been around awhile. "In Holland we start young. The Dutch are very liberal minded you know?"

I told them I was twenty three years of age to which one jokingly replied that she wished she was twenty again and knew what she knew now. I looked back at the group of teenagers and saw them smiling deviously. "Their perfume smells good, do you recognise it?" I asked the ladies.

"It's called "Chanel. We wear the same perfume but not as much as the girls. They drench themselves in it. Do you like it?" one asked.

"You can smell us any day," someone murmured and laughed out loudly at her witticism. "Looks like he only has eyes for the young ones," observed another "and who can blame him?"

After several bottles of beer I said goodnight to the ladies and left for my cabin. The teenagers it seemed were coincidentally going the same way. Some of their parents smiled but spoke loudly in Dutch to them; not that I understood a word they said. As I opened my cabin door they giggled and waved before disappearing down the ship's corridors.

Stepping into the cabin I was fully expecting to bump into the other three passengers who would be sharing the cabin but it was looking like I had the place to myself. As I lay in my bunk bed I wondered if the holy man who had predicted my destiny and had named me Krishna, was right. He told my parents that the boy will travel the world and be surrounded by beautiful young women. I tried to figure out if he was just saying that to please my dad or had really seen my future. I soon fell fast asleep.

In the morning I woke to the first bell at eight o'clock and was ready for breakfast well before greeting my companions at the breakfast table. Joining what I now considered to be my table I asked the other ladies what they had in mind for the rest of the day. I was told that some swam in the pool that could be found on the top deck; otherwise sunbathing or enjoying an afternoon drink at the bar. There's a dance tonight," I was told. "There would be tombola tomorrow and a film was being shown and was in the diaries for the following day."

When I asked what the movie was I learned it was Spartacus starring Kirk Douglas and Jean Simmons. That will do for me thought I. Afterwards; in my cabin again I pulled on my boxer shorts, flip-flops and grabbing a towel made my way to the swimming pool. Once there I was pleasantly surprised to find beside it a small gym. This gave opportunity for a good workout before diving into the swimming pool.

It wasn't long before I had company and was joined by some of the Dutch babes. They were now in their bathing suits, looking ever so good and looking forward to having some fun. Not at my expense I hoped. Before long we were cavorting about and getting on like a house on fire when one of them, Saskia, asked if I would be at the dance that night. I told her I would of course; there wasn't much choice in terms of entertainment on a ship no matter how large. I was fine with it and asked her if she had a boyfriend. She told me she did but he was in the Netherlands. When asked if I had a girlfriend I told her I hadn't, which was not quite the truth. I had been involved with several but my real girlfriend was being a martyr on an island known as the devil's own.

Saskia was a lively soul. She told me I would be better off settling down in Holland where there were lots of work opportunities. That didn't wash with me. I was wholly focused on reaching London. There wasn't a Plan B.

Shortly after her swim Saskia stretched out on her beach towel that was spread out beside my own. When I told her later that I was heading for my cabin her face lit up with anticipation: "Can I come with you and see what it is like?"

That was to me a pleasing thought but the alarm bells were ringing. "Sure, of course you can but won't your parents be wondering where you are, Saskia?"

She told me they were off the radar and not expecting to see her before lunch. To my way of thinking discretion was called for and I told my pretty companion that I would get some drinks at the bar; she could follow a little later. I asked her if she remembered my room number and deck. She did.

By the time I reached my cabin I had now more reason to be thankful that I had it to myself. My fingers holding the glasses were trembling with anticipation. I had better place them down. I left the cabin door ajar so Saskia wouldn't feel the need to knock. Before she did so the contents of the first bottle cascaded down my throat. It wasn't long before the door was cautiously pushed open. As she looked around her and expressed her approval the teenager settled on to one of the lower bunks. I passed her one of the bottles I had just opened.

Perhaps she was lonely and looking for a bit of fun while travelling the high seas. And if anything she was doing all the running. I suppose I wasn't putting up much of a fight; well there's no point of being alone when have a companion as beautiful as she was? There was the age difference of course. Five or six years is not a big deal for adults but I was then twenty three-years old. There was a disparity and I was conscious of it. I suppose I was old before my time. As we chatted I learned something of the liberal mindset in Holland at the time. If she was telling the truth she was seventeen but age wasn't an issue anyway. She had been on the pill for a couple of years and such intimacies by now had become more or less standard practice, with the right person. It seemed I qualified. It was I gathered typical of Dutch life. I learned that there was some of the others competing for me. I supposed that might have something to do with their being a surplus of women on board and as far as I was aware I was certainly not the only unaccompanied young male; there were others but mostly older men.

RETURNED TO DEVIL'S ISLAND

It was obvious that she was as experienced in lovemaking as was I and she was quite matter of fact about it. She told me that she would love to come to my cabin often to keep me company as I was alone and looked shy and lonely. Well, she was right I was shy and lonely and a bit of distraction will certainly jolly up my five weeks travel to England. Soon it was nearly time for her to join her parents for lunch.

"What kind of belt is that," she asked when she set her eyes on my boxing trophy and tried it on around her slim waist. I told her it was a boxing trophy and that I had earned it in Tonga. My sport seemed to surprise her; did she expect me to have a cauliflower ear or a broken nose?

"So, you're a boxer? That's interesting," she smiled as she replaced it on the hook over the bedside shelf. Within minutes of her departure I had dressed somewhat more conventionally and was soon to join my middle age women companions at the dinner table. By this time they had a few glasses of wine and were in a flirtatious mood. "Hey, you," one of them smiled. "Where did you disappear to earlier? One minute you were by the pool and then there was an empty space?"

I just shrugged the question off. I think I must have coloured. At least I felt the blood rush to my cheeks and looking around, a little furtively, I spotted Saskia sitting with her parents at the adjoining table. Her friends were there with them. They all looked happy enough. I was ravenous by the time the food arrived; working out, swimming and then making love does wonders for one's appetite. Not for the first time I was grateful for the nuns having taught me the arts of table etiquette. I can well imagine the fool I would have made of myself at such a sumptuous table amidst such surroundings had they failed to do so.

I noticed how my table companions supped their soup with their spoons just half filled; then patting the corners of their mouths with the white cloth napkins. Here was England at its best and Holland too I supposed. There was much small talk; banter mostly and by the time dinner was served I was glad to see the Indonesian kitchen staff had prepared one of their authentic rice based dishes. For dessert there was freshly cut pineapple followed by ground coffee.

As I was leaving I bumped into Saskia and her friends. I was a little dismissive as I had no wish to have my voyage and my life taken over by a group of teenage girls. They had other ideas and they followed me to my cabin and pleaded with me to be allowed inside. Saskia had obviously told them she had been here earlier and now they all were curios to have a look inside my cabin.

Sort of reluctantly I held the door open for my new friends; six of them in total. They were quick to make my cabin the group den. They weren't too much of a tribulation. They were full of fun and constantly fooling about with each other. Saskia had got my belt down from its hook and was again trying it on as were the others. I was just a spectator.

"Where are the others then," one of the girls asked.

"The others?"

"Yes, Jamie: you can't have a cabin all to yourself. We share. Who are the others you are sharing with?"

I told them I had no idea, that I had the cabin to myself since leaving Auckland and guessed that the situation might change once we reached Tahiti.

"I hope not," cried Ingrid. If not we can all sleep here and do things like the famous five in the Enid Blyton books. I thought of the earlier encounter with Saskia and doubted if that sort of activity ever went on in the Famous Five books. I very much doubted it. They all laughed at the suggestion that my cabin double up as a famous six hideaway. As they were leaving there were some hotly spoken words being exchanged between Ingrid and Saskia? I gather Ingrid might have been jealous of her friend's conquest and wasn't best pleased to leave her alone in the cabin with me as the rest went on their way.

I grinned and asked her: "What will your boyfriend say if he finds out that you had been unfaithful to him?" Saskia laughed and didn't answer me as she joined me on the bunk and curled into me. We made love again and relaxed in each other's arms.

"Better show our faces," I grinned. "Coming to the pool? We can always come back here later."

After we had dressed I opened the door a little to see if it was all clear and as I did so I spotted Saskia's friends running away down the corridor giggling. I let Saskia go first, promising her I would follow a little later.

The cruise dance that evening was pleasant enough and there were familiar and new faces there. The band was as good as it gets and it wasn't long before I was joined by the Dutch girls who had obviously made an effort. Their appearance was quite a contrast to their baggy jeans and light tops and they all looked much older than their years. My jaw dropped when I saw Saskia; talk about a diamond in dust. "You're going to ask me for a dance?" she queried. "You look out of this world. Which Christmas tree did you fall off?" She laughed and took hold of my hand. As we danced I held her tightly with my lips resting against her ear and inhaling the tantalising smell of her aroma. Over the top of my partner's head I could see her parents and her friends keeping an eye on us two. We danced to a few more slow tunes and returned to my table. As soon as we sat down at our table Ingrid whispered something in Saskia's ear. I asked her what that was all about; she told me Ingrid wanted me to ask her to dance.

Her friend was dressed in a white dress that hugged every curvature of her well rounded figure and she looked ravishing. Ingrid had legs that went all the way to her pert bottom and at the other end long blonde hair tied in a ponytail. She looked taller than she really was. Our eyes met and we exchanged smiles. "Go ahead; dance with her if you want." I looked at her; the last thing I needed was to rock the boat and on a cruise liner too. But she was serious; why not?

"Sure," she said and smiled as she got to her feet. Stepping out on to the dance floor we slow smooched to Elvis Presley's latest number. "You are so Young and Beautiful'. It somehow fitted the occasion perfectly well.

I held her knowing well that all eyes were on us and soon I began to gain confidence and I held her more tightly to me. The aroma of Chanel was overwhelming. When the singer stopped to pause before his next song we were still clinging to each other. The next melody was, "Save the Last Dance for Me." It was the same song I had heard on the jukebox in Auckland when I was with Grace. I tried to get out from her strong grips and dance with Saskia but Ingrid pulled me back and held me tightly. We fell into a clinch and were smooching gently to the music.

It was not long after midnight that the girls' parents said it was time for them to leave and dutifully they trooped off behind the adults like small ducks following their mother. I joined the older ladies.

"That was romantic and a little unexpected," observed one of my table companions. I queried what she had said. "I think the girl you were dancing with didn't wish to be with anyone else on earth from the look in her eyes."

Her companions were highly amused when one of them hinted that bed would surely follow: I don't think she was talking sleep. At breakfast the next morning, we were handed a memo from the captain. We learned that by noon we would be arriving in Papeete. Everyone was allowed on shore until 6pm at which time we would be setting sail for Panama. That would be the last time I would experience the Pacific I thought to myself.

After breakfast the girls trooped into my cabin as though they owned it. Clearly Ingrid and Saskia had issues and they were mouthing off at each other in Dutch. It was all double Dutch to me. Finally it seemed that Saskia got her way whatever had been decided. Ingrid left in tears and the others sympathetically followed the unhappy girl except queen bee herself.

I was due for an earful myself. It seemed that jealousy was rife and I did point out that I had danced with Ingrid at her invitation. "I suggested you dance with her; not fuck her on the dance floor. You two were fucking embarrassing."

I was told that was it; I was having no more 'fun with her'. The silence was broken by the sight of green vegetation seemingly flowing past the cabin's portholes. It was time to call it a day on that upset and carefully closing the door behind us we headed for the top deck to see where we were. On getting up there near the boat deck we could see our cruise liner was being lined up for berthing at the wharf; we could soon disembark and spend the full day in Tahiti. As customs and immigration came on board I spoke with Saskia. "I lived here awhile, Saskia. Why not ask your parents if I can show you and your friends around town?"

Her parents who were standing nearby didn't seem too comfortable with my suggestion but I assured them I would look them after Saskia and I shook hands on it; I meant it. I told them I used to live there and knew it as well as did any tourist guide. The parents muttered between themselves. This was followed by a cheer from the girls. This suggested the tour was on. It was—for the ten of them.

"Ten? Who are the others?"

They nodded in the direction of four small boys. I guessed they were about 8-years old. There wasn't going to be a language problem as everyone spoke English.

As we disembarked a young Tahitian women greeted us by placing a garland of frangipani necklace over each of our heads. I parted with $10 in full payment, which seemed to make the vendors happy enough before strolling off along the quays with my little party and then down the Boulevard Pomare. Fortunately for my pocket everyone bought their own ice creams. It was a pleasant tropical scenario. I was recognised in the post office and the staff came over to chat with our small group. Our next port of call was to be Le Village; there I would be really feeling at home.

Leaving the youngsters outside I engaged with the reception staff who were clearly pleased to see me but under the impression I was back to resume work. There were a few expressions of disappointment when I told them I was only dropping by on my way to England. Dan and Adam were off looking at the progress of their new hotel in Samoa so I wouldn't be seeing them. I wasn't too disappointed. I had neither the time nor the inclination to engage in men talk when I had this little party of youngsters to look after.

We dined when we felt hungry but there was something of a cloud as it was clear that Saskia and Ingrid still had issues and I was the issue. Even so we ate well and the real icing on the cake was my not having to plunder everyone's pockets to pay the bill. It was on the house. I was told by the serving staff that Dan would approve. I asked if I could show my small party around; there was no problem with that. Heading for the beach we stopped on the way to show off my old gym. There were brochures lying around and I could see they were the same ones in which I figured prominently. The group members were impressed; the more so when they saw the framed photos of me in my sparring gear in the gym.

A spell on the nearby beach and an explanation of its place in history, followed by a swim, took care of much of the rest of the guided tour. It was by this time 4pm and there was just two hours to go before we sailed off across the Pacific Ocean to draw a line under a very big part of my past life.

There was just a little shopping to do. I had my recollections as souvenirs, the rest of our party spent their money on the usual trinkets before strolling back to the ship and had our names ticked as we boarded.

The passengers were in a festive mood and many were singing and dancing whilst as many others had their cameras out and were adding to numerous family albums. In a way I pitied those who would be forced later to look through them. Otherwise there was no delay and promptly on the hour of six the head ropes and the rest of the lines securing the liner to the quay were cast off. As we looked down on the wharfs we couldn't help but notice the hundreds of Tahitians waving goodbye. They were certainly the friendliest of islanders.

Out of nowhere I was again overwhelmed by feelings of nostalgia as I realised that this was quite different from all of the other departures. This was for real and I was at last England bound. It seemed to me that all I had ever known was already over 12,000 miles away. They may well have been for there was no going back now. Even Panama was many thousands of miles distant. This really was time to say goodbye to the glorious South Sea Islands.

Filled with such thoughts I stayed partially hidden on my own on the higher decks; I really didn't want to be disturbed. I knew the feelings sweeping over me as quickly as the bow waves were sweeping past the ship's bows would never be repeated. This was for real and there was no going back. I had made my bed and now I was lying on it.

Gradually Tahiti disappeared over the stern's horizon and I stayed there looking back towards it until it was the faintest of smudges on the horizon. Had I not kept my eyes on it then it would have since disappeared from view but I couldn't take my eyes away from it. The islands held so many memories; they were the custodians of my soul, my very self; everything I was in those lovely islands. It was as if I were leaving myself behind and transforming into another person. Perhaps I was. I was certainly very thoughtful as I took the garland of frangipani gracing my neck and cast it into the flecked waters as they rushed by the ship's hull. The frangipani disappeared from view just as Tahiti had. I felt myself filling up but bit my bottom lip. This was no place for a display of emotions. There would be enough time for that. I was still only twenty three-years old.

One by one I could see other passengers desert the ship's deck. Some like me were on their own and harbouring their own thoughts. There were couples and there were families; small groups here and there. The one thing that everyone had in common was a touch of sadness but they were not as forlorn as was I. I felt sure the mood would pass and soon replaced by hope for the future. And, if I could depart then I could return. That was a much comforting thoughts. I had seen Tahiti fall below the horizon; I would wait to watch the sun slip over the horizon for in a way the sun was going out of my life too. As I was about to finally go and look for Saskia I felt a hand gently resting on my shoulder. Looking around I came face to face with Ingrid.

It was an emotional experience that seemed to perfectly complement the mood and the time, the place and the two people that we were. Only when I thought of Saskia and the possible consequences did I loosen my embrace. "No, this isn't right," I murmured. "You are Saskia's best friend. It is a betrayal, by both of us and we can hardly run away from the consequences on here."

I was also concerned about her youthfulness but she was of legal age and as she reminded me that there was only four or five years difference in our ages whilst there was eleven years difference in her mother and father's ages.

I told her again that I was seeing Saskia and on this point I was reminded that if we were going to talk betrayal then what of Saskia's boyfriend in Holland. She told me it was bullshit to think he wouldn't be upset if he knew of her behaviour. I had to admit it did seem a little hypocritical of Saskia. It also occurred to me that if she double crossed him then she could as easily double cross me. Maybe Saskia had round heels.

Our tryst didn't last too long anyway. We were soon joined on the now breezy deck by a new stream of passengers including Saskia and the gang. I was clearly hot property: "Jamie" I have been looking for you. I even went to our cabin."

I noticed the emphasis on 'our' cabin. I told her that Ingrid and I had been talking which seemed to cut little ice with Saskia. The suggestion then was that we retire to the bar.

CHRIS NAND

Just the three of us headed for the bar, the rest of the group choosing to stay in the freshening breeze and watch as the great ship plied its way to the east. As soon as we got to the lounge I was greeted by several parents who were appreciative of my taking their kids off their hands when in Tahiti. I think the children, and the young ladies too, had given some pretty good reports. I wasn't going to be buying my own drinks that evening. The price of the frangipani was sure returning to my pockets. There was no shortage of friendliness although there were still differences of opinion between Saskia and Ingrid.

I was a little confused and later when alone in my cabin I guessed I wasn't solving any relationship problems for me. I was learning that making love is all very well but there's a shit load of baggage that comes with it. All of a sudden the shine was going off the concept of romance. That baggage was now tapping lightly on my cabin door. It had Saskia written all over the luggage label.

"Are you coming to tombola?" It was a peremptory demand rather than an invitation.

To be honest I wasn't too enthusiastic about tombola; a sort of audience game. That is not to say that inviting in a cold-shouldered embittered girlfriend in to my cabin was much the better idea but it was all I could think of at the time.

Maybe it was an invitation she wanted anyway. She couldn't really have been serious about bloody tombola? That problem was resolved anyway by circumstance. It was her parents command that I show myself and play tombola. They were waiting at the bar for me and there would be hell to pay if I didn't return with her. I told her I would see her and her parents in twenty-minutes time. It was a long twenty minutes; I fell asleep on my bunk. It had been a very long day. Sleep it appeared was the answer to my problems.

It was the following morning before I awoke so I must have needed the sleep; I was woken again by a light tapping on my door. I wondered who it could be. Sure it was morning but morning as in 6am rather than 11am. Someone had clearly been more sleepless than I had been. It was Ingrid who responded to my non-invitation by pushing the door open and joining me on the bed. Well, in a ship's cabin there is nowhere else to sit so nothing too strange about that. Dressed in shorts and a baggy T/shirt she had run along the corridor to join me.

Ingrid had been thoughtless in not bringing me morning coffee but she sure made up for the oversight in other ways. Afterwards she whispered; "Will you be seeing Saskia again, Jamie?

So that was the price tag on making love to Ingrid. That was sure a head scratching question and I really didn't feel I was cut out for international diplomacy. "Er, maybe we should all be just friends. We might get on better that way," I said more in hope than anything else. It was a lesson I might have already learned in life but it was 'fail' for me. "Anyway," I added cheerfully. "We shall all be parting company anyway in the not too distant future."

I don't think it was quite the answer the girl was looking for. "No, Jamie. You don't understand. It is you and me from here on and I do not share. Remember, it was

RETURNED TO DEVIL'S ISLAND

me who approached you and welcomed you on board in the first place. It was Saskia who butted in on us and I am fucking annoyed about that; she betrayed me and she is a queen bitch. Promise me you won't be seeing her again, Jamie."

"Heck," she said as she noticed the time. "Have you seen the time? Where does it go? I must get back before the first bell for breakfast. I made excuses that I was going on deck to see the sunrise with the other girls."

Moments later she slipped out of the bunk, put on her dress and rushed off leaving the cabin door swinging on its hinges. I shook my head: Did that really happen I asked myself. As the bell sounded once more, almost imperiously as though demanding our presence, I hurriedly dressed and nonchalantly strolled up to my place at the table, being a creature of habit.

Ingrid looked happy enough so I was doing something right; as a matter of fact she was wearing the smile of a cat that had just had the cream. Our eyes met and the corners of her lips went right back to her ear lobes. When Saskia caught us two smiling at each other and in such a knowing and intimate way her looks said it all. She was not best pleased and one could almost read her suspicious mind. I glanced over towards their parents and then across to the group of ladies at my table. Everyone looked happy and bubbly, ready to tackle another day on the high seas. No sea sickness here then.

As breakfast progressed, a young brunette and a small boy of about eighteen months of age appeared through the swing doors leading in to the restaurant. As heads turned to look at her she smiled uncertainly as she flicked her shoulder length hair back over her shoulders. She was obviously looking for a place at a table. I expected her to be followed in by her husband but she was on her own. A little embarrassed by the curious dinners focusing attention on her I watched as a steward showed them both to a table set feet apart from my own. As she took her seat she glanced at all the others and in my direction, our eyes met and we both smiled.

As I enjoyed my breakfast that morning I wracked my brains trying to figure out who she was. Although I had been on the ship for quite some time and thought I was at least familiar with the other passengers I had no recollection of seeing this lady before. I imagined she must have boarded at Papeete.

I was attracted to her and if anything was fascinated by her unique loveliness; there was a chemistry or magnetism on my part at least. The curiosity and the suspense of not knowing were killing me. She was outstandingly beautiful and had flashing dark eyes that would have stopped the heartbeat of any red-blooded male. She was in a word, priceless. I kept on glancing at her and each time she caught my eye she would smile a response.

After breakfast I reluctantly took my eyes off her and strolled back to my cabin where I changed into my boxers before stretching out on the bunk. I was pleased that no other passengers had taken a berth in my cabin during our stopover in Tahiti. It had worried me at the time but there would have been precious little I could have done about it. It was nice to be alone; to not have one's thoughts distracted by the chattering trivia of others sharing a cabin. There were times when silence to enjoy one's thoughts is incomparable to all else. As my mind wandered towards the new lady who had added her beautiful looks to my tapestry of female images there was a light knocking on my cabin door. On opening it I was confronted by 'the famous six.' They were smiling and I gathered they wished to join me. In they came and spread themselves around, climbing on to the top bunks; everywhere they could find a seat. It seemed like my place, our peaceful den was going to be everyone else's too. There wouldn't have been room for more than those who had already crammed themselves in.

Ingrid was wearing the same light pair of shorts and T/shirt as she had done earlier; it clearly showcased the lithe but feminine curves. The contours of her youth were clearly outlined. Saskia was evidently edgy and less cocksure about herself or her place in the pecking order. Leaving baggage aside there was no place on earth like a cruise liner for a twenty three year old fit as hell young Fijian. Saskia was watching me like a hawk. I would like to say that reading her eyes and thoughts they were lustful; no, they were thoughtful and brooding and trouble may well have been breeding in that small jealous mind of hers. I hoped I wasn't going to end up in the briny with something heavy tied to my ankles, like Ingrid for example.

I didn't make eye contact with Saskia; I wasn't that brave. I had taken on the best boxers in the ring and won. I wasn't as confident about this presumed bout. Everyone stood silently by the bed and there was a curiosity in each of their eyes.

I took a deep breath. "Let's all go to the pool." I suggested. It was the first thing I could think of; anything to break the pervasive brooding atmosphere. This was all getting a bit too complicated for me and I should have learned to keep a civil tongue in my trousers. My suggestion was too little too late; Venus or Vesuvius; call it what you will, the simmering stopped and the explosion lit the place up.

Saskia began hurling abuse at Ingrid and immediately all hell let loose. Even though I had a rough idea of what the problem might be, for I couldn't speak Dutch remember, I stayed well out of the way. Hell hath no fury like a woman scorned it is said; you tell me about it. It was then that Saskia began waving her finger accusingly at me. "And you, Jamie, are a fucking bastard. You screwed her this morning didn't you? Go on, admit it you treacherous bastard. You fucked her this morning. Own up."

I looked sheepishly at Ingrid. I knew what I knew but I didn't know what Saskia knew or what Ingrid might have told her had she been eager to put one over on Saskia. I was getting no help from Ingrid. She was saying nothing at all and just turned away. She wasn't smiling but I bet her heart was. I felt like I had been set up. Without denying it I tried explaining to the jilted Saskia. "Listen to me, Saskia?"

She glared at me, her eyes filled with hostility: "No, I don't want to listen to you. I am going and I never ever wish to set eyes on you again." With that she flounced out of the cabin: Not to the ship's rails I fervently hoped. Saskia the underdog had the sympathy of the others. Her friends looked at Ingrid as though they had just discovered her on the soles of their shoes before marching out after Saskia. The slam of the cabin door nearly blew the wax out of my ears.

RETURNED TO DEVIL'S ISLAND

There wasn't much to say after that operatic performance. Ingrid and I lay silently on the bed for a few minutes before I apologised. "I am sorry to break up your friendship with Saskia," I muttered though clenched teeth.

"Please don't be sorry. She tries to control everyone and we are at each other's throats lots of times; I usually have to defend myself. She is a bossy bitch and thinks she is number one."

I stroked Ingrid's hair thoughtfully. "Your parents will wonder where you are. I don't want any problems for you."

She agreed that time was now up and we had promised to meet up after lunch before I watched her svelte figure disappearing down the deck's corridor. There not being much else to do I made up to the swimming pool where who should I encounter but Saskia stretched out on a sun lounger. Yes, life on a cruise liner for a single guy is good but there's no escaping from entanglements. Clearly she wasn't amused and I am not quite sure why I put myself in the firing line by sitting next to her. Self immolation you would call it as she was breathing fire and brimstone.

I tried to explain to her that we had a wonderful time but that in four weeks time we would be getting on with our lives; going our separate ways. Holiday romances don't last forever. We could all be either good friends enjoying precious moment of the excitement and adventure of our togetherness or let the ill feeling between us spoil the remaining days of our journey. Some day when we were older we could look back at this voyage with fond memories. Hating each other is not the right way. We all have to reach our destiny as good friends. If we were passengers on the Titanic it would put things better in perspective; live for the day.

Saskia sat up straight and looked at me carefully. "Yes, Jamie. I believe what you say but why mention the Titanic? How can you speak like that?"

"I had to speak like that to make you understand the reality of meeting each other on this floating tub where anything could happen. Just take a good look around you."

She turned her head this way and that and clearly visible the big green white flecked mountainous waves were sweeping by. Thoughtfully it brought realisation of how the ship was our survival chamber. We were like on a space craft in deepest space. It was a sobering thought. There was no sign of either land or birds to be seen anywhere; just endless ocean with the nearest land many days away. We looked at each other for a while and her expression changed and a smile appeared. She was the loveliest of girls when she was natural and not being self-centred. My ramblings had eased the tension between us and it was all hunky-dory again.

"Come on," I called: "Let's go swimming." As we used the ladder to get into the pool I unintentionally came face to face with the pretty brunette I had seen at breakfast that morning. She still had the child with her. I caught her eye and she smiled shyly before turning away and carrying on with her swimming. She remained close enough for me to introduce myself; I was curious about her. "Hi, my name is Jamie; James. There's no mistaking you; you're the lady who sat opposite at breakfast."

"Snap!" she smiled. "My name is Christine and this is my son, Stephen. We are on our way to London to see my parents; his grandparents of course. They haven't seen him yet."

I smiled. "I couldn't figure out this morning why I had not seen you before on the ship after ten days at sea. You seemed to appear out of nowhere. I guessed you must be a mermaid and you climbed on board during the night. I couldn't account for your little boy."

Christine laughed gaily at my take on things. "Oh, Jamie; I wish. I was seasick and Stephen was too; neither of us could leave our cabin until after Tahiti but we're over it now. I would never make a sailor let alone a mermaid."

I asked her where they were from and she told me their home was in Auckland and she was heading for London. I told her that we must both be mad; leaving the Pacific for cold and wet London.

As we two chatted Ingrid joined us and began to tease and play with Christine's little boy. He was as bright and as bubbly as was his mum. That gave me the opportunity to chat directly with Christine and it was what I might call the Nirmala affect. I was choked with wanting to know more about her; she had the kind of perfection you normally see only in the best glossy magazines. I had to learn more about her. I asked her if her husband was in Auckland or London. She told me he was in Auckland. He was a police officer in the city. He couldn't get the leave to go with her to London and anyway, the tickets weren't cheap and he was on a policeman's wage. She told me she had seen me when boarding at Auckland.

Ingrid had by now joined Saskia; it was good to see them both chatting happily again and I left Christine to look after her son as waving to my two Dutch friends I climbed out of the pool and having got the pool out of my system headed back to my cabin.

I was followed by Saskia and Ingrid so the cabin was still evidently the pivotal meeting place for my circle of acquaintances. At least they were both in good humour, which made a refreshing change after recent skirmishes. Yes, they were smiling but there was something a little odd about their smiles; deviousness comes to mind. I had every right to be suspicious.

There wasn't much said between us other than the usual niceties; both girls immodestly sprawled out on the bunk beds and clearly they weren't intent on confrontation of any kind. There was however much teasing.

One dare followed another and what started out as a swimwear party ended up as a nudist get together. Decisions, decisions; the last thing I needed to do was to show any kind of favouritism but I still recalled the books on lovemaking positions I had discovered at Nirmala's.

I remembered that not only was making love to two women simultaneously possible; it was fun too. I remembered my first time in bed with Monica and Isabel in Tonga which was my first threesome and again in Tahiti with the air hostesses who were insatiable when it came to love making. I was glad that they had warned me of

European women and their demands during love making. I couldn't be sure if it was Saskia and Ingrid's first threesome but we had the whole afternoon to find out. They were unlikely to tell me but it had the bonus of banishing the green-eyed goddess we call jealousy. There's nothing like a bit of sharing and I was like a dog with two tails. Well, I had two tails didn't I?

"Hey, that was good," I finally conceded as I lay exhausted by our lovemaking; I needed a breather; a bout in a boxing ring was less draining but this was far more enjoyable. I asked them whose idea that was and if they had ever done anything like this before. Neither had but they would say that wouldn't they?

Maybe they had just dared each other. Whatever, I wasn't complaining. I just hoped they were on the pill because otherwise the consequences of my dalliance were going to be born on the same day; I wondered if they could be classed as twins? I put such thoughts out of my head and re-joined the real world.

This was turning out to be a cruise and a half; who needs to be a millionaire thought I. Huh! Even Dan wasn't living life as good as I was. Was anyone? Not surprisingly my nostalgia for village life was quickly disappearing over the horizon as had the islands earlier. I was a very happy young man. Being involved with Saskia and Ingrid was the best thing happened to me it certainly was a distraction from my thoughts of being so far away in the deep of the Pacific Ocean.

Soon 15 days had passed by since we had departed New Zealand and our day to day routine had fallen into a predictable pattern with the usual diversions. Saskia, Ingrid and I began to meet clandestinely and enjoy each other's company for we were all on a learning curve and life wasn't likely to get better than this. At twenty three-years of age I could cope but only just. It was on the morning of the sixteenth day at sea that the ship's skipper, over the p.a system, told us that we would soon be sighting the Galapagos Islands and as it so happens crossing the equator too. The earth had certainly moved for me a few times recently; I might as well see what it was like in the middle. We were all invited up on deck after lunch; something enjoyable was about to happen.

During lunch the excitement and laughter at the tables suggested that everyone was in a party mood. It was good to have a break from shipboard tedium; we were all looking forward to the unexpected party about to take place. As soon as we finished dining we headed up the ladders to the ship's decks and gathered around the poolside. It wasn't long before the ship's captain, in the company of other officers and crew members, turned up to join us. Champagne was being served and cameras were clicking whilst some of the passengers focussed their binoculars on the Galapagos Islands. There was a great deal of good humoured revelry and after many empty glasses there were those who ended up in the pool.

As we all messed about and behaved like kids I noticed Christine and her son Stephen standing alone not too far from the pool's edge. Going over to the pair I invited them over to join the more joined up celebrators. It was a good move; Stephen immediately took to the fun and games and he delighted everyone with his presence.

CHRIS NAND

It was an occasion when it could truly be said that a good time was had by all. It was a moment to savour; we were now in the northern hemisphere of the earth. It was another first for me, which gave me some thought as I lay on my bunk bed day-dreaming as usual.

Another three days of shipboard tranquillity and trivia passed in which the east were as calm as a millpond. We were approaching San Cristobel and the entrance of the world famous Panama canal that would take us through to the approaches to another of the world's great oceans; the Atlantic. This is truly where east meets west; two different worlds in one.

After a day's sightseeing in that uninspiring poverty stricken city we sailed through the canal and into the Caribbean. It was then that the captain informed us that because of some political upheaval between America and Cuba our planned visit to the Cuban port of Havana had to be cancelled. It was a disappointment for everyone, and I suppose the hoteliers and the bar owners, the gift shops on the island but that is politics, we had to live with it. The ship was continuing on to New York.

Several days passed and the weather was becoming noticeably cooler as we made our way up the eastern seaboard of the United States towards New York. For some reason unknown to me or to anyone else Ingrid's mood seemed strange of late. She was very brooding and if anything obsessive; even threatening to throw herself over the ship's sides if I didn't agree to be her exclusive boyfriend. It is the way some young women tick I supposed. Reasoning with her seemed to have no effect whatsoever, she was totally focused on having my undivided attention and time after time threatened to take her life by going into the sea if I couldn't agree that we were to be from here on a couple.

No amount of sweet reasoning had an effect on her. It only seemed to make her more agitated. I had no desire to commit myself; there was no way I wanted a serious relationship and everything I had planned, all I had worked towards all my life would have been threatened by such a relationship. I had only one obsession and it wasn't Ingrid, it was London, England.

As a consequence of my refusal the relationship I had with both girls deteriorated. It was a sad ending to a great holiday romance but in other ways it had to happen; if anything it was a blessing in disguise and a timely one.

My friendship with Christine and her son Stephen was becoming more close and there was now a personal side to it; a togetherness that fell short of exclusivity. She knew London well and was great at helping me familiarise myself with the country so I wasn't completely in the dark on arriving there. She knew the best places to go to that I might get a job and how to go about getting lodgings; the places to avoid and especially important the prices I might be expected to pay. I wasn't carrying much financial fat and I had little choice but to be careful. I was grateful for the care she was showing towards me and began to spend more and more time in her company.

The afternoon before arriving at Manhattan we chatted together, with her son of course. She had told her small son about the tall buildings that we were going to see

RETURNED TO DEVIL'S ISLAND

soon. I was fascinated listening to her and was looking forward to seeing the Statue of Liberty and the then tallest buildings in the world. It was then that Christine asked if I might help her out.

"When we dock, Jamie, can you help me with the baby's push chair when we get off the ship as I would love to see Manhattan and I might never again get the opportunity to see the city." She said she would like to take some photos for the family album?

I was happy to oblige and maybe we could do the sightseeing together. I needed to take photos too and I was looking forward to seeing the skyscrapers. The tallest building in Fiji was just three storeys high and I was astounded to see the ones in New Zealand that had fifteen or so storeys. I couldn't begin to imagine what 102 storeys must be like.

As we laughed and enjoyed each other's company Saskia and Ingrid glared at us from their nearby table. Neither of them now liked my taste in women; there's no pleasing some people. Christine and I continued to chat good naturedly until the dinner gongs were being prepared to summon us to our tables.

As we dined we could see through the restaurant's windows a festivity of shore-based lights. It was a signal of sorts. Everyone began to get their fare share of food down their necks so they could get to the decks and not miss anything. Everyone wanted to see what the best cityscape on the earth's surface was really like.

Soon Christine with Stephen joined us and before long we could see the awesome spectacle of Manhattan in the distance. Already we could make out the Statue of Liberty; ironically a French building rather than an American one. The clicking of cameras was reaching din levels and there was great excitement. Interestingly the ship heeled over, not dangerously but noticeably to its starboard side. This was due entirely to the numbers of passengers now congregating on the starboard side to take in the sights of New York and its approaches. Carrying little Stephen in my arms I stayed close to Christine. We began to stare at each other and I suppose it was the shared experience that drew us closer together. It was then that Stephen, perhaps tired or overwhelmed by the excitement, began to cry and demand his bed.

"It is late for him. He is tired, Jamie. I must take him down to the cabin. Will you help me to carry him and I will take the rest of the stuff. Here, give me your camera case."

It suited me; we had all day tomorrow to explore the city. Christine smiled shyly and led the way to her cabin with me following dutifully at the lady's heels; Stephen was already fast asleep by the time we opened the door. As far as he was concerned we had already reached his cot. As we passed the small group of Dutch teenagers they stood and watched with silly grins on their faces. I shrugged. It didn't bother me.

The child's mother turned the key and let us both in before closing the door behind us. I lay the baby down to continue his sleep in his cot and turned towards the cabin door. They are small cabins and you couldn't swing a cat in them. Christine suddenly grabbed my hand and pulled me back towards her. As I held the young woman in my arms our lips met; gently at first and with an urgency that brought back memories of Nirmala. I sure envied her policeman husband. With our lips joined we fell on the small double bed and made love passionately before she suddenly stopped.

"I bet you were screwing those Dutch girls haven't you?" she laughed good humouredly as she sat astride my thighs. "Be honest or this is as far as it goes, pretty boy."

I gave a non-committal reply which seemed to satisfy her as I wondered what might else satisfy her.

"I don't blame you; frustrated littler virgins," she laughed as her nether parts were grinding into my lower torso. I grinned and went along with it. "They are unlikely to be virgins at their ages," I laughed.

"I bet you're not either. I know you guys from South Seas; I bet you were hardly out of nappies."

Somehow I thought of Susan and from the maturity I was feeling right now I was pretty sure she was right. That was a long time ago and sure I was young then but then so was Susan; furthermore, she was not a Dutch girl. That was a thought that made me think of my own contradictions. After making love there seemed little point in my returning to my cabin and so Christine became part of the Manhattan memory for me, and I suppose for her too. New York! New York! Indeed!

During our intense lovemaking the ship had berthed at Pier 92 and we awoke to the sound of stevedore shouts; commotion on the decks and vehicles coming and going. We gathered the gangways must be down and everyone would be getting ready to spend a little time in the city seeing the sights. Us too but priorities being priorities we made less passionate but wonderful tender love before I slipped out to shower and change.

There were many knowing smiles and familiarities exchanged between us as we enjoyed our breakfasts. A little later I found myself helping her get ready for our break ashore; I think we were going to need and enjoy each other's company that day. It wasn't long before, holding her hand in one hand and the pushchair in the other, we found ourselves on the teeming dockside. Without our noticing where they came from we found ourselves surrounded by tour guides touting their excursions and then we were ushered into a ferry that took us to the Liberty National Monument and the Ellis Island Immigration Museum. There we took photographs of empty suitcases belonging to the first immigrants who arrived to the U.S. from all over Europe. The guide told us that more than 12 million immigrants had first entered America through this immigration centre and were kept at this point before starting a new life in the United States.

After purchasing tickets we entered the massive metal lift inside the giant Statue of Liberty and went up to the balcony inside the statue's crown. After admiring the splendid views and taking even more photographs we took the steps rather than the lift before returning by ferry. Once back on Manhattan itself we hailed one of the city's famous yellow cabs and directed the driver to the city centre. As we sat arm in arm in the cab's rear seat we must have looked like a happily married couple. I wondered if her cop husband was at that moment looking equally the happily married husband of another woman in his wife's absence. I put such thoughts out of my head as with Stephen sitting happily in my lap I watched the passing streets on the cab's way up to Times Square and Broadway.

"Anywhere in particular?" asked the driver.

I looked at Christine. "Okay, just take us to Times Square please." In truth I didn't know much about the tourist attractions in Manhattan and went with what little recollection I had. I could remember only the pictures of Times Square so why not as a starting off point?

Alighting from the cab and paying the guy off we two took in the sights, which were truly awesome. Once seen, never forgotten. The city itself is far bigger than the imagination. From Times Square we took the walk to the Empire State building and entered through the giant glass doors. We were hardly the first to do so but to us it was sheer magic on a stupendous scale. Taking the lift up to the 86th floor we stopped to pick up a few postcards and from the post office situated there sent them to friends and relatives around the world.

I hadn't forgotten Susan, who by rights should have been with me. I of course sent her the loveliest card out of the batch I had purchased. I was far too sensitive to mention in my message that she should be here with me. I addressed it to the leprosy island where I presumed she was still living and working. There was a godliness to her being there I supposed. Instead of bringing comfort to a husband she was bringing soothing consolation to many who needed her care far more.

Just for curiosity and to be able to say we had been there we went up to the 102 storeys and gazed in admiration through the solid glass windows, across the city and the Hudson River, pointing out all the landmarks before going back down into the city.

There was much to see; perhaps far too much for a single day's trip but we were keen to see as much as possible. We strolled along Fifth Avenue to Central Park where we enjoyed lunch at a small café. The weather was hardly Fijian and I was glad of my leather jacket. The endlessly warm sunny days of the South Seas seemed to be a million miles away; they might as well have been compared with our surroundings now.

Following lunch we had a few glasses of red wine by which time the fractious Stephen was becoming restless. "He's tired," Christine smiled. "It's time for his afternoon nap."

After taking a few more photographs we flagged down a cab and made for our floating hotel. Once there we put the still sleeping little lad in his cot; made love and drifted off to sleep. It had been a remarkable experience.

It was dinner at eight o'clock as usual; a great time for by then we were all famished. As evening approached we assembled on the boat deck once again as the ship slowly sailed away from the harbour. We watched with mixed feelings and to each our own thoughts as the bright city lights of New York faded until darkness fell. As we passed the Hudson River and the Ambrose Lightship it occurred to me that we were entering the last leg of my South Sea Islands odyssey.

As the liner's bows were set eastwards across the Atlantic Ocean Christine and I found ourselves spending more and more time together. I am good with kids and during the day found young Stephen to be a delightful distraction. From the night we left New York I made her cabin my own. After the tumultuous relationships that marked the offset of my voyage it was a pleasant and relaxing finale to my ocean-hopping trek. Yes, the South Sea Islands were out of reach for me now. It was on the seventh morning that on the faraway horizon we could finally see land that bore the name of England.

As we approached Christine was always at my elbow to fill in the detail and gave me a running commentary on everything we set our eyes upon. "That," she said pointing to a finger of land, "is what is known as Land's End. It is where England ends and the rest of the world begins," she smiled. Her hair was flowing in the cool breeze and its whisks were brushing my cheeks. It was a delightful experience.

As the ship sailed along the English Channel it was clear that she knew her geography well. Some of the place names conjured up memories drawn from the books I had read as a kid. There was Cornwall and what she believed must be Falmouth Harbour. Then there was Dorset and the Isle of Wight.

It seemed we wouldn't be seeing the famed white cliffs of Dover; white because they were mostly made up of chalk I was told. "The white cliffs of Dover," she said with a faraway look in her eyes. "You must have heard the song? No, Dover is further up the channel. We would have passed the cliffs had we been going to London but we are going to Southampton. It is some distance away but an opportunity to see some of southern England."

An hour later and our great ocean-hopping cruise liner was nosing its way gently through an armada of small boats, mostly pleasure crafts.

"This is Southampton," Christine told me. "My parents will be waiting for us. Why don't you join us on the trip to London? They would love to meet you and I can help you find somewhere to stay not too far away; I am sure I can."

It was an offer only a fool would refuse. I knew absolutely nothing of England; transport or lodgings, or opportunities for work. My being pals with Christine was going to pay dividends. "I would love that, Christine," I said. "I think it is a terrific idea. I wasn't at all looking forward to us saying goodbye to each other. I was dreading it."

"Neither was I," she simply replied.

I was so glad that I had met her. Fate did seem to look kindly upon this Fijian village kid. As we approached Southampton docks it began to softly rain and I was beginning to feel a damp penetrating cold of a kind that was a completely a new experience for me. Pulling my jacket more tightly around me I hugged myself but it offered little protection. I was shivering; I hadn't done much of that in my twenty years.

RETURNED TO DEVIL'S ISLAND

"Are you cold, Jamie?"

"Yes, you could say that. I am freezing. Maybe it is the rain. It is winter here now?"

She laughed. "Winter, Jamie? This is summer. This is the hottest month of the year. It is August, my friend. You just wait until you see what winter is like here. You will want to go back to Fiji?"

I laughed. "It is a bit early to make a decision on that," I laughed. "Ask me in half an hour."

"Wait any longer," she grinned and held my arm more tightly, "and your balls will freeze off. I once heard a story about the first Pakistanis who came to live in England. It was a very cold winter so they went off back to Pakistan."

I was yet to find out. Maybe it was the reason the English did so much wandering around the globe; they weren't stupid; they picked the warm bits of it. Not even one of them was interested in discovering northern Russia or Siberia.

I did the rounds of the ship looking for friends and acquaintances. I said my goodbyes to the well off middle-aged ladies. They were as good humoured as ever they were. I found them very likeable: "You come to Rotterdam, Jamie, if England doesn't suit you. We will look after you, darling."

Two of them gave me their cards and another wrote her name and telephone number down. Clearly lodgings wouldn't be a problem but did I want to become a dependent trophy stud? I didn't think so. As I gave each a hug I turned and faced Saskia and Ingrid who had been cold shouldering me lately.

When Ingrid saw me she turned away and niftily looked the other way but Saskia held me tight to her and placed her lips on my own. Filled with thoughts both pessimistic and yet hopeful I picked up my case and turning my back I helped Christine get her stuff together and we descended the ship's gangway together. It had been a wonderful voyage and an experience that would stay with me for the rest of my life.

Again there were very much mixed feelings tinged with sadness. From somewhere deep inside a small voice said, "I wish they could see me now." I had left so many wonderful friends behind; I could only thank God that it didn't mean leaving the memories of the experiences behind too. That would be worse than death.

As I stood for the first time on English soil I did gaze longingly back at the great ship's hull. It seemed so different in these surroundings. The skyline was a mass of crane jibs and storage buildings, railway tracks and roads. The skies were overcast and there was a tumult of sound as everyone went about their business. I must have looked a forlorn figure. It had taken five weeks to get here; I had lived and loved life on that beautiful ocean liner and I felt like it was yet another old friend I was leaving. It had been great fun; indeed the greatest of adventures. I swear I had to wipe away a tear as among the multitude I could just discern Saskia amidst the group of Dutch teenagers. I waved; a sad sort of wave before again turning and following Christine through immigration and customs before finding ourselves in the waiting lounges of the Port of Southampton.

Immediately we went through the doors a middle aged couple spotted their daughter. With beaming smiles and wet eyes they called Christine's name and ran to her, their arms outstretched. Her father reached my friend first and while he was hugging and kissing her, the lady who could only be Christine's mum was doing likewise to little Stephen.

The child looked quite bewildered. He was only eighteen-months old and to him the two people who were making such a fuss were total strangers. He was yet to learn how much they would spoil him; there was obviously going to be plenty of that. Looking bewildered the toddler began to cry.

I just took a back seat and let them all get on with it. There's times when you have little choice. I suppose in a way it sharpened my senses about my own family who, if the situation was reversed, would be as ecstatic over my return. They were now on the other side of the world, 12,000 miles away.

My thoughtful meanderings were eventually interrupted by Christine turning her attention to the 'stranger' standing a few paces behind her. "Jamie, meet my parents will you. Do come and meet them."

Smiling a little shyly I greeted them both politely and with outstretched hand. My friend introduced them as George and Margaret. I told them how pleased I was to meet them both. I meant it. She told them that we had been shipboard friends; had done Manhattan together; she told of how I had been a big help with Stephen and not the least with her packing and luggage. She also told them how she was returning the favour and asked if I could join them on the drive to London.

They looked at me with some curiosity and then told me how pleased they were to meet me. As Christine called, let's go, we all trooped off to her parents car. It was a new Rover so the boot was spacious for our luggage; I then climbed in with George whilst Christine and Stephen joined Margaret in the car's rear seat. As we drove off I gazed one last time at the cruise liner and my eyes met Christine's. There was a delightful knowing look that passed between us; it spoke of fulfilment, hope and success.

Soon we were on the main highways and I saw familiar names such as Brighton, London and Dover. For me it was enchantment. Here was the realisation of a dream that had been with me all of my life; it was an objective that had shaped my life and guided my feet. It was the pursuit of an ideal far more important to me than all of my family and friends; otherwise I simply wouldn't be here. I was a magnet drawn to the seat of empire.

George told me they lived in a place called Croydon, which was in Surrey. One of the Home Counties I was told. He continued chatting and asking me questions about the South Sea Islands. "I've never been further than Cornwall," he laughed. In the backseat grandma kept on hugging, kissing and talking to her grandson.

Eventually we started seeing signs for Croydon before driving into a rather plush housing estate in Thornton Heath. Christine's father drew up in front of an enormous detached house with a sweeping lawns and carefully manicured flowerbeds. "Home sweet home, it's good to be back," laughed an obviously delighted Christine. "I see that nothing has changed since I was last here."

George smiled and opened the wide metal gates before driving up the drive to park in front of the double garage. Opening the front doors to the house he helped us get the luggage in; no mean feat and then, as we all went inside they all kissed and embraced once again, leaving me feeling something of an intruder on what was obviously a very private celebration.

"Please sit down, Jamie and make yourself comfortable."

I thanked Christine's dad and settled myself down as I wondered where we go from there. Whilst domestic routine continued I glanced around the room and could see photos of little Stephen, Christine and her husband neatly set out on the sideboard. It was the first time I had seen her husband; there hadn't been any pictures of him that I could see in her cabin; come to think about it she hardly mentioned him. I wondered if it was a good marriage.

As soon as mum and dad were off our radar screen, Christine approached me and gave me a light reassuring kiss. She must have guessed at my feeling a bit of a square peg in a round hole. "Come on," she said. "I will show you your room; everything is fine; I sorted it."

I hesitated. "Are you sure?" I whispered.

"Don't be silly. I asked mum and dad if you could stay a few days before finding somewhere to live. I'm glad we met. Make the most of it while we both can."

"What about your husband, Christine? They might mention me and you will have some explaining to do won't you?"

"Finds out what," she smiled? "I won't tell him if you won't," she chuckled at her own joke. I smiled apprehensively but followed her up the stairs to an empty bedroom. "It's yours," she said: "Until we can get you your own place."

My suggestion that I take a shower brought the riposte that in England, showers are not common, unless they are coming from the clouds. Here people take baths.

"Don't worry, you'll be fine here. Tomorrow, I'll take you shopping. I must find some warmer clothes for you and help you find a job. Then you can move on."

I asked her when she would be returning to Auckland. She reminded me that she was here for six weeks and then reading my mind, assured me that there would be opportunities.

The bath was another first for me. I had never experience a bath of this sort before but I enjoyed it and felt totally relaxed. I lay there for a long time, reflecting on my journey to England. There were no regrets at all. What a fantastic trip it had been! I thought of all the girls I had so far loved without necessarily having lost them. Their images were perfectly clear in my mind. First there had been Susan and Nirmala who had opened the floodgates of my youthful sexuality, and then the others leading inexorably to my present lover Christine. All those beautiful women; how lucky I had been. Krishna indeed I thought to myself as I lay there luxuriating in a bath that embraced me up to my shoulders. I was wondering what Christine had planned for me.

Downstairs was back to domestic bliss; Stephen was being cuddled and fussed over by Christine's mother, whilst George asked me if I would like a beer. Would I?

I would kill for one; my first British beer! It was the first time I had seen black beer. They make such stuff? Seeing my puzzled look they all laughed: "It is Guinness. It is brewed in Dublin, Ireland. It is the country where my parents were born."

I looked even more puzzled. "You know where Ireland is? You have heard of Ireland, Jamie?"

I did recall it but had little knowledge of the geography of it. "Yes," I told them. "Some of the nuns at my school came from Ireland and often talked about their country."

"How interesting," said George. "Are you a Catholic?"

"Yes, but not a practising one."

After a few bottles of the beer we had dinner; my first of fried chicken, chips and mushy peas. This was followed by apple pie and custard with the usual sweet cup of tea. That evening we watched and enjoyed the Lonnie Donegan show on a small black and white TV set. This was followed by a new soap opera known as Coronation Street. In between watching the programmes Christine and I snatched furtive glances and smiles. I was a little nervous in case her parents noticed the electricity that passed between us.

It was after midnight that the shows came to an end as did television; here was nothing else on after the midnight hour. Saying my goodnights and of course my thanks I headed for my bedroom. It had been perhaps one of the most eventful days of my life but I didn't think my thoughts would keep me awake for very long.

As I was dozing off I heard footsteps in the hallway. Others were using the bathroom and eventually I heard Christine chatting to a very drowsy Stephen before tucking him up. I never rally expected to see her again that night and wondered at Susan's living conditions. Could they be as comfortable? I very much doubted it. As for a hot bath such as the one I had just had; I doubted that too. She could so easily have been here in London with me. What will be, will be. Still, there were the warm island waters; life is full of compromises if you appreciate them.

There was silence for a while and I imagined Christine stripping off and enjoying her bath. Yes, it could so easily have been Susan. Suddenly the door of my bedroom gently opened and I saw her form in the light that reflected from the street below. She took her bathrobe off her and slid between the bed sheets next to me. We quietly made love before she tiptoed out to her bedroom.

It was just after dawn when I heard the clamour of the alarm ringing; the clock's alarm that is. This was followed by the usual domestic sounds and I gathered George was getting ready for work; thoughts that were proven right as I heard the car's engine and the sound of its wheels on the gravel driveway.

I was in no hurry and lay there quietly as I listened as the sound of traffic in the street below. It was 8 o'clock and the large bay window in my room reflected the sunlight behind the curtains while the smell of toast drifted up from the kitchen below. I turned over and snuggled under the sheets until I saw my door open and Christine step in carrying a small tray. "Hey Jamie, I've got some breakfast here for you," she said with a beaming smile. She asked me had I slept well.

"Yes but it would have been even better had you been next to me."

"Your wish has been granted," she laughed in her usual light-hearted way. I watched as she placed the tray carefully down on the bedside table before disrobing and slipping in beside me. I was elated but horrified. "Your mother," I asked.

"Mum and dad have both gone off to work and Stephen is fast asleep," she murmured as she curled into my arms. I learned that we would be on our own for several hours. Her mum would return after lunch, George her father in the evening. He was a customs officer at Heathrow Airport.

We spent much of the pre-afternoon making small talk during which Christine chatted with her husband who was calling her to make sure she had arrived in good shape. Afterwards it was opportunity for me to ask her if their marriage was going well and if they were as switched on together as we were.

They had once been as passionate about each other as we were, she told me. But lately it had waned and the attraction just didn't seem to be there anymore. The marriage was running stale. "Now," she told me: "He just mounts me, has an orgasm and falls asleep. It is like my backside is a substitute for masturbating. Who needs that?

"Please don't get me wrong I like being married to him but I need a bit on the side when there is so little excitement at home. I need someone like you so that I can have real sex; doing the things that I can't do with my husband. It's every woman's dream to find someone like you and live out their fantasies. I will let you do things to me that I would be too ashamed to do with my husband.

I asked her if her parents might guess that we are lovers. "No," she smiled. "They are too bloody religious to think that I could even think about sleeping with another man. They think that the Irish missionaries have done a remarkable job on you and you are near enough a saint from Fiji." I threw my head back and had a good laugh. "By the way, I have warned my mother to tell father not to mention you staying here to Richard. As far as they are concerned you were a big help to me and Stephen on the voyage and this is their way, and mine, of thanking you for it."

Ever the realist she knew that what was happening between us didn't have a long shelf life. She was just a substitute for the Dutch girls and there would be in time substitutes for her too.

"Wait until you see the girls here in London," she said with a look of lust on her face. "This is the sexy sixties and they are all into free love, peace and all that shit. The girls call themselves the flower children, take marijuana and have group sex."

"Sound interesting," I said with an expectant smirk. She added a note of caution. "Be careful. Always use a condom because when you sleep with them you sleep with every guy that ever screwed them. Think about that."

"You don't know who I have slept with?"

"I don't have to: All I know is that you have had lots of practice or you have a great imagination."

When Margaret arrived home after doing her shift at the florists where she worked she took over the mothering of Stephen and took him off to the local shopping centre,

"Come on," Christine said: "Let's go to the Army and Navy stores. They might have some nice warm clothes for you. You are going to need them. There is already an autumn chill in the air."

"An Army and Navy store? You mean uniforms?"

"No, that's just the name of the shop," she laughed. I told her that when the war ended in the South Pacific a lot of Japanese soldiers were captured by the allies. Their uniforms were confiscated and later donated to missionary schools around the world. I told her that I went to school for five years dressed as a Japanese Major.

Christine almost fell over laughing when I told her. "You are a pretty funny guy, Jamie. You are a real comedian. The people here in England will just love you."

We were still laughing as we went into the store and after trying out a few suits I bought a light-grey three piece outfit; white shirt, tie with tanned shoes to match. Christine made me change into my new clothes right there in the store's dressing room as she placed my old clothes in a large shopping bag. When I was more appropriately dressed for England I called out to her. As she came into dressing room she took a good look at me and smiled. "My, my, just look at you? You look like a real London businessman now; a very handsome one at that. I'll have to eat you when we get home."

I thanked her for being so kind. She told me there was no need; it was my money I was spending "I have only chosen the clothes for you, I haven't bought them."

We left the shop hand in hand like any other couple. "Come on! I'll show you a real English pub," She was obviously enjoying showing me around. We strolled into a pub called The Bull's Head where I enjoyed my first pint of real English ale before strolling home.

Once there I was duty bound to go into the lounge and show George and Margaret my new look. I saw them glance at each other and smile. My mind wondered to what they thought of their daughter's friendship with a coloured guy from the South Sea Islands. Did they guess that we were lovers?

The following day after Margaret's return from her work she babysat for us again. Christine took me into London on the train. I was thrilled to be looking at my lifelong picture books coming to real life; all the world famous landmarks. I wondered at the reaction if those back home could see me now. I must get some postcards, I thought to myself.

There were other things to attend to. Eventually we arrived at the Employment Office in Mortlake High Street where I registered myself as unemployed. At first, the officials scrutinised me carefully as they checked out my British and Commonwealth passport. They then gave me some forms to fill out. Just as well, Christine was on hand and helped me to complete these after which they were returned to the officer.

Within days I was called back to the same office where I picked up the all important National Insurance Number. I was now eligible for unemployment benefits. "But I don't want benefits," I told her. "I need work."

RETURNED TO DEVIL'S ISLAND

She looked at me carefully. "So do all those people out there," she replied. I looked in the direction in which she had nodded. All I could see were West Indians, Pakistanis and Indians huddled together in a group. "They were here well before you were," she admonished me.

I looked around the area and once again I remembered what Grace and Barbara had told me while I was in Auckland. The back streets of London certainly did look grim and the people looked poor. It was then that I felt the first pangs of homesickness and it seemed to me to be something of an anti-climax.

During my first weekend in the capital, Christine showed me everything there was to see. There was Tower Bridge, Buckingham Palace, and Westminster Abbey. It was then I remembered the Pathe News feature bringing to life Fiji's Queen Salote riding the open carriage in the rain on the occasion of the coronation of Her Majesty Queen Elizabeth. Yes, I had seen it all on the newsreels in our battered old theatre back in Fiji. But I still couldn't quite believe that I was actually here in London at last. I was so far away from that bamboo village and the old tomb and their fascinating and gruesome history; several great oceans separated us now.

My childhood dreams had come true. Finally, I was here and all I had to do was find the streets that were paved with gold. In other words find myself a job, earn a good living and send some money back to help towards my mother's keep in her Fijian home. Generally I liked the look of London. Not all parts were so shabby and poor. I enjoyed the hustle and bustle of the cosmopolitan atmosphere.

After burning layers of shoe leather pounding the city's streets I finally arrived outside the head office of the London Transport Company in Melton Street. There I saw posters advertising jobs for bus conductors. Within moments of showing myself to the desk I was hired. This will do, I thought. That is, until I find something better.

After two weeks training on the crowded double deck buses I was finally left to collect the fares on my own. I have to say that it was a nightmare not knowing the city and the bus routes. It was all very strange to me. I thought I would never get to fully understand them. In addition to such problems I was trying to come to terms with the pounds, shilling and pence system. It wasn't easy. There were occasions when passengers took advantage of me and got away without paying their fare or by paying less than they should have done. Some fooled me by giving me Irish and Scottish pounds; which I found difficult to tell the difference from the real thing; especially when the route was busy.

CHAPTER 9

Before long six weeks had gone by and it was time to say goodbye Christine and little Stephen who were setting off on their return journey. This time they were going by British Airways from Heathrow.

Once Christine was gone I thanked her parents for their hospitality and moved to a small bed-sit in Richmond. Christine had been right about the flower children and free love era. It hadn't taken me long to meet the eclectic genre of London but I didn't indulge in marijuana: It was a distraction from dwelling on what it might have been with Susan being here.

One evening as I walked to my bed-sit I saw a boxing poster on a wall. It was advertising a heavyweight contest between Jim Cooper and Kitone Lave of Tonga. I quickly grabbed a copy of the Boxing News from the news stand and tracked Lave to the Hilton Hotel where he was staying. He was overjoyed to see me; an old friend and so far away from our homes. It was just like old times; we had a few beers together and I was invited to see him box at the Olympia in Kensington. He floored Jim Cooper in round six after which I received a further invitation to his next fight against Dave Rent. This was to take place at a stadium called Belle Vue in Manchester. Unfortunately I could not make it to the northern city. It is some two-hundred miles distant; instead, I listened to the fight on my radio. He stopped Dave Rent in the fourth round by TKO.

A few weeks later I did have dinner with Lave and his English wife Patricia when they were back in London. They were getting ready to leave for Tonga and Fiji for a well deserved holiday. Lave told me that Johnny Halafifi (The light heavyweight champion of Tonga) had beaten the American Yolande Pompey. He had also drawn with Mike Holt. He was finally beaten by Chic Calderwood by TKO in the 12 round. I was pleased that my two boxer friends had done well in Britain. They deserved it. I had come a long way; they had come much further and that was a credit to them.

The weeks went by and I was about to experience autumn; there are no seasons as such where I came from so seasons here in England were interesting spectacle. I was fascinated by the green leaves turning to different colours and hues before falling to the pavements and parks where they formed large clumps; often being windblown. Then upon me my first English winter and I first experienced stinging hail, the lashing rain

RETURNED TO DEVIL'S ISLAND

was hardly new but its coldness certainly was. Then there was the spectacle of the snow. Christmas 1960 dawned and everyone was singing along to Elvis's Are You Lonesome Tonight. It was then that I experienced my first snowball fight, saw my first snowmen.

Goat curries and rice for my traditional Christmas dinner that we ate in Fiji were just a distant memory. Instead, I tried the traditional English turkey, roast potatoes, Brussels sprouts and Christmas pudding at my transport company's canteen. I missed my family back home and longed to see them all. But I was determined not to give in to my emotions and return to the islands. I had to stay and make the most of it until I was finally ready to return.

The news from my sister in Fiji was that Kitone Lave had been knocked out in the fifth round by the new Fijian heavyweight champion named Mosese Varasikete (nicknamed the Fijian Brown Bomber) Apparently, after Lave had beaten three Fijian heavyweights he boasted to the Fiji Times News and assorted media that Fijian boxers were inferior and no match for him. Mosese was determined to knock the living daylight out of him and finally succeeded. Unfortunately that was the end of Kitone Lave's boxing career. Once back in Tonga he was invited to the Royal Palace to meet Her Majesty Queen Salote and the royal family. He and his wife Patricia arrived at the palace gates dressed as tourists and were not allowed to enter the palace gates. Lave insisted that he was now a British citizen and was not obliged to wear a suit with the traditional crunchy mat around his waist. It cut no ice; he was still refused entry. He finally migrated to New Zealand where he lives to this day.

The festive season behind us and as 1961 got into its wintry stride I took driving lessons and passed my driving test with flying colours. I was very proud of that as passing a driving test in London was no walk in the park. Especially coming form an island where we had no traffic lights or the Highway Code. In many cases one had to bribe the driving examiner before passing a test. This was another culture our people had brought with them from mother India.

Within months I had become the very proud owner of a five year old Morris Minor convertible. This enabled me to travel around and in particular to see Brighton and Dover; the places I had so often read about.

There was no doubt about it: There was something about my feet for they were as itchy as they had ever been. The wanderlust was grabbing my gut again. I had to see a bit more of this fascinating country they call England.

It was exactly twelve months since first setting my eyes on England that I handed in my notice as a bus conductor; shoved all my stuff in that small car of mine, and headed up the M1 and M6 motorways to Manchester. I was curious: I wanted to see where Grace and Barbara came from.

Fortunately it was the middle of August and the weather at the time was fabulous; deep blue skies and lush green countryside surrounded me and everywhere looked so inviting! This is more like it I thought to myself; I was pleased to have left the crowds and congestion of London far behind me. I had enjoyed my stay there but it was time to move on.

CHRIS NAND

Spotting the sign to Manchester I headed first to Old Trafford. I wanted to see the home of Manchester United. Then my wheels frustratingly took me to Moss Side before I eventually found the internationally famous ground just as darkness was falling. Parking the car close to the stadium's high walls I visited The Seahawk pub. My mind sadly recalled what Grace had told me about the Busby Babes and the tragic plane crash that took so many of the great team's players in their prime. After a few pints in the pub I treated myself to fish and chips; they were wrapped in newspaper just as Grace had once described them to me.

As the night darkened and the midnight hour approached I climbed back into the car and spent the night there in its back seat. It was to be my lodgings for the night; far preferable to traipsing the streets to find more conventional lodgings. I was awake well before the hustle and bustle of the crowds making their way to wherever crowds go on a busy weekday morning. After reading my dog-eared crumpled map I somehow found the East Lancashire Road that would take me to the City of Liverpool, just thirty miles distant. A little under an hour later I pulled up in the city's Scotland Road and realised I was not too far from the great city's football team stadiums; Liverpool F.C and Everton F.C.

It was a Saturday afternoon and this was driven home to me when I was near overwhelmed by literally thousands of Everton fans; each wearing their distinctive blue and white scarves and heading in the direction of the Goodison Park stadium. Parking my Morris Minor behind a pub called the Everton Arms I tossed a pint of beer down my neck before joining in the parade to the match; this was something I wanted to be part of, even if I didn't have a scarf. I had chosen my day well: I watched fascinated as Everton beat Manchester City 2-0. It was the first time I experienced the din from 40,000 cheering fans. Once again I felt far away from Fiji where I was used to crowds of no more than a thousand and that even for such a prestigious event as the Fijian Cup final.

After the match I had fish and chips; I guess it was more or less my staple diet but it was nourishing and I liked the meal. I would look after myself with a more diverse diet when I had found myself somewhere to stay. Being August the city was full with visiting tourist and I found it difficult to find a bed and breakfast or a small room to rent. I settled for the night in my car again and returned to the pub when it opened at noon the next day. After a brunch of bacon and eggs I chanced upon the local newspaper, the Liverpool Echo. There was of course a situations vacant section and hopefully this ever optimistic Fijian wanderer searched for something suitable; hopefully something that paid well and might offer prospects. There wasn't that much on offer and in fact the only job vacancy I could find, and which I could do well was a job on the buses again. Not in Liverpool but a place called Birkenhead. I remembered Birkenhead from my friend Bill Bailey who had once told me that he had served his time at Camel Lairds in Birkenhead before he ventured out to the South Seas and finishing up as our foreman at Bish Limited in Suva. I was now intrigued and had to find Birkenhead. After seeking directions I was soon driving through the Birkenhead's

King's tunnel that took me right outside Camel Lairds. The smoke filled buildings and the tall rusty cranes was enough to drive anyone away. No wonder Bill ran away seeking for paradise to the South Sea Islands. Only the poor and the destitute were leaving the paradise islands to come Birkenhead, I thought. Perhaps I was one in a million. After twenty minutes driving I was at the Birkenhead Transports Head Office in Laird Street. In fairness my stint on London's buses had been lively and reasonably well paid; why not I thought. There and then I was interviewed and accepted for the job. Fortunately one of the busmen had a room to let and I moved into the attic of his home in West Bank Road, just outside the technical college on Borough Road.

After my first week's work I went into the Liverpool city and as I strolled down Church Street I found a store called Weaver to Wearer. A young sales assistant approached me and asked if she could help me. Telling her I was looking for some white shirts for work and was shown a selection of what was available.

Following her I couldn't resist glancing at her long slim legs as she trotted ahead of me. She seemed friendly enough and I shyly smiled and looked away. She was pretty and very polite so purchasing anything from her wasn't going to be too difficult at all. We smiled again as our eyes and body language began to flirt. I hoped she was on commission; I bought a couple of pairs of socks and other items that I was in no need of and she was still smiling really friendly as she placed my purchases in the shop's bags.

I thanked her as I took the proffered receipt from her well manicured hand. As I reached the door I turned around for a second look at her. My interest in her was obvious. I was alone and lonely in a new town and I needed a friend. As a matter of fact I needed distraction otherwise my mind will be twelve thousand miles away as it always was. Would we be just ships that pass in the night? She was still looking whimsically in my direction and smiling. I waved and went into a nearby coffee bar. As I sat down and enjoyed my drink I looked at the receipt to see there was a scribbled telephone number on it. There were also the words, 'Why not phone me then? Linda'

I was certainly intrigued by the city and whatever it had to offer; all I needed was someone to share it with, I called the number she had given me and I recognised her voice right away. I had been afraid a shop manager might have picked the phone up and was unsure of what he or she might do if I asked for Linda.

"Hey Linda; I have just come out of your shop and I found this number on the back of the receipt." She giggled nervously as though unsure as to where to take things from there.

"Well, is this a joke or what?" I asked. I was hopeful but a little confused. It was something of a direct approach but was she serious.

"No, I am amused because you are so cheeky; I never really expected you to call me you know."

I asked her if I could meet up with her later but that didn't look too hopeful; she wasn't going to finish until 8 o'clock that evening. I thought about it but I was at a loose end anyway: "That isn't a problem for me, Linda."

Again she giggled as though a little unsure or surprised at the outcome of her own audacity. I could meet you in the Leggs of Man; in the lounge bar," she suggested. "It is easy enough to find. It is right next door to the Empire Theatre."

I told her I would be happy to and putting down the phone I felt elated: I had made friends and I had only just hit the city. My luck was holding out. I left in plenty of time to find the pub and using my loaf and asking I found it easily enough. I arrived with a few minutes to spare. Getting myself a beer I took a seat unobtrusively in a small corner from where I could see the doorway. I must admit to a familiar pitter-pattering of my heart as Linda walked in, spotted me and came on over. As I stood to shake her hand I asked her what she would like to drink. It was going to be a Babycham; a drink I had never heard of but if that was what she wanted. Second question; would she like to visit a restaurant; we could have meal together. It was a little better than the pub. She thought it was a good idea but first of all she needed to call her mum who would be waiting for her.

As Linda used the pub telephone I couldn't take my eyes off her. She was tall and had shoulder length blond hair and a fabulous slim figure. She cut a friendly and attractive figure; factors that went a long way to my way of looking at things. I guessed she would be about twenty-years old. As she put the phone back on its cradle she smiled and said. "There isn't a problem, let's go, Jamie."

But where? I was the new boy in town and had little knowledge of where everything was. "I am new in town," I told her: "Have you got any suggestions?"

"Do you like Chinese food?"

"Yes, I love it. It sounds good," I grinned.

"Right then," she cheerily replied. "I know just the place. It is the best in town."

We walked on past the Adelphi Hotel and up to China Town where she found the restaurant she had in mind; it was called the Jangwhah. It was as good a place as you could find for a getting to know you better situation. After my usual travel stories had been exhausted we came on to a topic that was more or less of international interest anyway. I wanted to know more about the city's musical scene.

She looked at me as though wondering if she should be answering the question. Maybe she thought I came from Hicksville. "Have you heard of the Beatles, Jamie?"

I told her I hadn't but I had heard of Emile Ford and Helen Shapiro. "They are both in the top ten charts, aren't they?"

"Yes that's right," she smiled. Emile Ford's "I Don't Know Why I Love You" is the current number in the charts. Helen Shapiro is number two with Walking Back to Happiness. You know them?"

I told her I did; of course I knew of them and added that I liked Elvis Presley, Billy Fury and Buddy Holly."

At least I wasn't too much of a square. "Billy Fury is from here and we see him a lot but tonight I will introduce you to the Beatles. They have just returned from Germany where they made a name for themselves. I think they'll be world famous one day," she said confidently.

RETURNED TO DEVIL'S ISLAND

After dinner we headed down Duke Street and into Whitechapel and then on to Mathew Street where the Cavern is situated. "Be careful Jamie," she warned: "We have to go down eleven steps into the cellar before we reach the Cavern. You had better hold my hand; it can be pretty dark until your eyes get used to it."

I held her hand and together we went down the steps of the dingy old Cavern; they are really old warehouse storage cellars. I went straight to the small bar and got us both a drink and as I got back Linda introduced me to four leather-clad young guys who she said were the Beatles. I met John, Paul, George and the then drummer, Pete Best. Up on the stage was a teenage girl singing her heart out. Her name I was told was Priscilla White.

I was mesmerised by her powerful voice as she sang Summer Time at the top of her voice. "So what's Fiji like?" asked John. "Do the girls still wear grass skirts like we see them in the movies?" I saw Paul and George chuckling.

"He's bloody sex mad. If he finds out the girls wear grass skirts he'll be over there like a shot with a lawnmower in his hands," grinned George.

"Count me in", laughed Paul as everyone laughed. "Tell me about Indian music Jamie," John said as he took me in and made his own judgements. "I love the sitar and the tabla drums; that's music. Someday, when we can afford it we plan to go to India, just to listen to their classical music. We love Ravi Shankar he is an amazing sitar player."

"I would love to meet Ravi Shankar and learn from him how to play the sitar," added George. Pete Best just smiled and rolled his eyes upwards to heaven. He obviously had little idea of what the rest in the group were talking about. "Pete's quite shy," whispered Linda in my ear.

"Okay lads, let's do a few numbers and the get the hell out of here," said John. "I am famished. We must eat and we will meet the girlfriends later."

The band got themselves together on the small stage. There was plenty of screaming going on and obviously these four were popular. John took the mike. "These are some songs that we have written and hope to record some day," he announced.

They played 'Love me Do' and 'P.S. I Love You.' It was an opportunity for Linda to teach me how to jive. We had a great time and afterwards I drove her to her parent's house in Bootle where she lived. A few weeks later we went to support the Beatles in a night club known as the Majestic in Conway Street in Birkenhead. The headliner that evening was a singer called Lee Curtis. He finished the show with a current number one song called: Speedy Gonzales. At that time amazingly the Beatles were not headliner material.

As the days went by I became a regular visitor at The Cavern and soon became something of a Scouser; meeting many people not the least on my bus trips from Birkenhead into the city of Liverpool. It was different here to London; here everyone had time to stop and have a chat; life was unhurried and there was always a pause for a shared joke or to talk football. I also had the pleasure of meeting Ken Dodd, a young and up-coming comedian; He pulled my leg about my suntan.

Linda and I became good friends and lovers. She helped me repaint the ceiling of my small apartment and tidy up the peeling wallpaper in the corners of the room. At weekends we had great fun at the Blue Angel Club, the Beachcomber and the Grafton Rooms. Being a keen as mustard football supporter as are most Liverpudlians she took me to see Liverpool play in the second division at Anfield.

Towards the end of October Linda's boyfriend returned from Germany where he was stationed with the British Forces. This was no time for my being around and not long afterwards they were married and my now ex-girlfriend went off to live with him in Germany.

By this time my social circle was getting ever bigger; moving to Merseyside had been a good move for me. At weekends I went on trips to New Brighton and Liverpool; and Chester Zoo. They were all accessible by taking my small and reliable car through the Mersey Tunnel. There were times when a small group of pals would take the ferry across the River Mersey to the Liver building and spend the time browsing around the shops or the pubs round the Queen Victoria Monument on top of Church Street.

I joined Jim McCollough's Gym in Liscard Village where I pumped iron three times a week but I felt it best to keep my boxing background to myself. My good looks brought rewards other than purse money and I no longer had any desire to having my features misshapen. Weightlifting was just fine. It kept me reasonably fit and strong.

How times flies when you are having fun. Soon three years had flown past during which time I had met a French beauty whose name was Claudia; an art student at the University of Liverpool. During the summer of 1964 she invited me back to her home in Northern France for a visit. I was not sure my Morris Minor was up to the journey so we took her BMW to Plymouth and then the ferry to St Malo before carrying on to Bordeaux where her parents lived.

It was Claudia who introduced me to good French wine and the very best of her national cuisine. She also introduced me to the nudist beaches of Le Verdon Sur Mer where we camped. Eating seafood was now back as a normal diet; I had missed such cuisine since leaving the South Seas. Fish and chips don't quite qualify as seafood for those with good taste, much as I like the British national dish. Oysters and mussels were back on my menu once more. Here we didn't need the luxury of clothes and could go through life naked, for weeks at a time if we so wished and the weather allowed. We only dressed in the evenings to visit the clubs and the nicer restaurants of Bordeaux. After an idyllic three weeks we reluctantly packed our stuff and drove back to Liverpool and eventually back to my scruffy old bed-sitter in Birkenhead.

Soon afterwards Claudia arranged for me to model for them at the art department of her university. It was something for me to do although it didn't pay much; my doing shift work on the buses made it possible.

On my first day at the university Claudia met me on the campus and soon afterwards she introduced me to the art teacher and her students. Within minutes I was shown to a small dressing room and asked to put on my swimming trunks before standing on a

RETURNED TO DEVIL'S ISLAND

table and flexing my muscles. I did as I was asked and was soon surrounded by a class of about ten art students.

As I stood on the table posing I watched the wrapt expressions and the keenness displayed by the students. Some of them were sketching whilst others were fashioning small sculptures. I was very much reminded of the occasions I used to model for Ruth in Tonga.

My eyes focussed particularly on a young lady who was concentrating on a lump of black clay as she studiously carved a sculpture of me. Seeing my interest in her she shyly smiled before averting her gaze. I recall she had the most enormous brown eyes and with their ultra long eyelashes I was in no doubt they would haunt my heart forever and a day. I tried not to make it too obvious but couldn't keep my eyes of her. She looked absolutely gorgeous and again there were the now familiar stirrings; I became desperate to meet her. Each time she glanced in my direction our eyes met almost by telepathy. There was a definite chemistry between us. In fact, the last time I had felt like this was in Tonga when I had first met Claire; she had been the girl of my dreams back then.

My gaze fell on her again and again and I watched her intently until it was time for a coffee break. Pulling on my jeans and tee-shirt I joined Claudia for a coffee in the canteen before returning to their classroom and again posing.

After the class finished at two o'clock I hurriedly changed and left the college with Claudia. As we were walking towards the car park I noticed the girl who had so much caught my attention walking towards the bus stop. This was an opportunity not to be missed thought I. Walking Claudia to her car I made my excuses and told her I would catch up with her a little later. I then got into my own car and drove straight to the bus stop where I hoped to better acquaint myself with the young student if the bus driver didn't get to her first.

He didn't and when I reached her I lowered the window and leaning across the front seat caught her attention. I asked her if perhaps I could give her a lift. Was I going in the same direction; I wasn't sure but right then I sure was. I think I would have taken her to Land's End had she asked.

She smiled and warned me she lived quite some distance away. I didn't take the hint; in for a penny in for a pound thought I as I told her that this wouldn't be a problem and opened the door for her. She thought it very kind of me; I thought so too.

"Right now I just need to know two things," I smiled: "You name and where your home is. You are not going to tell me it is Land's End are you?" Weak humour I know but I was just trying to lighten the conversation up a little.

"Do you know where Formby is; I live there near the golf club. Is that too much out of your way? I can get the bus there. It won't be a problem; I do it every day."

I told her that is wasn't a problem; you see, that was the effect she had on me. I had only a vague idea of where Formby was but I was willing to stick my neck out for this one. As we set off she told me her name was Francesca and ignoring the Highway

235

Code manual I leaned across with my free hand and shook her own hand. I told her my name was Jamie.

We chatted happily away and at my suggestion we stop en route and enjoy whatever she fancied she was all for it. The place we chose was a pub called the Jolly Miller. I strolled into the lounge bar with the delightful Francesca at my side.

Hers was a glass of white wine, mine was a beer and we toasted our good fortune at meeting in such auspicious circumstances. You see a modelling career has its opportunities too and not for the first time I was glad that I was doing the workouts at the local gym.

This was getting to know you time and as she tenderly touched my hand in response to something I had said my heart skipped a beat; it was used to it by now.

I took my cue and held her hand; an affectionate gesture and knowing well how Western women like to have the backs of their tiny knuckles touched with the lips of those who have had their hearts captured by their beauty; I raised her fair hand and did just that.

The response was much as I expected which was of course pleasing and all too soon was reminded that it was getting on and she really did need to be getting home. Distance no object I asked her if I could see her later that same evening to which she replied that I could; about seven o'clock.

Sure I was on a guilt trip about letting Claudia down but these things happen. How could I possibly deny Francesca? I clearly could not. She was the most beautiful thing that had happened to me for a long time.

We did meet as arranged and off we went to see The Sound of Music at Liverpool's Empire Theatre. I must confess that we didn't see too much of the film and so watching it was going to be in my diary sometime in the future; my attention was focused in its entirety on the stunning beauty sitting beside me.

As days went by I quickly fell head over heels in love with Francesca and my friendship with Claudia was as quickly on its way out of the door. Eventually, I was introduced to her parents and was accepted in their home, their lives and their social circle. As love blossomed we began to see each other daily and were by now very much a couple. It was a nice life; far better than I had experienced in London. Sometimes we went out for enjoyable evenings, sampling Liverpool city centre's nightlife. Not too far away was the seaside town of Southport.

There were other times when we stayed in her home and listened to the music of the Beatles, Billy Fury, and Joan Baez and of course, the young lady whom I had seen at the Cavern once named Priscilla White. She had her first hit song under the name of Cilla Black—"Anyone Who Had a Heart".

Apart from a brief period when Francesca became ill with glandular fever we were inseparable. Fortunately September's sun that year was uncommonly warm and we spent many happy and languid hours on the town's beaches. Because of her natural colour Francesca quickly became sun tanned and with her dark eyes and hair she looked more like a sister that a girlfriend, especially given the age difference between us. She was eighteen and by this time I was twenty-five but what did age matter? We were idyllically happy together.

On our first night out after her illness I took her to see the Bolshoi Ballet at the Southport Pavilion. As we were leaving the spectacle we noticed a poster outside announcing the Miss Southport contest. I encouraged Francesca to enter and after a little persuasion she finally agreed to put her name forward.

I wasn't surprised and I don't suppose others were when she walked away with the title; she was a hard act to follow and we celebrated her good fortune at her home with her parents and her university friends.

Francesca had her own dreams and ambitions in life. She planned to finish her education and become the best in her calling as a fashion designer. After just four months together her father decided to move to Buckinghamshire to be nearer his ageing parents. Within a few days they had sold their home and were preparing to leave Formby. It was a heartbreaking parting; tears streamed down our faces as we kissed for the final time and the vagaries of life and circumstance separated us. After tearfully watching they car disappear from sight, thoroughly dejected I drove back to my bed-sit, parked the car and went into the nearest pub to drown my sorrows.

It felt as if my whole life had come to an end. Was God punishing me I wondered? After all, I had left many loved ones behind despite my still young years but now someone very dear to me had left me; it was as if it was payback time. I didn't like it one bit. This wasn't just a taste of my own medicine it was a glassful and I was as despondent as it was possible to be. When the pub closed at midnight I made my uncertain way back to my place and collapsed on the bed. Perhaps it was fate that separated us I thought to myself as sleep separated me from mournful reality.

The latest hit, Blue Bayou, by Roy Orbison, made matters worse. The lyrics seemed to have been specifically written for the drama of our particular separation. It had a double impact on me as the words furthermore reminded me of the tropical paradise I had deserted on the far side of the earth. It was still there but for me it might as easily have been on another planet. I remembered my own little blue bayou by the bamboo village where I had grown up. My love with Susan, Nirmala, and my two sons; I missed them all so dearly!

As the days of soulful depression passed I found it difficult to put Francesca out of my mind. We wrote to each other of course, and I would telephone her every Sunday but it was not the same as being together. We both spoke about how much we missed each other and longed to be together again. But it was not to be. I pined for her, missed her dearly, but somehow the distance was just too great and we drifted apart. Our letters eventually petered out and became less romantic and I was beginning to reclaim my life by meeting others on the bus routes of Birkenhead.

Christmas 1964 came and went. I was promoted to a bus driver but I wasn't happy as a driver. I no longer had contact with the passengers. There had always been time for banter and I was now isolated in the cab; only a cheery wave to the regulars at the bus stops. After a month's driving I volunteered to return to being a bus conductor and immediately felt far happier. The rest of my life returned to normal; meeting new friends and the nightlife.

The Cavern Club had in the meantime changed. John, George, Paul and their new drummer, Ringo Starr had become world-famous. Their dreams had come true. They were fulfilling their lifetime ambition by travelling to India, living with Hindu gurus, learning Indian music and topping the music charts all over the world.

Cilla Black, Billy Fury, Dave Clark Five and Ken Dodd, the young comedian I had once met all became world famous. Liverpool, within the space of a year or two, had become the music capitol of the world. It was a good place to be. Hundreds of fans from all over the world began to visit the smoke-filled Cavern Club and to stroll around Penny Lane to see the birthplaces of the Fab Four.

In 1965 myself and a Jamaican friend took a short holiday on the Spanish island of Majorca. After the 60's Liverpool nightlife of Liverpool we deserved a well earned rest to recharge our batteries.

As soon as I returned to my bed-sit I picked up the letters that had been delivered whilst I was away. Those I read first were those with the Fijian stamps on them. My sister Malti wrote lovingly and comforted me by saying that everything was fine. But she was a little apprehensive as there hadn't been any replies to the letters she had sent to father in India. He had we recalled promised to return to Fiji after eighteen months but since that promise nine years had passed and now his letters had stopped coming. Everyone was worried about his whereabouts.

In the post there was a letter and a photograph from Nirmala and my two sons Surendra and Narendra. The secret that I was their father remained a secret but I did wonder if my mother and sister had detected the resemblance between my kids and myself.

Otherwise the timing of my arrival and continued lifestyle proved to have been timely and propitious. In May 1966 I went to Wembley to see Everton win the FA.Cup Final where they beat Sheffield Wednesday by three goals to two. This was the cause for great celebration throughout Merseyside. A few months later I watched Portugal play North Korea in the World Cup at Goodison Park.

It wasn't looking too good for the small European nation at all; by half time the Koreans were winning by three goals to nil. Then in the second half dominated by a Portuguese player called Eusabio a hat trick was scored and Portugal was back in the game. There was going to be a nail-biting final and the game is probably still talked about today. It ended with a Portuguese victory of 5—3. Even though the Koreans lost they had earned acclaimed fame throughout the world and rightly so. It was a good time to be keen on football; there was thrill and excitement as on that old black and white television of mine I celebrated with England their defeat of Germany during the World Cup.

Elsewhere in sport, for I was still an avid follower if not a participant, the same year saw the arrival in London of Leweni Waga. He was the guy that I was too nervous to fight on my boxing debut in Fiji. Now he was in London as the undefeated heavyweight

RETURNED TO DEVIL'S ISLAND

champion of Fiji, South Seas and the Orient. While in London he had beaten four heavyweights including the unbeaten Johnny Hendrickson and was matched to take Mohammad Ali's sparring partner Jimmy Ellis at Highbury Stadium, Arsenal FC's home ground. Yes, it needed that kind of space. Unfortunately Waga was beaten by a TKO in the first round. His left eye brow was cut and swollen so the referee George Smith had no alternative but to stop the fight. The main event of the evening was between Henry Cooper and a very young Cassius Clay, who would afterwards become better known as Mohammad Ali following his religious conversion. Ali won the fight by a TKO as Cooper's eyebrows were cut; the referee had little choice in the matter but the Afro-American outclassed him anyway; it was a foregone conclusion.

It was sometime in 1970 that the UK Home Office informed me that my British and Commonwealth passport was now deemed invalid. Fiji had gained its independence from Great Briton and my passport in effect wasn't worth the paper it was written on. After several months of correspondence between me and the Home Office they finally relented and I received a new passport; this time as a British citizen.

Perhaps this fired me; it was liberation of sorts and again I was taken by the wanderlust. This time my thoughts were on Fiji. I couldn't escape the nagging persistence of missing my family and friends. I had roots and I needed to rediscover them. For the next three years I saved every penny I earned; it seemed that I was on an eternal quest; there was always the hunger to move on and to never settle. Perhaps it was the travelling I had done that whetted my appetite for more of the same? At what I considered to be the right moment I went along to the general manager's office at Birkenhead Transport where I had first applied for the job; there I handed my notice in.

As soon as I had done so I booked my Fijian flight on British Airways and then worked my two weeks notice bringing my contract of employment to an end. This breathing space provided me with enough time to say goodbye to the many friends that I had made. I said farewell to the sales girls from the city and the not so young; the retired who had so often handed me sweets. The fond farewells included dock workers who hadn't paid their bus fare when they were broke, and the schoolgirls who had given me food and biscuits they had cooked in class. Had I been a culinary test bed or rather guinea pig?

On my final day as a bus conductor a bunch of my 'on the buses' colleagues gave me a great sending off bash at The Farmer's Arms in New Ferry. "Do please return as soon as you can Jamie," they pleaded. They told me fervently that Birkenhead, not Fiji was my home now. "You will miss our beloved Everton," said one of my acquaintances. "Don't forget Liverpool FC," another reminded me. "They have just been crowned Football League Champions and they have also won the UEFA Cup. "Bill Shankly is our king," called another; which hardly went down well with the Evertonians.

"I'll be back as soon as I can," I merrily assured them. "I haven't found those pavements lined with gold yet." It was remark that much amused them for they had been in England for very much longer and they had not found them either.

CHAPTER 10

A few days later I paid two months rent in advance to my landlady with an option to return to Birkenhead if I didn't wish to stay in Fiji. Chin up but spirits down I took the train to London's Heathrow Airport and there boarded the 747 British Airways flight to Fiji. The pretty blonde and brunette air hostesses reminded me of the good times I had enjoyed. That had been an incredible fourteen years previous: I could hardly believe it.

I couldn't help but wonder at how their lives might have turned out. Had they married; retired, started a business or maybe done as I had and relocated elsewhere? Had any been attracted to the convent as had Susan; unlikely one supposes but it was nice to let my thoughts drift in their own fashion. Such thoughts would pass the time away. Even by air the South Sea Islands are a very long way away. I thought of Susan; was she still a doctor-nun and on the leprosy island? Would she have thought of me as often as I had thought of her; or would she have put me out of her mind?

I thought it might have been better had I been a policeman; imagine had I been able to track down her family and the story behind their disappearance; their abandonment of her? My reveries were interrupted by the sudden movement of the airliner as its engines burst into life.

The flight took me via Bermuda, Nassau, Mexico City, Acapulco, Hawaii and finally to Fiji. By the time it touched down I had been travelling for fifty-two hours; thirty-six of which was actual flying time; the rest was spent hanging around crowded airports in all of the five countries we had touched down upon.

This was not the time for English nostalgia or Birkenhead homesickness. As I stepped out on the tarmac of Fiji's Nadi Airport I was submerged in a tropical rainstorm that soaked me through to my skin. In that kind of downpour clothes are wholly ineffectual. They are good only for covering one's modesty and there's not much of that either when you look like a drowned rat. Welcome home, Jamie. I hurriedly rushed into the airport building and was met by an uncompromising Indian immigration officer. My cheery 'hello' didn't have much of an impact on his ridiculously severe demeanour. He just glared and abruptly snatched my passport as I offered it to him.

RETURNED TO DEVIL'S ISLAND

"And what are you doing here in my country?" he demanded. His uncalled for and unprofessional remark reminded me of the Indian and Pakistani customs officers at London airports. No smile or greeting, just po-faced insolence. They obviously think that the uniform removes them from necessity to follow the normal rules of civility. If this is how they treat travellers how would they treat invaders? I looked at him coolly: "It happens to be my country too."

"No, it's not your country anymore. You have a British passport. Fiji is an independent country now. Please do not seek employment here without government authorisation," he growled.

I studied him for a moment or two just to let him know that the feelings of dislike were mutual. "Excuse me for saying so but I have left this god-forsaken mud bank many years ago and I have no intention whatsoever of seeking employment here. From my travels I can tell you that this is very much a Third World country and your attitude is Fourth World. Why don't you just lighten up, you arsehole and get yourself a life?"

The best he could say to that was to tell me to go as he gestured angrily in the direction of the airport lounge. First there was a rain storm and now this unnecessary hassle, who needs it? I was agitated but somehow managed to stay calm.

As I walk through into the lounge I immediately spotted my mother. She now had grey hair and looked very much older than I remembered her. But, her smile was as warm and as memorable as it had always been. I loved her dearly. We had been through much. My sister Malti was carrying a few extra pounds around her waistline but time hadn't harmed her pretty features. Her husband, Ramesh, and their five children were looking at me excitedly. I did a quick head count. There were three boys and two girls all under the ages of sixteen. We hugged and kissed and then I handed around their presents all of which I had purchased at the Jewish owned warehouses around Liverpool.

Despite the weather and the uncivil civil servant I was glad to be back; it was all worthwhile. Soon we were in Ramesh's car heading along the Queen's Road towards home. Once we reached Lautoka we took the Kings Road and carried on towards the gold mines of Vatukola. I felt a sudden stabbing pang of deep regret as I saw the General Hospital where I had taken my dead sister, Sabita after her suicide.

My mind flashed back to that overwhelmingly sad day sixteen years earlier. Time had not dimmed the recollection of her mutilated body on the slab at the mortuary. It was like a permanent video recording that plays back in one's mind over and over again. I swallowed hard to keep back the emotions; this was no time for that sort of stuff. My mother read my thoughts and gripped my hand tightly as we swept past the hospital gates; we didn't mention anything of course: There was no need for that.

Ramesh drove on and after an hour we passed the beach fronting St Joseph's College. I remembered Sara of course. There were so many memories and not all of them sad by any means. There was though poignancy and I wondered if she had ever managed to make it to Los Angeles where she planned to visit her grandparents.

The car ride was a sort of 'This is Your Life' car journey. Much of it was taken in thoughtful silence. We passed through the town of Valabala, and on past St Mary's Convent School. This was where I first encountered true love as averse to lust. There was a difference. Yes, here was where I had fallen head over heels in love with Susan. Another hour and we were in my hometown. Except for a few new buildings nothing had changed.

Glancing in the direction of the river I could see it was still a very dirty river that looked even filthier than before. Not much in the way of environment concern there then. I was very much preoccupied with a kaleidoscope of recollections mixed up with thoughts. I thought of the ghosts of the past; Sara and of course Lisa Fong. Where would Lisa be now; still married and where? In the distance I could see our love island looking every bit as it always did. As we approached Nirmala's home my heart began to pound. How will I react to seeing my sons'? Will there be any recognition; bonding, empathy? Eventually Ramesh pulled up outside my old home across the lane from my former lover's home. "Do you remember this place?" mother asked.

I didn't answer her; I was too busy with my own thoughts. Stepping out of the car I thoughtfully looked at the little house where we once lived. The corrugated metal had rusted and there were holes in the tin roof; most of it was half hidden by a sea of tall wild flowers. I glanced over at Nirmala's veranda before nervously walking up the steps and tapping lightly on the door. So much had happened since I last tapped on it. She opened the door and let out a scream: "Jamie, you are back at last." Taking her in my arms I bear hugged her, kissing her on each cheek. "Nirmala! Where are my boys?" I asked feverishly.

"They're at school but should be here any moment," she laughed gaily. I stayed silent and just let my eyes gaze down that small dirt track that led to the school.

Her words broke the silence. "Would you like a beer, Jamie?"

I smiled and told her of course I would as she handed me a Fosters. I had taken her in my arms; now I took her in my eyes. She had put on a little weight, which was I suppose natural. Her hair was still jet black and her lower arms covered with bangles that could have graced any jewellery store's window. She hadn't lost any of her beauty.

"Look, there they are. They are coming now. Can you see them," she exclaimed as she pointed in the direction of a small group of schoolboys approaching her home. They were followed by several girls of mixed ethnicity. There was no need for her to identify my own two; they were miniature replicas of what I had been at their age; they were mirror images.

I watched as they drew nearer and as they reached their home I heard one of the girls call out: "I die there." They giggled and tittered between themselves before going on their way. As the boys stepped up to the veranda I stood and greeting them shook their hands. I was choking back the tears. Their dark brown eyes looked so much like my own. I felt like hugging and kissing them but under the circumstances that would have been far from appropriate. The secret had to remain for the sake and reputation of Nirmala's sake."

"You look well. How old are you, Surendra?"

He smiled the broadest smile imaginable and told me he was nearly seventeen years old and added that he was planning on going to college soon.

"Will you be going to St Joseph's?" I asked.

"No Hindus aren't allowed to go to a Christian college. I'll be going to the Hindu College in Suva."

"And you, young man," I asked turning to the younger of the two brothers. "What age are you?"

Narendra smiled a little shyly as he told me he was fifteen but would be sixteen very soon.

Feeling very emotional I stood and walked around the overgrown garden where in the privacy it afforded I tried to rein in my emotions and wiped away some tears caused neither by sorry nor sadness; just missed opportunities I suppose. I had missed experiencing their childhood whilst I was exploring my own worlds of wonder. From where I stood I could again see my old home; not so much a home now but a harbour filled with memories.

Standing there I remembered a little sadly of the day my father had left our home to trace his roots to India, just as I had returned here. I could still picture his hopeful and bright face and smile as he reassured us that he would be back in eighteen months. That was seventeen years earlier during which time; of late at least, he had it seemed disappeared off the face of the earth. Had he passed on? Had he been murdered or killed in floods or perhaps taken by some deadly epidemic in India? Or was he still alive and living in a commune with many wives and children? Could he really have turned his back on his family and his old home? All sorts of questions crowded my mind and it was only when I heard my mother calling my name did I come down to earth.

"Come on, Khrisna. Let's go before it gets dark. You can come back whenever you wish to. Right now we have things to do." Silently I walked back up the steps of Nirmala's veranda. She was watching me closely with a foolish grin on her face and was clearly happy to see me. "You must come back in the evening. Rajendra would love to see you again."

I forced a smile before walking to the car where I sat next to Ramesh who was doing the driving. Looking back through the half open windows I could see both the boys waving. Soon we were driving past the Vatuklola Public Works Department and nearby, Sara's old home. "Do you know where Sara is?" I asked mother.

"Yes," she smiled. "She is married and has four children. She is living somewhere in New Zealand."

There didn't seem to be the necessity of a reply as I looked intensely out of the window. I gazed in wonder at all the familiar sights from what seemed to be an unconnected past life; a fellow soul to the one I was now. Nothing much had changed, which was I suppose something of its rustic charm. The convent gates were just as I recalled them. The old church and the Fong family bakery looked exactly the same.

CHRIS NAND

There was only the wooden theatre that was gone; it had been replaced by a breeze blocked and cemented building. I noticed a few convent girls chatting animatedly to boys their own age. They were wearing the grey skirts I was more than familiar with as were their white blouses and socks; the black sandals just as Sara and Lisa Fong used to wear. I thought back to the day Lisa had left for Hong Kong. It was as clear in my mind now; well, it could easily have happened an hour earlier. The regrets hadn't changed either. There was such poignancy.

We hadn't been driving for very long when we pulled to a stop outside my sister's home. This was a wooden chalet surrounded by a blaze of tropical flowers. There was no grass hut now. Obviously, Malti's marriage was a good one for both of them and they looked happy. In fact, it wasn't difficult to see that they were likely better off than I was.

Once inside their home mother and my sister hugged and kissed me again. I couldn't believe myself that I had finally returned. They must have thought they were dreaming. I had literally circumnavigated the earth; all 25,000 miles of it. It had taken me sixteen years to complete. Certainly I had many fascinating stories to tell my family and friends and of course I had to do a little cherry picking as to which ones might be told; there were a few that would have to remain untold for the sake of propriety.

We chatted happily about everything under the sun and the moon too as my nephews chased around the garden. They were trying to capture a large white duck. It had been especially fattened for my coming home celebrations. The duck was a guest at the dinner table. It was slaughtered later that afternoon and we enjoyed a fine fowl curry and rice for dinner.

On the following day I visited and paid my respects at my sister's grave. What wouldn't I have given for her to be with us now, instead of asleep wherever she was. It was at moments like this that one is reminded of the importance of those who are still sharing our lives. I then visited my old boxing club where I was knocked out, metaphorically speaking of course, to find my old boxing coach, Naliva. I couldn't begin to describe the delight on his face when he set eyes on me. It was at moments like this that beers go down the best. We put the world to rights and I told him something of my adventures and he told me of his. It was good to be home; it was at its best when I chatted with my sons who hung on my every word as I told them of my boyhood and my travels since.

The second week of my visit I borrowed my brother-in-law's old Datsun car and decided on a visit to Suva via my old bamboo village. It was an interesting ride. I was astonished to see tall sugarcane now growing on the land where our home had once stood. Thoughtfully I strolled to the mouth of the Raki Raki River and then to the cove where I used to swim with the American servicemen before silently brooding over the ground where my grandparents had been cremated. Again, it was all as if it were yesterday. Time moves on but memories stay right where they are. From there I turned my feet to the old tomb of Ratu Udre Udre where I had played as a child all those years ago.

I was glad I was on my own. I needed only myself to talk through my past with; two would have been a crowd. As I gazed across the languorous Pacific I realised that there was no longer need for me to wonder about what lay beyond the horizon; I had discovered it and returned with the memories in my heart and mind. I had seen the places I could once only dream about.

Suddenly the sound of an approaching bus shattered the solitude of that lonely memory-filled oasis. I stood up to take a better look and could see a brand new Leyland bus drawing near. It certainly made its presence known painted in its bright Hindu colours.

From it lightly stepped some sari-clad women breezily chatting away to each other in Hindi. They laughed when the saw me standing there in my shoulder length hair, wide flared slacks and wooden Cuban heeled shoes. I heard one of them say: "He must be a tourist from some other country," before an old Ford Anglia pulled up and carried them on to wherever they were going. I stood there for awhile and watched as the bus went on its way. Patiently settling in behind it a small convoy of lurching Lorries on their way to the nearby sugar mill.

As quickly as it had disappeared the tranquillity of the place returned, which allowed me more precious moments of reminiscing. I thought back to the day when I was taken to boarding school by Father O' Donald and Sister Henrietta. It had not been the happiest of days and I was glad that adulthood didn't have the same fears of the unknown and in particularly was a life period when one made one's own decisions. I think it is too easily forgotten that a child isn't allowed a mind of its own; whatever happens in its life is down to the decisions of others. It is a very vulnerable period and I sure knew it.

I felt momentarily sad as I thought of Susan and it was then that I realised that I had little choice in the matter; I was bound to search for her, to go to the leprosy hospital and see if she was all right. Again my reveries were broken as a bus filled with Australian tourists drew up.

From where I sat I could hear the party's guide explaining: "This is Ratu Udre Udre's tomb." He was the Fijian King responsible for carrying out the sacrifices of 350 men, women and children; yes, sacrificed on this very spot before being cooked and eaten."

As he finished his presentation the tourists piled around with curiosity, talking away as they tried to picture the horror. I suppose they found it as difficult as I did. Many others posed on the cement tomb to have their pictures taken. This I thought was not a very noble way of commemorating such terrible events; there is little dignity in poses of grinning tourists at places where people were routinely picked up and smashed to death on boulders. The place lost some of its magic and I stepped into the old Datsun and drove along the dusty Kings Road towards Suva.

Four hours later I arrived in the capital and was relieved to see that little had changed except for a few new buildings dotted about here and there. When I approached Renwick Road I could see a swarm of people standing at the entrance of a four-storey building. They appeared to be excited; giggling and talking in loud-pitched voices. Inquisitively I strolled over to see what the commotion was all about. Evidently, Fiji's first elevator had been fitted in the building and people were a bit apprehensive about stepping on and off the moving stairs. Some were laughing and others were nervously giggling!

Just as had earlier happened my attire was notice and remarked on. They looked at my flared trousers and Beatle hair cut and laughed. Smiling I left the car where it was and strolled to the shipping office of Morris Headstroms Limited I booked a ticket for the ferry that would take me to the leprosy island of Mokagai. I then killed an hour purchasing a sleeping bag; a torch and a box of chocolates for Susan. The sleeping bag would always be useful and on that particular night it was; I slept in the car parked close to Albert Park Botanical Gardens.

CHAPTER 11

On the following morning, after making sure my car was parked where it wouldn't be any trouble to anyone I made my way down to the Suva wharf and boarded the ferry to the forbidding island. My reminiscing was assisted by the thought that this was exactly the same rusty old tub that had carried my Susan away all those years earlier. This old ferryboat had crossed her Rubicon and left mine in its wake. Symbolically that small ship meant more to me than the biggest liners in the world for it represented the most important part of my world.

During the small and otherwise uneventful voyage we chugged along across the ocean's placid waters to eventually moor at the wharf on the small island of Bau. Whilst we were moored there was much coming and going with plenty of chatter as parcel and luggage changed hands; some alighted and others climbed on board. It was a great way to travel; the only way to travel.

As we let go our tenuous hold on land, such as it was, the ferry's bow slowly swung south before settling down into its onward voyage. It gave me plenty of time to consider my reception. I had no idea of course if Susan would welcome my uninvited visit. Many years had passed by and for all I knew I might be only vaguely recalled. I might be no more than a half-familiar face of an old friend; a source of wonder that I should even bother myself to go out of my way to see her. I supposed it was unrealistic to expect a beaming welcome and embraces; nor could it be an opportunity to tell her that above all her presence and imagery had been a forever spectre throughout my life. Always the unseen presence and the intruding brooding thought. Her imagery had accompanied me wherever I had travelled. Places she could hardly imagine.

The sun was beginning to set as the small ferry made its way through a perfectly calm sea before settling on its course for the small island we could now see on the distant horizon. It was a speck in the ocean known only to a tiny few who have business or fate awaiting them there. I could only imagine the thoughts of so many others who over a great many years had first set eyes on the island that would become their destiny and for most their tomb. I had less reason to be mournful but it was all still very emotional for me. Not surprisingly I was elated yet apprehensive at whatever awaited me. Maybe I should have left the past where the past is best left.

CHRIS NAND

I gazed thoughtfully at the islands green hills and tropical fauna; it was straight from a tourist handbook but hardly its purpose. There must have been many a poor doomed soul whose thoughts I couldn't imagine when taking a one-way ticket to be an outcast on the island that was itself an outcast. It was as far away as it is possible to be from the hustle and bustle of the earth's humanity. My aunt Ram Kali must have seen what I am seeing now. She must have thought she is here to be healed and will soon return to her husband and children on the main island. How wrong she was. I just don't know how she managed to stay here for thirty years without a visitor or even a letter to let her know how her children were growing up without her. She had no idea that her dear husband had taken a young wife and all was hunky dory for him while the poor soul suffered here physically and mentally.

My thoughts came to an end as the engines cut out the boat gently glided to its moorings against the hanging rubber tyres of a small wooden jetty. The gangplank was then lowered for me to walk down. I looked around me and sure enough, I was the only passenger disembarking at this rather brooding isle. Those I was leaving behind on the ferry were looking at me with a mixture of curiosity and thoughtfulness. They must have been wondering what on earth my quest was to be. I could hardly blame them. This place was hardly Tahiti at the height of the tourist season. All was silent except for birdsong and the whisper of the breeze. The silence was otherwise broken only by the shuffling of passengers' feet and the squeaking of the ship's hull as it rubbed against the fenders. This island had quite a reputation throughout the South Sea Islands, rather like Devil's Island used as a penal colony by the French in the 19th Century.

As I stepped ashore the silence was shattered by the clatter of the ship's gangplank being raised. It seemed an intrusion to the idyll; this daresay paradise. The ropes were let go and with an insignificant little hoot, for what purpose I have no idea, the small ferry swung around and went on its way.

Taking the obvious route I stepped out on my way and followed a narrow stone-strewn path leading in the direction of the hospital. This would be a route that Susan would have taken, and I thought how many times since; she and so many others. By this time my heart was racing and it had little to do with the exertion of the long climbing walk. Where was everyone, I thought to myself. Why isn't there some sign of life here?

The truth dawned when I was brought to a stop by a half derelict building; its storm damaged windows and the overgrown gardens suggested that something had gone terribly wrong with my intentions. With a thumping heart I rushed headlong past several feral cats and dogs and rattled away at the battered old building's main doorway.

There was an air of wretchedness about the place. From somewhere inside I could hear light footsteps approaching before the door finally creaked open. A kindly elderly nun dressed in flowing white nuns' habits confronted me. Light of stature she was wearing darkened spectacles. They were not sunglasses but were so heavily tinctured that they might as well be; yet it appeared to be so gloomy inside. I could only guess that her eyes were unusually sensitive to light. From behind them she peered up at me with a clear expression of surprise. Her eyebrows rose as she looked at my unconventional dress: "Yes, may I help you, young man?"

I stammered my reply. "Please, may I see Susan? I mean, Sister Susan? I am sorry. She wouldn't be expecting me. Is she here?"

The nun's face darkened perceptibly and I could see her thoughts weren't exactly where I wanted them to be. "And who exactly are you?"

"My name is James. I was brought up with Susan at St. Mary's boarding school. I have just returned from England after being away for sixteen years. Please, can I see her now sister?"

Again she paused before muttering quietly almost to herself in wonderment. "So! You are James?" She paused for a while before she spoke again. I thought I could detect her voice quivering either with emotion or anger as she addressed me. "Yes," she said: "I know who you are. There are many of your letters and post-cards here, from you."

It wasn't exactly answering my question. "So, sister; where is Sister Susan? I have come a very long way. May I please see her?"

Shutting the door behind her she came down the steps of the convent. "Follow me please. I have something to talk to you about."

I did as she requested and followed the small sister of mercy as she made her way to a small church set in foliage behind the convent. Knowing Susan as well as I did I guessed she would either be praying or decorating the Alter as she loved doing at St. Mary's. As we entered the time-scarred building the sister placed her arm comfortingly around my shoulders. Instinctively I knew that something was dreadfully wrong; that she was going to tell me something that I had no wish to hear. I was filled with dread and felt as thought I had fallen into my own grave. "James, my son I have some heartbreaking news to tell you. Sister Susan is no longer with us; she is dead."

I never realised that grief could descend at such devastating speed. I cried out: "No, it's a lie. It must be the wrong Susan. It is a common name. My Susan was young; she was beautiful; so full of life. There has been a mistake; it must be a terrible mistake. Please don't tell me this."

Grief stricken at the finality of a relationship experience that had dominated my life I broke down and sobbed uncontrollably. I felt as one must when hearing the nails thudding into one's own coffin lid. The sister, bless her, held me in her arms while sobbing I sat on the bench and listened to her. She told me that in 1966, after being here for eight years, Sister Susan had contracted leprosy. The mind reels at the horror of the remorseless torture the poor young doctor nun had been subjected to by the whims of fate.

The sister told me how the disease spread; first it was just the one hand that was affected but then the other was similarly afflicted. She told me how they had cared for her, and treated the disease but it was all to no avail. Eventually the surgeons had little choice but to amputate both of her hands; the skin having by that time decayed to reveal the bare bones.

My stomach was churning at the thought of such suffering. I thought of those hands that had held my own ever since she had first held them out to offer me sweets after my being beaten as a child. Hers were the hands of Christ; never have I been as aware of the presence of evil as I was when I heard the aged nun describe Susan's fate. I had no wish to hear further but for some reason unknown to me, maybe she thought it would be better for me to know, she told me that after the removal of her hands, Susan herself requested to be transferred to the ward where the terminally ill were nursed. The leprosy had spread to her neck until she was completely infected.

I was told that she couldn't have possibly had better care than that which she received. It was in 1969, ironically it was just before better more palliative drugs were discovered that she succumbed to her illness. She had passed away peacefully in her sleep.

"Susan was interred there," the sister said pointing in the direction of what was clearly the hospital's cemetery. I had to force myself to look over at the mournful sight.

Weeping, I made my way over to the burial ground whispering to myself how much I loved her. Telling her how sorry I was. I wondered if her spirit was present and she realised that I had come back for her after all of those years.

As I made my way tearfully through grass and foliage that reached my knees I felt sick to the pits of my stomach. In the distance behind me I was aware of the elderly nun watching me as I stumbled through the headstones. Clearly there wasn't anyone here to maintain this garden of remembrance. It was half hidden in the tranquil setting of a remote isle, a dot on even the most detailed of maps.

I confess that such was the overgrown nature of the burial ground I unintentionally stumbled upon gravestones; I walked across the final resting places of those who once walked the earth; played as children, loved as adults, died in misery. It was then that I came across a cross; symbolically it had fallen over to one side, perhaps because it had never been properly mounted in the first place. On the hewn stone were the inscribed words: 'Sister Susan Jane Taylor'. This was her autobiography; a simple name on a simple headstone in God's garden.

I needed time and peace to be with her and as I crouched and held the headstone in my arms I felt as though I were holding her and that she was aware of my doing so. My confusion of faith suddenly returned and I felt a presence, was it Susan's soul or was it God. I never for a moment thought of her as being dead. She had gone to a higher plane, one to which I could never ever aspire. For all her suffering surely there was solace in the isle's purification of her soul?

Time passed; I have no idea how long I had sat there with my thoughts, occasionally wiping tears from my eyes for the sobbing came in waves. I would recover and then some imagery of a shared moment would impose itself and set me off again. I jumped when I felt a hand gently touching my shoulder. In the gathering dusk I could see a tiny pair of black shoes at my knees. There was no miracle; the only sight for me was a nun's tear-striped face. "Come, young man. I have some belongings of Susan's which you must have, just as she would wish them to."

Getting to my feet I took the elderly nun's arm and allowed her to lead me through the path leading back through the undergrowth. As we knelt in the chapel and prayed I again felt an uncanny closeness to Susan; I felt as though like an angel she was hovering and that she was crying too at witnessing and sharing my distress. My throat was sore, I have never felt so thoroughly wretched in my life as I did when kneeling and praying for forgiveness. Had I only succeeded in persuading her to come to England with me?

"If it is any comfort," the sister said to me, "I think Susan's death had purpose to it. It was a sign that her work and ours was done. You see, my son, Susan was the last martyr to leprosy on this island of ours. When she was taken from us, God's work had been done in other ways. Do you know no one else died here after she had gone; she had closed the door behind her as she went. Leprosy was completely eradicated from 1969. Have faith, my son; she died a martyr's death and as such she will live far longer than we lesser mortals can hope for."

I looked bleakly at the distressed nun. I picked my words carefully. "I am not sure if you know this, Sister Helen. Susan's mission had two purposes: She had God's work to do and she was also on a quest to find her mother whom she believed had been sent here to this island as a penance for a sin she had committed. She was ever in search of her mother. It is all so terribly sad."

I paused as the emotions were threatening to again overwhelm me. When I again found my voice I asked Sister Helen if Sister Susan had achieved her second ambition; had she found her mother here at the leprosy island.

I thought her reply strange. Holding my hand firmly the nun told me Susan had found her mother and she had not. I couldn't understand what she meant, it didn't make any sense to me at all and my bewilderment showed.

"How well did you know Susan?" she asked quietly.

"I knew her as well as a man could," I said dejectedly. "I was the only one who ever loved her completely, apart from God."

Sitting on the bench the kindly nun turned towards me and with her sweet saintly face close to my own she carefully removed her spectacles. I reeled from the shock as she bared her eyes. I felt as though I had been kicked in the stomach. The eyes of Sister Helen were light-brown and in her right eye was a beautiful dark speckle; a freckle on her iris. "James. Do you better understand now?"

My hands went involuntarily to my mouth at the shock of seeing eyes that were so unusual and so like Susan's. I don't how much time passed before I chokingly whispered: "You are Susan's mother?" She didn't reply. There was no need to.

"Then she did get her wish?"

"No, she never did, my son. You see, by necessity I have always worn dark glasses as God's light has always been too bright for me. My ailment worsened when I entered the work of the Lord and since coming here to administer to the sick and the dying I had little choice but to wear them constantly. No one has seen my eyes for twenty years or more. Since then only you, James, have seen my eyes as God made them."

I was more confused than ever. "But, why didn't you let Susan know, or to see your eyes? She was your daughter?"

"James. It is a long story that could have only two outcomes; both painful. I took the hardest decision of my life and denied her that knowledge. I told her what I call God's lie. That the lady who had given birth to her was never on this island; that I was sent here in her place. Isn't that the truth? You will want to know the reason I did so?"

She didn't wait for my reply; there couldn't be one as such. The kindly nun paused thoughtfully before continuing. "There was much truth in it because the woman who had sinned, lived and loved and then later became her birth mother was no more. I, a Sister of God's Mercy, had taken her mother's place: I was now mother to all."

She continued: "On the island back then you have to remember that it wasn't as it is now. It was a thriving well populated parish of God's children. Many of them had been abandoned, exiled, were homeless and in the greatest distress. They had neither a mother nor a future but they all had love and faith. I was representative of their faith and I was the bringer of unconditional love. I was their mother too.

I listened intently as the sister continued: "Had it ever been revealed the manner of my sin that faith they had in me would have been no more. My children, all of them, had little enough to hold on to. Their faith in our God and my integrity as his unsullied wife was paramount to all things on earth. I kept that faith. And so you see, my son, Susan did achieve both her calling and her quest. She carried out God's work on earth and she met her mother. To her I was her mother and of course I was everything to her a mother could be. She was not aware of my being there with her when she was born but she was comforted by my being there when she said her final goodbye. I hope you can understand."

I asked her if she thought Susan had ever guessed. The elderly nun shrugged. "Who can read the minds of others? She may have done. If she had any doubts she chose to keep them to herself. I was glad of that. I do not think I had the strength to either deny her or accept her as a daughter. The Lord spared me that decision and for that I am eternally grateful."

Should her words have brought me comfort? I don't know but there was little comfort in knowing that Susan was with us no longer. I had daydreamt for sixteen years; those daydreams had sharpened upon my return. I wanted so much to tell Susan of my adventures and perhaps give her pause for thought. I wanted her to know that I still loved her as I could no one else. I wanted her to know that our parting had been her decision, not mine.

As I sat there deep in thought the nun picked up a small brown suitcase and she handed it to me. "Here are some of Sister Susan's belongings, James. I want you to have them for she has no one else. I can be equally sure that you are the only person to whom she would entrust them.

RETURNED TO DEVIL'S ISLAND

"You were her all and her everything, other than her calling of course. You see, all your letters, I saved all of them as did she. And when she had passed away I saved the unopened ones too for they still belong to you and Susan alone. They are here for you. I know that when you were writing them to her you were with her in spirit Now that you have them you still are in spirit with her."

I recognised Susan's shabby old suitcase and gently I opened it with trembling hands. I cannot describe my feelings as I held Susan's small crucifix and other simple belongings. Simple but things she obviously cherished as icons of the heart. With her hairbrush with the strands of her hair still present; and other small items of everyday use and comfort, there were all the letters and the postcards I had sent to her. They were postmarked before and after her death.

One didn't have to look at the dates; the unopened ones were those delivered after her passing. I brushed with my fingers the sepia tinted photograph I had sent to her from England; she had kept it too. How often had she held it while she too remembered our moments together, so many of them stolen moments? Images flowed through my mind. They were of her as a small child stuffing my scattered belongings back into my fallen bag. As might a saint I looked up and her child image was caste in light across the harsh stone facades of a place called St Mary's.

"Did you speak often with Susan, I mean Sister Susan, sister?" I asked when I had recovered something of my composure.

"Yes I did," the nun replied in a soft voice. "She held the opinion that she was being punished by God for her sins and she didn't question her suffering. Father Donaldson took her final confession and administered the last rites; holding communion for her before she passed away. It was later that night that she left us; she was very peaceful and there was a small but unmistakable smile on her lips as we prepared the poor girl."

"Is Father Donaldson here?"

"Yes, he is but he is visiting one of the other islands. He will be back soon and I am sure he would be pleased to meet you. We here are left behind to serve a handful of ex-patients who still live here on the islands."

By the time we had exchanged our thoughts night had descended on the island. "I wonder if I might ask; is there anywhere on the island where I might find lodgings. Perhaps I should have found some first. I would like to spend the night on the island so that I can feel more as one and at peace with Susan."

She looked at me kindly: "If you walk past the cemetery, you'll see some lights over the hill. That's where some of our ex-patients live. They will I am sure be pleased to see you and to find a bed for a pilgrim."

I thanked her and apologised for my loss of self control. She said it was perfectly understandable given the circumstances. She added that I mustn't let such thoughts enter my head. Taking the path I had discovered a little earlier I walked on and past the graveyard. I was still absurdly clutching the gift of chocolates I had brought for Susan. Also in my hand the shabby little suitcase she had hauled around in her travels; inside her modest belongings. I say modest but how priceless they were to her. My face was still tear-stained and only by self control was I able to keep my composure. In the distance I could see a cluster of village lights in the dusk and headed in the direction.

As I approached the group of grass huts the village dogs began to yap and bark. I could just make out some curious soul walking slowly towards me carrying a hurricane lamp in his outstretched hand. As the figure drew closer I smiled and when he came close enough I nodded. "Do you have a bed for one night, sir? The nun at the hospital suggested that there would be someone here who could oblige me."

Holding the lamp up to see me better he searched my face for heavens know what. Was he curious about my apparent distress? "Oh yes," he said. "That can only be Sister Helen; she is a kind lady."

I followed the bare-footed man who was dressed in a sulu but shirtless. I was soon brought face to face with a small group whose curiosity mirrored my own. With the moon barely visible behind the clouds they were no more than ghostly silhouettes. It was only when kerosene lamps were lifted to see me better that I took a step back. Horrified, their ghastliness was now apparent and I felt as though I had walked into some medieval biblical depiction of hell. All of those confronting me were disfigured and deformed in one way or another.

Some of the figures before me had just holes where their eyes, noses or mouths used to be. They stared in my direction but some couldn't see me. There was an odour I didn't like; I had never endured it before and I couldn't identify it with anything I had ever experienced.

Others had stumps where their hands and feet had once been, or were missing fingers or toes. Some were far worse off than were others. It was a vision of hell and I doubted very much if any Hollywood horror film producer could have matched the unsightly apparitions. They stood in silent curiosity lit only by the dull glow of the hurricane lamps; to each their own thoughts about the sight I must have presented to them. These unfortunates were like the walking dead; it was as though a burial ground had in the night come alive with corpses reluctant to leave the old world of the living behind them. My mind reeled from the appalling sight and my stomach was churning but for me there could be no retreat.

Some of the women were shyly trying to conceal their disfigurements behind their saris. Human dignity doesn't abandon the living dead. "You can sleep in this house, sir; there are some spare mats in there."

"Thank you," I said although I am not sure if I sounded as thankful as I should have done: "You are very kind." I told him.

"Are you hungry?"

"No. Thank you. I have eaten quite well today. All I need is rest, to sleep for the night."

He nodded in acquiescence and I followed my guide into the nearby small hut where in the dim lights, some lanterns and others bare-flamed, I could see a group of people huddled fairly closely together. I nodded in their direction without being sure if they could see my greeting.

I could see enough to make out their disfigurements; these were perhaps made more hellish by the poorly lit hovel. Each in the group were sitting in traditional fashion with legs crossed; some were playing cards although how they could see the detail of them in the poor light was beyond my comprehension. I apologised for disturbing them and directed to a mat in a corner I set my few belongs down. Pulling my sleeping bag free I climbed into it adopted the foetal position.

I doubt if I had ever felt so desolate and abandoned in my life. Nothing could have told me better what Susan had given her life up to; words could never describe the sights I was seeing, the smell, the atmosphere of decay; of lost hope. As I lay there sleep eluded me and in my misery I was haunted by visions of Susan. I imagined her, like an angel, visiting this small community with her raised hurricane lamp in hands that were doomed. I knew then that I could never be as close to God as she had been or was now. It was with those thoughts that eventually I drifted into a deeply troubled sleep. I dreamt that I too was in my coffin.

There was no need for an alarm of any kind; dawn's light and the social activity of the birds in the fauna was all one needed to wake to the day. Without disturbing others, for some were deep in sleep, I found a small beach and a fresh water stream. As I gazed around me the outlook was transformed from that of hell to that of heaven.

I might easily have been in the Garden of Eden, such was the lushness of the fauna. I picked some wild guavas from the bush and bolted them down; they were perfect for breakfast and I felt far happier eating direct from nature's bounty than taking anything that might be offered by the unfortunate exiles that made up the small colony.

As I was packing my bag to leave a man approach me with a small billycan full of hot tea. "We don't often get visitors," he smiled and as he did so revealing his broken gravestone teeth. "We have made some breakfast for you. Please, come inside and join us."

Taking the Billy-can offered I reluctantly followed him into the large hut that served as a communal centre. In there was a huddle of men and women; children too. They were sitting cross-legged on their reed mats eating freshly prepared chapattis and vegetable curry. Sitting among them I managed to disguise my feelings. They were after all humans just as I was; they had the same feelings and their disfigurements could never disguise their common humanity; their wish to offer a haven and friendship to a wandering stranger.

Looking at the smiling faces of the children I was much relieved to see that they all looked in perfect shape; unlike their parents it was clear to see they were each as God intended them to be. Theirs was a natural inquisitiveness. "What is your name, mister?"

"My name is James," I told them. "I came here to visit Sister Susan."

There was a momentary silence as though the group was waiting for someone to speak. "Sister Susan? Do you know what happened?" a man asked gravely.

"Yes," I sighed, without particularly wishing to go over her ghastly end again. "Sister Helen told me what had happened. I am dreadfully sorry. I was Susan, Sister Susan's friend from school."

"She was not just a sister," said an elderly lady half hiding her face behind her sari to disguise her own disfigurements. "She was an angel and she still visits us you know."

No one interrupted her but whether or not they shared her views about Susan visiting them I had no way of knowing. The old lady broke the silence once more: "Sister Susan was an angel and we loved her. When she went to heaven we cried for days. We buried her there in the cemetery you know."

I was trying to keep my emotions in check. I had no wish for a repeat performance of the night earlier when I had disgraced myself. "Was it you who laid her to rest?" I asked.

"Yes," she replied earnestly: "We all did. It was very sad and then we burned her clothing. She used to come here and help us when the children were being born."

"She was our white angel," said another to murmurs of approval. Each of them sat with their own thoughts as they examined my face for a reaction. I glanced at their sad faces, their scars and their dreadful disfigurements.

"Susan was a doctor. Do you have a doctor who comes to visit you here?"

"Yes, Father Donaldson is a doctor. He comes here all the time." Again there were nods of agreement.

I was curious: "And where do you get your food supplies from?"

"A mission boat comes every month and it brings with it essential supplies."

I asked if any of them had relatives. I was wondering if they were ever visited. Several answered and I learned that yes they had relatives. These were living on the mainland and these exiles were never visited. I was the first visitor for many months. I was told that they were the untouchables. They quietly told me something of their grim past.

"Everyone abandoned us and we wandered in exile, like dogs in the streets. Eventually the missionaries took pity on us and brought us here where there would be no one to stare at us and remind us of our circumstances. It made us feel much better for we are not different to each other; only to those on the mainland. They are different."

I felt very sad and there was a charitable part of me that desperately felt for them and wished fervently to help them as a sort of thanks for my own health. It was but a dream; I had none of the qualities necessary for that sort of sacrifice.

I told them I had a mother who was waiting for my return. I think they understood and didn't think badly of me. Thanking them for their hospitality I assembled my few belongings, taking great care to put as priority Susan's shabby suitcase and set out for the path that had brought me to what was almost but not quite a God-forsaken place. Never forsaken as long as there are earthly saints like Sisters Helen and Susan; men like Father Donaldson.

RETURNED TO DEVIL'S ISLAND

The small group of ghoulish individuals followed in my steps as I walked through the undergrowth to the cemetery where Susan lay at peace. I can only guess that they read my thoughts for as we arrived at the forlorn little corner they voluntarily began to tidy up the undergrowth surrounding it. Perhaps they were ashamed of its neglected state and wished to make amends, my having reminded them of her saintliness. As they completed their task they collected some wild posies and placed them over her cement tomb.

It was then that I remembered the box of chocolates I had brought for her. I took the carton from out of my bag and handed it to the small group of curious children watching what we were doing. Shaking hands I completed my stroll to the small chapel where I found Sister Helen. I didn't see the point in prolonging my misery; I had seen and heard all I wished to and all I now wished for was to leave this sad small island to its place in history and take with me memories that I had no choice but to take with me. Walking down to the jetty I waited patiently for the ferry and as I boarded I was met by the same searching looks of inquisitiveness as I had received on disembarking.

The ferry's skipper smiled in recognition. "You know, we are not going to Suva for several days yet. I'll be glad to take you to the island of Levuka."

I told him I didn't have a problem with that at all for I knew the island and I had sentimental reasons for visiting it too."

As the boat pulled away from the island of Mokagai I stood on the deck with my eyes fixed on the distant cemetery. There was emptiness inside and I was wondering if during my short visit my heart had somehow joined Susan's in her little bed of clay. Thankfully I was left alone by other passengers as tears streamed down my cheeks. All I could think of was the terrible waste of a young life filled with such promise. I realised that we are surrounded by Calvary; people and placed who as did our Lord thanklessly give their lives for others.

"I will always love you above all else, Susan," I whispered. I promised that one day I would return to tend her grave. The boat sailed on and before long the small island abeam and abaft disappeared over the horizon. Or had it? Was it me who was disappearing? It would surely seem that way to those on the tiny island, alive and dead.

On arriving at Levuka I thanked the captain and paid him my fare in English pounds before stepping on to the jetty. I reflected that this was the very same jetty where my grandparents, Chand and Gulbi, had arrived as children from India on that ill-fated steamer, the Leonidas. It had been such a treacherous journey from Calcutta and all so many years ago.

Finding a seat to myself I sat and gazed across the ocean. I was trying to visualise what it was like for them to arrive here as children, their hearts filled with a mixture of hope and trepidation. They would have been bare-footed and alone; totally dependent upon each other, trusting in each other. Their clothes would have been threadbare and the islands completely strange to them. These islands were as far removed from India as it was possible to be and they couldn't have had any idea of what lay before them.

As I sat there thinking such thoughts I felt depressed. I had to find a pub to do more than merely slake my thirst; I was humbled by the world and its history, and the part I was playing in it. I felt as a star among billions; undiscovered in my own firmament.

As I strolled into the very small town that was hardly more than a village that had big ideas about it I found a pub.

*   *   *

After a few days in Suva I finally climbed into that old Datsun and took the road for the gold mines and my sister's home. Unashamedly I got very drunk that evening and wept until my eyes had gone beyond sore. Perhaps I should not have taken such a painful voyage into the past; doubtless was there much wisdom in my getting drunk so soon afterwards. As I confessed to my mother and sister that two of Nirmala's boys' were my own; their grandchildren, I wept as copiously as did they.

Mother said between tearful questions. "I had my suspicions about those two boys. They looked exactly like you when you were that age. I often wondered if there was a connection."

The following morning we went to Nirmala's home where my mother and sister sat talking together on the veranda. I had a pretend fight with the boys and gave them boxing lessons. They for their part touched my biceps and felt the ridge of my stomach muscles. I gave them my boxing photographs taken when I had been a champion. I parted with a few brochures of Le Village in Tahiti; the ones that had my photos displayed in the centre pages. As we played and talked together some teenage girls arrived. I heard them call out, "I die there" and watched as the boys ran towards them following which they all disappeared over the small hill leading to the riverbank. I wondered if they were doing what I had done with Sara, Lisa Fong and their mother Nirmala. There wasn't much of an age difference between me then and the age they were at now.

We sat on the veranda and Nirmala brought me a beer. I thanked her and drank straight from the bottle. It was time for coming clean: "I am sorry, Nirmala, mother had to know about the boys. I told her. They are really her grandsons."

Nirmala seemed to colour but she held her tongue and otherwise appeared calm at my confession. After a moment she said quietly: "It's alright, Jamie. Your mother and sister are welcome to come and visit them as they wish. But please, no one else must ever know. Rajendra's family must never find out otherwise that will be the finish of us all. They would destroy us; the humiliation would be too much for them to bear."

We promised that no one would ever discover the truth and after mother and Malti left us I stayed and talked to Nirmala while waiting for Rajendra to return from work. There was awareness that things had changed since I had returned; that things would never be quite the same ever again.

"Nirmala; please do not arrange the children's marriage as most Hindus do," I asked passionately: "Let them date girls and find the right one for them when they

RETURNED TO DEVIL'S ISLAND

are ready. In Britain thousands of Asian girls commit suicide each year because their primitive thinking parents force them to go back to India or Pakistan to marry."

"We'll never do that," she assured me. "Once they finish their education here we will send then to New Zealand for higher education."

I added that I would be only too pleased to help them if they wished to come to England to finish off their education. She wasn't too happy at that suggestion and replied thoughtfully: "England is too far for my babies to go; Rajendra won't agree to that."

I was tempted to remind her that they were my boys too but perhaps it was just as well; Rajendra arrived. We shook hands as if there was no big deal in my returning home. It was the same informality as if I had been there the day before. A few courtesies exchanged I left Nirmala and her husband to themselves and headed back to Malti's home.

As the days went by I couldn't stitch together the past and the present; there had been too much change over a very long time. I was trying to recapture something that was more than elusive. I felt like a foreigner in my own country of birth and there was a feeling that this was no longer a place for me. I was trapped on an island.

Its beauty was inescapable but I wasn't. It was still a Third World country and I knew I would never again be a villager with small horizons. Strangely I missed England and I knew I had to return without delay. Fiji was not for me. I missed the modern way of life, the lifestyle, and the comforts of England. I was homesick but not for the land of my origins; I missed my other family; the people of Liverpool. Since I had left the South Sea Island my sense of humour had changed. I missed the comedians on television; I had laughed at the 'racist' jokes of Bernard Manning, Josh White and Charlie Williams. As an Irishman or Jew might laugh at the stereotypes of their ethnicity I too could laugh about my own ethnic differences, as could the people of England. They told jokes about the Irish and the Poles, so why not us, the non-whites?"

With such thoughts and harmless pastimes spent with family and friends I wasn't sorry to be leaving after my six week anti-climax of a revisit. If I got itchy feet again and England's permanent winters got too much for me there was always the California of Europe; Spain, the South of France and Italy.

On my final day I said goodbye to Nirmala and Rajendra and took endless photographs of the boys. After a hug and cuddle with the customary good wishes I stepped into the car and took with me many mixed feelings and memories, not all of which were good. That was life. As we drove off for Nadi Airport I sat next to mother and Malti in the back seat. Ramesh at the wheel had the front of the car to himself.

CHAPTER 12

After a heartbreaking farewell and a great deal of soul searching, for I was still unsure as to whether or not I was doing the right thing, I boarded a British Airways 747 en route to London. This time it was a thirty-six hour flight via Hawaii, Los Angeles, New York and finally we touched down at London Heathrow. Every soaring mile took me further away from Susan's small shrine and I couldn't help but feel guilty about it. Was I running away from something far more important than whatever the future held for me?

I arrived back at Heathrow Airport after the epic journey. From there I boarded the train to Victoria station where I caught the train bound for Liverpool and finally to my old landlady in Birkenhead. I had been happy there and felt I would finally be home when I alighted at the towns Central Station.

There was little evidence that my journey back had lifted my spirits; I was still sad and unsettled and the falling September rain did little to lift my gloominess. The leaves were already changing colour to autumnal hues and the warm southerly winds had changed direction; replaced by a chillier northern wind. I shivered and pulled my coat closer as I wondered what I was searching for. The cold was seeping through my clothing and I knew from experience it would find its way through to the marrow of my bones. When that happened the only relief was complete immersion in a hot tub. Perhaps I would have been better off making tracks for the south of France; Spain had a certain appeal too.

Leafing through the weekend newspapers I began to look for employment opportunities along Spain's Mediterranean coastlines known as the Costas. They were favourite locations for the British; the holiday-home owners and the retirees. There were others there too; those younger who were attracted by the warmer sunnier southern California climate not to mention the more laid back Spanish lifestyle.

As I leafed through the pages of the Daily Mail I saw a familiar face on the fashion page; it was Francesca, who as a 18 years old young lady been a student at the Art College and had sculptured my physique in clay. She was the fabulously beauty contest winner who had won my heart before her father whisked her away to live in Buckinghamshire to be near his ageing parents.

RETURNED TO DEVIL'S ISLAND

As I read on I learned that she had become a famous fashion designer. Her success was not confined to the UK but in Paris, Milan and New York. Many mail order catalogues had marketed her fashion designs through their centre folds. I looked at the picture over and over again. A little self consciously I cut the article out and put it away with other paperwork I couldn't ever be parted from.

A few days later I saw Francesca being interviewed on a television broadcast called Look North. Francesca was now 26 and as beautiful as she ever was. My heart skipped a beat as I heard her voice again; how self assured she now was; again I realised how privileged I had been to be part of her life.

After much searching I found her old telephone number and called her to congratulate her on her success. Mixed fortunes, it was her mother who took the call. She told me that Francesca was in Paris. Over the next week I telephoned her again and again but ever the success, she was always on the road somewhere. There again, she was now a rich and famous young lady with the whole world at her feet. Why would she want to talk to a guy who used to work on the buses? I was under no illusions; I was no longer in Francesca's league. In the end I opted for a postcard and a small message of congratulations.

Cheerless and feeling alone I wandered through the streets of Birkenhead and again considered if I had made the right decision in coming back. Perhaps if the cultures had been more similar; if the distances that separated us had been less vast, I could have been more certain. Wherever I had been in my South Sea Island travels there had been reminders of Susan. Here there were none; it was a planet removed.

Maybe I had seen far too much of the wonderful sides of life and life at its worst. There were to be no new experiences for me and I was haunted only by the images of the small overgrown cemetery where Susan's fragility lay asleep. I think the unexpected opening of old love wounds in seeing Francesca and her success was affecting me. I went to the nearby Prenton Park Hotel that was next door to Tranmere Rovers football ground; got myself pissed and mournfully sought my bed. Maybe the answer to my troubles would be revealed but that was not going to happen today.

During the weeks that followed I visited the French and Spanish consulates in Liverpool and obtained visitor's visas to both countries. Feeling better about things I sold the Morris Minor and bought myself a second hand Volkswagen Camper van and took the road for Dover on England's most southerly coast. From there I boarded the Brittany Ferry for the French port of Calais. After parking the van between decks I made my way up to the ship's lounge bar; I needed a beer.

Taking in my surroundings from the bar stool upon which I was perched I watched with amused detachment the excited faces and high spirits of the ship's complement of holidaymakers. Children were running about; excited by their great adventure whilst small groups of teenagers huddled around tables drinking. As they did so they peered earnestly at the maps trying to make sense of the routes; arguing between themselves the best routes to take for the sunnier climes in France and Spain.

CHRIS NAND

As I sipped my beer I again found myself ruefully considering what the future might hold for me. Uppermost in my mind, would I find work or would I return a dispirited failure to Britain? I had enjoyed mostly a lucky life; was my luck now running out? Time alone would tell.

Such were my thoughts when my eyes caught sight of a huddle of young ladies who had just that moment entered the lounge bar. I watched as they removed their travelling bags from their backs and after letting them drop to the carpeted floors they looked around for somewhere where they might sit. The bar caught their attention and I watched disinterestedly as they got their drinks in before selecting a table situated more or less behind me.

Although I couldn't pick up the detail they were clearly excited about their trip and their destination. I heard the names of several of the places mentioned and thought I detected Australian accents. They had same twang as Susan had. I couldn't help myself; I swivelled around to have a better look.

They were typical of their class and age group; wearing cut off jeans, trainers and yes, they were mostly lookers. A couple were blonde or at least appeared to be; there were two who were brunettes and a redhead. It amused me to see them drinking straight from their bottles; not a lot of finesse there then. This mannerism too was typical of all the Australians that I had so far met on my travels. Finally plucking up courage I picked up my bottle of beer and sauntered over to join them.

"Hey," I smiled. "May I join you? I'm from the same neck of the woods as you are. I'm from Fiji." I thought the fact that we were geographical neighbours would help open up the conversation and reduce the risk of them telling me to piss off.

"Fiji?"

I grinned. "Yes, I am from Suva but I have lived here for several years," I told them as I pulled up a chair.

"Are you on holiday?" the redhead asked.

"Well, not as such; I am footloose and fancy free though so is there a difference," I asked as I warmed to them and hoped they weren't considering me an intrusion. I told them I used to work in Liverpool. "I am running away to warmer pastures; I will be looking for work. I am not planning on coming back."

They were curious and asked if I had anywhere in particular in mind. I told them I was heading in the general direction of the south of France. I was also thinking of Spain or even Morocco. I followed up by asking where they were going.

"We've just finished university," they told me. "We want to see as many places in Europe as we can before we return home to Australia."

The ladies were chatting excitedly together and were all in high spirits. From what I could gather three of them were of Jewish decent and were going to parts of Germany to visit the sites of the holocaust. Another two were of similarly mind to me. "Are you driving to the Mediterranean?" I asked.

"Good Lord, no! We are all going to Paris by train and from there we are going on our separate ways." The German bound trio was separating from the two ladies who had their hearts set on St. Tropez.

As big hearted as ever I told them I would be happy to drop them off in Paris as I was going that way. Heading for Switzerland, Italy and on to the South of France I had little choice anyway. They thought it was a great idea and thanked me, telling each other how lucky they were to have bumped into me.

Suddenly the tall brunette asked: "Can two of us stay on until the South of France? We would love to see Switzerland and Italy and will contribute towards petrol expenses."

I shyly smiled. "It's no problem. It would be great to have some company; be my guests?"

After an hour's chatting during which the crossing had almost been completed the ship's engines came to a stop and peering through its windows we could clearly make out the French port of Calais. The girls wanted to go up the ladders to the decks; this was time for the cameras to start rolling.

As we took in the views, my first for France, the girls took photographs whilst we waited for the foot passengers to disembark. Soon it was our turn. Helping them with their luggage, for mine was already in the camper van, we reached my happy-clapper wheels. We loaded up and off trundled through the ship's bow doors. There was just the usual immigration and customs barrier to negotiate before we were finally on our way.

I laughed; I was filled with good humour and the depression I had been burdened with in England had by now evaporated. "Please keep on reminding me to drive on the right hand side of the road," I called out. "I have never done it before. Just say passenger on the pavement and I will know what to do."

The girls were full of fun too and shouted 'passenger on the pavement' at every crossroads and roundabout. Time and distance passed us by quickly enough and before long we were on the Paris ring road called the Peripherique. It was for me quite an awesome and intimidating highway. I was in a ten lane River Amazon of fast moving traffic. Yes, me and the ladies were in there somewhere and I was having difficulty figuring out just where we were.

The girls were more familiar with the place than I was and kept on excitedly pointing out the various landmarks. They were constantly urging me on whilst telling me to look out for Eiffel Tower. We got there too, surprisingly. As we pulled up I parked the van near Pantheon on Rue Soufflot and making sure all was secure six of us strolled to the metro station nearby. I looked on bemused as the five young ladies hugged each other and said their goodbyes. We then watched as the three girls companions disappeared through the boarding gates and climbed into the waiting train.

Back in our camper van we studied the road map and decided that the road to Dijon was the best route for us to take. As we ambled happily along we listened to the

CHRIS NAND

English pop songs being played on Radio Luxembourg. "What are your names again?" I asked now the confusion of five girl's name had come to pass.

"Oh, I am Marianne," said the tall brunette introducing herself before turning to her blonde friend; "And Karen is Karen aren't you Karen?' The blonde giggled impishly.

Having detected some familiarity with the French language and pronunciation I asked them if they could speak French. Yes they could; German and Spanish too. They laughed: "We have just graduated from Oxford University where we studied languages."

As we chatted away their Australian accents took me home time after time and inevitably I supposed to Susan's tragic end to her life. It all felt so unfair for again she too could have been enjoying life. What pulls most; self-indulgence or ideals I thought to myself.

Glancing at my watch I noticed it was already 2 o'clock in the late afternoon. It was time to eat. Pulling into a motorway restaurant we caught our breath; it was our first chance to truly relax since leaving the ferry. Perhaps tiredness and the effect of a couple of glasses of red wine caused my despondency to increase. I couldn't have been good company for the two high spirited girls sharing the front seat with me. They were both singing at the tops of their voices; their shoulders rocking and rolling' to the songs being broadcast. All I could think morosely of was Susan's grave. Would I take its image with me wherever I was to go? Would its reflection take me eventually to my own tomb wherever in the world that might be?

As we eventually pulled up at the Swiss border crossing we could see we were in a town called Besancon. The official at the barrier checked our passports and smiled as his little rubber stamp of approval came thumping down on each of our passports; it was another milestone reached on our journey. Spotting a sign for Geneva, which to us sounded Swiss enough, we took that one. They finally got around to asking me: "Do you speak French, Jamie?"

"Just a little," I told them. "I picked up a little in Tahiti."

"Tahiti!!" they chorused. "Wow. You have been around."

"Yes, Tonga and both of the Samoas' too," I told them. "I have been all over the South Sea Islands."

"That is our dream to go there someday," Karen said thoughtfully as she pictured in her mind the touristy images of the place. I thought it best not to mention the methods by which they killed suckling pigs or used the trees as lavatories.

Before long we were driving along the banks of a vast lake where we spotted a small camping area. A good place for a pause thought I. Parking the van I took out the map to discover we were on the banks of Lake Lausanne. This suggested we weren't too far away from Geneva. Stretching our legs we strolled along the beauty spot as the evening sun was setting behind the snow capped Mont-Blanc and other Alpine mountains in the distance. As we went on our small walk of discovery we chanced upon a small bar where we three sat on the patio surrounded with trellises and

RETURNED TO DEVIL'S ISLAND

bougainvillea. After the meal we climbed aboard again and as far as I was concerned we had done enough of the open road for one day. We had done well.

Up went the elevating roof of the van to give us more walking about space though neither of the girls was as tall as I was. Out came the red wine and bottoms up and we toasted our friendship and good fortune in crossing each other's paths. The evening passed pleasantly enough as one might expect in such circumstances but we had done much since boarding the ferry. There was plenty of small talk and eventually time for some shut-eye.

One of the van's beds pulled out in the roof over the steering wheel in the driver's cab. The other was in the elevated roof area whilst mine, the roomier one was in the middle of the van. Well designed, the dining table and settee fitted together and made into a double bed for me to sleep on. Room for two or at a push three thought I but just as well the five hadn't been going south?

As the girls were about to brush their pearly whites and change into their night-clothes I did the gentlemanly thing and took a moonlit stroll before returning and slipping into my sleeping bag on the double bed.

As morning broke and the world came alive I pulled on some shorts and trainers and strolled along the banks of the lake before getting some provisions in. The girls were already up by the time I returned and somehow the mood had gone; none of us were as chatty and high spirited as we had been and sat silently with our own thoughts as we motored along the pleasant lanes of Switzerland. Soon we saw the high jet sprays of the famous Geneva fountain.

"Please Jamie, can we drive close to it. I need a photograph for the album," called Marianne. We found the La Rade and the giant water fountain "Jet d"eau". Parking the van close to it we took usual touristy photos and I grabbed the opportunity to study our map.

Karen broke into my thoughts. "Jamie, Lets go to Chamonix. I've seen postcards of that place and it looks out of this world; it's a ski resort."

These place names meant nothing to me so I was happy to go along with whatever they suggested; their familiarity with Europe was better than was mine. Marianne knew her French onions for as we travelled back across the border there it all was in its full glory. Manhattan? Eat your heart out. The beauty of the snow-capped Mont Blanc was truly magnificent and after a further hour's drive we arrived at the snow-covered houses of the town of Chamonix.

"Look up there, Jamie. You can see the chair lifts going up to the mountain top?" called Marianne. Heck, I was trying to negotiate the van through the town's narrow winding and very packed streets. "Okay, I told her. "Let's find a place to park."

Parking the van close to a narrow fast flowing, frothy stream we took a stroll around the picturesque township. As we did so we bumped into many skiers heading towards the chair lifts that would take them to the mountain's ski slopes. It was a dull and chilly day so the girls went back to the van and changed into warmer clothes before we entered a small bar. As we sipped our beer our eyes met. The girls were looking at me with undisguised curiosity.

CHRIS NAND

The previous evening I had been certain the two girls were sound asleep. Again I was troubled by my experiences during my visit to Mokagai the leprosy island and unwisely I had allowed those events to fill my mind. I hadn't been able to suppress my restlessness; I had been overwhelmed with my sentiments. It had never occurred to me that I might have been overheard. I realised then that they had probably heard me and were inquisitive to know the reason for my emotive restiveness. They kept their thoughts to themselves and after awhile we took the Mont Blanc tunnel and headed south again.

The seven miles long tunnel behind us we crossed the Italian border at Aosta and continued along the banks of the winding river before seeing a sign for Turin. This just happened to be again one of the girls' must see locations. They wanted to see the Shroud of Turin; it wasn't something I was particularly keen to encounter but if that was what they wanted who was I to argue?

It was too far away for us to reach that day and as night fell we discovered a camping site with more facilities and a chance to shower. We felt a lot better, especially after changing into fresh clothes and soaking up the atmosphere of the small restaurant. Making small talk I asked them why they had left it until October to travel around Europe. Surely, July and August would have been far warmer," I suggested.

"We had to see England and Scotland first. Then there was the graduation to attend; our parents were flying in from Australia and they had been looking forward to seeing us in our caps and gowns all their lives," Karen smiled as Marianne nodded.

"I bet you both looked beautiful. I would love to see the photographs; very appealing. I bet they were as proud as Punch."

They promised to send me some of the photographs as soon as we were settled, wherever that was to be. They were looking at me again a little thoughtfully, which I found a little unsettling. I couldn't help but wonder what was on their minds. Maybe I needed to shower again?

The silence was broken by Karen: "Jamie, why were you sobbing last night? Please tell us? We would like to help you out of your sadness; you seem to be a nice and honest guy."

I looked at their faces and hesitated before I apologised for disturbing them. I told them their Australian accents reminded me of someone who was very important to me and it was rather a long and sad story.

"Our accents?"

They were intrigued and begged me to tell them. They told me we had all evening before us and they loved a good story. Hesitatingly at first I told them something of my background; how the holy man who had named me Krishna predicted my future. I told them about my love affair with Susan and my visit to the Leprosy Hospital where I had discovered her grave. I also told them about my children and my travels to the South Sea Islands. In fact I told them everything since my childhood days at St. Mary's to when I first saw them on the ferry.

Their silence suggested they found the story of my experiences absorbing. Their moods changed as I recounted my adventures and I saw them wipe away a tear occasionally, especially when I told of my visit to Mokagai the leprosy isle. I suppose they contrasted my own life with theirs of relative security and prosperity.

"You poor soul," said Marianne with an attempt at a reassuring smile. "I am glad you got it off your chest, Jamie. You shouldn't be keeping such thoughts in."

They asked if I believed in one's destiny. I told them that at first I had my doubts but with the passing of time and experience I wasn't too sure anymore. I was open minded; more than I had ever been before. "I do believe that there is something, a presence that we can't but have an instinct for. Some power beyond our understanding that might have brought us together for a reason."

"Do you think that we have been thrown together for a reason?" asked Karen"

We all laughed. Karen wasn't a lady to beat around the bush. Her questions were direct and right to the point. I smiled, looked at her and kissed her hand. Her beautiful face looked intriguingly beautiful or that might have been the romance of the intimacy of the restaurant and surroundings.

"I believe our meeting up like this was no coincidence." I told them. "This was predestined," I added. I lightened up a little. "That's if you believe in all that shit! How else would we meet on a floating tub and travel in a ragged old van together? Anyway, it was very good planning by whoever brought us together," I laughed.

We all brightened up considerably. "Well think about it. We are from the same neck of the woods; I mean the Pacific basin and here we are meeting up on a ferry on the exact opposite of the world. That can't be a coincidence," smiled Marianne. They both agreed that there was more to destiny or fate than was otherwise known. As we chatted away I caught sight of the waiter preparing the meal at an adjoining table: Turning towards him I asked; "Is that pilau rice?" I asked.

"Pilau rice? What is that?" he asked. "This is called risotto and is cooked Italian style."

It looked good to me and from the exclamations of my attractive companions it suited them too. I ordered some of the same. This was later washed down, as the local culture requires, with copious amounts of wine.

By this time it seemed to me that the two girls had either taken a shine to me or felt sorry for me; I was the centre of attraction and they were increasingly flirting with me. During our drunken walk back through the shrubbery and winding paths to our camper van we paused several times to embrace and to kiss too. My hands were shaking as I fumbled with the van keys; a fear of what might happen once we enter the van. Two very beautiful European young ladies reminded me of the very aggressive air hostages in Tahiti and New Zealand. As we entered the van their kisses became more intrusive.

"It's called taking your mind off things," breathed Marianne after we had familiarised ourselves a heck of a lot more than had hitherto been the case. Our alcohol fuelled lovemaking was intense and afterwards Marianne was still breathing heavily as was her friend. It had certainly worked for me. What I had just experienced was far better than seeking a drink for solace.

I was glowing at my good fortune for bumping into such company and who had helped to alleviate my pain. As Marianne snuggled into me I asked if they were both on the pill: one Nirmala was quite enough for any guy in a lifetime. They put my mind at rest so clearly they had been expecting more of their trip abroad than a little sightseeing.

At the crack of dawn I left the girls where they were and climbing into the driver's seat took the road to the Holy Shroud. Once reaching Turin I got caught up in the early morning traffic and having had enough of it we pulled into a lay-by. Anyone who has ever driven in peak time Italy will sympathise. Traffic lights? They took not a damned bit of notice. It is said that if one Italian jumps the lights they all do, to show solidarity.

As soon as Marianne and Karen pulled their jeans and jumpers on they joined me on the van's bench seat in the front. Not a word was said about our nocturnal exploits; as if nothing out of the ordinary had happened instead they blithely showed more interest in the architectural triumphs of the Italians than the architectural triumphs of the night. We studied the map and found the route to the Cathedral of John the Baptist. On the way we stopped at a small coffee bar and had breakfast before heading for the basilica. It was well after midday when we finally arrived outside the holy place. Should I be taking confession thought I. Parking up we walked towards the high steps and entrance of the Cathedral.

"Do you think they will allow us inside dressed in jeans?" Marianne asked.

"I think so. Look, other people around us are in jeans. Plus they need our cash on collection plates I guess. All churches have collection plates for a few coins to keep them going."

We sinners joined the queue and shuffled along inside, admiring as we did so the magnificent building and its structures. "Look? There is the Royal Chapel and the shroud should be in the chapel," supposed Karen.

We followed the line of people and went inside the Royal Chapel. Breathtaking, there was the shroud protected by a glass frame. My hands shook as I made the sign of the cross. My thoughts took me back to Susan and I thought of how thoroughly she had been indoctrinated by the nuns of St Mary's and for what? By sacrificing her life to bring comfort to others? Well Marianne and Karen were bringing comfort to me otherwise I would have been driving a lone figure crying my heart out for what it could have been; that was my take on things. However, I had to concede that the image on the faded cloth put the fear of God into me. My hands began to tremble as I lit a candle for the saint in my heart, Susan. Hurriedly I put a few liras into a collection plate and rushed out with Marianne and Karen right up close behind me.

"You look like death warmed up," said Marianne. I didn't answer her and walked back to the van before opening the van door.

"Well, Jamie! Did you see it?"

"Yes, I saw it."

"Is it really the shroud of Jesus?"

"I don't know but it sure as hell put the fear of God into me. Look, my hands are still trembling."

Karen was a little affected by the experience too. "We were very lucky to see it because they only display it on certain times of the year. It is normally kept in a vault."

I was still feeling edgy but the comforting hugs from my companions picked me up and putting the experience in our rear view mirrors we headed off in the general direction of France's Mediterranean coast. By sunset we had crossed the Italian border and like a yo-yo on a rope we were back once again in France. The cooler weather of Switzerland and Italy was also behind us and the weather had a warm sub-tropical feel to it. As I parked the van in a quiet corner of the small port of Menton we changed into our beachwear before sneaking into the Mediterranean for a swim. This was as far as we were concerned a pivotal part of our quest. Here in front of us was the Mediterranean and you don't get any further south in Europe than where we had found ourselves. It was symbolic of everything we were doing together.

"The water sure feels cool," Karen said with a shiver. She sounded disappointed.

"I know what you mean," I laughed as I paddled and splashed. "We are comparing it with the warmer waters of the Pacific."

The symbolic moment attended to we decided to turn our attention to the van, food and whatever might be on offer for dessert that day. Last night was surely only a taste of similar things to come.

Afterwards we took our showers to freshen ourselves up. Sure the sea was cool and by contrast the beach shower, especially with the two naked girls cavorting and having fun, was a welcome relief. They certainly brought me relief; and here was me thinking their purpose in getting a shower was to fresh up. After their attention only a nap would freshen me up.

That late afternoon we did the town and the ubiquitous restaurant before the meaningful night's nightcap was followed by sleep. Monaco was to be our next port of call. These two definitely had the lust for wandering and adventure. I knew what they were after and who could blame them? There was bay after bay of enchanting harbours, inlets and wooded havens. This was as far away from rainy England as it is possible to get. It reminded me of some of my South Sea Island retreats.

The girls were bouncing up and down with anticipation. "I have just got to see the royal palace," screamed Marianne. Spinning the wheel, up the hill we trundled. This was the way to go thought I. It was a long time since I had been in a royal palace. Once we had reached the top of the hill we took photographs of the cannons placed around the façade of the magnificent edifice and the palace grounds. Filled with excitement we followed the crowd towards the palace itself, taking photographs of the palace guards standing on either side of the main entrance. They were dressed in white uniform and carried rifles over their shoulders.

CHRIS NAND

From there we three visited the Royal Chapel before returning down the hill to see the Jacques Cousteau Oceanic Museum. I was surprised to see a whale's tooth that had been presented to the Principality of Monaco by the government of Fiji. It made me feel much closer to home. A short walk from there took us to the casino where we watched the wealthy clients being dropped off before being ripped off; or so I thought. This was the best place on earth to apply for a chauffeur's job; there was obviously a need with all those Bentleys and Rollers scattered around. Somehow my camper van didn't quite cut it in such exalted company but it was better than the Morris Minor I supposed.

It was another been there done that tee-shirt and after a few drinks we headed off in the direction of another glamorous watering hole; that of St. Tropez. That was it had to be remembered the girls' destination. En route we passed Nice and Antibes before discovering a small secluded beach just before reaches Cannes where we had decided we would be stopping overnight. It was almost dark by this time. The sun had set and the beach deserted. It was a great opportunity for us to skinny dip. It was hardly my first experience at cavorting in the sea stark naked and probably not theirs either, their being Aussies. It was a great place for three youngsters to be; it was a great time in the greater scheme of things.

Cannes was as fascinating as we had imagined it to be; it was also as pricey as we anticipated. We checked the menu out at the Charlton Hotel. It clearly suggested that the world's hoi polloi need not cast their shadows across its portals. We took the hint and went on our way. What is wrong with pasta enjoyed in a camper van anyway? Besides, I think it would have been more enjoyable to dine that way than at such a hotel table being patronised by flunkies.

The following day we found a hypermarket and bought our groceries in bulk. These easily fitted in to the empty compartment under the double bed of the van. The girls insisted on paying for everything and giving me some cash towards the cost of petrol. At first I refused to take the money but they insisted so what the hell; why not?

They told me it was their fathers' money and both families were well loaded. "You take it Jamie, you've been good to us and we know that you really need it."

I took it because gallantry aside I was going to need it. The engine started without a hiccup and onwards and upwards, the beaches of St. Tropez were beckoning and couldn't be ignored. Here we discovered our sandy hotel for the night. This beach was called Pamplona Plage and there on the glorious white sands we enjoyed our cheap Chateau de Plonque whilst the girls did what girls do best; they prepared the food in the dinette. The plastic plates didn't do the meal justice; they were dab hands when it came to dishing up some tasty meals. Again, it was becoming habitual; the wine went right down our necks.

In the morning we woke startled to a sharp rapping on the sides of our van. Pulling on my shorts I got to the door first. It was just as well, the girls were starkers. There outside with a smirk on his face was this guy writing down the van's registration. He looked at me and sort of smiled. "How long are you planning on staying here?"

RETURNED TO DEVIL'S ISLAND

I thought about it: "Oh, just a few days," I replied.

His English wasn't that good but it translated into "This is a naturist's beach. You must pay five francs a day to stay here. There are showers and toilet facilities over there."

As he chatted he pointed to some grass huts nearby. I smiled and clamoured back into the van. Inside the van the girls were hysterical, laughing their heads off for being on a nudist camp and having to pay five francs for showing what others should be paying to set their eyes on. "Hey, this is wonderful," Marianne screamed. "We don't have to dress for breakfast."

Karen laughed. "Had we been wearing our jim-jams we would have had to take them off. "There's no need to be conformists anymore," she squealed. "We know what we look like. Now let's see what the others look like."

I took out the fifteen francs for the anticipated three days stopover and paid the guy; it was my second nudist camp receipt. As we breakfasted we peered out of the van windows and saw a beach filling with naked bodies, some of them children and all as comfortable as imaginable. It looked really rather strange; perhaps not quite as much for me but who knows? We didn't have any wish to not conform either so stripping off we hesitated for just a moment before picking up our towels and going with the flow.

We giggled like children as we made for the water's edge and one ball short of a game so to speak we were encouraged to join in a game of volleyball. There was no getting away from it. We joined in the fun, sniggered some more and joined in the fun again. Those balls sure bounced; so did the bare breasts. It was amusing to see the group of men and women playing the game in their birthday suits but there was no embarrassment and no feelings of immodesty. In point of fact I thought it one of the least sexy situations I had ever been in. "Have you two ever been to a nudist beach before?" I asked.

"No never! I feel a little strange without my clothes," Karen smiled before asking if it was a first for me too. I told them about my Liverpool University French girlfriend and of how we had once gone to nudist beaches in northern France."

Before long, the beach was packed with nudists; all ages and sizes with all kinds of sports being played while others exercised or swam. We mingled among the crowd feeling perfectly at ease and getting used to being naked.

CHAPTER 13

When our stay was up we turned our backs on St Tropez and drove towards Marseille which was further on along the coast road. After getting lost through the Pyrenees we three wanderers eventually arrived in Andorra and carried on to the Spanish border. Our passports and visas were carefully scrutinised by the frontier guards before we were nodded through the barrier. We were in Spain. The Land of the el toro.

The road to Barcelona was reasonably good so I put my foot down and it wasn't long before we found ourselves on the city's Paseo Maritimo. Although it was already almost November the sun was still hotter than one might reasonably have expected in August in England. We had a good feeling about things and I guessed we wanted life to be always like this.

Finding a parking bay outside what appeared to be a British pub; well it was called Hemingway's, we had a few bottles of San Miguel beer and watched the sunset sinking over what we presumed direction in which the Dark Continent lay. "Can we try some sangria? I have heard a lot of travellers talking about it?" asked Karen.

Marianne said of course we should and asked the waiter for it in near fluent Spanish: "Una jarra de sangria porfavor".

Karen and I laughed as the waiter smiled and walked to the bar. There he chopped up a variety of fruit and placing them in a jar added a mix of cocktails and served it to us in large glasses. We toasted our good luck and drank the ruby red liquid whilst tucking enthusiastically into the fruit. "This is bloody good," said Karen.

"Too bloody strong," added Marianne with a pretend hiccup and a giggle.

"Fucking good and fucking strong," I echoed as I remembered drinking plenty of it when holidaying in Mallorca with my West Indian friend. The girls laughed and Karen looked quizzically at me. "It isn't like you to swear, Jamie."

I reminded them they were both Australian; a country which in my opinion didn't know the difference between a conventional and a swear word. After freshly fried sardines and salad for lunch we showered at the open air shower on the beach and dressed up a little for a site seeing trip of the famous city. I hadn't seen the girls in skirts before; they should wear them more often with legs like theirs. They strolled beside me and as they did so they turned a few heads with their undulating hips swinging. "Let's take a taxi around the city," suggested Marianne. "I must see the famous Cathedral."

That agreed we hailed a passing taxi for a short inclusive tour and after a brief visit to Barcelona Football Club we eventually arrived outside the Cathedral. It was impressive.

"Magnificent" breathed Marianne enthusiastically. It seemed to us to be more interesting on the outside than it might have been on the inside; rather a novel idea for a cathedral thought I. As we toured inside I listened to my better informed companions. They had obviously read up on the outstanding edifice. "This was designed by Antonio Gaudi, the famous Spanish architect," Marianne sighed with bated breath. Karen, the other culture vulture agreed with her. "But it was finished by Picasso. It had to be: Poor Gaudi was knocked down by a bus and killed before he completed the Cathedral."

"Thanks for the history lesson, where would I be without you both?" I smiled. As we approached the altar we lit candles before visiting the main central spire and finally exiting the building. It was mentally and physically draining. That night it was night out, lights out and straight to sleep for us three travellers.

We slept right the way through and it was late morning before we were moved on by a traffic cop. We had it appeared parked in a prohibited zone. Breakfast down our necks we took the road south to Valencia, hugging the Mediterranean coastline as our van swept graciously and sometimes ungraciously around slopes and curves with occasional sharp turns. It was dark when we finally arrived in Spain's third biggest city and fabulous port. While I took care of the road the girls looked out for a convenient stopping off point and finally found one at a beach called La Albufera. It provided us with another good night's sleep.

Karen looked thoughtful: "This is what is known as the Costa Blanca," she said quietly as she gazed across the endlessly blue sea.

Our companion sitting between us nodded. "Yes, it means the White Coast," added Marianne which was unnecessary for we knew that much Spanish. What we didn't know was that the description had nothing to do with the white sand beaches. The term is a description of how the region looks in February when the almond blossom appears and makes the entire countryside look as though it is snow covered. "I always dreamed of coming here, ever since I was a little girl. I always wanted to see a bullfight."

"That is not for me," I ventured. I am far too squeamish for that sort of crap. Anyway, I think it is cruel. You're on your own in this. I have no intention of going anywhere near a bullring. I will find a bar nearby and wait for you both but you must promise me one thing; I don't want you talking about it. The thought of those guys killing such a magnificent animal as a sport and for the pleasure of spectators I think is a real turn off."

As we huddled into bed together that night heavy rain began to fall. The noise on the metal roof of the van was deafening. It was far too noisy for us to get to sleep and we ended up laughing our heads off. Finally giving up I opened up the bottle of brandy we had purchased at Hemingway's Bar and poured the drinks. It was a heady drink and the moment was right. After a long chat we went to sleep snuggled up together.

The following morning after a brisk walk along the beaches we had a late brunch before carrying on to Alicante. The sun again was setting as we arrived outside a small hostel near to the beach called Hostel Nevada. We appeared to have a thing about sunset arrivals. Parking our camper van in the car park adjacent to the hostel we entered its dimly lit foyer, rang the welcome bell and asked the middle-aged owner for a double bedroom for the night.

He wasn't quite as welcoming as was the bell sitting on what passed as a reception desk. Looking the three of us over carefully it was clear that he disapproved of one bloke sharing a room with two babes. He knew that the room would only have one bed and I didn't look like the kind of traveller who would even think of sleeping on the floor.

Shaking his head he told us in perfect English that it was not possible for him to let a room for two females and one male. He didn't say it, we guessed it; this is a strongly Catholic country with a different take on morality than the more liberal northern Europeans. He let us have one double and one single at a discounted price. We had something to eat in the restaurant and went straight to our rooms. After a good shower and a scrub we met in the double room. Everyone was happy; morality had been restored.

We were all too knackered for hanky-panky we slipped beneath the sheets and as quickly slipped into deep slumber. The proprietor did rather well out of us; we stayed the two nights before finding the road to Malaga. That Spanish port city was almost as far south as you can go in Mediterranean Spain. From there on there is only one way forward and that is backwards; to retrace one's steps.

On arriving there we found the Hotel Torreblanca Del Sol in the small fishing village of Fuengirola. Here the hotel proprietor was much more upbeat about such indelicacies and had no qualms about us three booking the one room. Perhaps he thought it only natural; he would have done the same thing. Who wouldn't? It made economic sense too; this was the quiet season and there was no getting through it if one got picky about one's hotel guests. Thank the good Lord for Spanish winters.

The two girls and I stayed there for just two nights during which we did the usual sightseeing tours. We visited the small Spanish mountain pueblos of Mijas and Coin. At the latter we enjoyed dinner at a local Venta called Las Palmeras. Then, after taking several photographs of the charming hillside villages we took the road for Marbella. It wasn't too far away, which was just as well. I think we were all feeling sore arsed through spending too much time on the road. The van had been good value for money; I felt sure that it needed a rest as much as we did.

On reaching the city we found a bar in the Puerto de Marbella where we relaxed a little before spreading the map out once again on the table before us. "Look for Estepona," I told the girls. "I don't know much about the Costa del Sol but it is a place that rings a bell. We are so close we may as well go and see what it is all about."

"Money, that is what it is all about," said Karen with a grin. "It is where the wealthy live down here; you just got to believe it. Here, I can see Estepona on the map and it is only about twenty miles from here," she added.

"Thirty kilometres," interrupted Marianne.

"Whatever know it all. Let's go and find it." Clambering aboard once again we drove towards the then small resort and on the way pulled up at Puerto Banus. There we found a newly opened bar called Sinatra's. Why not? Afterwards we strolled around the marina gaping like tourists at the rich assortment of yachts coveted by not only their owners but the rest of the world's aspirants too. So this is how the other half lives. You don't see such self indulgences moored at Mokagai leprosy isle I recalled dreamily.

As soon as we reached Estepona Marianne screamed. "Stop, Jamie. I think I can see Gibraltar. Whoopee. We fucking well made it." We gave ourselves congratulatory hugs as we took in the scene before our eyes. It just wouldn't have been the same had I done this trip on my own. Surely my luck had been in when I met Marianne and Karen with their friends on the ferry almost two months ago.

It was indeed quite a moment for us. This is as far south as it gets in Europe. It had been a long way, a long time and a great adventure. This was the final full stop on a long exciting book of adventure. There was somehow finality to not only the trip but to my quest. I was tired. I had done enough travelling; I didn't want any more new experiences. This was it. It was as far as it goes for me. It was time for this South Sea Islands sloop to drop anchor. I had to think long and hard as to where I went from here.

I stopped and alighting joined the two girls as we walked up a hill and looked over the Mediterranean from where we allowed our eyes to wander across the horizon. "Yes, she was right. It was unmistakable. It was the Rock of Gibraltar alright.

"Do you see what I see?" breathed Karen excitedly. Without waiting for either of us to reply she pointed across the languid blue waters where the Mediterranean Sea meets the Atlantic Ocean. "Those mountains over there in the distance, they must be the Atlas range of mountains. That is Africa can you believe?"

We were all jumping up and down but torn by our inner feelings too. Our journey could never have been planned this way; it had taken its own course but it might just as easily have been guided by God. It had been the experience of a lifetime. It was going to be the hardest act ever to follow.

It is a strange way in which the mind works for until this moment there had been a sense of permanence to our idyllic way of life. There had been more stability to our shared adventure than with any of my previous relationships. There had been so many moments when its ending would have been inconceivable. It was certainly something we never discussed.

Compared with this journey being shared with Marianne and Karen the other relationships had been ships that pass in the night. Only Susan had been permanent. Never ever had I envisaged life without her even if Fate had separated us as it had done. I knew her image was ingrained in my heart and there was no escaping it even if I wished for respite.

Ours had been a marriage of the heart. I was married to Susan more so than many others who had their relationships formalised. All else that had happened between our meeting had been escapism but there could be no escape; no comfort in distance and no release from longing for her.

I had tried again and again to defeat the magnetism of her attraction; at times like this I could not only look back but look forward to being with Susan. But, how does one look forward to life with a memory, a woman who has died? It cannot be possible.

I am not the erudite type but I remembered the line of an anonymous writer: 'In a world of women I searched, and then I found you.' Those words had stayed with me for years because in my case they were meaningful where Susan was concerned.

Now with Marianne and Karen there was an alternative sense of permanency. But, like those that had gone before it I knew in my heart that this was as far as it goes. That the two who had shared my adventure, their images and our shared memories would become wisps of recollection on an old man's face. That was as certain as the knowledge that there would be one image that would stand out in stark relief; it was the enduring image of Susan when she had joined me on our ferry. If only? How often had I thought that? The ship that would eventually have led us both to Europe had she not at that final moment responded to the call of God.

Now we had reached the end of our trail I knew that the girls' objectives and my own no longer coincided. There wasn't much left for us to do as we flipped the pages in our diaries, filling in our days and nights with sampling what this coastal stretch of Andalusia had to offer us.

We visited the famous mountain town of Ronda where we took snaps of the magnificent views down the gorge. As we lunched in the bar opposite the famous bullring the girls insisted on their seeing a bullfight. Surprisingly I relented and after lunch we bought the tickets and we were swept along in the crowd as the river of excited spectators poured through the bullring's grand doors and into the arena. This I thought was what it must have been like in the Coliseum of Rome and other Roman arenas throughout the Roman Empire.

Once inside we were visually stunned by the colourful crowd seated in several tiers from the ring level to the top. It undoubtedly made a magnificent spectacle. The golden sand on the ground was neatly swept and the fence around the arena brightly painted in red and yellow, Spain's national colours. It was about then that a small band began to play their instruments; this was mostly brass. This spectacle was followed by the appearance of two brightly uniformed men on horseback, who in turn, were followed by three men dressed as bullfighters.

We walked side by side behind the men on horseback as the crowd went wild with enthusiasm. From all around we could hear the clicking of the cameras and exclamations from the spectators surrounding us.

"The two horsemen taking the lead are picadors," explained Marianne who had been reading up on the subject ever since we had reached the Iberian Peninsula. "The man in the middle of the three bullfighters is the man who is going to fight the bull. The two very young men walking either side of him are novielleros meaning young bullfighters. In other words they should be wearing a L-plates on their backs.

"You'll see them drawing the bull away from the fighter if there's a problem. They also stab sharp darts like arrows called banderillas into the bulls back."

I listened quietly as I saw a man in a black suit wave a white handkerchief to another who nodded in response and opened the heavy gate leading into the arena. By now the bull was approaching down the run unaware of its fate of course; ambling slowly and warily weighing the situation up. I was sure glad it was the bull and not me entering the stadium. This man waved his hat towards the emerging bull to attract its attention and then hurriedly departed climbing over the barrier to get out of harm's way.

By this time the crowd was watching in expectant silence and then a gasp went through and around the stadium as the magnificent beast, perhaps expecting a threat, came charging into the arena. Its head proudly held high and its horns straight pointing directly towards the matador we three held our breath.

Marianne and Karen who were sitting either side of me gripped my arms tightly. I was tense and not comfortable at all at even being there. I felt their fingernails dig into my skin. My throat dried and I far wished I were in the bar across the road instead of watching this barbaric so called sport.

The bull had paused, a little uncertain and there was only one way to help make its mind up; that is what the banderilleros are there for. As one they rushed towards the confused beast from where we were sitting they appeared to thrust something that looked very much like a short lance into the bull's back, drawing first blood.

"Those little spears are called banderillas," Marianne whispered. "Its sting distracts and weakens the animal and this helps the matador to take control."

As she spoke the bull charged towards the matador grunting and snorting as its adversary with great agility stepped to one side, drawing his cape away from himself to further confuse the enraged creature. But the stubbornness of the animal as it spun and lurched again towards its tormentor forced the matador back. As this was going on the novilleros and the banderilleros kept on tormenting the poor beast until it was exhausted by the confusion and its injuries; gasping its life out as it instinctively experienced the futility of the duel. By now blood was mixing with the saliva dripping from its nostrils and mouth and its awesomely beautiful black hide was now coated unevenly by its own blood. Such was the excitement in the stadium that the spectators were now in a state of frenzy and screaming, 'bravo, bravo!' I presumed they meant the matador rather than the unfortunate beast.

I wasn't comfortable with the sight at all and again regretted that I had been coerced into accompany the girls. As far as I was concerned it was taking companionship too far. I should have stuck by my guns; I was now regretting having not done so. I felt disgusted and sick to my stomach. We looked on in transfixed horror as the matador finally stepped forward to deal the death blow. By this time there was no fight left in the beast. It was trying vainly to catch its breath; shuddering from its exertions and its knees were beginning to buckle. Clearly it was not going to take a further step forward but at least it tried. Surveying the creature with a mix of bravado and contempt the matador paused for effect and then theatrically raising his sword, that looked to me like a rapier, he sank its blade deep into the lower part of the beast's neck. As I understood it this piercing would, if deftly and expertly delivered, impale the animal's heart and bring to it sudden death. Did it suffer? No one thought to ask the bull.

Blood was now bucketing out of the animal's mouth and its tongue was hanging as it slumped heavily to the blood-soaked sand of the area. The final death blow couldn't have been that effective; it refused to give up and again attempted to stagger to its feet but it was clearly finished; the fight had completely drained away. At this point the coup de grace was more expertly delivered and the magnificent beast finally succumbed to its sad fate; it was what it had been reared for. All of its life had led to this spectacle; it had cost us a few pesetas to witness but I would gladly have paid far more not to have witnessed it. I was not at peace with myself at all. It occurred to me that Susan would have thought my being there intolerable; this made me even more ashamed and I vowed to never again witness a bullfight.

I was greatly moved and it was showing. The two girls rushed after me as I left the stadium almost at a run. It thought of the killing boulders and the other killing fields in the islands that had once been my home. I thought of the piglets being broken to pieces by sticks whilst still alive and shrieking unmercifully and wondered why I was different from so many others. I couldn't figure out what pleasures people derived from seeing their fellow creatures killed. Worse, they seemed to take greater pleasure if the killing was done in a cruel or ritualistic way. It was beyond my understanding.

"That was so barbaric," said Karen. Her voice trembling and I imagined it had been something of a challenge to her but that she too now felt as nauseated as did I. "How can they be allowed to inflict so much suffering to such a magnificent animal?"

"How can it bring them pleasure?" I grimaced.

"Those bullfighters are fucking cowards," declared Marianne. "They should fight someone who can fight back on equal terms; not some poor bloody animal that hasn't got a snowflake's chance in hell of turning the tables."

We three felt distinctly queasy as we made our way back to our rented apartment where we could talk things through over a glass of wine. We needed space and time to look at things more objectively.

"You were involved in blood sports, Jamie, weren't you? Don't tell me the spectators weren't screeching for blood as you and your opponent knocked seven kinds of shit out of each other. They went there to see blood; you were getting well paid to make sure they got what they wanted. That is the truth now isn't it?"

RETURNED TO DEVIL'S ISLAND

"Yes, Jamie, You can't deny it. Yours was a blood sport too so there's no point in your claiming the moral high ground on the issue," ventured Karen. I didn't argue; was there a point in doing so.

The following morning after breakfast we drove the few kilometres to the port of Algeciras, the gateway to Gibraltar but for the van at least it was a kilometre too far. It had served us well but it could go no further. There was the most awful sound of metal against metal, it came to a halt and the engine would no longer turn over. It completed its last 100 metres to the beach, freewheeling and being pushed by the two girls whilst I steered the thing. That night we slept where it had finally rolled to a stop.

As dawn broke we walked into La Linea and looked through the gaps of the strong metal gates of Gibraltar. General Franco had suddenly closed the boarder in 1969 and Spanish Military took control of its frontier. Eventually we found a breakdown truck and had the van towed to a local garage. There the mechanic had a good look at the engine and we were told that the engine had seized; it was kaput. Marianne and Karen spoke Spanish well and communication between them and the mechanic was perfect. After talking to el hombre for several minutes we learned that getting a replacement engine for a Volkswagen wasn't easy. It would need to be ordered, cash up front; waiting for delivery and for installation and checks. He was willing to strip the lot down and recondition the old engine but even that would take a month; and that being Spanish time too. We were well and truly fucked up now.

This meant the separation of the ways; not just for the abandoned van but for the three of us. The van had been our life support system. Now the girls had little choice but to bring their adventure to a close; to catch their flights back to Australia via Malaga and England.

Our funds were depleted and we sort of bedded down in a clapped out hostel not too far from the Gibraltar border before catching a bus to the seaside resort of Torremolinos. From there we took a taxi to the small airport of Malaga where the girls were able to purchase their tickets. It was understandably a sad farewell and there was much embracing and words of truly felt endearment before I watched them both disappear through the doors after negotiating check in.

Our exciting journey had lasted just over two months. It is said that time passes quickly when you are having fun. It wasn't true in this case. For a little while afterwards I thought we had been together for much longer than that. I guess it was because we had crammed so much into those ten weeks. How thankful I was for having had the courage to approach and make their acquaintance on the ferry.

Making my way to the airport bar I sat with my beer and gazed at my navel for awhile. I had never given any thought to where I might be going from here on. It had simply never occurred to me to do so.

Whenever I was alone my thoughts would drift back over the past and across the circumference of the earth to where the palm trees swayed over blue lagoons. My past experiences and the girl with the freckle in her eye. There could be no going back or could there? The unthinkable was now thinkable and as I sat in deep thought my situation concentrated my mind.

The UK was out of the question. Yes, it had been home to me for several years and it had brought me many friends, new experiences and a home of sorts. But the weather wasn't appealing and let's face it, there was no real future in conducting a bus. I thought I deserved better than that.

Here in Spain I was basically an illegal immigrant. It was only going to be a matter of time before my papers would be checked. It would then be the calaboose for me until a decision was made. There could be only one decision: I would be dumped in Gibraltar or put on a plane to follow the girls. Neither held much appeal; I was in between a rock and a hard place.

CHAPTER 14

As I was drowning my sorrows I saw a man talking to an English couple and showing them a brochure of properties for sale in that region. I moved closer to them and after eavesdropping for a while I discovered that they had just purchased a holiday villa in Malaga and were returning back to England. I waited till the salesman shook hands with the couple and was heading towards the car park when I rushed after him and asked him if he could please give me a lift into town. The kind young man agreed and soon we were heading to the town of Torremolinos. On the way he told me that his name was Ted and also about the property boom in Spain and how he was earning a good salary and commission by meeting potential clients at the airport and finally selling apartments, villas and land to them. He also told me that there could be vacancies for English speaking salesman but first I will have to visit their office in Calle San Miguel and speak to the boss. I was intrigued and I thanked him and waited outside the office till the boss had arrived. Beaming with confidence I knocked on the door of his office and was interviewed by the general manager named Mr. Jack Butterfield. Fortunately he was from Liverpool and we had something in common to talk about, like football, the Beatles and the friendly people of the city. Once the formalities over he went straight to the point.

"Have you done this kind of work before?"

I thought how best to answer the question posed by the hard-edged estate agent even though he was a friendly sort of a guy. "Not as such," I smiled. "But, I worked as a rep' at holiday resort in Tahiti for quite some time. I was selling health and spa packages to tourists. I have references from them."

"You have paperwork? How does that stack up?"

Taking my passport from my hand he studied it with some degree of gravity whilst again looking me up and down before reaching a judgement on my suitability. On his answer I guessed was the decision as to whether I stayed in Spain or got enough pesetas together to head for Liverpool and Birkenhead buses. "You want to work and stay in Spain?"

I nodded.

"You ever worked on a commission basis before; you can drive?"

I nodded eagerly. I sensed I was sending all the right signals. "You're in luck, son," he smiled. "I am one agent down and I have a couple of buyers coming in on a flight on Friday. They're yours. Fuck up and you're still broke, and so incidentally am I so please don't fuck up. And do not make it too obvious that you are working in Spain otherwise you'll be picked by the police and deported back to the UK. Work permits in Spain are hard to come by, understand?"

He paused as if to weigh up his words before adding that I should return at 9am the following morning. Ted would be picking his client up at their hotel. I should accompany them to learn the ropes and it was pointed out to me that I should not expect payment for it. He did add that Ted would include me in any meals.

He said 9 o'clock: I was there half an hour earlier but the office was closed and so I hung around until the affable Ted turned up. Climbing into the company car he sort of introduced me to my interrogator who had given me the job.

"That was Jack you spoke to yesterday. He looks tough but he is a real pussycat when he gets comfortable with you. There's a lot of suspicion in this job; there's a lot of stealing and switching potential clients. Once he is sure you are genuine he will look after you."

As the weeks went by it seemed to me that my stay in Spain, its Costa del Sol region at least, was assured. There were several confrontations with the Guardia Civil over unauthorised employment and overstaying one's welcome. Somehow Jack, who was on the mayor's Christmas card list, always seemed to smooth things over. Perhaps he bribed them but we had no idea why no one was being deported, as yet. Months went by and Jack began to like me and he liked the sales I was making. I was a natural holiday homes representative he once told me. I thought it fun meeting the clients at the airport. They were always in a holiday atmosphere mood; I shared it. It was genuinely a good time for buying after the dreadful austerity of the post war years in Britain. There was a new mood and expectancy of a better lifestyle beckoning; some were grabbing the opportunity with both hands. I was part of living the dream. Besides the property gold rush the Costa del Sol was also being glamorised by the glitterati form Hollywood. Yes, Frank Sinatra, Ava Gardner and Debra Kerr had also visited here and rumours of other stars from sport and the silver screen were soon to follow. It was a good time to be alive and there was no better place to be alive. Best of all I was earning fabulous money; it was like taking sweets from a kid. Working all kind of hours god sent me was a distraction from my past life while I was earning hard earned cash too.

There was just one shadow persistently blighting my life and it was brought into sharp relief self-gratifying lifestyle I was leading; it was the contrast that was bothering me for there were two sides to the one coin I had experienced in life. I had seen at first hand humanity at its most despairing and foul. People, who didn't have a penny to their name, had no future and as if all that wasn't bad enough they were burdened by disease. Here I was seeing humanity and it's most self-indulgent and in many cases foul.

RETURNED TO DEVIL'S ISLAND

Sure, within the bounds of human weaknesses and indulgence, myself included, there were few here who could be considered saints. But there were at the other end of the pole those who had been blessed with wealth and good fortune not to mention health. They were the worst abusers of their good fortune. That may be dismissed as being their own business but not when those who were doing the paying whilst others were doing the slaying.

Where I was operating there were arms dealers and child exploiters, there were those living off the immoral earnings of those who had little lifestyle choice. There were plenty of crooks and the region had already earned the sobriquet of Costa del Crime.

Here on this part of Spain were those who had made their money from the recent wars, including World War Two. For every battlefield corpse there was a war profiteer; all part of life's rich tapestry proclaimed the bard.

There were many who were making big money from sweatshops and filthy factories situated throughout Europe; there were bankers; the leeches of all societies; the public service fat cats, the politicians and the parasites who grow fat on the underdog. I had seen the underdog and the images once seen never once left me. I constantly thought of the poor wretches, the exile, and the untouchables on Mokagai. I thought of their comparatively simple pleasures and their coming to terms with what Fate had given them. Strangely, they weren't bitter about their fate and accepted it as their Karma but here in Spain it was different. The more affluent purchases of second homes were constantly complaining about the cost of property and asking for fat discounts before they parted with their pounds shillings and pence to invest in Spain. Bundles of cash from the UK was being smuggled into Spain and invested into properties. Hundreds of English bars and restaurants were being inaugurated along the coast. Mind you I was not complaining as a salesman I was doing extremely well. Yes, I was doing very well thank you: My only dilemma, which constantly pestered my conscience, was how I should spend my good fortune. I could do what everyone else was doing; invest it in property and ride to heaven on the property boom. I could well imagine my glowing pride in explaining that to my maker when my time cometh. On the other hand I could party and have the fun of my life at the region's most expensive watering holes where money was no object. Quite frankly, my love and friendship with Nirmala or Sara, Clair or Ruth was meaningful that brought me far more joy than could any romp with a grasping hooker escaping the deprivations of Belarus or Romania.

Sure I was in a reflective mood. I had achieved all I had set out to achieve. In fact I had been far more successful than anyone could reasonably have hoped for. I was never tired of saying truthfully that my lifestyle was far superior to that of many who in later years were absconding from the United Kingdom with millions of ill gained cash hidden in their cars or under garments. I was satiated but unlike others I was not complaining. There was just one thing left that would complete my life. That was to square things up.

Don't misread me. I was no penitent and nor was I aiming to be a Christ like figure. I wasn't into wearing hair shirts and I couldn't remember when I had last gone to confession. Nor was there any intention to remove myself from the comforts and a bit of wealth I had acquired. I did however feel as though I should be giving something back. I believe in the adage: what goes round comes round and I had no desire to end up in a leper colony when I was reborn.

There was awareness that a small investment that would have no effect on my new Spanish lifestyle could radically change the lives of others for the better.

To use my assets to purchase swathes of property whilst living in fear of a collapse in the market wasn't an option. I wanted guaranteed returns and I knew where to get them; I even had a partner in my venture. She was a lady so light in form she might easily have blown away; she was a true saint who had as the mark of her uniqueness a small brown fleck in her right eye. I decided that I wasn't going to go home but some of my wealth was.

* * *

The Blue Lagoons office was uncharacteristically quiet. In fact there was only Melanie there and she was painting her nails. In answer to my question as to where Jack might be she yawned and said: "Coming!"

I hung around and sure enough I saw him pull up outside and making small talk with Carmen who ran the cafeteria nest door. He was a little surprised but after the usual civilities I broke the subject: "Jack, it's coming up to December and there are not a lot of clients around. Can you get by without me for three months?"

He looked a bit puzzled.

"Fiji's is a long way away; it's not a weekend in London. I need to go," I told him.

"Family?"

I smiled a little sadly: "Yes, you could say that and if I am going to go then better now than when the season kicks off after in the spring."

"Sure, Jamie. Ted will look after things until you're back. He isn't going anywhere.

By the same weekend I was boarding my flight. As I did so I thought of how my fortunes had changed since I had last climbed an airliner's steps. There had been the anti-climax of arriving in Liverpool. Had I any regrets at making the city little more than a stopover? Not at all. I thought of Karen and Marianne. I could have married Karen but as well as we got on together I had my doubts if marriage to her could have been sustained. She was happy to run with things when she was on holiday but did she really want a husband who had so happily shared a bed with her and her best friend?

It was such thoughts that between siestas kept me occupied for the flights to the South Sea Islands hadn't become any shorter. On arrival it was a relief to meet my mother and sister, Malti. We certainly had plenty of catching up to do but I guess I had changed while I had been away; in fact they remarked on it. Jamie had been reborn but as what? Even I couldn't hazard a guess at that.

I was older and wiser; more weather beaten and certainly worldlier. I had dropped much of my laddish behaviour. I still had a keen eye for an opportunity but only when it came knocking; I was no longer skirt-chasing as such. That was the way most men were wired I suppose. There was a new and softer side to me now. There was an innocent idealism and ever optimistic aura that I had captured from somewhere.

I had a yearning for everything to be sweeter in the world than it was and this I supposed was the purpose behind my mission. I didn't reveal a lot to my immediate family; I had already made my decisions and didn't feel the need for the opinions of others. Nor did I visit Nirmala and my sons' for I had learned that they were both away at college. The last thing I needed right now was small talking offered by my former lover.

If there was going to be any going back it could only be to the one woman I had vowed to be with for the rest of our lives; this is what I intended to do. Fate had separated us; desire had not.

There was a quiet acceptance of what I needed to do as I knocked on the small convent's door. As soon as my rapping was answered by the door swinging open I grinned: "Sister Helen, you are looking well."

It was as if no time had passed since I had last left her and headed down the small track towards the ferry carrying Susan's battered little suitcase in my hand.

"James? Yes, it is you isn't it, James? My eyes aren't what they used to be, my son."

"Your eyes will always be very special, Sister Helen," I smiled. "I think you know that more than anyone else on earth."

Somehow her graciousness and devotion to God, supported by her compassion, reminded me that there weren't necessarily faults with her religion. It had its weaknesses as did all others but the fault lies in those who interpret religion for their own ends. The suffering endured by me and Susan when we were children and placed at the small mercies of St. Mary's School was not God's fault or even that of the Church. The sin could be laid at the feet of those who abused their power. They and not the Church would be answerable to a far higher being. Now I felt at peace with myself; the truest disciples of humanity's goodness were here on Mokagai Island.

The elderly and frail nun read my thoughts: "I am afraid Susan's grave has not been as well attended as it should," the kindly sister smiled as she handed me a cup of tea.

I suppose she realised why I was there. "The villagers have hearts of gold but they lack the motivation. Other than that there's just myself with everything to do. Oh I get a little outside help occasionally; the boat arrives with the provisions. But you know, James," she added as she gently patted my knee. "The island doesn't need much now for we already have God's bountiful blessings. This is to us God's island. Can you understand that? It is not the devil's island it was once rumoured to be."

I supposed I could. From where we were sitting I could see cascades of bougainvillea and other tropical blooms. The palm trees were waving to the zephyrs as they approached from the sleeping Pacific Ocean. The air was filled with birdsong and it was planets removed from the pleasure-seeking fast moving lifestyle of the Costa del Sol; the constant pursuit of money, power and social acceptance.

"You have everything, Sister?"

"Well of course, my child. What else could we possibly need?"

I smiled at her sweet innocence for it seemed that we too were on separate planets but unlike Mars and Venus we were strangely empathetic; I doubt if me and Sister Helen would ever find anything to disagree with. There was just the quiet acceptance of whatever was to come our way be it good or bad.

I stretched out on the lounger the kindly sister had pulled up for me and I thoughtfully looked across the gardens. Although I couldn't see it from where I sat I could picture the small overgrown plot surrounded by weather beaten crosses where Susan had been laid to rest. There lay the remains of the saintly woman with a fleck in her beautiful eyes.

Without looking at her I asked Sister Helen if she had given any thought to the future of the colony. She told me this was hardly her concern; it was God's. He alone would decide on what might become of it and it would be God who would choose who was to be instrumental in its future. I am sure that to her my question seemed rather silly. She probably put it down to my youth.

"You know," I said thoughtfully. "Leprosy has been mostly eradicated and colonies such as Mokagai will one day be living not dying museums."

She allowed me my thoughts and no doubt she had her own as the aromas of the gardens drifted to the breeze. From somewhere in the distance I could hear children laughing and playing. I thought of the idyllic days when I had played happily with other village children and then later with the American servicemen. There hadn't been a penny to our names either. "They seem very happy, sister."

"They mostly are," she smiled. "They expect and get little and they make the most of what they have. It is human nature I suppose."

"Or God's ointment?"

The elderly nun smiled. "Now, my son; you are starting to talk out of character and it is a long time since I had the pleasure of chatting with a man of the cloth."

I smiled thoughtfully. "Someday the laughing will be lost; taken away by the sea breezes and replaced by the wind in the trees, and the bird song of course," I said whimsically. "On the other hand there will be tourists who will visit. They will find it difficult to comprehend what you have achieved and how the villagers once lived."

"Then, maybe that is the way it should be," she replied. "Maybe it is time to do what we need to do during our time on earth and allow the future to care for itself."

"There should be a memorial, Sister."

"Do you know that out of 4,500 patients treated on Makogai only 1,500 died and remain buried on the island. Most returned home, their condition improved or in remission. Maybe someone should write a story of Makogai?"

RETURNED TO DEVIL'S ISLAND

I told her that it was a distinct possibility and using my experiences on the Costa del Sol I tried to picture the future of the island. Just as the great resorts dotted along Spain's Mediterranean coasts were once insignificant fishing villages with sparse populations this island would change to.

"Do you remember telling me that because of advances in medicine Susan had been the last to die here as a direct consequence of the disease?"

I didn't wait for Sister Helen to reply; there seemed no need. "Her job was done and so will mine one day. What then?"

"You are speaking in riddles, my dear boy. I am an old woman now and when I was young, as Susan once was when she knew you, I would talk the sun down and up again. But I am tired; your thoughts tire me though it is lovely to see you again. Spare an elderly sister your riddles."

I smiled. It was so typical of me to give thought only to myself. I came to the point and picking up a small bamboo cane, which I used as a pointer, I waved in the direction of the village. As I spoke I remembered Dan who had invested in the good life. I was going to go one better and invest in the afterlife.

"There's just one thing left for me to do, Sister Helen," I smiled. "You won't find it arduous at all."

Her frown did little to stop my spoken thoughts. "I would like the work that you have done to be immortalised as a memorial to the goodness and charity of humanity."

I then went on to explain my purpose and how I was to achieve my aims. As I envisaged the shape of things to come my eyes took in the landscape, the rolling wooded hills and the vales that lay between.

With her agreement I would begin commissioning without delay. Press releases would be prepared, investors encouraged but only those charitable in their intentions. There would be need for an archivist who would double as a curator. He or she would be able to work with both the Church and the South Sea Islands media to build a living working museum as a living memorial to the colony's final years. They would require a modest salary; I would until the island was self-sustaining take care of that.

Throughout the world's churches there would be publicity that would encourage religious tourism, the rewards of which would be earmarked for recognising the part played by those who gave their lives to assisting those stricken with leprosy throughout the world and through the ages.

I could already imagine the visitor centre. There would of course be a need for a larger chapel where visitors and those living on the blessed island could offer their thanks and receive blessings. This would be situated at the bottom of the Garden of Rest where Susan was now resting. She would be laid to rest in a sepulchre: I had already arranged for her sculpture to be placed atop it. There would be adjacent plots for her mother and myself for I would need my little home in the clay and where else but next to my Susan.

CHRIS NAND

As I set out my plans, for I had already done my homework, I looked at Sister Helen. I thought it important to get her compliance; besides I needed to get her input to my investment ambitions.

The saintly sister was fast asleep but there was a smile on her lips. I took that as unqualified agreement. It was just as well for I had already engaged the stonemasons and the sculptures; the craftsmen would build here, those with the gifts to create the stained glass story of God's greatest gift of all; charity to the less fortunate.

One has to make a start somewhere. As I gently rose to avoid waking Sister Susan I strolled hands in pockets through what would be a garden of remembrance and in my mind's eye I could see Susan smiling too; the girl with the fleck in her eye and God in her heart but with a small place set aside in it for me. Soon there would be a small place in God's still beating heart for her. ©

Lightning Source UK Ltd.
Milton Keynes UK
UKOW050625041111

181458UK00001B/42/P